VIKING DAWN

C R DEMPSEY

CRMPD MEDIA LIMITED

KINGDOM OF
BREGA
STORMONT
RING FORT
VILLAGE
HIBERNIAN SEA
KINGDOM OF
LAGIN
MASIN
OBSERVATION
TOWER
WICKLOW
MOUNTAINS

CONTENTS

For Mena and Poppy

CHAPTER ONE

A TEMPER COAXED FORTH

AFFRAIC GENTLY HANDED HER brother his bag, a proud smile on her lips. His eyes lit up as he gripped it, the weight of his victory heavy in his arms. His back was dotted with a smattering of red marks from the congratulatory slaps he received from his fellow villagers. Angry scratches and dark bruises covered his arms and legs. His sweat mingled with the drops of gentle rain that had been a constant companion for the duration of the hurling match.

He reached into his bag and pulled out an old rag, wiping down his hurley stick before carefully stowing it away.

"They won't be so smug down the market for the next couple of weeks," Finn said, the memory of the defeated faces of the men from the other village taking pride of place in his mind.

Gormlaith draped her arm over her son's shoulders. "Your legend grows," she declared proudly, daring anyone in the vicinity to challenge her son's status as the hero of the team. No one did.

Finn glowed in the company of his family. Gormlaith was his rock, his protector, his advisor, and his comforter. She had always protected him, right from the time when he was a little boy and the family crisis was at its most acute. Angry men came when their father was accused of cowardice in the face of the Norse raids and they thought he might be hiding in their house. She was the one who slammed the door shut on them. They banged the pommels of their swords on the door and called their father all sorts of names demanding that he come out. She hid her young children and shouted abuse at them through the door. Finn cowered with Affraic in the corner of the house as their mother screamed all sorts of curses at the men, words they had never heard her utter before. Finn was frightened, but not as frightened as he would have been if he was on the wrong side of his mother. The men left and did not return. Given the gravity of the accusations made against her husband, most mothers would have left or been driven out of the village. But not Gormlaith. She faced up to all the rumours and accusations, placing the blame back with King Tigernach and saying he was covering up his own failure to drive the Norse away. In the absence of any evidence against her husband or the production of his body, the villagers eventually accepted her side of the story that he had disappeared and still was the hero he once was. Now, here they stood, village pride sitting comfortably on Finn's shoulders as he led the village hurling team to another in a series of victories over their rivals.

His sister Affraic was also his constant support, rarely leaving his side. In their younger days she was more like his shadow as Finn was far more likely to be the victim of bullies because of their father rather than her. She may not have her mother's bark but she had inherited her mother's cunning and then some. Few who bullied Finn did it again after Affraic's retaliations, be it through rumour-spreading, using her looks to get other boys to do her dirty work or other methods. She had grown up to be quite a beauty, with her inky tresses cascading down her lithe frame. Warriors and young lads alike stole glances at her, drawn in by the captivating beauty and enigmatic aura that seemed to shroud her every move. There was a certain aloofness about her, something they could never have, as if she was destined for a different path. But for the moment that path was her family. Finn smiled and imagined himself like a wolf cub, safe in a cave up in the mountains protected by two fearsome she-wolves.

They turned to leave to go back to their village to celebrate. But suddenly, a noise came from a distance, causing Affraic to turn and search for its source. She noticed a commotion coming from the path through the woods and quickly stepped in front of her brother to shield him from whatever may be causing it.

"Enough sport for today," she urged, trying to distract him. "Let's go home and revel in your victory. I can make you a nice pie. You'll like that."

But her brother, who ignored his aching muscles, easily peered over her head of black curls to see what was happening in the distance.

The villagers watched with a concoction of awe and fear as King Tigernach made his grand entrance on the back of a magnificent steed, its coat shining in the sunlight. It was a horse unlike any other they had use of in the village, for only the king could afford such an animal and he wanted everyone to know how he lived. Tigernach had always been a cruel and demanding king, always asking for more from the village. More men to fight his wars, more of their time to till his fields and more of their daughters to sew and mend so he could maintain his soldiers in the field. His presence, especially with such an entourage, could only mean he wanted something.

Behind him strode Ultán, his beloved son, his shoulders broad, his dark brown hair protruding from beneath his cap, his muscles honed by years of wielding a sword and shield. His eyes, as sharp as a hunting bird, betrayed no emotion, yet they seemed to command the very air around him.

In one hand, he gripped a freshly carved hurley made of strong oak, its surface still smooth and unmarred by the game it was destined to play. A small smile tugged at the corners of his lips as he caught sight of Finn in the distance.

"What's he doing here?" Finn growled to his mother and sister as he pushed past them. "Why did he bring his son? I hope he does not expect us to bow in deference to him."

Gormlaith stood in front of her son and rested her hands on his chest.

"Ignore them. Don't cause trouble or aggravate them. Decline any offers for a match. Say you're injured. Nobody will think any less of you."

Finn glared at the entourage and gritted his teeth. The weight of his father's legacy always sat heavy on his chest when he saw Tigernach and Ultán.

"Oh, they will, Mam, they will. Our only pride these days is on the hurling pitch, especially mine. I can't take that away from the villagers. I can't."

Gormlaith looked up at him with pleading eyes.

"Pick your battles, Finn, pick your battles. I know I don't always follow those words myself, but be better than your Mam." But she could see his attention was already gone, now fully focused on the advancing Ultán.

Ultán stopped a few yards before Finn. He held his hurley low in both hands and gave Finn a smug grin.

"I have come with my men to challenge you to a game. I heard you have some reputation as a hurley player but I don't believe it. I told my men you'd run away when I challenged you. Just like your cowardly father did when he served mine."

Ultán gave a smug grin. Finn snarled in response, taking the bait. But Gormlaith pinched him on his side, hoping to bring him to his senses.

"I can't. I'm injured," Finn muttered.

The embarrassment of this lie burned on his face. Ultán roared with laughter.

"Injured? You don't look injured to me." Ultán shook his head and smirked. "Well, I hope you're not going to show yourself up in front of your mother and your sister and refuse to play against my men and me? If you are, you can go along home and we'll have a different sort of fun and games with them."

Finn stood tall, gripping his hurley tightly and stood in front of his family.

"Leave it now, son. Come home with us before anyone gets hurt," his mother said, tugging on his shoulder.

Finn waved her away.

"No one threatens my family like that. Not even the king's son," he declared.

He squared up to Ultán. They were the same height and across the antagonism their noses almost met.

"If you've recovered from your 'injury', we'll have a match," Ultán goaded Finn. "What'll the stakes be?"

"I always play for pride," Finn said.

"Pride is for fools," Ultán said as he grinned. "So I can see how it could appeal to you."

Finn squared up again, refusing to back down from the challenge.

"So what do you suggest?"

"If you win, I will give you my new hurley stick. It is said the tree it came from was planted by Cú Cuchulain himself. Look at how it is hooped in embroidered bronze. Now I have it. A hurley fit for kings that draws the sliotar down from the sky to cover the stick bearer in glory."

Finn stepped back and grinned.

"I bet the merchant who sold you that lie is long gone to count his money."

Ultán stuck his face into Finn's.

"Then you would be a coward if you did not want to face me if you think my hurley will shatter in the middle of the game."

"You may be the king's son, but he did not bless you with either pleasant breath, or any sense. I accept. What do you want from me if I you win?"

"I will come to you to do me a good turn. It may not be today, but sometime in the future."

"And what if I refuse this 'good turn'?"

"Then I shall tell your fellow villagers you broke your oath just like your cowardly father and see you and your family are cast out into the woods to live like beggars."

Finn sneered at Ulltán.

"I will consult my men to see if they wish to accept your challenge."

Finn turned and looked behind him. He ignored the pleading faces of his mother and sister and looked further behind to his men. They all stood grim-faced and slowly nodded. King Tigernach had humiliated or treated them badly in the past too many times for them to turn down this opportunity for revenge and they did not want to appear to be cowards.

Finn nodded to Ultán in acknowledgment.

"It looks like you have a game."

It was Ultán's turn to smirk. He turned to the watching crowd.

"Hear ye," he exclaimed to all within hearing distance. "Finn and the villagers have accepted my challenge. He swore before God that if I beat him he would do me one task without quibble. No one trusts a coward's son to keep his word so I make this declaration before all of you. If he does not keep his promise I will return with my men and take the value of my promise from your grain stores. If he wins, he gets my hurley stick."

Gormlaith's face dropped.

"My fool of a son agreed to that?"

Finn reached out his arm to protest at the declaration, but Ultán had already turned his back and his men took up their positions on the field. Finn had to win.

CHAPTER TWO

THE WAY OF THE SLIOTAR

THE SCENE WAS SET for a hurling match, and a cacophony rose from the spectators, their cheers weaving through the air like threads of an intricately spun tapestry. The first set of threads was somewhat soured as a bully in the form of the king's son had appeared on the pitch and not all the villagers had the nerve to cheer against them for fear of retribution. The second inter-twining set of threads was bright and vibrant as the king's men cheered loudly for Ultán and threw curses and multiple slanders at Finn and the other prominent villagers.

King Tigernach settled into his throne, a specially crafted seat made for him. His smug grin stretched across his face, confident that none would dare challenge him or defeat his son in front of him. The thought crossed his mind as to how ungrateful these villagers were for it was he who protected them from Hibernian raiders and worse, the Norse sea wolves. How could they not celebrate his son when it was he who would stand in the way when raiders came to burn their homes down? But Ultán would teach them respect, starting by winning this hurling match.

As the clouds parted and the sun shone down, it cast a dull glint on the modest crown perched atop his head. He remained silent, but the fierce warriors surrounding him let out thunderous roars, eager for the game to begin. The anticipation hung thick in the air, like a storm waiting to break.

Men, women, and children of the village pressed close to-gether, their bodies a patchwork of colour and movement, each person jostling for a glimpse of the heroes of the hour. The smell of damp soil rose from the trampled ground, mixing with the scent of sweat and excitement that clung to every woollen tunic and leather boot.

Gormlaith and Affraic stood amongst them biting their lips, standing still in a swaying sea of people. They both gulped for they knew Finn was prone to bouts of foolish male pride but not before to such an extent that it placed him in active danger before their eyes. They moved forward in front of the group of villagers hoping they could steer this almost irretrievable situation into something that resembled a neutral outcome and pride saved on both sides.

The two teams came out, made up of young men in their prime, both team captains renowned for their skills on the pitch. But this was no mere game. It was an epically proportioned grudge match: the king's son was keen to assert his own skills and powers independent of his father; for Finn and his team, it was a legitimate chance for a village to get some payback on a cruel overlord and regain some pride.

The sliotar, a ball made of leather made to bounce on the end of a hurley stick, rested upon the earth at a carefully selected mid-point, around which all the day's tensions pivoted. Around it, each blade of grass shimmered with rain, mirroring the glistening spears of warriors under a reluctant sun. Ultán spat, crouched and snorted like a bull. "Ready yourself, Finn," he boomed with feigned camaraderie. "Today is no different from any battle we've faced."

"But it is," Finn replied, eyes ablaze with competition. "My whole village watches."

"Even worse for you then, boy," Ultán sneered, hurley at the ready.

"Begin!"

The elder's staff slammed against the ground. He cast the sliotar into the air between the two men, signalling the match to begin.

Finn lunged forward, his hurley a blur of ash wood slicing through the air in pursuit of the sliotar. Ultán matched his movements with the precision of a seasoned predator, his eyes fixed on the small orb of solid will that soared between them. The world seemed to fade away as they focused solely on the sliotar, their own heartbeats pounding in their ears.

With a ferocious swing, Ultán's hurley missed its mark by a hair's breadth, the sliotar dancing out of reach under Finn's precision control. "Protect and prevail," Finn growled through gritted teeth, the memory of his father burning behind his eyes.

Finn could feel Ultán's searing gaze burning into him, urging him to falter. But he refused to be swayed, using ancient tactics and pure instinct to outmanoeuvre his opponent.

The gap widened between them like a gaping chasm, Finn bounding ahead like a hare and Ultán the wily fox chasing at a distance. Finn delivered a powerful strike that sent the sliotar soaring over the line. A roar erupted from the villagers, but Gormlaith's face remained clouded with concern.

"You've made your point, Finn. Now take it easy," she cried through cupped hands.

At the referee's signal, the match resumed again. Finn could see the determination in Ultán's eyes. He would not be humiliated again. Finn bent his knees and leapt, ready for anything. This time, Ultán got the sliotar first. Finn moved to block him, but Ultán barrelled forward, using his superior strength to force Finn aside.

Jaw clenched, Finn raced after Ultán. He would not make it easy. The crowd held their breath as the two men struggled for control of the sliotar, skill against brute force. Ultán shook Finn off and charged down the pitch, sliotar in hand. Finn sprinted after him, hurley poised to strike. At the last second, Ultán feinted left, then pivoted right, trying to fake out the younger man. But Finn was too quick. He adjusted seamlessly, swiping at the sliotar, now at the end of Ultán's stick, and sent it rolling free.

The crowd cheered as Finn regained control. He dribbled the ball steadily towards the goal, but Ultán was on him in an instant. The larger man slammed his shoulder into Finn's back, sending him sprawling. The sliotar rolled loose once more.

Finn gritted his teeth, ignoring the flare of pain in his lower back. He would not be taken down so easily. As Ultán scooped up the ball, Finn was there to meet him. As they tussled sinews stretched, muscles taut, hurleys cracking together.

"Getting tired yet, boy?" Ultán taunted. "Why don't you quit before you embarrass yourself?"

Finn's eyes flashed. "I don't quit," he spat.

With a burst of effort, he ripped the sliotar free and took off down the pitch. Ultán lumbered after him, face reddening from exertion and rage. The ball snapped off the flattened wood with a sound sharp as a blackbird's call. The sliotar soared through the air and smashed into the net. The crowd erupted, chanting

Finn's name again. Ultán stared at the goal, chest heaving, fists clenched white-knuckle tight around his hurley.

The sliotar was tossed up and the match resumed. Ultán charged forward like an enraged bull, all pretence of skill abandoned. He battered at Finn relentlessly, not caring if he made contact with hurley or body. There were very few rules in this game and even fewer when you were prepared to play dirty. Finn ducked and wove, avoiding the worst of the onslaught. He had to keep his head. If he lost focus, even for a second, Ultán would crush him.

Finn's family watched anxiously from the crowd. His sister's face was drawn, his mother wringing her hands. They could see no way out of Finn's humiliation at the hands of someone who had no desire to play fair. Finn set his jaw and stood firm as Ultán bore down on him again. At the last second, he pivoted and let the warrior's momentum carry him past. The crowd cheered Finn's clever manoeuvre.

Enraged, Ultán rounded on him again. Finn was ready, eyes blazing with determination. Their hurleys cracked together, the force of Ultán's blow vibrating painfully up Finn's arms. He stumbled back a step, but quickly regained his footing. The crowd was hushed now. The earlier cheers turned to anxious murmurs. Ultán pressed his advantage, raining down blow after blow. Finn blocked what he could, but several painful strikes slipped through his defences. His ribs ached, his shoulders burned. Still, he would not yield. With a mighty swing, Ultán knocked the sliotar from Finn's hurley. It rolled free as Finn crashed to the ground, the wind knocked from his lungs. The crowd gasped. His family watched in dismay as Ultán scooped up the ball and pelted towards the goal.

Finn forced himself to his feet, lungs heaving. With a burst of speed, he pursued Ultán, throwing his body recklessly at the larger man. They tumbled to the grass in a tangle of limbs. The crowd roared at the audacity of Finn's tackle. Finn grappled for the ball, finally wrenching it from Ultán's grasp, and knocked him into the mud. Before Ultán could react, Finn was up and sprinting for the opposite goal. His lungs burned, his muscles screamed, but he ran on. Ultán could not keep up, but gave the nod to his men. One man mountain ran straight for Finn and made no attempt for the sliotar. He collided into Finn, sending him and the sliotar flying in the air. Finn crashed to the ground and remained there as the sliotar was returned to Ultán. No one dared to tackle him as he trotted up to the opposing line and scored. The king's section of the crowd, until now stood in silence, roared their approval.

Finn lifted himself to his feet, his face a storm of anger. He lifted his hurley as if to whack Ultán over the back of his head as he accepted the cheers of his supporters. But he saw his mother, watery-eyed, with her index finger planted across her lips. He would keep his temper, but she would not get it all her own way. He would still go out and win the game.

The sliotar was once more cast in the air and Finn clashed sticks with Ultán to bring it under his control. But no sooner had his feet left the ground than he received a sharp pain in the ribs and once more he went down in a heap. Ultán gained control of the hurley and ran down the pitch. Finn picked himself up and ran after Ultán. He saw Ultán wind his body up to belt the sliotar over the line. Finn threw himself forward to block Ultán's shot. The sliotar, as if destined by the fates, slipped with a whisper past Finn's outstretched hurley and over the line. A hushed gasp rippled through the onlookers, the sound of it slicing into Finn's pride as effectively as any sharpened blade. The silence that followed felt dense, a fog of collective disbelief that descended upon the field, suffocating cheers and jeers alike.

There Finn stood, his black hair now a limp banner as he stood on the brink of defeat, stark against the overcast sky. His chest heaved, each breath a laborious draw as though the very air conspired to weigh him down. The muscles that had served him so well throughout the match now tensed with a different sort of anticipation, dread.

Finn trudged once more to the point deemed the centre of the pitch. Ultán beamed as if a hungry wolf was about to devour its prey.

"The Brehon will hear about your conduct today," Finn growled.

Ultán laughed.

"The Brehon is my father's man. So much so, he has a wager on me to win today. If the wind has died in your sails, you can always forfeit the game. As long as you do it in front of your mother and your pretty little sister."

Finn cringed at the reference to his sister. He turned to the referee.

"Throw the sliotar."

"As you wish," and the man grimaced at Finn's stubbornness as everyone seemed to know he was beaten accept he.

As the sliotar soared, Finn's emerald eyes mirrored the grey expanse above, stormy and brimming with the threat of rain. Time slowed, and the world around Finn narrowed to the echo of the ball against wood. But as soon as his eyes were distracted by the dot in the sky he felt the thud of two bodies collide into either side of him. He fell, and the damp earth beneath his feet seemed to swallow his boots as his body folded into the ground where his failure was laid bare for all to see. He saw blackness and his head spun. This time, there was no getting up.

Little blurry shapes ran in front of his eyes. He felt the breeze on his back and then drops of rain on his face. His eyes focused. He raised his head to see Ultán throw his hurley up in the air in celebration as he took the lead in the game. Finn's head dropped once more into the mud and all he saw was darkness.

CHAPTER THREE

A GREATER MENACE

GORMLAITH AND AFFRAIC RAN onto the pitch, ignoring Ultán and his men, who were lined up to restart the game.

"STOP THE GAME! STOP THE GAME!" Gormlaith screamed, waving her arms in the air as if her shouts alone were not enough to get everyone's attention.

Ultán went to raise his fist against Gormlaith but decided against when his father stood up to object to his potential action.

"Get these women off the pitch," Ultán cried, signalling to his men. "They're trying to rob me of my victory."

He pushed Affraic, who unleashed a mighty punch to his cheek.

"THE NORSE," Gormlaith cried. "Their ships fill the bay!"

"This is cheating," Ultán cried towards his father while pointing at Gormlaith and rubbing his jaw. "I won. Tell her I won. We need to resolve this first."

Tigernach instructed his men to ignore his son and see if what Gormlaith said was true. A hush fell over the crowd as they left Ultán open-mouthed and waving his arms in protest in the middle of the pitch.

Gormlaith and Affraic rushed over to Finn as he lay stirring feebly in the mud. He rose with their help and exchanged an uneasy glance with Affraic. Without a word, they took off for the cliffs overlooking the sea, hearts pounding. A marauding band of Norse meant certain death. As they crested the rise, the blood drained from Finn's face. An enormous fleet dotted the horizon, sails billowing, oars churning the surf.

"By Brigid's grace," Affraic whispered.

Through the sea of panicked faces, Finn's gaze locked onto the horizon. The setting sun cast an ominous glow over the bay. The dark silhouettes of longships sliced through the waves like a swarm of predators closing in on their prey. Finn scanned the ships and grimaced. He counted to at least fifty before he got confused. More than he had ever seen. Fear coiled in his stomach even as determination steeled his spine.

"Gods above," Ultán said, now standing beside Finn and his mother and sister. The rivalry that had consumed them moments ago now seemed a distant memory, trivial in the face of such impending doom.

"Back to the village!" Finn's voice, though strained, carried over the din of the crowd. "We must prepare for the raid!"

Without waiting for a response, he turned on his heels, his mother and sister on either side as his crutches. The others followed, a tide of villagers surging away from the shore, their previous revelry replaced by the clatter of urgency and fear.

"Ultán, we need every man wielding whatever they can!" Finn shouted without looking back, trusting his rival to marshal the men while he raced ahead. His breath came in ragged gasps, his muscles screaming from the exertions of the game, now repurposed for survival. In the bustle of the crowd, Finn soon found himself alone in the clamour of villagers.

"Affraic! Mother!" Finn's thoughts were with his family, his feet pounding the earth, each step a silent vow to protect them at all costs.

"Move, move!" Ultán bellowed behind him, the authority in his voice undisputed, his tall frame pushing through the throng of villagers.

The noise of the village grew louder as they approached – the cries of children, the barking of dogs, the hurried commands as the community scrambled to fortify their homes. Finn could smell the peat fires burning, a scent that usually brought comfort now tinged with the acridity of dread.

"Into the roundhouses! Barricade the doors!" Gormlaith's voice rose from the centre of the chaos, her tone brooking no argument as she directed the younger ones and the elderly.

"Where is Affraic?" Finn's pulse thundered in his ears, his eyes darting around in search of his sister's familiar form amidst the melee.

"Here!" Her voice cut through the turmoil, calm and resolute, as she emerged from a dwelling, her hands already distributing weapons to the able-bodied. "I've hidden the little ones. The caves will shield them."

"Good." Finn nodded, a surge of pride warming him despite the cold grip of apprehension. His sister, once again, proving her cunning and strength.

"Prepare yourselves!" King Tigernach's proclamation echoed above the fray, his presence lending a semblance of order as the villagers looked to their aging ruler for guidance. "Send messengers to the other kings and Malachy that the Norse have landed."

"They won't take us without a fight," Finn declared, grasping the hilt of his sword, the leather familiar and reassuring in his grip. The warrior spirit within him hardened like iron in the forge. Defeat was not an option, not against this Norse horde, not when everything he cherished teetered on the brink of ruin.

As the shadows lengthened and the first stars pricked the velvet sky, the village transformed into a bastion bristling with weapons and anticipation. Every heart pulsed to the rhythm of war drums, every breath hissed with the promise of battle. Through it all, Gormlaith and Affraic attended Finn's wounds so he would not disgrace them in the upcoming battle ahead.

CHAPTER FOUR

THE EAGLE'S CLAW

SIXTY LONGSHIPS DESCENDED UPON their prey, their dragon prows slicing through the serene waters of the bay. Each ship held at least thirty-five men to its bosom, all of whom craved the plunder and destruction promised by their leader, Thurgest, if their conquest of Hibernia was successful. Some saw the journey as merely a raid and would seek to return home when they had all the plunder they could carry. Some were there purely for the adventure, seduced by the tales of old warriors who had returned from previous successful raids to Hibernia. Then there were those who had been banished or chose exile, seeking to make Hibernia their new home. They were the most determined, since the stormy seas had not sunk them on the way there, it was Hibernia or the oblivion of taking to the waters again to find another home that awaited them.

Thurgest stood tall at the helm of the lead vessel, as if his mere presence should terrify the Hibernians into submission. His gaze was as sharp as the steel blade he clenched in his calloused hand. He was a beast of a man, heavily muscled, covered head to toe in intricate tattoos of the variety only the wealthiest of warriors could afford. His hair protruded in blond braids out of the back of his weather-beaten helmet, his face was drawn down into a point by a long straggly beard.

He had been to this island many times before, but having extensively raided in the north he was now turning his attentions south, for he considered it a softer target. He was a jarl in his homeland, but these lands were to become his kingdom. His lust for conquest drove him, his motivation to be the most famous Norse of his age, the burning fire in his soul. That, and the territorial squeeze in his homeland meant that his brother had pushed him out and he had to seek fame and wealth elsewhere. But he was a wandering soul not afraid of the daunting task of landing on hostile shores with a small army of men to conquer the whole island.

But even he, as stubborn and fearless as he was, had nagging doubts in the back of his mind. He had promised so much to the various warbands and jarls that had supported his venture that he needed almost instant success. If he could not pay his men, and quickly, they could turn on him and his dream would turn into the nightmare that led to his death. He also had his ambitious brother to think of at home, who was already probably plotting and conniving to take all his lands while he was gone. But he had taken his son Einar along as part of their compromise agreement on the pretext of making him a man but really he was a hostage to ensure his brother's good behaviour. But all of this could only be a twitch on his impassive face for no one could know of his doubts. For if he showed weakness to his men it would be his death sentence for there would always be someone ambitious enough to try to kill and replace him.

"Steady now," Thurgest murmured.

His warriors, a sea of hardened faces, clenched fists and determined eyes, nodded in quiet acquiescence. They trusted Thurgest, for his cunning had steered them through many a peril, his leadership an anchor in the tumultuous tides of their raids and conquests. They feared Thurgest for his wrath could be at any moment turned against them for the slightest infringement of his will. But jumping out onto the shore if it were full of natives armed to the teeth could only mean death. They squeezed the hilts of their weapons all the tighter.

As the ships neared the shoreline, the Norse leader's gaze pierced the darkness, examining the coast before him. He sought somewhere to land uninterrupted – a place where they might dig their claws into Hibernia's rich soil and claim it as their own.

"Here," Thurgest finally said. "On that beach."

His outstretched arm directed their attention to a beach with a shallow incline of dunes behind it. The spot was flanked by thickets and shadows, an ambush spot for sure, but the incline would be easy to assault if they ran into resistance.

"That's where I have been told a natural harbour lies behind. It is known as 'the Black Pool' according to our Hibernian friends. This is where we will establish our longphort."

Thurgest squinted into the darkness to ensure where he had chosen was correct.

"Drop sails!"

The sails fell as one, the ships slowing as they approached the banks of the river where it met the sea.

"Ready the grapples," Thurgest said. "We land here."

Thurgest stood tall, his silhouette imposing against the moonlit night as the prow of his longship scraped the gravelly shore.

"Disembark."

His men responded with the dexterity of the greatest craftsmen. Oars lifted in unison, sliding softly onto the deck; shields gave the faintest of noises as they were unslung from backs; swords whispered from their scabbards. Bodies waded through the water, securing the boats so their comrades would not get wet. Boots met earth, heavy and purposeful, leaving deep impressions in the wet sand. The tang of seaweed mingled with the scent of anticipation emanating from the men.

Thurgest's gaze never wavered from the shore that beckoned them forward. He stepped off the ship last, his own boots sinking into the gravel and sand. He felt a pang of satisfaction that he had crossed the storm-riven seas with his army intact, but knew the hard work started here. For with each footfall, he claimed this land, an unspoken vow etched into every step. His warriors gathered, and their weapons and shields formed a metallic forest bristling around him.

"Form up," he instructed, his tone allowing no disobedience.

They obeyed, finding their places with the ease of many battles fought shoulder to shoulder. Their shield wall was sleek and deadly. Each man knew his place, ready to protect their fellow warriors and leader. They scanned the surrounding sand dunes but all their vision inspired was fear and apprehension for it was all shadows and darkness with the spindly shoots of grass on top of the dunes silhouetted against the inky black sky.

They began their march, their progress a measured cadence over root and stone. Eyes flicked from shadow to shadow, seeking out any hint of threat. Yet, there was only the rustling of leaves and the distant cry of a falcon cutting through the night sky. The world held its breath, the moon and the stars watching these Norsemen with wary eyes.

Thurgest halted his men and listened into the silence. He heard only the sound of distant nocturnal animals going about their own business. They climbed the sand dunes and beyond that they saw the moon shimmering over what appeared to be the perfect body of water for a protected harbour.

"There's no one here," Thurgest said. "This must be the Black Pool our Hibernian thralls told us about. Make a camp and tomorrow we'll explore our new lands."

The men dispersed at their leader's command.

Back at the bay, where the black pool mirrored the dark sky, Thurgest watched over his men with the acuity of a seasoned chieftain. He pulled his wolfskin cloak tighter for there was a nip in the air and even the Norse were susceptible to the cold of the night. Broad shoulders squared, he surveyed the managed chaos of preparation. The Norsemen worked methodically, erecting shelters and tents they carried up from their ships. Their camp stood out under the starry night like a wart on the back of Hibernia's hand.

"Keep sharp," Thurgest's voice cut through the muted din of activity, "you never know what could strike us out of these woods. These Hibernians can fight like trolls when properly motivated."

His men grunted their acknowledgment, the sound a low rumble of assent. They knew their leader's reputation had seen him carve victory from the jaws of defeat more times than they could count. But if faced with defeat, he always had a smartly placed ship he could run to if he needed to escape. In Thurgest's presence, there was no room for doubt, only the unyielding drive to succeed and claim their place in legend.

They all thought he had chosen well, for he had listened to the treacherous Hibernians who he had brought with him, captured on previous raids. They now were branded with Norse tattoos, which meant they could never go back to their homelands. They would be dead by a nervous arrow before they could blurt out their sorry tales of capture and abuse, and that they had only changed sides on pain of death. They had brought their new Viking masters to a sheltered pool known as the Black Pool that was off the entrance to the river Liffey but was the most defensible position on the river. It was free from the tides of the sea and could only be approached in one direction over the water. It was a perfect base from which Thurgest could start his conquest.

A figure approached, casting a long shadow in the light of the campfires that flickered in the moonlight. As the shadow neared, it became the huge hulk of a man, shoulders and arms a dense bulk of muscle. The shadow became more detailed to show the wolf's head on his shoulder, a reminder he kept on the pelt he used as his blanket to always be alert. It was Torstein, returned from seeing the scouts off. He was a man whose loyalty to Thurgest was as steadfast as the ancient rocks that lined the shores of their homeland.

"The men have their instructions and make all haste," Torstein said, his voice a low rumble. "There is no sign of any enemy force in our immediate vicinity."

"Good," Thurgest replied, his gaze never leaving the edge of the forest from where any potential attack would come. "Until the camp is finished, we are at our weakest. We will need every advantage this night. Split the men in two, some to make the camp and the rest to keep watch and prepare for tomorrow's raid. But there will be no sleep for us to be had this night."

Thurgest pointed to Torstein and himself. Torstein nodded and turned to relay his master's instructions to the men.

"But spare the ale. The men must have their full wits about them this night."

Torstein scowled.

"They won't be happy with that. The men like a drink after such a long and perilous journey."

"If they complain, tell them I like them alive to do my bidding, not lying in a ditch with their throats cut because they were too drunk to see the Hibernian knife coming."

Torstein nodded. He had his orders.

By the glow of the fires, the warriors sharpened their axes and swords, sparks dancing into the night like fireflies. Their faces, illuminated by the orange light, were masks of determination etched with the stories of countless raids and battles. This was their element – the anticipation of the raid, the promise of glory and riches, and the camaraderie of brothers-in-arms.

Meanwhile, beneath the vast expanse of stars, and the nocturnal howls of the beasts of Hibernia, Thurgest waited, for either an assault by the natives, or for the scouts to return.

CHAPTER FIVE

THE LURE OF GOLD

THE SOFT RUSTLE OF leaves and the indistinct murmur of voices broke the stillness of the night as shadows detached themselves from the darkness, materialising into the forms of Thurgest's chosen warriors. The blades that faced them were withdrawn when their faces became recognisable in the flickering firelight.

"Thurgest," one of the scouts called out. His tone carried the delight of good news and hope of ingratiating himself with his master. "There is a monastery but a few hours' walk from here that lies unguarded. Its doors are wide open to us, as if the sheep are inviting the wolf into their fold."

"Tell me," and Thurgest beckoned him forward. He squeezed his fist for if the monastery had much of value it would solve his immediate problem of paying his men and maybe even supply some thralls.

"Gold, my lord!" exclaimed another, stepping forward with eagerness etched on his rugged features. "Chalices, crosses, all wrought with precious metal." His hands gestured with greed-driven enthusiasm, painting the air with visions of their spoils. "And books... so many books. Their covers glint with jewels that catch the moonlight like the eyes of a dragon hoarding its treasure."

"Books," Thurgest mused aloud, the word rolling off his tongue like a foreign coin, unfamiliar yet laden with potential. "Knowledge to be bartered or burned."

"Indeed, and more," the first scout added, not to be outdone. "Icons of saints and relics said to perform miracles – at least by those who believe in such things."

"Belief is a weapon as much as any blade," Thurgest said, his mind already weaving the threads of opportunity into a cunning tapestry. "But so is fear. We shall relieve them of these burdens.

May their once holy relics to their cowardly god be the first of many repayments to those who have been loyal to me and brave enough to cross the great waters."

He paced before the flames that licked at the darkness, casting a giant's shadow upon the ground. The glow of the fire danced in his eyes, revealing a mind alight with strategy. Thurgest stopped, planting his feet firmly on the earth as if drawing strength from its core.

"Brothers," he began, his voice a resonant growl that rumbled through the ranks, "we strike the monastery at dawn. It will serve as our spearhead, a diversion to confound any who might oppose us."

"Will we not draw the ire of the locals?" Torstein wondered. He worried that if they revealed their position too soon they would bring the wrath of all the Hibernian kings down upon them and the once black pool where they made their camp would be red with Norse blood.

"Let them come," Thurgest replied with a fierce grin. "When they see the smoke and hear the cries of their foolish priests, their attention will be ours to command. They will flock to the monastery like moths to a flame, and once they are defeated they will have left our true prize, the land and its riches, exposed."

"By Odin, it's a daring gambit," another warrior exclaimed.

"Fortune favours the bold," Thurgest declared. "We are the storm that comes without warning, the tide that sweeps away the unwary, the wolf that sinks its fangs into the helpless lamb. Tonight, we are fate's hand, and we shall grasp this opportunity with iron resolve."

He looked upon his warriors, their faces illuminated by fire and the burning desire for glory. He knew how to conjure up the right words to get their blood pumping.

"Don your armour, sharpen your steel, and ready your souls for the glory of Valhalla," he ordered, turning his back to the fire, casting his face into shadow while the light outlined his powerful silhouette. "Rest, if you must. But keep your weapons close and your spirits closer. Be warned we leave before this hour is settled. We sail on fortune's wind, and she blows ever in our favour. In favour of the brave and valiant men from the north."

The men shook their weapons in silence to acknowledge the words of their leader. The warriors dispersed, each man a tight knot of pent-up energy, murmurs of strategy and fate entwining like smoke around their hushed conversations. They adorned themselves in chain mail and warpaint, their movements methodical, a ritual honed by countless raids and skirmishes.

As the men dispersed to tend to their duties, Thurgest stood alone, the weight of leadership resting on his shoulders like the yoke of a mighty ox. He gazed up at the sprawling canvas of stars, and allowed himself a moment to savour the anticipation of conquest. Tomorrow would bring blood and spoil, but tonight, the world held its breath, waiting for the axe to fall.

Thurgest's silhouette cut an imposing figure against the lowering moon, his voice a low thrum that wove through the ranks of his assembled warriors. "Brothers of the sword," he began, each word deliberate occupying no more of the night than absolutely necessary. "I have called you back together for tonight we strike with the silence of a shadow and the suddenness of thunder." His gaze moved across the upturned faces, their expressions a mosaic of anticipation and ferocity. "Our enemies slumber, their monastery walls unguarded, their treasures gleaming and unclaimed. But it is not the gold nor the silver that we seek this eve". He scanned the eyes of his men for the true source of their greed, for those rebellious eyes that betrayed those who did not realise their true mission. He continued upon noting no dissent. "It is the terror we shall sow in their hearts. For once the terror takes hold, it will rot their will and these green and rich lands will then be ours."

The men shifted, resisting the urge to cheer their leader's inspirational words, leather creaking and metal clinking softly, a chorus of readiness. Thurgest stepped closer, lowering his voice to ensure every man leaned in to catch his murmured plan. "We will move as phantoms through the dark, swift, and unseen. The monastery will be our lure, its pillage, a message written in flame and fear."

Eyes smouldered in the torchlight, reflecting a kindling resolve. Thurgest raised his hand, palm flat, a silent command for attention. "For it is fear that is our greatest friend. It makes them who are in its possession drop their swords, forget their duties to their masters and families, and leave the field to us, the children of

Odin. We are the wolves at the door, the storm that breaks upon these foreign shores. Let no man falter, for tonight, we carve our destiny with the edge of our blades."

A ripple of excitement surged through the gathering. The warriors gripped their axes and swords tighter, the air thick with the promise of battle. There was no dissent. This is what they came to Hibernia for. They were united in purpose, a single entity guided by Thurgest's indomitable will.

"Go now," he instructed. "Follow your leaders, who in turn follow the scouts that know the way. We strike at the hour of the wolf, when the moon stands guard and the world holds its breath."

The landscape, bathed in the hues of twilight, lay hushed and unsuspecting as the chosen warriors, silent phantoms in Thurgest's formidable host, wove through the undulating terrain. They moved with the stealth of a hunting pack, each step deliberate and soft upon the fresh earth, eyes vigilant for signs of life around the monastery that sat like a slumbering beast unaware of the predators at its doorstep.

Their movements were but whispers against the backdrop of nature's chorus, the distant call of an owl, the rustle of leaves in the gentle evening breeze. The air was cool on their skin, carrying the scent of damp soil and the faintest trace of smoke from some far-off hearth. They communicated not with words but with gestures, a language of war-hardened kinship, each nod or hand signal enough to convey volumes.

Thurgest watched them, his heart a drumbeat of nerves and expectations. He turned his face towards the distant monastery, a dark outline against the star-pricked sky, and felt the old thrill of conquest surge within him. Soon, he would give the signal, and they would descend upon the monastery like a tempest from the old tales. And as he waited, the world indeed seemed to pause, the very air holding its breath in anticipation of the coming storm.

"Torstein, Einar" he called, selecting his men as one might choose arrows for a decisive shot. Torstein was one of his most trusted warriors whose axe had sung beside his own in many a fray. Einar was his nephew who he was supposed to blood and make a man. This would be the easiest opportunity.

"Approach the monastery and see who guards it," Thurgest said. "Then signal at the opportune time to strike."

"Understood," Torstein said.

He nodded and signalled to Einar who followed him into the twilight.

CHAPTER SIX

THE GREEN BEAST

Torstein's breath misted in the cool dawn as he led Einar through the thicket, their bodies low to the earth. The dawn was but a whisper against the sky, barely touching the treetops that towered above them. Each man moved with a predator's grace, their leather and chain mail scarcely rustling the undergrowth, despite the bramble's clutching fingers.

The mist of twilight clung to the woods like a lingering spirit, shrouding their advance towards the monastery. Einar trailed just behind Torstein, his eyes scanning the shadows, senses honed for any hint of resistance. He was well used to hunting and had some fighting experience, but all of this was back in his homeland, where he was familiar with the land. This was completely different, a foreign land in the twilight, the death of the night punctuated by the howls of unknown beasts. They were only supposed to be fighting priests, but he could not prevent his hand from shaking. Something he did not want Torstein to find out. So he tucked it in his pocket only to be rewarded with the sting of branches in his face that his spare hand should have warded off. He asked the gods to help a novice warrior to smooth his way to Valhalla should it come to that.

Torstein did not need to evidence a shaking hand to resent the young man for in his opinion his very presence detracted from his opportunity to win favour with Thurgest. He had served Thurgest faithfully for years and had yet to receive his just rewards for all his efforts. This boy could only ruin it for him and cast him back to the front of the shield wall.

Torstein squinted towards the horizon where the sun began its ascent, a blood-orange disc heralding the new day. It bathed the trees in a gentle luminescence, casting long shadows that danced with the retreating night. The woods themselves seemed to hold their breath, awaiting the unfolding drama.

As they neared the clearing, the hushed murmurs of morning prayers whispered through the air. Monks, clad in simple robes, emerged from their stone cells like a procession of ghosts. They lined up one by one, their heads bowed in reverence, oblivious to the two Norsemen concealed by the woodland's edge.

"See," Torstein said, his voice no louder than the rustle of leaves, "no guards. No spears nor swords. They think praying to their God will protect them, but their God will not shield them from Odin's blades."

They juddered when they heard the bang of a door from one of the monastery buildings and scoured the yard for its source. A boy with a bucket appeared executing some chore or other, but his loud yawn indicated he had not long risen. The boy's head jerked back at the crack of a twig. Einar raised his hand in apology. Torstein scowled and wished that Thurgest had sent a man with more experience than a fool who would carelessly give their position away. The Hibernian boy's head darted from side to side and into the nearby woods where the Norse were hidden. He dropped his bucket and ran back towards the monastery.

Torstein ground his teeth for a quick decision had to be made. His hand tightened around the haft of his axe, muscles tensing with anticipation. Einar secretly pinched himself on the thigh so he could concentrate his mind on the brief pain and not the pit of fear in his stomach. Torstein gave a nod. It was time. Torstein rose first, his axe held high above the bushes. Einar surged from their cover, the suddenness of their charge cutting through the serenity of the morning.

Their roar shattered the calm, fierce and bloodcurdling, a sound to freeze the heart of any man. The priests halted mid-chant, their peaceful line thrown into disarray. With terror wide in their eyes, they dropped to their knees upon the dew-soaked grass, hands clasped, praying to their God for deliverance from the wrath of these northern invaders.

Thurgest also heard the roars, hidden as he was in the woods with the main body of men.

"It is time for the men of the pale Christ to meet Norse steel," he cried as he raised his axe to signal the charge. The men roared and charged behind him.

Steel glinted in the soft light of dawn as the Norse descended, the sharp sound of their battle cries mingling with the muted whispers of morning prayers. Thurgest led the onslaught, his silhouette a spectre of death against the burgeoning light that struggled to chase away the night's shadows. His men, fierce and relentless, followed in his wake, axes swinging with brutal precision.

The monks stood no chance. They were lambs amidst wolves, jumping for the blade alleviated the pain all the quicker. The air thickened with the smell of sweat and fear as blood blossomed upon the verdant grass. Robes of simple cloth sliced easily under the unyielding bite of Norse steel. Several of the holy men fell, their last breaths gliding on the chilled air before their lifeless bodies fell to the ground. The remaining priests huddled together as there was no longer a means of escape.

"Enough!" Thurgest's voice boomed across the clearing, halting the massacre as abruptly as it had begun. "We have not come for death but for gold."

The remaining priests huddled together, their eyes wild with fear, yet as they could still clasp their hands together in prayer, some spark of defiance flickered within them. Thurgest beckoned forward one of his Hibernians to stand between himself and his prisoners to translate.

"Know this, priests," Thurgest proclaimed, one foot on the head of one of their fallen brethren. "I am Thurgest, he who commands the winds and tames the waves. My name is feared across the breadth of Hibernia. Your God has abandoned you to cower beneath my blade. Now your choice is simple. Say your prayers and we will send you to your God and you can see if all the time you spent on your knees was worth your effort. Or, think to yourself, I am under the blade of Thurgest, yet he is merciful. What can I do for Thurgest that will stop the blade from coming upon my neck and cleaving my head from my body?"

The abbot, an elder whose spine was bent by both age and years of devotion, rose from his knees. His gaze never wavered as it locked with Thurgest's.

"I care not for your name, heathen," he spat. "Even if I knew thee, it would change naught. You are damned, damned to the deepest pits of hell for this sacrilege."

A moment hung between them, as Thurgest digested this defiance from someone so old and frail, without the strength to back up his words. Then, swift as a falcon's dive, a talon of steel found its target. Thurgest stepped back to show the dagger in the defiant priest's heart. The old man's eyes rendered a final flash of surprise before he crumpled to the earth, his soul departing on the morning breeze.

"He wasted his last breath," Thurgest said with a nonchalant wave of his hand. "If he chose to die, it would have been better with a prayer on his lips."

Thurgest turned to survey the remaining priests. His eyes were those of a hawk ready to swoop down on any lingering defiance, his chest heaving from exertion and exhilaration. But all he saw were the tops of bowed heads, all shaking in a cacophony of muffled prayers.

The dawn had crept in with hesitance, as if wary of disturbing the aftermath of Thurgest's wrath. The scent of fresh blood mingled with the earthy aroma of the dew-kissed grass, the juxtaposition to the serene chorus of morning birdsong not being wasted on the priests.

"Tell me," he began, "who would like to save their life by telling me where you've hidden the gold?"

The nearest monk, a wiry man with fingers interlocked in silent prayer, raised his head. His eyes held the remnants of fear, but his voice was steady. "We have taken a vow of poverty, lord. Our coffers are empty save for the instruments of the sacraments, which repose within the church."

"Poverty?" Thurgest's laugh was scornful as he turned to face his men. "They mock us with tales of empty purses and holy trinkets!" His gaze whipped back to the monks. "You'll each meet your God just as your master has, unless something of value is offered. Or else I can help you fulfil your vows of poverty as I will ensure you gain no earthly possessions as you live as my thralls. Now, what is it to be?"

Priestly heads bowed. The silence was their defiance, or in some cases resignation to fate.

Thurgest cursed the pale Christ and unsheathed his dagger, its blade catching the first rays of the sun. The metal sang a song of death as it glinted in the morning light. He stepped forward, his face grim and resolute. The decision was made. Two priests fell before the rest, their bodies crumpling to the ground, their blood seeping into the soil of their homeland.

"Enough!" A young monk stumbled forward, his habit soaked with terror and humiliation. "Mercy, please! The only... the only thing of wealth we possess is knowledge. The ford over the river Liffey. It's the lifeblood of trade on this side of Hibernia." His breaths were ragged, the words tumbling out in desperation. "He who controls the ford, commands the trade. Knowledge and power, my lord... that is our treasure for you."

Thurgest paused, the heavy breaths of his warriors the only sound to break the hush of dawn. His eyes narrowed, weighing the monk's words like coins on a scale. Control. Power. These were currencies he understood and valued far more than the glitter of gold.

"Then you will show me," Thurgest growled. "If it holds value, it shall be mine. If not..." His eyes flicked over the remaining priests, each one pallid as death itself, "the river will claim you and the only thing of value this ford of yours will be covered with is your blood."

Without another word, they set off, the nascent light of dawn casting long shadows across the land. The mists clung to the earth like spirits unwilling to depart, ensnaring the priests' legs in cold tendrils as they were frogmarched towards the fabled ford. Their long robes, damp with the morning dew, whispered against the foliage, a mournful chorus accompanying their grim procession. A prayer for help. A prayer for hope.

Thurgest led them, his thoughts a tangle of anticipation and scepticism. Control of trade meant power, true, but could such a claim be trusted? It was a gamble, and Thurgest was not a man to leave his fortunes to chance. He signalled to his senior hersirs to be ready in case it was all a ruse.

The river's murmurs reached them before its waters came into view. A promise of life – and for some, perhaps, a harbinger of death. It depended whether their promises contained a kernel of truth. As they emerged from the woods, the mist began to retreat, drawing back its veil to reveal the ford in all its strategic significance.

"See," the young monk said, extending a shaky hand. "This is the heart of trade, where goods flow as freely as the river itself."

Thurgest studied the ford, the way the water rippled and danced over stones worn smooth by countless crossings. He imagined longboats laden with wares, the clink of coin, the haggling of merchants, but more importantly, he could build a bridge and instantly strangle any trade not controlled by him. The monk saw a green beast grow in his eyes.

"Control here means dominion over the wealth that passes through," the monk continued, his voice gaining strength. "But also responsibility for its safeguarding. But be warned."

Thurgest raised an eyebrow that this monk thought himself so familiar that he could issue a warning to the mighty Thurgest. The monk gulped, but stuttered out his warning all the same, as if his and the lives of his fellow monks depended on it.

"The kings of the region also derive their wealth from this ford, so any attempt to possess it would immediately incur their wrath."

"Thank you, priest," Thurgest said, his tone softer, yet still edged with steel. "You show me wealth and a way to meet the local kings. I would not have accomplished so much today if it had not been for you." He turned to address the priests, their faces drawn with dread and exhaustion. "The river will not feast today." His proclamation seemed to lift the fog from their hearts, if only slightly. "Back to our camp," he ordered, his command brooking no argument. "We are in need of thralls and you have a vow of poverty to keep. My offer was to spare your lives only. If you were so ready to offer me up the wealth of Hibernia to one you would call your enemy, I can only imagine how your mouth would gush forth if you met someone you'd call a friend."

The monks' mouths dropped, but they were shoved at sword point towards the Norse camp. As the monks shuffled away, Thurgest stood alone by the Liffey's banks, the weight of potential conquest heavy on his shoulders. The river flowed on, indifferent to the fates of men, as eternal as the mist that now retreated before the relentless rise of the sun.

CHAPTER SEVEN

THE STUBBORN CHILD

WEEKS OF INTENSE APPREHENSION melted away. Muscles tired of being tense, minds exhausted of mulling through every permutation of the future which ended in their cruel and horrible death, the contemplation of an imminent threat at their door became rationalised away. The mind settles on a new equilibrium, the new melts into the present to become confused with the old. What was once a real and present danger blurs into the landscape called a possible future. Hope springs as life sprouts. Minds settle down and find peace once more.

So it happened in Finn's village. The air in the village was cleansed by the rain and had softened into a gentle rhythm of tranquillity. Children's laughter once again wove through the thatched roofs and mingled with the clucking of hens foraging in the commons. The scent of freshly baked bread from the communal oven carried on the breeze. Once more, they brewed ale. Tendrils of smoke from peat fires painted hazy trails against the azure sky as it caked everything in its path with its oppressive smell and grey ash. In the distance, the anvil's song chimed a steady beat as the blacksmith worked, shaping ploughshares instead of swords.

Hemmed within the modest confines of his family hut, Finn sat hunched over his collection of old weapons, most of them from his father's day, their blades dulled by time rather than use. Shadows danced across the walls, cast by the flickering flames of the hearth, which filled the space with the earthy smell of burning turf. Copper pots hung above the embers, their exteriors stained with soot, mute witnesses to countless shared meals. The aroma of dried herbs lingered in the air, mixed with the musky scent of leather from Finn's armour, now resting unused in the corner. All sat above the smell of smoke embedded into the walls of the hut and every item that entered it that could absorb its smell.

Finn's hands moved with grace from years of practice, polishing the tarnished metal, yet each stroke of the whetstone was a grim reminder of his recent shame at the hands of Ultán. His broad shoulders slumped slightly and he set the blade aside, flexing his fingers to ward off cramp and the creeping cold that settled not upon his skin, but deep in his marrow, where no fire could reach. The memories festered longer than his physical wounds, refusing to heal. They relentlessly turned over again and again, a cacophony that swelled in his mind, ceaseless and cruel. How could he let himself be cheated so? Why did he not fight back? How could King Tigernach or the villagers who had cheered him on in the previous game allow such an injustice to stand? He turned his gaze, praying for some distraction. The unfinished blanket on his mother's loom told of quieter days free of Ultán and Tigernach, before his pride got trampled into the mud of the hurling field.

The door creaked open, and Gormlaith entered, her arms laden with a basket brimming with root vegetables, the scent of the soil still clinging to their earthy skins. She moved about the hut with an ease born of years tending to her family, the rustle of her woollen dress blending with the soft thud of produce placed upon the wooden table. But the sullen face of Finn poisoned her jovial morning mood.

"Will you not rest, Finn?" Her voice, laced with concern, broke through the steady rhythm of his brooding.

"Rest is for the weary, not the wronged," he replied, his tone sharper than intended.

Gormlaith ignored the sullen tone of youth and took the vegetables carefully out of the basket, examining each one for defects or signs of rot that would render them unusable. Gormlaith's hands, calloused from toil, began the familiar dance of meal preparation. She sliced through turnips and carrots with a seasoned hand, the sounds crisp in the quiet room. She cast a glance at her son, noting the furrow in his brow and the set of his jaw, a mother's eye for her child's unspoken hurts.

"You've got to know when to give up, Finn, to step aside. The world doesn't always work in the way you want it, and we all have limited control over our lives. You should have stepped aside and given the king's son his day and everyone would have understood and not held it against you. But no, you are now so battered and bruised you are useless to attend to either pig or hen and you sit there wasting your time moping."

"You don't understand."

Finn jabbed his index finger in his mother's direction as if he had returned to being a child. Gormlaith was a patient mother used to two strong and emotional children. The rhythm of her vegetable chopping did not miss a beat.

"Oh, but I do. Time progresses for all of us. I was not always the grey-haired wrinkly woman you see before you. I was once a youth, full of vim, vigour and folly, just like you. But life caught up with me and I learned sometimes you have to swallow your pride and step aside."

Finn snarled at such foolishness coming from his own mother's mouth.

"Is it pride that has you locked up in this hut, your husband long in the grave? A woman of your looks and abilities should have been able to snare herself a good husband long ago."

Gormlaith slammed down her knife.

"This woman of good looks and 'abilities' also had the misfortune of giving birth to a conceited son too prone to act or speak without thinking of the consequences first. I can easily feed your dinner to the pigs. At least I'd get a snort of gratitude."

Finn's face dropped along with the whetstone to the floor as he realised the consequences of his anger-tinged words. He ran over to embrace his mother, but found himself facing the cold shoulder. Gormlaith picked up her knife and finished her chopping. She ignored him and selected a pot for that evening's dinner.

"Water, and make sure it's clean this time."

She thrust the pot into Finn's chest and resumed her chores. He returned several minutes later with a half-full pot of water. Gormlaith took it off him and peered inside.

"It'll do. It'll be your fault if it makes us sick."

Finn held his hands out, seeking his mother's forgiveness.

"If only you were as handy with a dagger the way you stab words into the heart of your mother."

Finn bowed his head.

"No one has a sharper tongue than you, not even Affraic. You also know how to stab straight into my heart."

Gormlaith paused, for it was not often she got her son's thick ears to be receptive. She would pick her subjects carefully and try and plant a seed in her son's head she hoped would eventually germinate.

"Well, if it's forgiveness you want from me, you can have a serious conversation with me."

Finn sighed, for he knew he was cornered.

"Such as?" Finn asked, though his interest was feigned, a thin veil over the turmoil within.

"Marriage," Gormlaith ventured, her voice gentle. "You're of marrying age, Finn. Strong, brave, I see the way you look at Affraic's friend Étaín. Are you a bit sweet on her?"

"Marriage?" Finn cut her off with a scornful laugh, the raw edge of his pride bleeding into the word. His mind had flown straight back to the public humiliation given to him by Ultán. "I've no need for ties when my honour lies in tatters. Who would want to tarnish their own standing in the village by entering into marriage with me?"

"Son, there's no shame in seeking happiness."

She reached out, her touch warm against the chill of his arm.

"Nor is there any in seeking vengeance," Finn snapped, pulling away.

His heart raged against the notion of domestic bliss when every fibre within him thirsted for retribution.

"Vengeance is a flame that warms naught but itself," Gormlaith murmured, her words floating like smoke in the heavy air.

But Finn was deaf to her wisdom, his spirit alight with the fire of his own indignation. He stood abruptly, and turned towards the doorway. It seemed, in that moment, the walls of the hut pressed in upon him, suffocating him under the weight of a peace he neither desired nor could endure.

He was half out the doorway when the clamour pierced the tranquillity of the village. Boots pounded the earth, stirring a rhythm that heralded urgency and unrest. Outside, the voice of a messenger cut through the air like a swift arrow.

"Hear ye! By order of King Tigernach, all men of fighting age are summoned to his hillfort with haste!"

Gormlaith's hands stilled, the knife she was using to chop root vegetables falling silent upon the wooden board. She turned to her son, her eyes wide and fraught with worry. The scent of peat smoke hung heavily between them, a silent witness to the stifling tension.

"Stay, Finn." Gormlaith's voice was a plea wrapped in the steel of maternal command. "Heed not this call to arms. 'Tis your pride, wounded and raw, that would march you to folly."

Finn's gaze swung towards her, a storm of resolve brewing behind his eyes.

"Do you expect me to cower while others stand for our land? I will not!"

His voice was a growl, a steaming broth of indignation and injured honour.

"Your heart seeks a battle to mend what's been torn," she said, reaching out as though she could hold back the tempest within him with her bare hands. "But vengeance is a path that leads only to more sorrow. Be a man, but not like your father."

"Don't bludgeon me round the head with my father's memory as if it were a blunt sword to control me," he said, his voice softening just a fraction before his resolve hardened once again. "This is my path to tread, and mine alone. Fate leads me out this door."

With a swift motion, he shrugged off her touch, the finality in his movement echoing louder than the anger reverberating in his voice.

"Your father..." Gormlaith began, invoking the memory of a warrior who knew the cost of wrath.

"Is not here!" Finn snapped back, sealing the past with the present. "And I must stand where he cannot."

Silent tears pricked at the corners of Gormlaith's eyes, but she blinked them back with proud ferocity. It was not the time for weeping. Her son, so much like his father, bristled with the same stubborn pride that had led many a man down a perilous road.

"Promise me, then," she implored, her voice breaking as she clutched at the woven fabric of his tunic, "promise me you'll return. Not for vengeance, nor glory, but for me, for us."

"Mother—"

The word caught in Finn's throat, rough with unspoken emotions. He placed his hand over hers, the callouses of his palm pressing into the softness of her skin.

"Promise me, Finn," she repeated, her voice steadying with the strength of her conviction.

"I promise," he said at last, the words feeling like stones within his mouth. He gently pulled away from her grip, gathering his weapons, a sword inherited from a fallen father and a shield battered in past skirmishes.

The door creaked open to the world beyond, where honour called and destiny awaited. With one last look that held a lifetime of love and fear, Finn stepped out of the hut, leaving the warmth of hearth and home for the cold embrace of an uncertain future.

Affraic's shadow stretched long across the earthen path, the sun dipping low behind her as she hurried towards home. Her basket was heavy with herbs, her hands stained with their scent after spending a day picking. The village was abuzz with the movements of men; their clanking armour and muted conversations told Affraic something big had either happened or was about to happen. Her mind immediately went to her stewing brother and how she must stop him from doing anything stupid.

"Mother?" Affraic called out as she pushed aside the woollen drape of their hut's entrance, her voice tinged with concern at the unusual haste outside.

Gormlaith sat by the hearth, the firelight casting a warm glow on her weathered face, a stark contrast to the cold worry in her eyes. "They have been summoned," she said simply, gesturing towards the open door where the sounds of urgency grew louder.

"Summoned?" Affraic's brow furrowed, and she set her basket down with a soft thud. "By the king?"

"Aye, to Tigernach's hillfort." Gormlaith rose, crossing the room to stand beside her daughter. "Finn has gone with them."

"Without a word to his sister?"

"His pride..." Gormlaith's voice trailed off, laden with a mother's sorrow. "It clouds his reason. I fear for him."

"Then we must follow," Affraic stated, the resolve hardening within her like the sharpening of a blade. She was not one to watch from the sidelines.

"Follow?" Gormlaith echoed, trepidation knitting her brow. "And do what, exactly? We cannot interfere."

"Interfere, no. But witness, we must." Affraic's hand found her mother's, a silent pact forming between them. "We will keep to the shadows, but we shall be close."

"Witness what? I don't have to move from his hearth to see my son's stupidity. Why would I place myself in jeopardy to see him do it in the hillfort?"

Affraic arched her eyebrow.

"For all your complaints about your children, I can see where we got our stubbornness from."

Gormlaith tutted and turned her head to ignore her taunting child.

"Remember he made a bet with Ultán that he owed him a favour if he lost the game? It doesn't take a soothsayer to predict that Ultán will call it in now."

"But the game was called off, so the bet was off."

"Do you think Ultán and Tigernach will see it like that? Especially in their own fort?"

Gormlaith pondered a moment and saw all the ingredients for her son's demise neatly chopped up and laid before her. She leapt from the hearth and picked up her shawl.

"Why didn't you tell me that sooner?" she growled at Affraic.

Together, they stepped beyond the safety of their home, leaving the comforting smell of peat smoke behind. The grasses whispered secrets beneath their hastening steps, and the shadows threw off visions of doom and gloom as they trailed after the procession of men. Each warrior carried the weight of impending confrontation upon his shoulders. Fields and forests passed by, streams were crossed and lakes circumvented.

The groups of warriors grew and Gormlaith and Affraic could move around more freely with these different groups for cover. They saw the tension etched in the warriors' faces, more prevalent in the older warriors than the young. The tales of the Norse had spread from the north where they had been a blight for many a year whereas where they lived had been infrequently pestered by raiders, and if they had, they were easily beaten off.

The hillfort loomed ahead, an ancient sentinel watching over the land. It was as if man had made a mountain and hollowed out the middle for his home. As the sky bled into twilight, the silhouette of its palisades cut into the horizon, a jagged line dividing earth from the heavens.

"Be safe, my son," Gormlaith murmured under her breath, a prayer to the gods old and new. Affraic squeezed her mother's hand tighter, her thoughts echoing the plea.

In the distance, the men's figures became indistinct, merging with the encroaching darkness. Affraic glanced at her mother.

"Whatever comes," Affraic whispered, strength and vulnerability intermingling in her voice, "we face it together."

"Always," Gormlaith answered, her gaze fixed on the shadows that danced ahead. "Now to get in there unnoticed."

CHAPTER EIGHT

FROM A MOTHER'S LIPS

THE DARKNESS LIFTED, REPLACED by the soft glow of early morning light that crawled through the mist. The sun's rays painted the sky a pale pink and orange, casting a gentle warmth over the fort. Gormlaith and Affraic rose from their slumbers, their ribs aching from sleeping on the floor of a hut of a friend and their muscles protesting as they rose from their slumbers. But all in all, the accommodation was not too bad, considering the overcrowding of the fort.

The air was filled with the aroma of freshly baked bread from nearby ovens and the scent of burning wood from cooking fires. But it always paid to have friends in the regional marketplace. They took the hunks of bread given to them by their hosts and said their goodbyes with promises to see them again soon. As they made their way through the crowds, they could feel the press of bodies against them, as everyone was trying to get into the hillfort for an audience with the king.

The hillfort bore the weight of the morning's mist. The earthen walls held the murk at bay, its ancient stones a huddle of shadow against the pallid sky. The priests, dressed in ornate robes with animal skins draped over their shoulders, lit a fire in the circle, calling the men for an audience with King Tigernach. They then lined up on both sides of the fire, their painted white faces lending solemn authority to the ceremony. Thick grey royal smoke tinged the smell of damp earth and woodsmoke from more domestic fires clung to the heavy woollen cloaks of the warriors, tattered at the edges by countless battles and seasons. The men followed the plumes of smoke and clustered in the central meeting circle, their breaths billowing like spectres in the chill air. A mixture of leather and iron clad their sturdy frames, while hands calloused from toil rested upon the hilts of swords and axes, the weapons' presence as familiar as the heft of a plough or the grip of an oar.

Finn stood with the sinewy throng of his kinsmen. His armour was older than most of theirs, slightly ill-fitting as it was the inheritance from his father along with his sword. He had added a couple of straps so his armour could be pulled into a more snug fit to offer a more even level of protection. It also saved his pride for he looked less of a boy dressed in his father's armour. The sword was a fine blade which made an impressive whoosh as it cut through the air. Finn had no idea what it sounded like when it cut through a man for he had yet to hear the din of battle. As a result, the sense of anticipation coiled tight in his stomach. There was one good thing all could say about King Tigernach: no matter what else he did or how he did it, he had brought about several years of peace.

King Tigernach perched uneasily on his throne, a chair carved of knotted oak and draped with threadbare furs. He fidgeted with the chain at his throat, a man uncomfortable in himself, looking from left to right like a rabbit caught in the open field. His eyes, once sharp as a hawk's, now held a sheen of uncertainty that belied his reputation for cunning manoeuvres and political intrigue. The greying hairs along his beard bristled as if charged by the whispers of doubt, of his crown slipping, of the silent dagger coming in the night, slithering through the ranks of his own court.

Finn's gaze narrowed, observing the king's uncharacteristic nervousness. He knew that look from the hurling pitch. It was the look of a man who knew he was beaten before the game had even begun. Leadership, he knew, was as much about appearance as action, and the sight before him drained the confidence the excitement in his veins was trying to sustain. When Ultán, the king's son, rose to stand beside his father, the tension in the air tightened like a bowstring. The younger man's features were wrought with a seriousness that mirrored the storm clouds above. His attempt at looking confident always had a touch of arrogance, with a sliver of cruelty, but today he could barely lift his eyes to meet the crowd.

"Father," Ultán murmured, leaning closer so only the king could hear, yet the apprehension that danced across his face was clear for all to see. His words were a murmur lost beneath the cawing of crows who had now gathered on the roofs of the huts, and the rustling of uneasy feet.

Finn felt the silent questions ripple through the crowd, each man exchanging wary glances. Ultán straightened, his hand briefly clasping his father's shoulder, a gesture attempting re-assurance but laden with gravity. It was then Finn sensed the inevitable approach of a tide that might very well sweep them all into realms unknown. Whatever news awaited them on the whispering winds of fate, it was bound to test the mettle of every soul within the weathered walls of their refuge.

Tigernach rose, the creak of his leather tunic competing with the groan of the makeshift throne beneath him. The men hushed, their murmurs snuffed out like torches in a gale. Heads subtly angled forward, afraid the wind would steal the king's words and they would miss out on something their lives could depend upon. The grey sky pressed down upon them, the chill of the day seeping into bone and sinew and stirring melancholy into the hearts of faltering men.

"Brave, strong men of my kingdom," Tigernach began, voice faltering as if each word were wrested from a reluctant tongue, "ill tidings have reached my ears and may have reached some of yours. A grave blight has come upon us." His gaze darted among the faces before him, seeking perhaps an anchor in a sea of uncertainty. "The Norsemen..." Tigernach's words trailed off, a hand rising to clutch at the silver chain around his neck, a symbol of power now tarnished with dread.

Finn leaned forward, his breath forming clouds that mingled with the heavy air. "Speak it, king," someone urged from the crowd, voicing the restlessness that gnawed at their patience.

"The ford... The ford over the Liffey. They've seized it." The declaration fell upon the crowd, stark and cold as the stones they stood upon. A collective gasp moved through the assembly, the import of the loss descending like a shroud. The ford was the lifeline to the kingdom, and the tax placed on every consignment of goods that crossed it, the very pulse of Tigernach's domain. It meant not only doom for Tigernach, but that the kingdom would now become a target, not only for the Norse, but for any of the many hostile kingdoms that surrounded it.

"Who will stand?" Tigernach's voice broke through the shock, a plea wrapped in the demand. "Who will reclaim what is ours by the right of blood and sweat?"

Silence pervaded, thick as the fog that rolled in from the hills. Doubt furrowed brows, swords and spears slackened, suddenly burdensome in the hands of men who had long endured a ruler's gambles. Trust was a currency Tigernach had spent with abandon, and now the coffers were bare.

"Your son!" The shout sliced the quiet, and every eye turned to Ultán, whose stature seemed to diminish under the weight of expectation. "Let him prove the mettle of your line!"

Father and son, their heads bowed in clandestine conference, spoke in hushed tones that none could discern. Tigernach's fingers gripped Ultán's arm, their shadows entwined on the ground. As Finn watched he tasted the metallic tang of unease on his tongue, as leadership's mantle was bartered in whispers between kin.

Ultán straightened, the whispered counsel with his father ceasing as he faced the restless throng. The air, raw with the chill of uncertainty and the smouldering embers of betrayal, seemed to pause in anticipation of his words. "Yes," Ultán's voice rang clear, a steely resolve tempering the tremor that had once been there. "I shall accept this charge, but as your prince, my duty binds me to these ramparts, to rouse the courage of more men, to forge an army that will purge our lands of the Norse scourge."

Ultán's next words cut through the din, sharp as an axe. "But fear not! For I name a champion in my stead. Finn Ó'Braonáin, son of our soil, heart of our hearth. A master on the hurley field, he pledged to me when I inflicted his first defeat on him in many a year. I call on him to honour the pledge he made to me in front of his family and fellow villagers. He will be my sword, my shield, my wrath upon the invaders."

The announcement hit Finn like a punch in the stomach. All eyes turned to him and he knew not what to do or where to look. So he looked to the ground, for he could no longer see the eyes upon him. He broke into a cold sweat, his stomach knotted with panic. What should he do? He was no warrior. Surely he would die if he accepted Ultán's invitation. But if he refused, he would bring shame to his village and family. But in the end, the hurling match, a contest of village pride, had ended in his defeat, and with it came a promise, a forfeit owed to Ultán. But that game was forfeit for it never finished. Everyone knew the rules. Finn tried to swallow but coughed due to a lack of saliva. He raised his head to be surrounded by eyes.

"The game was forfeit," he said in a barely audible croak. "It was never finished. It was interrupted by the invading Norse."

Ultán grinned like a man prepared.

"I have asked my father's Brehon." Ultán invited the Brehon forward. "He says no matter the game was interrupted, the final score still stands. Therefore, you owe me a promise which I ask for today."

Finn dropped his head and began breathing heavily.

"Do you want to defy the law?" Ultán asked. "If so, I will take what I am owed from your village grain stores or else cast the villagers out and not offer them protection from the Norse. Which is it to be? The choice is yours."

"Ultán speaks true." Finn's voice emerged, croaking but audible to those who mattered. He stood tall to conceal his nerves and project gravitas. "I'll stand for him, for all of you. I'll face the Norsemen and reclaim what they've stolen." Commitment laced his words together, a vow made before a nervous crowd and a very relieved king and son.

The silence that followed wrapped around each man, woman, and child present. Finn walked through the crowd, expecting it to be a victory parade, where he would be showered with pats on the back as the crowd greeted their hero. But the crowd parted like the Red Sea and looked down, as if they were at a funeral, unable to meet the grieving family's eyes. The only people who were grinning were Tigernach and Ultán, who awaited their hero at the end of the tunnel.

Gormlaith bit so hard down on her lip, blood dribbled down her chin.

"How on God's earth did I get such a fool for a son?"

Affraic looked at her to see if she wanted a reply.

"Oh, yes, his father. That's how," Gormlaith said confirming Affraic's thought that she was not looking for a reply. "But what does that make me if I married one and created the other?"

Affraic opened her mouth only to be shoved out from their hiding place my her mother.

"Don't you start answering me back," Gormlaith said with a face on her no one dared cross. "All I need now is cheek from you to wind me up."

Gormlaith stood at the edge of the crowd emitting a string of curses to rid herself of her frustrations.

"Shh, mother," Affraic said. "Finn will find out we are here if you keep drawing attention to us like that."

Gormlaith shook her head in disgust.

"At least I'm not standing here like a statue at a funeral, pretending he's already dead."

Gormlaith placed her hands on her hips and looked to the heavens. Above her, the simmering greys yielded forth a patch of blue and a shaft of light. The anger and frustration dissipated. She tearfully turned to Affraic.

"You know what this means, don't you?" Gormlaith's eyes searched her daughter's face for some semblance of hope.

"Of course, I do." A pause, heavy and thick as the clouds above passed between them. "But Finn is no foolhardy youth led astray by dreams of glory. He understands the weight of his word, the bond of a promise given."

"Bond my arse. That Brehon has a full back pocket for perpetuating Ultán's lie. My son has to go in that coward's place because everyone is too afraid to stand up to his lie. Promise me, Affraic," Gormlaith implored, her hand finding her daughter's, "promise me you'll watch over him."

"Like the wolf guards her cubs," Affraic vowed, her grip firm and unyielding. "I will keep close, ever the unseen sentinel. Should fate cast its shadow too darkly upon him, I shall be there to kindle the flame anew."

Gormlaith scowled, for such verbal flourishes seemed to detract from the seriousness of the situation.

"Just both come back alive."

Finn's boots squelched atop the muddy rise as he turned to face the gathered crowd, a sea of anxious faces that flickered like candle flames in the twilight. His voice, usually a clarion call of confidence, faltered slightly as he embraced his fate, but also sought to carry the fate of others with him.

"These Norsemen are not wild beasts from the depths of some dark forest. They are skin and bone, just as we are. The blade of a sword will sink into their flesh as easily as ours." Finn threw his arms out and tried to look the men in the crowd in their eyes. "Who here will stand with me against the marauders? Who will join in defence of our kin and soil?" His plea hung lonely in the damp air.

A weighted silence blanketed them all, heavy as the woollen cloaks upon their shoulders. Eyes shifted, feet shuffled, and not a soul stepped forward. Finn's chest tightened. His heart beat like a lonely drum. An island in a sea of silence, his spirit began its descent into despair. He tried to blink away the panic in his eyes. He looked for faces he knew, neighbours he could rely upon, but all he saw were the tops of heads. His mission was about to fall at the first hurdle. For him to go alone was a useless death, barely worth the effort of digging a grave. Finn's head hung as he thought of all those who cheered him on when he was on the hurling field, only to abandon him now.

A cloud hung on Ultán's face, a fiendish plan to save his own skin about to fall short. He had whispered hope in his father's ear and won himself some esteem and was not about to lose it so easily.

Ultán strode from his father's side and draped his arm over Finn's shoulder like a protective cloak.

"You'll not be alone, Finn." Ultán's deep timbre offered a semblance of solace. "I'll send two of my finest men with you to the ford. Deliver the king's ultimatum to the Norsemen there. If they do battle with you, then so shall follow all the glory. If they decline, you will expose them for the cowards they are. My men will be behind you all the way. They'll see you're safe."

Finn glanced at Ultán, and his eyes were firm. The offer was a double-edged sword, one that Finn had no choice but to grasp. Finn nodded and looked at the smirks of his new protectors. He understood the unspoken condition. The men were his escorts as much as they were his wardens.

As the last vestiges of twilight waned, the crowd dissipated like mist upon the distant mountains, leaving Finn standing with his newfound shadows. Broad-shouldered and stern-faced, they flanked him and, as they did so, they enveloped him in their own silence. They matched him step for step, guiding him towards the exit of the fort. Why was Ultán so determined to deliver him to the Norse?

Finn turned away from the emptying field, his mind awash with the grim reality. He left the ring fort and its protective walls of earth. The heavens seemed to weep for his plight, as droplets of rain began to descend, gentle at first, then growing more insistent. Water trickled down the sinewy lines of his face, mingling with the sweat and resolve etched upon his brow.

His journey home was a slow trudge, boots sinking into the increasingly sodden earth, the rhythmic squelch accompanying the beat of his heart. The rain painted the world around him in hues of grey despair, turning the path ahead into a murky stretch of uncertainty.

Finn felt the weight of leadership heavier than ever, pressing down upon his broad shoulders as if he bore the very sky. But he only heard the roar of the crowd or saw the elated faces of his friends in his head. When the chill of the wind brought him back to reality, only the relentless patter of rain and the muffled steps of his silent sentinels remained.

Yet, once he saw the lights of his village, his stride became purposeful, fuelled by the burning need to rally any soul brave enough to accompany him.

CHAPTER NINE

THE THREE SHADOWS

THE RAIN-SOAKED STREETS OF the village lay before Finn, the puddles in the mud glistening like teardrops in the muted light. The three shadows loomed down the central track of the village, elongated by the morning sun. With every step closer to the heart of his home, doorways darkened and shutters snapped shut, as if the very houses themselves were bracing against an ill wind.

He passed by his mother's abode, its once-welcoming facade now shuttered and barred. The decision pained him deeper than any blade, but keeping distance was his safeguard for her. He did not want the two shadows who followed him to find a way to hurt him should things work out in his favour and to their master's detriment. But he knew why his mother had locked him out, for a fourth shadow followed him. Fate stalked him in the form of the shadow of death.

Yet it was not just the silence of closed doors that followed him. A murder of crows had gathered, their black forms stark against the grey sky, their calls a haunting echo amidst the hush. They seemed to mock the solitude that cloaked him, their beady eyes watching with a knowing glint, as if they too sensed the pall of doom he carried.

Finn felt like his father would have done had he ever returned, or so Finn imagined; the returning hero having fought for his village and willing to do so again, yet cast out by a lie. Finn's was that Ultán had really won the match when it was forfeit and his father's was that he was a coward and had fled the battle with the Norse. Both lies had been disseminated by Ultán and Tigernach, both father and son tainted by the same brush.

At the edge of the village, where the last house stood guard like a sentry at the borders of the known world, a trio of figures emerged. Familiar faces appeared as the shadows subsided. Seamus, with hands like leather from years of smithing; Aengus, whose laughter could once lift the darkest spirits; and young Padraig, barely more than a boy, his eyes wide with a mix of fear and awe.

"Seems we're fools alike," Seamus grunted, the corners of his mouth twitching in what might have been the ghost of a smile.

"Or perhaps just loyal ones," Aengus added, trying to infuse some warmth into the damp air.

"Is there a difference?" Padraig asked, the tremble in his voice betraying his attempt at bravery.

Finn met their gazes, reading the resignation etched onto their faces. It seemed that fate too cast its shadow over them as they emerged from their hiding place. They were no seasoned warriors, their hands were meant for tools, not swords. Yet here they stood, offering their lives to a cause that had already left them orphans in spirit.

"Thank you," Finn said, his voice steady, though it took all he had to muster such composure. "We fight not because we are unafraid, but because we hold something greater than fear."

Seamus noticed the two men standing behind Finn and how they did not smile or bear the demeanour of volunteers on a righteous quest.

"Who are these, then?" he asked, pointing behind Finn.

"Your best hope of living," one of them growled and both of them laughed. It was the kind of laugh that sent shivers down the spines of the three boys, and Finn could see fear clouding over their eyes.

"They are two warriors volunteered by Ultán," Finn said quickly, his cadences measured to maximise assurances. "But we should begin our journey so we reach the ford with good light."

"Lead on, then," Seamus replied, his hammer-swinging arm flexing instinctively.

"May our courage outshine our skill," Aengus quipped, a hollow attempt to dispel the dread.

Padraig simply nodded, swallowing hard, the Adam's apple in his thin throat bobbing with resolve.

With the weight of a thousand stones rattling around in his heart, Finn signalled to his friends to follow him. They turned away from the village, stepping beyond the veil of familiarity into the realm of legend and loss. Behind them, life resumed in hushed tones, but ahead, only the unknown awaited, as vast and unforgiving as the sea that brought their foes to Hibernia's shores.

Unbeknownst to Finn, his sister crept around in the shadows, mimicking his every step. She was determined her brother would come to no harm. Hers was a much easier request to persuade companions to follow, for sisters were well used to having to bail out foolish brothers from the messes they created. Gobnat, the older sister of Padraig and Étaín, the younger sister of Seamus, were easy to persuade. God certainly topped up those wayward boys with foolishness, but cursed them both with being useless with a sword, partly for their own good no doubt. The girls' best bet was they would get waylaid on the road to the ford and be forced to abandon their mission and have to hide in the woods until King Tigernach's anger with them subsided when something came along to distract him.

But never one to leave matters to wishful thinking, Affraic followed at a distance, keeping to the shadows of the path so the boys would not see them. They made use of bush and rock, knoll and tree, and the boys did not notice them. When they saw the boys were determined to pursue their quest, they slipped around them and found a hiding place with a good view of the ford. They dredged their brains for the names of every saint they could think of that could intervene on their behalf and divert the boys from their quest. But their prayers were to be disappointed as Finn emerged from the nearby woods.

CHAPTER TEN

AN OLD SWORD RAISED TO THE SKY

FINN RELUCTANTLY LEFT THE embrace of the ancient oaks, their gnarled limbs gripping the soil below, holding it together as if protectors of this ancient land. The roots weaved a basket to protect those who slept, and the branches formed a steadfast shield above. This was his sanctuary, his home from home, where the damp earth cradled his every step and the whispers of leaves spoke of how the woods protected his kin and his ancestors before them. Here, among the sentinel trees, he drew breaths scented with oak and peat, cloaked in a verdant shroud that dulled the outside world to mere echoes.

But as he edged beyond the woodland's grasp, the sky loomed, an open expanse that left him naked to prying eyes. His heart thrummed a wild rhythm against his ribs. Fear seized him, a feral beast with claws that raked at his insides, roaming freely in his heart and mind. It often ran with him and whispered of all he could not see, of the dangers lurking in the exposed terrain that stretched before him, of foes far stronger or more cunning than he. Yet it was not for himself that Finn feared. It was the thought of failing those who depended on him, of allowing harm to befall his people. A thoughtless promise wickedly kept had brought him here, but Finn's loyalty coloured it with meaning. Such dread coiled tight within, the feral beast ever ready to strike at the core of his soul.

In front of him, where the road met its end and he would meet fate, was the ford, where the waters murmured tales of passage and trade and the route to distant seas from where the Norsemen came. There, a merchant, a familiar face weathered by sun and time, stood head bowed surrounded by the new trolls of the ford. Even from afar, Finn could see the tension etched into the merchant's stance as he reached for his money pouch, pleading for his life. The same tension that now knotted his own sinewy muscles.

Beside the ford, the foundations of what would become a bridge jutted from the water like the bones of some great beast, rising from the deep. Massive stumps bore the scars of axes as the Norsemen shaped their beast that would drain the riches from Finn's green and pleasant land.

The bridge was the final straw for Finn. Those timbers were not merely wood; they were the shackles of foreign dominion, the bloodletting of a gaping wound sapping the strength of the people, and he would not let them take root in his soil. Not while blood still surged hot through his veins, not while his hand could still grip a sword and wield it to protect his family and the land he loved.

He cursed his foes and strode with purpose towards the ford. His three friends followed, with Ultán's guards shepherding them forward to block off their means of escape.

Finn thought of his father and the stories he used to tell him as a boy of how he would lead the charge for the men of Tigernach and how many Norse he had slain. Finn wanted to be just like him, leading the charge against the Norse. They had the same sword. He could only be successful.

Seamus hooked his hand through Finn's arm.

"Now is not the time for hotheads, but for cunning and guile. We must see how many of the invaders there are and assess their weaknesses before charging at them with our swords."

Finn wrestled to free his arm while Seamus tightened his grip and scanned the landscape for a wiser course of action.

"Look, there lies a well-trodden path." Seamus pointed to a long patch of mud from the woods to the ford, where the soil was jagged and bare. It had elongated trenches cut into the muddy ground that had become puddles. "Let us see what is there first, for if the enemy is to ambush us, that is where they will come from."

Finn scowled at his path to glory being diverted by sense and signalled to everyone to take cover so they could observe what had created such a blot on the landscape.

Hidden amongst the tangled underbrush, Finn tracked the procession of broken men down by the ford as they dragged massive logs through the muck and mire. The forest floor, once a tapestry of greenery and life, had been churned into a landscape of desolation beneath the burden of these wooden behemoths. The men's rags hung from their bodies like tattered ensigns of defeat, each step forward told of their gruelling servitude.

As he crouched low, the coarse bark of the oak against his palm, Finn felt the damp earth seep through his boots, the same earth that clung to the labourers in thick, odious layers. A sudden movement caught his attention. One of the downtrodden figures lifted his head, and recognition flared within Finn. It was Father Cian, a beacon of piety from the local monastery, now reduced to this pitiful state.

Finn could see the stark terror etched across Father Cian's face. His eyes, wide with an animalistic panic, met Finn's for the briefest of moments. They held a silent plea, a wordless counsel screaming louder than any sermon ever could. *Flee.* In that gaze lay the naked truth of their predicament, the understanding that what transpired here was more than mere thievery or skirmish. The Norsemen were here to conquer and enslave them, destroying their very way of life.

Drawing back into the shadows, Finn cast a glance at his own men. Their faces were set in grim determination. Their hearts raced like his, in a rhythm of anticipation and fury. With a nod, Finn set his jaw and threw off his fears. He rose from his hiding place and held his sword with menace. His stride was deliberate, a prowling wolf emerging from its den to confront the intruders in his territory. The ford would be the Norsemen's no more.

Three hulking brutes led by Torstein guarded the ford, their skin adorned with intricate tattoos that spoke of battles and bloodshed. Long beards, woven with the filth of their labour, framed smirking mouths. They released the merchant to cross the river and congratulated themselves as they counted the toll they had extracted. Torstein turned towards the woods. His eyes lit up for the gods had rewarded him for his bravery and adventurous spirit with the opportunity to make as much money as he could ever wish for. All he had to do was seize it with both hands.

"Where are those damn lazy priests?" Torstein roared in the direction of the woods. "No wonder they are banished to kneel and pray to their weakling god, for they are good for nothing else."

Then he caught sight of Finn striding towards the ford with a face as red as the priest's raw hands and an old sword threatening violence. The Norsemen reached for their weapons, the air suddenly thick with promise. Axes and swords glinted dully in the waning light, singing softly as they were drawn from their slumber. The Norse amusement was palpable, their laughter rolling across the air like thunder, all further winding up the coil of Finn's fury.

"What have you come to poke with your father's sword, boy?" Torstein bellowed. "Let us tickle you with our axes and then playtime will be over and you can join the priests in their work."

Finn stepped onto the ford, the stones beneath his feet slick with algae and the blood of conquest. He did not answer the Norse taunt straight away with words. Instead, he first let the glint of his sword in the sunlight speak for him. Then he had to free his nerves.

"Release the priests and begone, heathens!" Finn roared. He glanced over his shoulder to ensure his friends were behind him. "This bridge will serve King Tigernach, not a band of thieves!"

The Norsemen roared with laughter.

"Little cub wishes to reclaim his den?" Torstein boomed. "We need strong backs for our work. Your men will suffice once you fall."

Finn stood legs astride, attempting to intimidate his much larger enemy.

"My back will not do your work today, tomorrow or ever."

Torstein grinned as he looked back at his warriors, signalling for them to be ready for whatever eventuality.

"If we are to fight, at least make it entertaining. I need a story for the mead hall this evening." Torstein stepped forward, his lips curling into a sneer.

"Then come," Finn countered, the fire of challenge blazing in his emerald eyes, "and let your fate be sealed by the hand that wields it."

Torstein gave a guttural roar as he charged, axe raised high, its blade catching the dying light. The earth trembled under his assault. Finn's heart provided the drumbeat.

Finn braced, his sword an extension of his arm. Torstein slammed his axe down upon the sword, and Finn was barely able to keep it steady. The shock of the blow reverberated up his arm and exploded in his side where he had spent a couple of weeks nursing his wounds obtained on the hurling pitch. Would the misdeeds of Ultán and his men be the spear in his side, the final death blow?

Finn parried blow after blow, forcing him back. Each impact sapped more strength from his limbs and confidence from his heart. No wonder Ultán sent him here to fight his battles. This Norseman was a natural-born killer. His only thought was the most entertaining kill he could wrap in a story. Finn began to look for a way out in between parrying blows. But each blocking move jarred his injuries, whispering treachery to his muscles.

"Is this all the fight you have, boy?" Torstein taunted, his breath a tempest.

"Enough to send you to your gods," Finn spat, parrying a blow that would have cleaved lesser men in two. Finn looked around for his means of escape. The beginnings of the bridge were water-soaked planks that made a small jetty out across the river. He was sure of his footing. It was many a time he had to ensure he did not slip on the mud of the hurling pitch. This hulk of a Norse relied on brute force and was heavy-footed. The kernel of a plan took root. He skipped to the side and backed up the jetty. Blows showered upon him with rhythmic certainty. Finn saw out of the corner of his eye a particularly slimy plank and moved to the edge of the jetty, his back to the water to tempt the Norseman forward. Torstein had nothing to fear except his victory being too easy and robbing him of a tale. He lumbered forward, timbers creaking ominously below. With each collision of steel, Finn's world narrowed until there was nothing but the foe before him and the relentless river below, eager to claim its due.

In a moment as fleeting as a shadow's passing, the Norse feinted, and Finn, betrayed by throbbing sinew, faltered. The axe's butt met his temple with a sickening crack, the world tilting precariously as he teetered on the edge of consciousness. With the roar of the river crashing in his ears, Finn felt himself falling, the chill embrace of the water rushing to meet him.

CHAPTER ELEVEN

A DEAFENING HEARTBEAT

AFFRAIC'S HEART HAMMERED AGAINST her ribcage as she gripped the gnarled trunk of an ancient oak. So fixated was she the trunk imprinted itself on the palm of her hands. She winced with every blow her brother took, all the while her grip tightened on the trunk. She saw her brother fall as the butt of the axe connected with his head. She went to cry out but a friendly hand slipped over her mouth. Her two friends rested their hands on her shoulders as if that would be any kind of reassurance.

"By Saint Patrick, we must go," whispered Affraic's friend Gobnat, her voice barely carrying over the rush of the river and the distant clamour of the fray. Affraic's other friend Étaín nodded in agreement.

Affraic gave a fleeting look towards the water where Finn had disappeared, saw his friends drop their weapons and enter servitude with the Norsemen. Ultán's guards immediately took to their heels.

Affraic and her friends turned to melt back into the protective shroud of the forest. Affraic stumbled her way through the underbrush, blinded by images of her brother being struck down. The shadows of the trees cast long, sinister fingers across their path.

"Shh, you'll get us all killed," said Gobnat, who crossed her lips with her index finger.

Suddenly, the muffled sounds of their flight collided with a chorus of harsh voices. Affraic's breath hitched. The guttural tones of Norsemen's speech cut through the woodland's hush like a blade. Her mind raced, fighting the blind panic brought on by witnessing her brother's demise. She knew it would take cunning to evade such seasoned warriors. The dread surged in her veins as she switched to survival by instinct.

They froze, listening as the voices grew louder, nearer. Heartbeats pulsed in Affraic's ears. Swells of emotion overwhelmed her, depriving her of her senses. Deaf as well as blind, she prayed for the clarity to decide the best course of action. Images of the impact of the axe butt on her brother's head dominated her mind's eye. The sound of breaking twigs meant the owners of the voices were getting closer.

"Split up," she hissed, her voice as sharp as the cold air biting at her cheeks. "Meet at the cairn by moonrise."

With a nod, they parted ways, darting like startled deer into the dense foliage. Affraic's chest tightened as she ran, brambles tearing at her skirts, the threat of capture and what happened to her brother pressing down on her like the dark clouds overhead.

Her footfalls were silent whispers against the loam, but even the breaking of a twig felt like a scream. She wove between trees, her black hair like a banner flying behind her. Then she felt it. The unmistakable sensation of being watched.

She stopped, scarcely daring to breathe, and turned slowly. Through the lattice of branches, she saw them. Norse, their armoured silhouettes emerging from the dimness like spectres. Their eyes gleamed with the thrill of the hunt, and she knew that her ruse had failed. She backed away, only to come up against a tree. She looked around to see the Norse were closing in from all sides.

"Come out, little bird," Torstein called mockingly, his voice laced with amusement. "We've no quarrel with you unless you make it so."

But Affraic was not one to be cowed. Her spirit, fierce as her brother's, burned within her. She stepped forward. Her gaze was defiant, though her hands trembled at her sides.

"You'll find this bird has talons," she retorted, her accent thickening with every word spoken through clenched teeth.

"Your scratching and clawing will only be practice for my bed tonight," Torstein said, a smile breaking on his face, for he could not decide which he admired most, her looks or her spirit. "Don't worry, you'll have plenty of friends where you're going. Why, we just rounded up a couple of girls who'll make splendid company for you. You may even get to sail on the wide oceans and visit my homeland. Maybe even with a child in your belly."

Affraic panicked at the thought of becoming a Norse bed thrall. She looked around her for a stone or a stick to use as a weapon. She heard the rustle of the Norse getting nearer, their heavy-footed steps and their panting breaths. She picked up a stick that looked as if it had a sharp end and stabbed the back of her hand to test its sharpness. She winced as it drew a small amount of blood, but a lot of pain. She closed her eyes as her tears forced their way past her eyelids. She said a prayer to Saint Bridget and thrust the sharp end of the stick towards her face. A hand clasped her wrist before the stick made its impact.

"Don't ruin your pretty face, little bird. Let me do it by filling your womb with my children."

The hand did not let go, for now she was a prisoner.

CHAPTER TWELVE
RESCUED TREASURE

F INN HIT THE WATER hard. His head throbbed but he still had his wits about him. He could not surface for all that would greet him were a hail of Norse arrows. The tides of the Liffey had him in their grip, carrying him along like an invisible hand. He felt his grip loosen and a weight fall from it. His father's sword! He could not let the sword fall at his first defeat. He could not do that to his father's memory. But he had little air left in his lungs. It was the sword or be within arrow range of the Norse when he surfaced. He kicked his legs and swam down towards the riverbed. If he protected his father's sword his father would protect him.

Finn could barely see for all the silt at the bottom of the river. He could make out the blurry shapes of large boulders and that was about it. He looked behind him and could just discern the faint outline of the bridge that was being built over the river. He may be able to trace his way back if he had enough air left in his lungs. He kicked his legs again so he could search the riverbed with his hands. A rock, an old pot, a dead fish. His hands searched and his brain guessed. His lungs pressed against his ribs, compelling him to seek fresh air. He resisted and searched behind one more rock. Pebbles, slimy plants, OW! The sharpness of a blade. He carefully felt the face of a blade until he found the hilt. Success. He secured the sword in its scabbard. His lungs felt as if they would explode. He looked up to see silhouettes on the bridge. He was elated now he had his father's blade but had no wish to drown. He had to get air. He kicked his legs and swam away from the bridge but at such an angle he would not break the water. He turned to see where the bridge was. Bang! His head collided with a discarded log. He floated downriver and there was blackness.

CHAPTER THIRTEEN
A MOTHER'S CURSE

THE EARTHEN FLOOR OF the hut bore the imprint of Gormlaith's restless feet as she paced, her worn soles tracing the same relentless path. Each step wrought a silent plea cast upward through the smoke hole in the roof, where the light of day waned, diffused by wafting tendrils of hearth-fire. Each prayer bead left behind an imprint on her thumb before being moved along as the next prayer took its place. Her whispers danced amidst the flickering shadows, a litany to the Almighty, to Jesus, to the revered Saint Patrick, and to any of the old gods she could remember and thought may help. Each name was a desperate invocation for the preservation of her son, Finn.

"Lord above," she murmured, fingers threading through the wooden beads of her rosary, each one an echo of her heart's cadence, "I may not have the poetic words of the priest, or be able to recite all your stories and prayers, but I am a poor mother and no less devotional for it. Shield my boy in battle, cloak him in your grace. And although it may take on the dimensions of a miracle, please make him see the stupidity of his ways and send him back to me."

She blessed herself and wrestled with the guilt of whether her prayers were selfish or not, for even though she prayed for her boy, could her prayers be interpreted as praying for herself? Would her selfishness condemn her to hell? She always found what the priests said to be confusing, a jumble of the new god and the old gods, and they seemed to skip from one to the other at their convenience. But they would say she was being blasphemous by questioning them and only they could give God's instructions. But despair returned and so did the prayers.

A sudden cacophony from the outside world shattered the rhythm of her prayers. A horse's hooves thundered against the moist earth, urgent and foreboding.

"Tigernach sends word," the rider began, his voice carrying the toll of sorrow across the gathered throng.

The room caved in on her, the claustrophobia of impending catastrophe, her heart cleaved in two by the blunt axe of dread. She turned, knocked over everything in her path, and fumbled with the lock on her door as her eyes welled up. She opened the door, throwing it back on its hinges in retribution for the inconvenience it caused her.

The villagers were gathering like crows to carrion around the rider. He was a silhouette against the dimming sky and bore the weight of tidings upon his slumped shoulders. Gormlaith took one look at his expression and elbowed her way to the front, tears streaming from her eyes.

The rider's gaze met Gormlaith's, and in that glance, eternity passed, a mother's hope extinguished beneath the veil of twilight. He decided not to mince his words and put the poor mother out of her misery.

"Finn... Finn Ó'Braonáin is dead."

The words tore like fire through a bone-dry forest, leaving nothing in their wake except despair and empty hearts. The rider spoke of escapees, of Ultán's guards, the fortunate few untouched by death's indiscriminate hand. But for the rest, chains awaited prisoners to an unknown fate. But Gormlaith was so preoccupied everything sounded like distant muffled grunts.

"Dead?" Gormlaith's voice, though soft, cut through the murmurs. She staggered back, throwing her arms behind her to maintain her balance. A sharp pain pierced her heart. Sorrow? An ailment? A desire to be with her son? Her neighbours took her weight and held her until she threw them off, steady on her feet.

"I... I also had a daughter, Affraic. She went to protect her brother. Is there any news about her?"

The rider dropped his head.

"Taken prisoner," the rider said, heavy-hearted at having to be the bearer of such tragic news to the one mother.

"Prisoner..." she echoed, the word foreign, sharp on her tongue. The surrounding crowd swelled, a sea of faces etched with concern and curiosity, yet none bore the weight of a mother's despair. Finn, her proud warrior, felled, her daughter Affraic, God knows what to a horde of Norse.

In the shadows of the failing light, Gormlaith fell to her knees as she absorbed the gravity of the message. The air was thick with silent questions, laced with thunderbolts of anger. Anger at the Norse and also anger at the king for leaving the village boys to their fate. Amongst it all Gormlaith knelt and grieved for her son and the trust in her king lay shattered among the trampled grasses of the gathering place.

The villagers veered a sharp path away from Gormlaith when she finally rose off her knees in the early evening light. No one would take her arm and guide her home by the light of a fire torch. All were too afraid of the emotional volcano they saw brooding in the mud of the central meeting place.

Gormlaith rose and staggered back towards her house, whose shadow she could still make out through the tears in her eyes. She felt prying eyes upon her, niggling beaks of judgement pecking away at her sorrow. But they would niggle no more.

"You cowards!" she turned and screamed at the huddled neighbours who watched from a safe distance. "Cowards, the lot of you! Not one among you stood with my Finn! Your bellies are full of fear, content to let your betters bleed!"

Her words fell like lightning, searing the skin of collective guilt.

"Ultán, you viper," she spat the name like venom towards the sky, "you and that withered husk of a king!" Gormlaith's fists clenched, her nails biting into her palms as she swore, "By all the saints, there will be vengeance for my blood!"

The surrounding air seemed to quiver with the force of her vow. But her rage was not yet done, her energy not yet spent.

"Tigernach, you gutless worm!" Her voice was a lash, a whip that sought to strike at the absent monarch. "May the gods curse your name for a thousand generations. May your tongue rot in your mouth until you can no longer utter your spineless decrees. May your fingers wither and blacken until you cannot grasp your ill-gotten gold. May the ghosts of all those you have wronged haunt your every waking moment, their wails of anguish echoing in your ears until madness takes you.

"May your kingdom crumble to dust, your crops wither in the fields, and your livestock drop dead where they stand. May the rivers run red with blood and the skies rain fire upon your wretched head. May your enemies gather at your borders like a plague of locusts, devouring all that you hold dear. May your allies desert you in your hour of need, leaving you alone and despised.

"May your every waking moment be filled with agony and despair, as you realise the depths of your failure. The very air you breathe will turn to poison in your lungs, and every step you take will be on a path of molten fire and thorns.

"And when at last death comes for you, may it offer no release. May your spirit be doomed to wander the desolate wastes for all eternity, forever tormented by the knowledge of what you did to my children."

She paused to catch her breath and to wrack her brain for sufficient curses to condemn the loathsome Ultán. But then she gained a twinkle in her eye, the kernel of an idea that would constitute her revenge. She stopped cursing at the sky and hurried home. All eyes of the village followed her home hoping her curses and next course of action would not bring the wrath of the king down upon them.

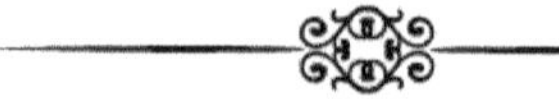

With the last of her curses dissipating into the cool evening air, Gormlaith's eyes, red-rimmed and swollen from weeping, fixated on the distant silhouette of Tigernach's hillfort. It rose against the horizon, a large jagged tombstone that had condemned her children to death and enslavement, respectively. Her heart, a cauldron of sorrow and fury, bubbled over as she trudged towards the looming structure. The twilight seemed to gather around her, cloaking her movements in shadow as if meant to amplify her sorrow.

The path ahead was treacherous and untamed, but Gormlaith's resolve did not waver, even as brambles clawed at her skirts and the earth beneath her feet turned to slippery mud in the deluge. The sky wept with her, rain pouring down in sheets that blurred the world to shades of grey. Droplets mingled with the tears on her cheeks, washing away the salt, but not the sting of loss.

"Gods above and devils below, witness this mother's plight," she whispered between shuddering breaths, each word punctuated by her boots squelching against the sodden ground. "I fear I may have use for both of you before the sun sets. I may weave my sorrow with my tongue, but give power and potency to my curses. You gave me blight. At least let me redirect it back to its human originators. You have taken so much away from me, at least give me this back."

As she traversed the woods, the trees themselves seemed to recoil from the force of her grief, their branches creaking and groaning in the wind. The darkness of the forest was oppressive, yet it could not smother the fire that raged within her. Memories of Finn's laughter and her daughter's wide-eyed innocence flickered before her like phantoms, haunting every step.

"Children of mine," she murmured, the confession lost amidst the howling of the storm, "I blame myself for giving you my stubbornness but not the brains to use it wisely. For it has come back with a vengeance against its bestower."

Gormlaith's thoughts were a torrent as tumultuous as the rain-swollen rivers she skirted. She recalled the prideful tilt of Finn's head, the same obstinate angle that the king himself often adopted. And her daughter, sweet and trusting, misled by promises as empty as the hollows in ancient oaks.

"By the saints, I taught you to be strong, to be wise." A sob caught in her throat, her voice strangled by despair. "But 'twas not enough to save you from the scheming of men who sit high and look low."

The fields, once a tapestry of green and gold, now lay desolate under the relentless downpour. Each blade of grass bowed beneath the weight of the heavens' sorrow, and so too did Gormlaith feel the burden of heaven upon her shoulders.

"Tigernach," she hissed into the driving rain, her words like serpents slithering through the tall grasses, "your fortress of stone and timber may stand tall, but your legacy shall crumble beneath the weeping of a mother wronged." She took a breath for it was her anger that gave her the strength to place one foot in front of the other. "I call upon the ancient spirits of this land, the ones you have forsaken in your lust for power. May they rise from the depths of the earth and the shadows of the forests to haunt your every waking moment. Your dreams shall be plagued by the screams of the children you have orphaned, and your days shall be filled with the weight of your sins."

Exhaustion clung to her bones, an unwelcome companion urging her to succumb. Yet she pressed onward, propelled by a force that defied the weariness of her flesh. She would not rest. She would not falter. For within her breast beat the heart of a lioness robbed of her cubs, and no tempest, no king, no curse of fate could still its ferocious rhythm.

By the time the hillfort's gates loomed before her, Gormlaith was more spectre than woman, her form a wraithlike vision etched against the storm's fury. Her voice, when it rose to challenge the stones, was the lament of the broken, the battle cry of the bereaved.

"Here I stand, o king!" she declared, defiance ringing clear despite the lateness of the hour. "A testament to your failures, a herald of your downfall. Never may I leave this place again, nor place a morsel of food in my mouth until I have damned you to hell and your kingdom has collapsed for all the ills you have caused. You may have an army and a fort and I just the clothes on my back, but mark my words, you will fall to a mother's curse."

As the rain continued its relentless assault, Gormlaith knew that this was but the beginning. Her vigil outside the fort's walls would be a beacon, a flame that would ignite the hearts of those who had remained silent for far too long.

Dampness seeped through the woven fabric of Gormlaith's blanket as she settled its frayed edges upon the sodden earth, her figure a solitary silhouette against the sprawling shadow of Tigernach's hillfort. This would be the perfect spot for her vengeance against Tigernach: under the shadow of the walls made of mounds of earth, at the southern entrance that led to the ford which had robbed her of both her children. She sat and made herself as comfortable as possible, for she did not know if she would ever leave this spot again.

The sentries, clad in mantles of wool that had succumbed to the deluge, peered across from their seats on the other side of the gate. Curiosity sharpened their gaze.

"Move on, woman," one guard called, his voice carrying the weight of duty yet lacking conviction. "This is no place for your grief."

"Nor was it a place to plot my child's slaughter!" Gormlaith retorted, her voice a raw scrape against the stone-cold air. "Tigernach has failed us all, failed my daughter, sent my son like a lamb to his doom. I shall not feast nor find comfort until this truth is known by all!"

The guards exchanged uneasy glances, their hands resting upon the pommels of their swords, yet they found no enemy before them, save an anguished mother. When they advanced to usher her away, Gormlaith's form erupted into a flurry of resistance, her worn boots kicking at the muddied ground and her cries piercing the veil of rain.

"Back, you heartless curs! I will not be moved!"

Her tumult drew the eyes and ears of the village folk, who emerged from the shelter of their dwellings, drawn to the spectacle unfolding beneath the king's very walls. Murmurs rippled through the crowd, a chorus of discontent that mirrored the storm's relentless drone.

The Brehon, the man of law, wrapped in the dignity of his office and the wisdom of years, stepped forward from the swelling sea of villagers. His voice, when he spoke, carried the gravity of law and tradition.

"Let her be," he decreed, his tone unyielding as bedrock. "She speaks from a place of loss, and her actions stand within the bounds of custom. Someone who thinks their king has failed them has the right to show it through letting themselves go hungry until the king provides a remedy for their ails. She has the right to show the king's failure to protect his kin and kind and you have none to interfere."

Gormlaith gave the smallest of smug grins and reclaimed her seat upon her blanket, the simple cloth now a throne of defiance. Her eyes, alight with the fire of vengeance, fixed upon the gate each time it opened to admit one of the king's men. Her voice, hoarse and relentless, cut through the air.

"See how Tigernach hides behind his walls while his people suffer! See how he sends our sons to die in foreign fields and leaves our daughters at the mercy of fate to become slaves to barbarians! Where is your protection now, o mighty king?"

Her slanders rapidly became more coarse as the wind and rain took their toll in the passing days. The villagers took pity on her and made her a small shack to sit in. They left food on the side of the blanket for it to remain untouched and get stolen by dogs as Gormlaith remained vigilant.

And there, outside the gates of power, she remained – a sentinel of sorrow, a spectre of accusation, all under the protection of the law of the Brehon who even King Tigernach dared not cross.

CHAPTER FOURTEEN

A DROWNED COIN

Finn's consciousness flickered like the flame of an oil light in a tempest, each wave of pain rekindling the world into sharp, brutal focus. His body lay strewn across the harsh embrace of a stony shore, where the chill of the sea gnawed at his bones. Salt-laden air filled his lungs as he drew a ragged breath, tasting the bitterness of brine and blood. He tried to lift his head, but the weight of it proved too great, and he flopped back onto the pebbles with a soft crunch.

The sky above was a vast expanse of grey, indifferent to his plight. The wind assaulted his body, enveloping him in a blanket of wet and cold. His body shivered, revealing his most vital sign of life. Finn's mind clawed for memories, but found only tendrils of fog that slipped through his grasp as quickly as they appeared. How had he come to rest upon this desolate strand? His thoughts were muddled, an echo of distant battle cries lingering in his ears.

"Are you all right?" a voice broke through the haze, youthful and edged with urgency.

Eyes squinting against the muted light, Finn discerned the silhouette of a young boy standing over him. The lad's form wavered as though seen through water, shimmering as Finn struggled to focus.

"I am not here to rob you and take advantage of your unfortunate state," the boy said as he bent down and cautiously stuck his finger out to prod Finn to see if he was really still alive. "Saint Patrick must have thrust you upon these shores himself to allow me to do penance for my sins. It was not but one day ago the priest said that prayers alone were no good to free me of the sins I inflicted on my poor mother."

Finn managed to lift himself onto his elbows and focus on the boy. He had blond hair and a face far too innocent to have committed the sins he claimed to have done.

"It is not for me to question the motives of a Good Samaritan," Finn said as his voice bore the rasp of all the seawater he had swallowed. "I'm glad it was only you here when I washed up on this shore."

Finn lifted himself onto his knees, his head throbbing, and his ribs stabbed him with every movement.

"Give me your hand, boy, and help me up."

The boy nodded, offering a grimy hand. Once Finn was on his feet a noise from behind the boy startled him.

"You had better go, and quickly," said the boy.

"Why is that?" said Finn only half paying attention for he was surveying the landscape, trying to work out where he was. His eyes settled on the Wicklow mountains, always a good guide to tell where you are.

"Norse," the boy spat out the word like a curse, "they land here, taking those who dawdle as thralls."

"Norse?" Finn's voice was a hoarse whisper, his throat raw as though scoured by sand.

"Indeed, they'll be upon us soon enough."

The boy shifted from foot to foot, casting wary glances towards the sea.

"Then we had better leave. Can you set me on my way to there?" Finn said, pointing at the mountains.

The boy's head sank.

"I haven't cleansed my soul just to go adding another sin by disobeying my mother."

Finn looked at him and smirked. He remembered when he was in that state, when his father was still there.

"There'll be a reward for you," and Finn smiled at the boy, hoping to win his confidence.

"Of what?" said the boy, his eyes now lit with curiosity.

"Whatever you desire from my pockets. Now lead the way."

The boy was not for moving; he squinted at Finn, sizing up this drowned beggar straight from the sea. Surely the fishes would have robbed him of any value he may have on his person?

"Is there anything good in them or are the contents of your pockets all hell spawn, designed to tempt me?"

Finn scowled for such resistance did not sit well on a throbbing head.

"I have not seen the hell your priest or mother describes, but I am sure men crafted the coins in my pocket and they are acceptable in any market. Will you continue your good deed for a stranded stranger, for who was ever sent to hell for helping someone in need?"

The boy pondered, then smiled as he made up his mind and skipped ahead.

Steadying his breath, Finn set his gaze upon the distant Wicklow mountains. They rose like slumbering giants cloaked in verdant green, their tops lost to the heavens in a soft embrace of mist. The ache in his limbs was but a whisper compared to the clamour of thoughts racing through his mind. He had heard tales from his mother, stories spun before the hearth's warm glow, of a man named Aodh the generous – an appellation that danced on the edge of legend and reality. Legend because of the number of men he killed, importantly including Norse, and reality, for he fought with his father. The story went he had his fill of killing after all his good work was undone when Tigernach took power on the back of it. If any man could help him avenge himself on Tigernach and Ultán and be easily motivated to do so, it was he.

"Boy," Finn's voice bore the rasp of dried leaves, "have you heard of a man called Aodh the generous?"

The child, with his mop of unruly hair, paused mid-step, eyes widening as if the name conjured spirits from the earth itself. "I know of him. Lives deep within the woods, where the mountain's breath grows cold."

"Then you will take me to him," said Finn, not as a question but as a statement sternly stated to impress it on the child.

The boy turned to Finn.

"For a journey that perilous, it would take me more than a night. With me just having my soul cleansed by helping a stranger, it would cast my mother into a pit of worry and I'd descend into my sinful chasm again, without even a night having fallen."

Finn grimaced, looked to the heavens, and stuffed his hands in his pockets, hoping the sea had left him with something. He felt the rounded edges of a coin, one cast away by his mother in his youth. It was one of the last memories of his father for Tigernach, once he had assumed his throne, had come round to his house. He had placed the coin on the table and said that was for her now deceased husband's wages. The coin hit off the back of the door as Tigernach left and Finn had retrieved it and kept it for luck. Finn smiled, for he thought it might finally bring his mother's revenge.

"Will you do it for this?" and Finn held up the coin, hoping to appeal to the child's greed.

"Of course, I'll lead you," the boy grasped out at the coin only for Finn to pull it away.

"You can have the coin when you have brought me to Aodh, and I have brought you back to your mother. I cannot have it on my soul that I tempted you with coin and then you ran away without fulfilling your promise."

The boy's head sagged, but he gestured for Finn to follow.

CHAPTER FIFTEEN

CHASING GHOSTS

Finn and the boy set forth, the forest swallowing their forms, a tangle of roots and earth beneath their feet. As they ventured deeper into the heart of the ancient forest, the air grew thick with the scent of damp earth and the sweet fragrance of wildflowers. The sunlight filtered through the dense canopy, casting a soft, emerald glow upon the forest floor.

The trees grew ever taller, their trunks gnarled and thick with age, adorned with intricate patterns of moss and lichen. The green hues of the foliage seemed to pulse with an inner light, as if the very essence of life flowed through its veins.

The path wound through the forest, guided by ancient spirits and ghosts, as if the very earth beneath their feet knew the way. With each step, they could feel the presence of the gods and spirits that had once walked these same trails, their whispers carried on the gentle breeze that rustled the leaves above. The birdsong grew louder, a symphony of trills and melodies that filled the air, as if the feathered inhabitants of the forest were welcoming the travellers to their domain.

The boy led on, his small frame navigating the forest paths with ease. Then they climbed, as the incline grew steeper, the earth changing beneath them to the craggy bones of the mountain itself. Here, the air grew cooler, the scent of pine sharp against the backdrop of damp moss and decaying leaves.

"Be mindful of the stones," the boy cautioned, his words floating back to Finn, who navigated the rocky terrain with care, following the smaller figure who flitted through the landscape like a wisp of smoke.

"How much further?" Finn asked, though not from weariness, for his strength was returning, but from an eagerness that gnawed at his insides.

"Close now," came the reply, a promise carried on the wind.

As they ascended, the woods thinned, revealing a landscape scarred and shaped by ancient forces. Great boulders lay scattered, thrown by the hands of giants, it seemed, and amidst these titans of stone, a shadowy opening beckoned – a cave concealed by nature's artifice.

"There," the boy pointed, triumph in his tone, "that's where Aodh the generous makes his abode."

Finn nodded, drawing a deep breath as he prepared to meet the man of whom his mother spoke, his father's great warrior friend, the man who might hold the key to his next path. His heart thrummed a warrior's rhythm, eager to face what he thought was his fate.

Finn stepped past the threshold of the cave, his eyes adjusting to the dimness within. The air was cool, tinged with the earthy scent of moss and the smoke of a distant fire. The walls were wet to touch, covered in large parts by green algae, slime and moss. He moved cautiously, aware of the multitude of shadows that danced along the walls, cast by the flickering light of a solitary flame. The shadows played tricks upon him, his heart jumping with elation, then spiralling down to hell, for the shadows crept into his memories and played them out on the walls before his eyes. The shadows mixed with the rock face and there a monster lay. The light danced upon protruding stones and an inviting path lay before him.

"Who ventures into the mountain's heart?" The voice that echoed off the stone was as weathered as the crags themselves. "Are you here because you wish to see the generosity of my axe?"

Finn straightened, squaring his shoulders. "I am Finn, son of Cathal the wide-eyed," he announced, his own voice steady, though it bore the tremor of anticipation. Laughter echoed through the cave.

"Ah, Cathal's boy." A figure emerged from the gloom, the shadow on the walls gradually reducing from that of a giant to a muscled old man. Aodh, once a formidable warrior, now bore the lean look of a life lived in austerity. His hair fell like rivulets of molten silver down his back, and though age had claimed some of his strength, his sinews were taut, reminiscent of twisted branches clinging to the cliff side. He bore a thin smile hidden amongst the wrinkles on his face, which were partially obscured by an unkempt white beard.

"Men have taken to calling me generous," Aodh said with a dry chuckle, his blue eyes sharp beneath bushy brows. "A jest, for I am generous indeed, with the blade of my axe."

Finn studied the man before him, noting the undercurrent of sorrow that lay beneath the bravado. Here stood one who had given much and lost more to the relentless march of time.

"I know you are Cathal's boy," he continued, "for no one called him wide-eyed except for Gormlaith. He used to hate that nickname as much as Gormlaith used to hate the way I used to drag your father off on more adventures."

"Is it true then, you live here with Babo also one of my father's former companions?" Finn ventured, recalling the tales woven into his childhood.

"Aye, Babo the slayer," Aodh replied, a hint of fondness softening his weathered features. "Built like the very trees we dwell amongst, but alas, swore himself to Lugh and became too fond of battle's embrace." He gestured to the depths of the cavern where a silhouette loomed, still and silent, an old oak in human form: Babo, whose violence had rendered them exiles even in their own land.

"Then Lugh took away what he once gave. He got a spear to the side of the head and he was never the same again. He had saved me in many a fight, so it was only right that I look after him as he had saved my life so. We came to the mountains to seek the help of the witches for no one else could help him. But even witchcraft could do him no good."

"Then the stories hold truth," Finn murmured, absorbing the reality of the legends etched into his memory.

"Stories often do, boy. It is how much is the real question. Now, what brings you to my hearth? Don't tell me your mother sent you?" Aodh asked, settling onto a worn stone, the makeshift throne of an isolated kingdom. "If she did, I can only think it would be to be an assassin. But I do not want to take the blame for taking another male from her family."

Finn smiled for he took the comment as a compliment and a joke. Then, with the solemnity of one seeking justice, Finn recounted his tale, the wrongs inflicted by Tigernach, and his desperate need to stand before Niall Caille, the High King in Tara.

Aodh listened, the firelight casting shadows that played across his face, accentuating the lines carved by time and toil. When Finn finished, the old warrior nodded slowly, the weight of decision heavy upon his brow.

"I will lead you," Aodh declared, his voice the growl of distant thunder. "But not to the High King, instead to Malachy, the king of Mide, for he is your overlord, to speak your grievance against Tigernach. But mark my words, young Finn, that is all I will do for you. Babo and I have dipped our axes in too much blood and we have no wish to do it again. But we will do this one task for your father's memory. Then what I owe him and whatever your mother thinks I owe her will be repaid and you will then leave me in peace to live out the remainder of my days."

Finn bowed his head, a gesture of gratitude mingled with the understanding of the old warrior's terms. They sat in silence, punctuated only by the crackling of the flame.

CHAPTER SIXTEEN

ONE OF THOSE THINGS YOU ALWAYS REGRET

THE LONGBOAT PITCHED AND rolled in the choppy waves, icy spray stinging the girls' faces as they clung to each other, desperate for warmth and comfort. The vessel was a sleek predator, its dragon-headed prow slicing through the iron-grey waters with relentless determination. Oars rose and fell in perfect unison, propelled by the powerful arms of the Norse warriors who manned them, their faces grim and implacable beneath weather-beaten beards.

Affraic's teeth chattered uncontrollably, her sodden wool dress offering scant protection against the biting wind that whipped across the familiar river, now transformed into the trail of a fearsome dragon and her entombed in its belly. Beside her, Gobnat's fiery red curls were plastered to her pale, pinched face, while Étaín whimpered softly, her delicate features etched with despair. She clutched a small wooden cross hanging around her neck, her lips moving in silent prayer.

The three maidens had been torn from their families, their homes, everything they knew, and now faced an uncertain future as thralls in what had become a foreign land. The ship lurched suddenly and Étaín lost her grip, the cross clattering to the deck. A brutish Norse of bright tattoos and braided beard snatched it up with a grunt, pocketing it with a cruel sneer. Étaín let out a sob, burying her face in Gobnat's shoulder. Had even God now abandoned them?

As the longboat drew closer to shore, the girls could make out the crude structures of the Norse harbour. The ramshackle dock looked like broken teeth jutting from swollen gums, adorned with the grisly trophies of past raids. Skulls leered down at them from atop pikes, empty eye sockets seeming to mock their plight. The air was thick with the stench of fish and unwashed bodies, mingling with the acrid tang of wood smoke from the fires that dotted the beach.

"Get up," came the harsh voice of one of their captors.

The guards yanked them to their feet, and they found themselves forced down the plank of the ship and onto the shore, as all the while they clung to each other for some sort of protection.

"Keep yourself scarce in their gaze," Affraic murmured to her friends, her voice barely audible over the din of the harbour. In a world of mud, rags and chains, bruises and matted hair, Affraic and her friends still managed to stand out as beautiful. She knew her beauty in this situation was a double-edged sword. It could be her salvation or her doom.

She set her eyes on the slaver stalls, instantaneously recognising them for what they were. The glint of cruelty and greed in the eye of the slaver contrasted with the look of total despair among the new thralls even though they stared at the ground. Affraic knew this was her fate unless she could wriggle out of it somehow. She looked around for a means of escape, but with the number of Norse milling around the harbour, there was none.

A sudden commotion near the head of the docks drew Affraic's and everyone else's attention. Thurgest, a mountain of a man clad in chain mail that glinted like ice, strode into view. His presence commanded immediate attention, from both guard and slaver alike. The slavers were the first merchant mission from back home in Norway. They had landed onshore with supplies of men, weapons, and the necessary tradesmen and farmers it would take to establish a colony. Now they had to fill their ships with goods for the return journey to ensure their trip was profitable and repeatable. Now, before them, stood the fruits of the fledgling colony, ready to be picked. Thralls.

"Five silvers each for this lot!" a slaver barked, gesturing towards a group of weary men paraded in front of him, whose shoulders sagged under the weight of unseen burdens.

"Ten," Thurgest countered without missing a beat. "They've strong backs, fit for work."

The slaver shook his head and smirked.

"If they are so fit, why don't you keep them yourself? The walls are barely built and you still need a lot more houses for your men. I have plenty of other stops on these islands I can get thralls from, and reliable too. I will give you six, for if you are looking to give them away, they probably have a plague or something else equally unwelcome."

Einar and Torstein stood behind Thurgest like twin sentinels. Both wore anxious faces, the worst kind to bring to a negotiation. Thurgest turned and scowled at them.

"I know what you want to say, but if you stand behind me looking like that, I never will achieve anything."

He turned back to the slaver.

"I need ten and you need a steady supply of thralls. This land is ripe for the taking, but I also need to pay the men and incentivise others to come if you are to get this supply. Give me ten and I will consider it a favour to me. That favour will be repaid multiple times by giving you first call on the next batch of thralls, this time at market price. What do you think? It could make us all rich."

The slaver's face did not twitch.

"Seven is the best I can do."

Thurgest leaned in towards him and prodded his own chest as if he was beating a war drum.

"I am Thurgest, the scourge of this land and a legend in his own. All the Hibernians will bow before me and accept my yoke. Those who trail in the wake of my glory may find themselves rich if fortune favours them. But I do not offer such favours easily, and you should be grateful to be the recipient of one. Accept ten or I will have to compose a tale for your widow about how you got lost at sea. I may spare the detail of any glory or neglect to add some embellishment to your demise so as not to give your wife and mistresses a false impression."

The slaver gulped and stood back out of the range of Thurgest's rancid breath. The slaver weighed his options, greed warring with pragmatism in his narrow eyes. Thurgest snarled for this slaver had a spine. He turned to Einar and pointed at Affraic and her friends who stood at the front of a crowd of female thralls.

"Grab one of them and bring her to me. We may need to sweeten the deal."

Einar strode up and circled the women. He etched a cruel grin on the side of his mouth as he built up the courage to complete Thurgest's task. These women were all around his own age and pretty too. He could not help but feel a pang of nerves.

Affraic and her friends all dropped their heads and trembled as they fixated on the ground. Whatever prayers they could re- member were muttered, skipping ahead if their memories failed them. They could feel the hot breath of their Norse tormentor as he circled them.

"Which one of you pretties would like to come with me?" Einar hissed. But his voice shuddered as he posed his question.

Affraic's mind suddenly flashed to her mother and the one word etched on her lips. "Survive." She grabbed Étaín by the arm and tried to pull her back into the crowd of female thralls. She looked back to see if Einar had noticed her trying to hide amongst the thralls. She was violently shoved in the back.

"Don't try and hide behind us," came a shrill voice.

Affraic fell forward and clattered into Étaín who fell before Einar's feet.

"It was as if the gods picked you out themselves," Einar smirked, and grabbed her by the arms. "It's much better if you come willingly."

Étaín lashed out with all her strength and punched Einar in the cheek. Einar gave an excited grin and grabbed her by the hair and dragged her towards Thurgest. Affraic let her hair fall to cover her face as the Norse guards blocked her way from saving her friend. She turned to the crowd of women behind her.

"Who did that?" she hissed. "Shame on you. Come and face me, you coward."

Affraic was met by a wall of silence and hard faces. Finally one of them spoke.

"We may be dead by the end of the day so it is every woman for herself."

Affraic made fists and her knuckles turned white.

"May the coward who will not face me rot in hell for what she did."

Affraic still had enough sense to know she should not draw attention to herself while the slavers were still there. She watched as Einar dragged Étaín away, pain and anguish on her face. Then it hit her. Her friend was about to be lost to her forever, probably this day to be beaten and raped and then to be dragged off to some farmhouse in a far-off land to be some old man's thrall and plaything. It was her fault. At least some of it. If she had only held her balance and not collided into her then she would still be here with her and the coward who pushed her would be being dragged down the street instead of Étaín.

She watched Einar drag Étaín by the hair through the mud and the whole of the docks seemed to turn to witness what she did.

She could feel hard eyes bearing down upon her, judging and condemning her while the real culprit hid.

Bile rose in her throat and she fought the urge to retch. Étaín's screams would haunt her until her dying day.

Einar pushed the screaming Étaín into Thurgest's arms. Thurgest held her out to the slaver.

"How about you take her as a gift to warm your bed on the way home? I bet she'll be compliant after a couple of beatings. Now, shall we say ten for this batch and see what the price is the next time you come?"

The slaver eyed Étaín up and down. Eventually, he spat on his hand and thrust it forward. "Ten it is then. If you are a man of your word, I will take as many as you can spare and we shall draw up the terms of our arrangement."

Thurgest clasped the slaver's hand, sealing the deal with a warrior's handshake, calloused fingers locking in mutual understanding of the brutality of their world.

"I expect you back before the end of the month," Thurgest said. "Torstein here will draw up a list of our requirements which you will bring back. He will also go with you, for I have a separate mission for him. Meanwhile, take the cost from what you owe me and give the surplus to Torstein so he can pay the men. The next time you can pay me to build you a long house for yourself and some cages for your thralls." Thurgest waved his finger at the slaver. "You will be rich from our arrangement. You will be rich."

Thurgest turned to Einar who stood behind him, noting every detail as to how his uncle negotiated.

"Take what you need to build the walls and houses and sell the rest. We need coin to make this a success so only take what you need."

Einar nodded and signalled to his men to follow him to inspect the rest of the thralls.

Torstein stood pale-faced before his master, as this was the first he had heard of this new mission.

"Yours is the most important mission of all," Thurgest told him. "I have a letter for you to give to my brother and offer him whatever he wishes for in exchange. But do not come back without what I ask for. But first, sort out the thralls with Einar."

Torstein gulped but nodded his acceptance. He knew from Thurgest's tone that he should not come back if he had not fulfilled his mission.

Affraic lifted her head and watched the exchange, her mind whirring with calculations. She put Étaín as far out of her mind as she could. There was no point in her friend being sacrificed only for her to die under the same sun. She drew a slow breath, the scent of salt and pine mingling with the less savoury odours of the docks, and prepared herself for whatever fate would come next.

Einar and Torstein organised the thralls into groups. Most of the thralls went with the slavers, but they selected some of the prettier women and stronger men to stay. Within this, Affraic saw her chance. Torstein was edging ever nearer, and she cringed at the thought of being made his bed slave.

Then she caught a better look at Einar. He was much closer in age to her and lacked the poise and confidence of the older Norse, as if he was too eager to prove himself. He reminded her of Finn and she knew how to wrap him around her little finger. An added bonus was that he was quite handsome, his long blond hair braided in the Norse fashion, trailing down his broad back. He was a far more attractive proposition than Torstein, who smelt like a bull in heat and she knew he liked her. Involuntarily, her breath caught at the sight of Einar. Her imagination had done much to fill in the parts she did not know about him. He seemed to have a magnetic pull on all those around him.

As he passed by her, his ice-blue eyes did not deign to acknowledge her existence. Yet something was stirring in that briefest of glances, a recognition of spirit perhaps. But there was definitely ambition in that blue steely stare, something she could share with him. Before she could ponder it further, her attention snapped to Torstein, his heavy boots thudding on the earth as he approached. His eyes, as they locked with hers, bore another glint she recognised, animalistic desire.

Panic fluttered in her chest, but Affraic's resolve hardened. She would not show fear. With a swift motion born from desperation, she lashed out, her foot connecting with the shin of one of Einar's guards, who passed in front of her. The man whirled, surprise turning swiftly into anger, and his hand cracked against her cheek with a force that sent her head snapping to the side.

"Insolent wench!" he spat, raising his hand for another blow.

The commotion drew Einar's attention, his body turning with a predator's grace. Their eyes met again, and a shimmer went down Affraic's spine. Without a word, he strode over, his hand fastening around her arm with an iron grip, pulling her up to face the gathered throng. Her cheek stung, but Affraic offered him a defiant smile, refusing to cower under his scrutiny.

"Take her to my house," Einar commanded, his voice carrying the weight of authority. "She'll learn respect there."

As she was dragged up the hill Affraic looked over her shoulder to see if Einar was coming. But all she saw was her former friend Gobnat being chained and forced to board a slaver ship. She now had no one and was being dragged off to become a bed thrall. She thought of her mother's cunning and determination and the heroics of her father. She would need the best of both of them if she was to survive.

CHAPTER SEVENTEEN

THE SWEET TOUCH OF A FIRM GRIP

AFFRAIC'S SLENDER WRIST FELT the grip of Einar's fingers as if they were iron manacles, the sinews of his arm taut as bowstrings. With a heave that sent crows scattering from the cloth-covered roof, he wrenched open the heavy oak door of his nascent long house. The structure loomed unfinished; its skeletal timber frame gave away the ambition but also spoke of the lack of available labour.

"Inside," he growled as he released her with a shove. He would have no more insolence from her, nor would she undermine him in front of the men. A good beating would sort out this thrall once and for all.

Affraic stumbled across the threshold, losing her footing in the abrupt transition from the uneven earth outside to the dirt floor within. As she fell, the scent of freshly hewn wood and cold iron filled her nostrils. She landed unceremoniously on the ground, her once fine gown now torn and covered in mud. She sat up and felt the sting of her grazed palms. She looked around her new temporary abode; the half-finished walls offered neither sanctuary nor a means of escape, only the hollow echo of her laboured breaths. Was this to be her home, her prison, or her tomb? She met Einar's steely blue eyes with a heady mix of defiance and hatred. Einar's eyes gave a revealing glint, for he regarded her as one might a feral cat – curious, but always aware that at any moment the cat could strike.

"What is your name, or should I address you as thrall?" Einar asked, a cruel grin growing on his face as he loomed over her in an attempt to intimidate.

Affraic lifted herself up and squared up to him for there was little point in handing him the whip hand.

"You can call me Affraic, for I am no thrall," she said with steel in her voice. She stuck her chest out and raised her chin.

"Tell me, Affraic," Einar said, "why should I not have you stripped of flesh before the others, a spectacle of blood and pain? We would have no more insolence from the other thralls and I could even sacrifice you to our gods so as not to waste your death."

His shadow fell over her, an eclipse presaging doom. There was no warmth in his eyes, no hint of hesitation as he crept ever nearer her. A wolf about to pounce. Affraic knew her life hung by the slenderest of threads, and yet, amidst the peril, her mind worked with the cunning of a fox.

"Because, Einar," she said, her tone laced with a daring that bordered on insolence, "I know you are not a stupid man for how else would you have got to the position you are in? I could be far more useful than to be reduced to a hunk of blood and flesh to cower thralls into submission. I am a Hibernian princess in search of a prince. I am not too particular as to where he comes from, be he of Hibernian royal blood or a Norse warrior. But I need a man with vision, who sees and wants the world and wants me beside them to help him conquer it."

Her words hung between them, a challenge wrapped in velvet. She gulped, for this was her best shot at surviving the night. She could see the question flicker behind the facade of Einar's indifference. Her eyes narrowed for she sensed the Norse in front of her had a sensitive side, one that would prevent him from doing wanton acts, especially to a woman he had a soft spot for.

Einar tried to hide his emotions behind his impassive face. But his chest tightened, and he twisted a ring on his finger presented to him by his father the day he departed for Hibernia. His father had sent him here to become a man and yet surely he was still a boy, for this thrall was still insolent to him even though he could kill her in an instant. But even in her defeat, her words had some resonance. Could her claims of being a Hibernian princess be true? Could her claims of power and influence be real? If he was to marry a Hibernian princess of true stature, how could his father and uncle fail to be impressed?

Affraic tilted her head at Einar's confused stare. Any Norse worth his salt would have slapped her across the face by now but this one did not. Beads of sweat gathered on her forehead but she shook her hair to hide them. The very earth seemed to hold its breath as the balance of power teetered on the edge of a knife. She had to be very careful with her next move but she was convinced she had already struck the right note. With a voice that wove confidence through the threads of vulnerability, she laid bare an alternative fate.

"Consider the folly in flaying such a woman," she said. Her words danced like firelight against the encroaching shadows of the long house. "What you perceive as defiance could be the very asset you require. I am more than capable of overseeing the completion of this dwelling while you pillage distant shores."

Einar's eyes betrayed a flicker of intrigue. The merest hint that her gamble had found purchase in the ambition that lingered in his soul.

"Your men grow weary of strife," she continued, softening her tone. "I could turn their hearts, persuade our fairest captives to join your ranks as willing partners. Joy would replace their sorrow, and in time, loyalty and trust might just bloom where resentment once festered."

"Trust?" Einar's voice was the crack of ice beneath a winter's sky, for he did not want to fall under her spell of deceit. "What reason have I to trust a woman who I know nothing of, whose loyalties are as shifting as the sea's tides?"

"Trust is earned, not given freely," Affraic conceded with a tilt of her chin, her cunning eyes locked onto his. "You cannot trust me, not yet. But imagine what we could accomplish together if you gave me something to lose. Bind me to you, make me need you."

Einar's cheeks flushed for Affraic excited him.

"And how would you suggest I do that, Princess of Hibernia?" Scepticism ran through his gruff inquiry like veins of silver through rock. His hand squeezed into a fist as he tried to imagine what his father or uncle would do, but his mind faltered when no answer came.

"Make me your wife," she declared, her eyes ablaze, designed to seduce. "Not merely a bed thrall or overseer, but a true partner. Elevate yourself to the leader of all Norse in Hibernia, and together we shall rule this land. My lineage is the key that unlocks the loyalty of clans and kings."

Silence fell, heavy and thick, but the pressure squeezed upon Einar's head. She was a temptress, but a beautiful and intriguing one at that. But what if he fell for her lies? What if she were merely a low-born woman and he, in his foolishness, agreed to marry her? What would his father and uncle think then? He would make his family a laughing stock and would be banished in shame. Yet, on the other hand, in the audacity of her proposal, there was a glimmer of ambition that resonated with his own thirst for dominion.

"All I know is that you have a silver tongue. I cannot attest to your blood," he blurted out as his ears and cheeks layered crimson upon red.

Affraic put her arms out and walked towards him. Cautious, for she did not want to be on the receiving end should he lash out, but assertive, for a faint heart would not beat for long.

"Who would protest should you see fit to kill me one day? A lie to cover your deed would not have to be elaborate to be believed. It is so easy to be rid of me, yet it is so difficult for you to take a chance. What I propose is an alliance between us. You have the axe in your hand, so you can end it any time you wish to do so. Why go to bed with a thrall when you can go to bed with me, beautiful and willing?"

Einar's whole body tensed as he wrestled with temptation.

"What are you afraid of?" Affraic goaded. "I am a helpless woman, do with me what you will. But if you take me, take me all. Listen to my counsel and you will have it all."

Einar stood pale-faced and dumbstruck as inwardly he wrestled with indecision. Affraic knew the whip was changing hands but an embarrassed and confused man could lash out, especially when he carried an axe. But an image of how Einar treated Étaín flashed into her mind and the glint in his eye when Étaín struck him.

"Oh, damn you to hell," she exclaimed and slapped him across the face.

Einar's eyes lit up. He could resist no more. His hand once more became an iron manacle as he dragged her towards his bed. Affraic's heart jumped. She had made the connection.

CHAPTER EIGHTEEN

A SERPENT'S PARADISE

FINN'S BOOTS SANK INTO the soft, marshy earth at the edge of Lough Owel as he peered across the mist-laden waters. The morning sun glinted off the gentle ripples, casting a shimmering pathway to Malachy's crannóg that seemed to float ethereally in the distance. His breath formed clouds in the chill air, and he rubbed his sweaty hands on his trousers, for soon he would come face to face with the king of Mide.

"And what do you hope to accomplish, meeting with the king?" Aodh queried, scepticism lining his weathered face.

A muscle twitched in Finn's jaw, his green eyes hardening like emerald ice. "I'll rid us of the Norse filth, free our ford from their greed, restore my father's good name and cast Tigernach down from his lofty perch."

"And who would you put in his stead?" Aodh challenged. "You?" Then he laughed. "No one hereabouts would support such a reckless claim from a boy, an old warrior and his sidekick, who is a danger to all those who cross his path."

"Give it back to the king," Finn snapped, his voice rising with the passion of his conviction. "He can rule from afar and leave us be, to live in peace."

Aodh threw back his head and laughed, a deep, rumbling sound that seemed to emanate from his pot belly. "You speak like a bard spinning fantasies, Finn. Your story barely has the substance to impress a wee naive girl and persuade her to give you a kiss behind an oak tree, never mind persuading the king of all the lands. I'm here because I owe a favour or two to your dead father. An old man, when he warms himself by the fire at night, has his memories and his supposed reputation to cling on to in the stories he tells himself. Do not destroy my reputation and make me a laughing stock."

"Such a ridiculous tale worked on you, didn't it?" Finn growled.

Aodh's face hardened.

"Don't get cheeky, son, for I can still turn around and go home with my reputation intact. The fire still smoulders and the tales I tell myself are still fresh." He pointed his finger over his shoulder in the direction they had come from.

Ignoring the sting of Aodh's words, Finn strode on, determination fuelling each step, each thud trying to block out excitement and anxiety clashing swords in his head. The woods embraced them, ancient oaks whispering secrets of bygone eras as they passed, abandoned gods whispering in the shadows. Birds sang and wolves howled, but all that did was make the hairs stand up on Finn's arms.

Upon reaching the water's edge, they were greeted by the sight of the crannóg ahead. A testament to old-world craftsmanship, its wooden walls and thatch roofs were an organic extension of the land itself. Little boats bobbed gently in the water, tethered to jetties that led to the crannógs clustered around a natural island at Lough Owel's heart. Jetties stretched like skeletal fingers, from the natural island linking the crannógs to one another, forming a silent community upon the water, united against the encroaching mist.

"Looks like paradise, doesn't it?" Aodh murmured, more to himself than to Finn.

"Paradise with serpents lurking beneath," Finn replied, his gaze never leaving the island where the High King resided. His fists clenched at his sides, ready for the battles to come, fuelled by the fire that had burned within him since he'd first lifted a blade in defence of his people.

Finn's boots thudded against the worn planks of the jetty as he approached the crannóg, his heart beating a war drum rhythm beneath his woollen tunic. The air tasted of brine and moss, the clammy fog clinging to him like a shroud. Aodh followed, quieter, less certain, his eyes darting to the water where reflections danced, fleeting and distorted.

"State your business," called a guard, his voice as weathered as the timbers that held up the structure before them. He stood in front of Finn, barring his way.

"I am here to speak with the High King," Finn announced, his voice cutting through the mist.

Laughter echoed back, raw and mocking. "And what matter brings you to disturb His Highness?"

"Expelling invaders, securing our ford, and dethroning Tigernach," Finn replied.

"Go home, boyo," came the dismissive retort. "Such talk is for men, not dreamers."

Finn's jaw set hard, the muscles in his neck tensing. Aodh laid a hand upon his arm, but was shaken off. Several men appeared from the boats on the shore, grim-faced, and axes by their flanks. Aodh shook his head at Finn, gesturing that he would go no further. Finn's cheeks brightened, and he pinched his leg to release his fury.

"You mock me now," Finn said, stepping closer, his green eyes alight with a fury unquenched by the surrounding waters. "But I'll prove myself worthy."

"Ha! If it's proving you be after," the voice returned, less amused, more intrigued, "there's a feast in three suns' time. Fighting men will entertain, test their mettle. You wish to join, do so, for that is the only way you are going to get on a boat. But know this – many step onto that island for glory. Few return."

"Then prepare a space for my victory," Finn snarled, turning on his heel, his cloak billowing behind him like a storm cloud about to burst.

Aodh and Babo looked at each other, wondering what they had got themselves into.

CHAPTER NINETEEN

FINN THE UNREADY

As Finn disappeared into the tangled woods, Aodh and Babo exchanged a wary glance before following him into the shadowy depths. The ancient oaks loomed above them, their gnarled branches twisting and reaching like skeletal fingers. But was this supposed to be a deterrent or to drag them in? A thick fog hung low to the ground, swirling around their feet and obscuring the uneven path ahead. The air clung to their bodies as if they had entered the lungs of a living being.

Finn's angry footsteps echoed through the stillness, snapping twigs and crunching leaves with each forceful stride. He was not a boy, he was a warrior and those guards who had insulted him so would soon feel his wrath. His cloak snagged on thorny brambles, but he paid no heed, allowing the fabric to tear as he forged ahead. The woods seemed to close in around him, the dense underbrush and low-hanging branches blocking out the fading daylight.

Aodh and Babo struggled to keep up, their own cloaks catching on the same brambles that had ensnared Finn's. The eerie silence was broken only by the occasional rustling of unseen creatures scurrying through the undergrowth. A sense of unease settled over them, as if the forest resented their intrusion into its dark domain. Aodh signalled to Babo to slow down.

"I have sired enough boys in my time and heard enough tales from their mothers that brought them up to know it is best to leave the headstrong be until they have cooled down. At least he had the sense to storm off in the direction of home, which will make our journey tomorrow all the shorter."

Babo nodded, his thick brows furrowing slightly, and let out a low, gravelly grunt. His calloused hands twitched slightly, revealing a man accustomed to hard labour and decisive deeds. He rarely spoke, preferring the silent language of movement and execution, even when those actions carried a shadow of dread and menace. They held off, following the boy at a distance, and filled their pockets with berries and mushrooms as they went, pointing at the abundance of rabbits in the vicinity. Babo held up the fruit and mushrooms.

"Babo make."

"Yes, Babo can make the dinner," Aodh said. "But first, we have to make sure the boy comes to no harm."

Babo shook his head and scowled.

"Boy end up dead."

Aodh did not flinch.

"As Lugh gave you his blessing, he also took it away. You gave me your blessing and saved my life. The boy's father extended his blessing over both of us and saved both our lives. So now we must extend our shadow over the boy and offer him our protection."

"Cathal was great, the boy not so great," Babo said.

"He has the body of an athlete but the temperament of a fool," Aodh said as he sighed.

"Three suns don't make magic from lumpy clay," Babo nodded firmly.

Aodh shook his head, for he knew he must persevere.

"We must make the king underestimate him and send a beast to squash him like a fly. Then we hope the boy can dance and weave as he claims to do on the hurling pitch and wear the man out."

Babo vigorously shook his head.

"Boy can't dance, Aodh never show his face to king again."

Aodh's face stiffened.

"Then we must teach the boy a proper dance."

Finn had now stopped in a clearing and had taken out his sword. He wielded it as if the bushes were beasts and he the mighty warrior, sent to slay them. He cursed as he slashed and cursed even more when his sword did not slice through the bushes as he so desired.

"Rusty swords are only a threat to the air," Aodh said as he approached him.

Finn scowled as a boy would at a parent who disapproved of his work.

"This is my father's sword," he said as he shook it at Aodh. "The blood of many a man and beast has trickled down its blade, according to my mother."

"Your mother?" Aodh said, raising an eyebrow. "Have you not blooded this sword? If not, you may wish to get your mother to do your fighting for you in three suns' time, for she has a tongue sharper than any blade and her foe would dare not step into the circle with her."

Finn's face flushed.

"Such is the reward for years of peace that many of the village's sons have not held a sword in anger. Do not concern yourself, for I have had much practice with the wooden sword. Albeit, the metal blade has a different swing in the air. Nonetheless, I will soon be its master."

Aodh looked at Babo, who had lost the ability to control his facial movements since he received the blow to the head with the spear.

"Raise your sword," Aodh said wearily to Finn.

Finn pointed his sword at Aodh and looked confused at the instruction.

"No, raise it as if you are going to block a blow from above. Your training has already started."

Finn raised his sword. Aodh tutted and shook his head.

"Place your feet so you can distribute the weight of the blows. I am not going to strike until you are ready, but your unreadiness does not hold you in good stead."

"Why would I learn to cower beneath a sword like a coward?" Finn snarled.

"Because of this."

Aodh whirled his sword around his head and slammed it down towards Finn's head. Finn raised his sword, but his arm buckled at the sheer force coming down on top of it. Aodh rained blow after blow until Finn was on his knees. Aodh twisted the final blow, so Finn's sword flew out of his hand.

"Boy is dead now," Babo said.

"Along with my reputation," Aodh said as he walked away.

"Now it is mother's turn to dance at dead boy's funeral."

Aodh glared at Babo. He could swear he was grinning back at him but he still bore the same fixed expression. Finn sat on the ground in a daze, contemplating what had just happened.

"We may as well leave," Aodh said. "Those guards at the lake did not recognise us, so our reputation is still intact. We may have to say a few prayers to Lugh to make it up to your father, but at least he would be happy for us not to have played a part in his son's death."

Aodh turned to leave and Babo followed. Finn scrambled to get up and stumbled as he ran in front of Aodh.

"You can't leave. You can't abandon me now."

"Watch me," came the curt reply.

Finn ran after him and grabbed his shirt. "I'll give you anything you want."

Aodh stopped and stared down at Finn's hand. Finn snapped out of it and released his grip.

"You have nothing to give," Aodh said as he brushed past him.

Finn stood flabbergasted and shaking as he watched Aodh walk away.

"What about the debt you owe my father?"

Aodh turned and looked over his shoulder.

"Setting his son up to die will not repay that debt."

"Train me for three days, so I will survive. You can come but pretend not to know me. Therefore, you can pay back the debt to my father and if I die, it will be no reflection on you."

Aodh looked at Babo, and Babo nodded.

"I suppose our cave can wait for three days. However, the first time you do not listen or resist my instructions, then we will be gone."

Finn nodded and smiled.

"I will follow your every word."

CHAPTER TWENTY

WARTS AND ALL

THREE SUNS ROSE AND fell, but these were merely drops in a stagnant pond compared to how many times Finn rose and fell in the woods over the same period. Yet despite his diligence, Finn could not shake the feeling that he was still woefully unprepared for the quest that lay ahead, partly because such a feeling was mirrored in Aodh's face. The woods seemed to sense his unease, the trees whispering their doubts in the wind that sighed through their branches. The very earth seemed to shift beneath his feet, as if testing his balance and finding him wanting.

After three suns even the woods seemed to tire of his inadequate efforts. The trees drew back their branches, the undergrowth parted, and Finn found himself stumbling out of the woods and into the harsh glare of sunlight. It was as if the spirits of nature were casting their judgment on him without him even raising his sword in anger.

As he walked the first steps of what he hoped would be a glorious quest, he felt queasy in his stomach. He prayed the nerves would dissipate once he was on the boat on the way to the island. Once on the island, he would find the king and make him listen to his tale before any combat began. When he had convinced the king, he would be dispatched home with a band of warriors behind him to oust Tigernach and the just rule of Malachy would begin. They would then all unite and turn on the Norse, and he would be the hero of his village once again.

"What do you want, boy?"

The growl brought Finn out of his daze. He had somehow wandered down to the jetty without realising. He found himself standing behind the square cut mane of a young man maybe a couple of years older than him and he could see how his leg shook. But he did not turn around to speak.

"What do you want?"

Finn looked to his right and down onto a scrunched-up face covered in warts. The blade of the axe over the man's shoulder gave him all the authority he needed.

"I am here to take part in the king's trials by combat," Finn said, assuming the bark in Wart Face's voice meant he spoke with some authority.

Wart Face looked him up and down.

"You're a bit skinny," he sneered as he poked at Finn's side. "You won't last long. We don't want the quality of the entertainment to decline for the king. Who are you with? No one gets in without someone to vouch for them. We don't want to send an assassin onto the island. Lots of Norse about, you know."

Finn gulped. He was not expecting to be accused of being a spy for those who had wronged him so.

"I am here to offer my services to the king. I am an orphan and have no one to speak for me."

Wart Face shook his axe in front of Finn's face.

"We don't like orphans around here. What happened to your family? Being an orphan is always a reason to kill. You could be here seeking your revenge against the king. Find yourself someone to speak for you and quick, before I set the dogs on you."

Finn edged away only to get shoved in the back by the young man behind him who was also queuing for the boats to get on the island. The commotion attracted the attention of the other guards on the jetty, and they began looking for the source.

"I... I'll get someone to vouch for me," Finn said as Wart Face's axe crept ever forward.

"If you are not on the last boat, I will hunt you down in the woods with my dogs. Then there'll be no more orphan."

"I will be back with a great warrior who will know me."

"I'd better know him too, or else I will take that as a threat."

Finn took to his heels and ran into the woods to find Aodh.

Finn stood on the weathered wooden planks of the jetty, his heart pounding in his chest as he watched the small boats gliding across the shimmering surface of the lake. The morning sun cast a golden glow across the water, making the ripples dance and sparkle like a thousand tiny diamonds. He shielded his eyes with his hand, squinting to make out the distant forms of the other young men on boats who had already set out, all vying for the same opportunity to serve the great king. A gentle breeze carried the scent of wild heather and fresh water, but it did little to calm Finn's nerves.

He shifted his weight from one foot to the other, his hands clasped tightly behind his back as he waited for his turn to board a boat. All around him, other young men stood in similar poses of barely contained anxiety, their eyes fixed on the distant island where the king's crannóg rose from the mist like a mythical beast.

Finn had heard stories of the king's legendary warriors, men who had fought in countless battles and emerged victorious time and time again. He had grown up on tales of their bravery and skill, dreaming of the day when he too might join their ranks and prove his worth to the king.

But now, as he stood on the shores of the lake, watching the boats carrying his potential opponents towards their destiny, Finn felt a flicker of doubt. What if he wasn't good enough? What if the king found him lacking in some way?

He took a deep breath, trying to steady his nerves as he watched another boat push off from the jetty, its occupants huddled together like a flock of nervous birds. The wind picked up, whipping across the lake. Finn gulped, for soon a boat would come for him and he would step on seeking his destiny.

Now the jetty was almost empty, with only two boats left as Wart Face and his guards sifted through the final hopefuls wishing to go to the island. Finn looked sheepish as he came towards the front of the queue, with a red-faced Aodh behind him. Babo took up the rear, oblivious to it all, staring at the hawks as they flew out of the woods and circled the sky. Wart Face pushed aside the queuing youths and signalled to his guards to follow him.

"What is the orphan doing back here? And bringing such burly men with him? Shall we get these eager youths to chop them up for the king and feed them to the fishes?"

Finn halted at the sight of the guards pointing the tips of their axes at him. He went pale, trying to figure out how to react. Aodh pushed past him as he shook his head. He knew how to deal with this.

"Get out of my way, for one of the king's most formidable warriors wishes to pass."

"I assume you speak of yourself and not the boy?" Wart Face turned to smirk at his men, who laughed in return.

Aodh's jaw stiffened and he stuck his chest out and strutted towards Wart Face. A bristle of axe blades and sword points barred his path. Aodh stopped and held his chin in the air.

"I vouch for the boy," Aodh said, holding Wart Face firmly in his gaze. "Do you know who I am?" Aodh stared daggers at the man.

"Too old for me to remember, and unless you possess magic, you're too old to get past my men. Now, what has brought you here to disturb the king's peace?"

"The boy wishes to take part in the tournament and afterwards serve the king," spat Aodh, now getting infuriated that he was not recognised and was being treated so disrespectfully.

"I suppose you want to get in the boat too?"

"If there is room."

Wart Face signalled for his men to let him pass.

"No weapons for you, but the boy can keep his toothpick. And the big burly brute behind you stays."

Aodh turned to Babo.

"Go into the woods and if we are not back in two moons, go home."

"Babo go home in two moons."

"Good," Aodh said as he turned to Finn. "Now you get on the boat." Aodh did little to hide his displeasure at coming on Finn's adventure.

Finn grew more nervous and more agitated with every row of the oars. The boy in front of him was lean and muscular, probably from training all day with a sword. He could beat me. Him over there, with the scars running down his arm – he got those from combat. Real combat. Not what he had done with wooden axes and swords. And he at the back. He was a hulk of a man, like a giant wild boar standing on two legs. Finn had taken a boar before, but he had a lot of help, and he only held the legs, never delivering the final blow. If he had to fight the likes of these, he would surely lose, no matter how much of Aodh's dancing he did.

He scratched, fidgeted and rubbed his hands with such frequency Aodh placed his hand on Finn's forearm and guided it to a position of rest.

"Calm before battle, calm," Aodh whispered. "Remember what I told you. Follow my instructions and stay in the fight."

Finn twisted uncomfortably on his seat and, heeding Aodh's advice, switched his attentions from his potential opponents in the boat to the looming island ahead.

Finn had not been to many places in his life. He had been mainly confined to the flatlands of his home and to go to the Wicklow mountains was seen as a big adventure. He had seen the forts of kings, but these had been the kings of small kingdoms such as Tigernach. He had witnessed the massive ancient hillforts, occasionally deserted and believed to be haunted by the spirits of fallen warriors or forgotten gods. But he had never been at the fort of a proper king, a king that oversaw all the minor and petty kings like Tigernach and could exert his influence all across the land.

Finn's heart pounded in his chest as he peered out across the shimmering waters towards the mysterious crannóg. The island seemed to float like a mirage amidst the vast expanse of the lake, its wooden structures rising proudly from the water like a sentinel guarding ancient secrets. A reed bed guarded the island, forcing any visitors to land on the jetty protruding into the lake rather than attempt a sneaky landing and assault.

As his small boat drew nearer, he could make out the intricate thatched roofs and rough-hewn walls that comprised the dwellings of those who called this enigmatic place home.

A cacophony of bird calls filled the air as they swooped and dived around the island, their vibrant plumage flashing in the sunlight. Herons stood stoically in the shallows, their long necks poised for a strike, while ducks paddled lazily in the reed beds that encircled the crannóg like a verdant halo.

The jetty was ringed by serious-looking warriors with freshly painted shields and spears held at the ready. Finn gulped. Would he soon have to fight these men? He turned to Aodh for reassurance but all he got was a finger pointing forward, directing him where to look. But Finn had no time to be nervous. He had arrived.

CHAPTER TWENTY-ONE

THE POOL OF DEAD SOULS

A ROUGH HAND WAS thrust at Finn.

"Take the hand, boy."

Finn hesitated and glanced timidly at the hand.

"If you want to stay in the boat and shit your pants, you should've stayed at home with your mammy."

Finn was about to snarl at the insult until he laid eyes on the man who said it. The grimace on the one-eyed man's face kept Finn's mouth firmly shut. He took the hand and was yanked off the boat.

He found himself on the quay fighting for space in a clutch of warriors, young and old, waiting to be directed to the meeting place. The quayside stank of men's odours far worse than any pile-up on the hurling pitch. Finn shuddered at the thought of holding his nose for fear of insulting anyone he may face in combat in the near future, so he grinned and bore it. When several more boats arrived and the quay was full, the king's captains bellowed out instructions to the waiting men. The warriors trudged forward, following the fingers of the instructors. Finn followed, propelled by the momentum of the crowd, making sure he kept Aodh in sight.

They made their way past the perimeter huts as the king's men funnelled them forward. At the centre of the crannóg was a circular assembly place with what looked like a pool of black water beside which the king sat. The pool was surrounded by stones covered in ancient carvings with a large flat stone on one side where Finn imagined the king sometimes sat beside the water. Around the circular assembly were numerous spears stuck into the ground. Most had a head on the spike and were frequented by visiting crows, picking away at the loose flesh with the lucky ones gobbling down an eye.

But as the circle was quickly filled all eyes turned to the king. Malachy sat upon a throne carved from ancient oak, its back and arms decorated by intertwined ancient beasts. It was an apt throne for a king whose legend for brutality and cruelty extended across lands far away from his. But what drew all these men to him was that while he was cruel to his enemies, he treated his friends and loyal subjects generously and with kindness. He extended his protection as long as they did what he said. Finn saw the king's smile extend as more and more warriors filled the circle. The king's lean frame belied the strength coiled within. His long brown hair cascaded over broad shoulders, framing a face etched with the confidence of a ruler who commanded all he saw. Behind him stood a wall of guards whose eyes combed the crowd for any would-be assassins who might attempt to kill their king. It may have been foolish for the king to allow so many armed men in front of him, but it was no different from a battlefield and some of the men would have to prove themselves through combat in front of him.

Malachy's piercing gaze swept over the assembly, a faint smile playing at the corners of his mouth. He relished the fact that his reputation swept all before him, including these mighty warriors, with their battle-hardened hearts and welt-riven hands. Yet how few of them dared to look him in the face as they bowed their heads in homage! Mide was only the beginning. In his heart, the ambition to be the high king of Hibernia burned brightly. All he needed was the opportunity. The Norse may just provide that. As he swept them out of Hibernia, he would ensure he would occupy any vacuum they left behind. He drummed his fingers on the armrest, the rhythmic tapping echoing in the hushed silence.

"Bring them forward," he commanded, his voice demanding obedience.

Three Norse, bound and bloodied, were shoved to their knees before the throne. Their once proud visages now bore the haunted look of defeated men.

Malachy leaned forward, his long nose casting a shadow in the flickering light that no man dared linger on. How could he make the most use of these beaten men? At least two of them still possessed the backbone to glare at him. But he could see the anger in his men's eyes, which dictated the direction he should go in. Malachy left his seat to slowly prowl around his victims.

"Tell me, Norsemen. How many of your kind infest our shores? What ill-conceived plans fester in your minds that make you think you can rape and pillage in these lands with impunity?"

The Norse remained stubbornly silent, their eyes fixed on the muddy ground.

Malachy's smile widened, as if a wolf were bearing its fangs. He looked down upon them and dramatically swung away and looked to the heavens as if seeking a message from an angel as to how he should exact God's vengeance. "Very well. If you can be no use to me here on earth, you can be useful to me in the heavens."

He gestured to his men, who dragged the first Norse to the dark pool near his seat. The captive's eyes widened in terror as he was forced beneath the murky surface.

Bubbles rose and burst, the shoulders of his bound arms shook from side to side in a macabre dance of desperation. Malachy watched impassively, his thoughts turning to the delicate balance of power in his realm. These Norse raids threatened everything he had built, every alliance he had forged, and they had not even the gall to give him enough information so he could gain an advantage.

As the bubbles slowed and then finally ceased, Malachy felt a familiar tightness in his chest. But it seemed to irritate him less and less as he filled his pool with the last breaths of dead men. He rose from his seat and pointed to the heavens.

"The lord God above will bless us for sending these heathens to hell. But feel no guilt, my brothers and sisters. These men rape our nuns and kill our priests and bring the wrath of God down upon us. So feel no sorrow for them, only sorrow for those we have lost. But we are nothing if not forgiving."

Malachy stood over the two remaining Norse and whispered to the sky above them.

"But only if you let us forgive you." He then swooped down and placed his hands on their shoulders. "Have you anything to tell me?"

Both grimaced and wrestled with the ropes that bound their wrists.

"No? Then may God forgive you." He sauntered towards his seat with his thumb and forefinger on the bridge of his nose as if the decision of what to do burdened him. "Next," he said softly, his voice carrying a hint of weariness.

The second Norse was dragged to the pool. He spat at the king and sent Odin's curses after his spittle. His head was held under the water until he drowned.

The final man was dragged before the king, his breath fast and shallow. He twisted his neck around to see the bodies of his two comrades and thought of how they would never make it to Valhalla the way they died. He bit his lip until it bled for the feeling of pain reassured him he was still alive.

"If I answer your questions, will you release me, king?"

Malachy grinned.

"It depends on what you have to tell me and how valuable it is to me. I have many spies, so you need to tell me something I don't already know."

The man stared at the ground before him, searching for a piece of information that would set him free.

"Thurgest, the scourge of Hibernian kings, leads us."

Malachy laughed.

"He bellows his name at my men every time they meet him. He does little to hide who he is. You'll have to do much better than that for me to spare your life."

The man curled up inside himself and searched for some secret a mere oarsman would know that would impress a king.

"He means to conquer Hibernia," he blurted out.

"Again, he shouts that at us every time we meet. My men, God, and I all tire of this charade. Tell us what you know or face the water."

The man went white and began to sweat profusely.

Malachy tutted and sat forward in his chair.

"Let me help you, for the clouds swirl in the sky and I don't want my men to get wet as well as bored. How many men does Thurgest have?"

"It depends, as there are many war bands."

Malachy threw his hands to the sky.

"My men should ensure it is a man of value they bring before me and not waste everyone's time."

The Norseman struggled in his ropes.

"What is to be done with me? I never asked your men to bring me here or brag that I was a man bigger than I was. I am a poor farmer just searching for some land on which to scratch out a living."

Malachy shrugged.

"Yet, I am a king. I have a responsibility to both my people and God. You and your people have come and massacred my people and God's priests. However, a king must be benevolent, even to his enemies. Here I have in my hands my prayer beads. Let me use my prayer beads and if by the time I finish God has seen it in his wisdom to spare you from the pool, then I will set you free."

"No, no!" But the man was dragged away and his head ducked into the pool.

Malachy closed his eyes and turned his head to the sky. By the time his prayer beads had passed through his fingers, the pool had stopped bubbling. His men dragged the bodies beside the pool and beheaded them so that the blood drained back into the pool. Other men brought spikes, and the freshly dismembered heads were rammed on to them. The men around him roared in celebration while Finn tried not to vomit.

Malachy rose from his throne to make this dramatic moment his. "Let their heads serve as a warning to any who would threaten our lands," he declared, as he radiated confidence. "Place the heads at the entrance, so that all may see the price of defiance."

As his men carried out the grisly task, Malachy gazed out over the assembled warriors. Their faces reflected a mix of awe and fear – precisely the reaction he sought to cultivate.

"We face dark times," he said, his voice carrying to every corner of the crannóg. "But we are Mide's sons and daughters. Our strength lies not in numbers, but in our unity, our resolve."

His long hair caught the firelight as he turned, casting his profile in sharp relief. "Let the Norsemen come," he growled. "For they will meet nothing but death here."

Malachy's eyes swept across the crowd, his gaze piercing. "Soon, once more, we head off to war. It will be hard, it will be bloody, but in the end we will be victorious, for we have always driven off the Norse in the past and will do so again."

The men roared and shook their weapons above their heads. Malachy signalled for silence.

"We have many young fighters who have come to us to seek glory. Some have come from other clans, be they new allies, or that these astute youth recognise a winner when they see one."

The men roared and laughed again.

"Who among you youths seeks my favour? Who dares to stand against the Norse hordes?"

Finn felt his heart pound against his ribs. This was his moment. He stepped forward, his hand shook as he raised it in the air. "I do, my king," he declared, his voice steady despite the nerves fluttering in his stomach. "I'll throw the Norse back into the sea and rescue my sister from their clutches."

A ripple of murmurs swept through the gathered warriors. Opinions swirled like a stormy sea, serious whispers in support, howls of laughter in derision, but every neck was now craned towards Finn. Malachy's lips curved into an amused smile. "And who might you be, boy, to make such bold claims?"

Finn drew himself up to his full height. "I am Finn Ó'Braonáin, son of—"

"Ó'Braonáin?" The king interrupted, his laughter echoing off the wooden walls. "I have so many men pass through my ranks, I know not this name, nor do I have men to spare for unknown warriors and their personal quests."

Anger flared in Finn's chest. He clenched his fists as he fought back the assault of the king on the memory of his father. He gritted his teeth, determined not to fall at the first hurdle. "My father served you well in the past, my king. The memory of the deeds he committed for you still lingers in our village. I am his equal in strength and surpass him in determination. Give me the chance to prove my worth in combat, and I'll show you I'm more than capable of leading your men."

One of the king's advisers leaned over and whispered in the king's ear.

Malachy's eyebrows rose. "Ah, yes. I remember your father now. Cathal the wide-eyed. An unfortunate nickname but he was a good warrior all the same." His eyes narrowed, assessing Finn. "But I've no desire to see you killed, lad. Your father's service earns you that much consideration, at least."

"I am here to prove myself worthy to serve you, Lord. Be it not with words, I can prove myself with deeds. However, my village needs urgent assistance, and it would be best for them if you could see it in your wisdom to test me sooner rather than later."

Malachy's face hardened, for he did not like even the merest suggestion of someone of such a low status telling him what to do.

"If you want speed, then the fastest way is trial by combat. But because of your father's service, I will not insist on a fight to the death. Who will fight this young man on my behalf?"

"I'll fight him, Father!"

All eyes turned to Donnabhán, the king's bastard son who stepped out of the group of bodyguards standing behind his father. Finn had heard whispers of his prowess in battle, and his eyes told of his eagerness to prove himself worthy of his father's name.

Malachy's lips curled into a sinister smile, the glint in his eye sending shivers down the spines of those who dared to look into it. He had sired numerous illegitimate sons and took pride in his ability to create more. But now, it was time for one of them to step up and prove themselves worthy of being part of his grand schemes. "I've heard whispers of this one's prowess on the hurling field," he sneered, pointing at Finn. "If he refuses my kindness based on his father's service, let us test his mettle in combat."

The gathered warriors roared their approval, the blood lust from the earlier executions still fresh in their minds. Malachy hesitated, waiting for Finn's acceptance.

Finn's mind raced. His heart beat like a war drum, and excitement ran through his veins. This was his chance, perhaps his only chance, to gain the king's favour and the men he needed to save Affraic. He couldn't back down now.

"I accept the challenge," Finn declared, locking eyes with Donnabhán.

Donnabhán's eyes lit up for this was the chance to impress his father and be accepted into his elite band of warriors.

Malachy nodded slowly. "Very well. Let combat commence."

The warriors quickly formed a circle, their bodies pressed tight to contain the combatants. They began to scream and jeer at the young men as bets were placed behind the first row of men. Finn's heart hammered and the palms of his hands became covered in sweat as he faced Donnabhán, the bastard prince's bulk dwarfing his own lean frame. He said a quick prayer for his father to give him guidance in using the sword and tried to remember in the heat of the moment what Aodh had taught him to do. All he could remember was to dance. He was at the mercy of three days of muscle memory.

Donnabhán lunged forward, his blade whistling past Finn's ear. Finn ducked and weaved, calling upon the agility that had served him so well on the hurling field. Another jab came dangerously close to his chin.

He's strong, but slow, Finn thought, remembering Aodh's teachings. He began to circle, looking for an opening.

But each time Finn neared the edge of the circle, rough hands shoved him back towards the centre. The warriors' jeers and shouts filled his ears, their breath hot on his neck as they pressed closer.

No escape, Finn realised, his stomach sinking. *I'll have to face him head-on.*

Finn's moment of hesitation cost him dearly. Donnabhán's blade flashed in the torchlight, and a sharp pain erupted in Finn's side. He staggered back, pressing a hand to the wound. Warm blood seeped between his fingers.

"Not such a little dancer now, are you?" Donnabhán taunted, his eyes gleaming with expected triumph.

Finn gritted his teeth. His mind raced. But he picked himself up just as he had many times on the hurling pitch. *I can't let this wound slow me down. I have to end this and quick.*

"Is that the best you can do?" Finn shot back, forcing bravado into his voice. "I've had worse scrapes from a bramble bush!"

Donnabhán's face contorted with rage. He lunged forward, his blade aimed at Finn's heart. But this time, Finn was ready. With a burst of speed born of desperation, Finn sidestepped the attack. As Donnabhán's momentum carried him past, Finn struck. He rammed the pommel of his sword into the side of Donnabhán's head.

The bastard prince's roar of pain was cut short as he crashed to the ground. The circle of warriors fell silent.

Finn stood over his fallen opponent, chest heaving. *I did it*, he thought, a mixture of relief and disbelief washing over him. *But will it be enough?*

He turned to face Malachy, awaiting the king's judgment. The fate of his sister and himself lay in the balance.

CHAPTER TWENTY-TWO
AN UNEXPECTED OPPORTUNITY

T HE AROMA OF ROASTING beef wafted through the air as Finn entered the great hall of the king's crannóg, his eyes widening at the sight before him. The hulks of what were once the pride of the king's herd turned slowly on spits over blazing fires, their juices sizzling and popping as they dripped onto the flames. Warriors crowded around long wooden tables, already deep in their cups, faces flushed with ale and merriment.

Malachy sat at the head table, his brown hair gleaming in the firelight as he surveyed his subjects with a calculating gaze. Finn couldn't help but notice the king's tightened jaw, a telltale sign of the tension that lurked beneath his regal exterior.

As Finn made his way through the boisterous crowd, a hand clapped him on the shoulder. He turned to see Aodh, grinning widely.

"Finn, my friend! Come, sit with us," Aodh said, gesturing to a group of warriors nearby.

Finn hesitated, his instincts screaming caution. But the other men nodded in welcome, and he couldn't deny the allure of acceptance. With a slight nod, he followed Aodh to the table.

"I didn't expect to see you here," Finn remarked as they sat down.

Aodh shrugged, reaching for a tankard of ale. "The king's feast is for all warriors. Even those with... complicated histories."

Finn's eyes narrowed. "And what of your history, Aodh? Can it be trusted?"

"Ha! You wound me, Finn," Aodh replied with a wink. "How goes your wound? It looked as if the cut was a deep one."

"I'm young and the healer had some good medicine. I fear I will be bothering you for some time yet."

"Oh, do not taunt me so," Aodh said as he smiled. "But come, let's not speak of such things tonight. The ale is flowing, and the meat smells divine!"

Finn sat down and after a few minutes, Aodh leaned in to whisper in his ear.

"Nice move there not to kill the king's son. He would not have returned the favour, but if you had killed him, I'm sure you would have found an early grave."

Finn grinned.

"I am well used to having to pull my punches or to remove my foot to spare the blushes of those born into privilege. One day I hope to be such a man that can leave his foot in there and not have to care about the consequences."

"Be they the words of a brave man or those of a fool?" Aodh said. "Only time will tell."

Finn grinned and then turned serious.

"Which one of those was my father?"

Aodh slapped him on the back.

"Drink your ale and enjoy the night. He, like most men, is a mixture of both."

As the night wore on, Finn found himself relaxing despite his misgivings. The ale loosened his tongue, and soon he was regaling the other warriors with tales of his exploits.

But even as he basked in their approval, a nagging voice in the back of his mind whispered caution. *Can I truly trust these men?* he wondered, his gaze drifting to Malachy. The ageing ruler's eyes met his for a brief moment, and Finn felt a chill run down his spine. Was he supposed to lose to his bastard son all along and his men would be waiting for him to get his revenge?

As the fires began to die down and the revelry showed no signs of abating, Finn found himself overcome with exhaustion. He stumbled to his feet, swaying slightly.

"I think I've had my fill for the night, boys," he mumbled, earning good-natured jeers from the other warriors.

"Off to find a soft bed, are we?" Aodh teased. "Don't let the bedbugs bite, Finn!"

Finn waved him off, his mind already drifting to thoughts of sleep. As he made his way out of the great hall, the sounds of laughter and song faded behind him. The cool night air cleared his head somewhat, and he found himself wandering aimlessly through the darkened paths of the crannóg.

Where can I rest my head without lowering my guard? he pondered, his warrior's instincts warring with his need for sleep. Every shadow seemed to hold potential danger, every rustle of leaves a possible threat.

Finally, Finn spotted a small alcove tucked away beneath the eaves of a nearby building. It was not ideal, but it would have to do. As he settled down on the hard ground, his back against the rough wooden wall, Finn's last thoughts before drifting off were of the uncertain alliances forged in the firelight of the king's feast.

The harsh light of dawn pierced through Finn's eyelids, rousing him from his fitful slumber. His head throbbed, a reminder of the previous night's excesses. His side pained him where he was wounded the day before as he must have slept awkwardly and provoked it. As he stretched his aching muscles, a commotion drew his attention to the centre of the crannóg.

Malachy stood atop a raised platform, his voice carrying across the gathering crowd. "Men of Mide, hear me!" he bellowed.

Finn pushed his way through the throng, his curiosity piqued. What news could be so urgent?

"News has reached me that Thurgest and his Norse dogs have set sail," Malachy announced, his eyes gleaming with the glint of a predator. "They've gone raiding. They are coming towards us, but have left their base vulnerable."

A murmur rippled through the assembled warriors. Finn felt his pulse quicken. Could this be the opportunity they'd been waiting for?

"We will pursue them," the king continued. "We'll catch Thurgest on the river Boyne and crush him like the serpent he is!"

Cheers erupted from the crowd, but Finn remained silent, his mind racing. *Why do I feel uneasy? This is the opportunity I wanted, isn't it?*

As the crowd began to disperse, a hand clasped Finn's shoulder. He turned to find Aodh, looking surprisingly alert despite the previous night's revelry.

"The king wants to see us," Aodh said, his voice low. "Both of us."

Finn nodded, and swallowed hard. "Lead the way," he replied, trying to mask his apprehension.

They found Malachy in his private quarters, his face grave. "Finn O'Braonáin," he began without preamble, "I have a task for you, or you could say, I am here to give you what you want."

Finn straightened, his chest swelling with pride. "I'm at your service, my king."

"I'm giving you a hundred men," Malachy said. "While we engage Thurgest on the Boyne, you'll strike at the heart of his power. Destroy the Norse base."

Finn's eyes widened. "A hundred men? But surely—"

The king held up a hand. "There is one condition," he said, his gaze shifting to Aodh. "He goes with you."

Finn felt his jaw clench. *Why Aodh?* he thought, struggling not to reveal his inner doubts on his face. *Can I truly trust him at my back?*

Aodh stepped forward, his voice steady. "I accept, my king. It would be my honour to fight alongside Finn."

Malachy nodded. "Then it's settled. Gather your men, Finn. They will meet you on the mainland. The fate of Mide may rest on your success."

As they left the king's presence, Finn's mind whirled with conflicting emotions. Pride at being chosen, fear of the task ahead, and lingering doubt about Aodh's loyalties.

"Well," Aodh said, breaking the tense silence, "shall we meet our men?"

Finn took a deep breath, steeling himself. "Aye," he replied, his voice gruff. "Let's see what kind of warriors the king has given us."

As they made their way to the jetty to get a boat, Finn could not shake the feeling that everything was about to change. For better or worse, the die had been cast.

CHAPTER TWENTY-THREE

A THRALL'S WORK IS NEVER DONE

THE FURS ENVELOPED AFFRAIC in a cocoon of warmth, their musky scent filling her nostrils as she stirred from her slumber. Her hand reached out in remembrance of the night before, searching for his bulk. Her eyes fluttered open, adjusting to the dim light filtering through the tent's hide walls. But where Affraic's hand should have met warmth was cold, where there should have been a warm feeling of love was now struck cold with fear.

Affraic's mind raced as she nestled deeper into the furs. Had she done enough to sway Einar's heart? The previous night's intimacies replayed in her mind – the tender caresses, the passionate embraces. Surely, she had proven herself worthy of being his wife no matter who may wait for him back on the shores of his homeland?

The tent flap suddenly flew open, startling Affraic from her reverie. Einar's imposing silhouette filled the doorway, his face an unreadable mask. Without a word, he tossed a bundle of clothing at her, the rough fabric landing with a soft thud on the furs.

"Get up," Einar growled, his voice as cold as the morning air. "It is time for you to work."

Affraic's heart sank, her hopes of a morning embrace dashed. She sat up slowly, clutching the furs to her chest. "Einar, I—"

But he had already turned away, ducking out of the tent without another glance.

Affraic sighed and reached for the clothes, her fingers trembling slightly as she dressed. "Men," she whispered as she shook her head. It was not as if it had not happened before, a man ignoring her after he had got what he wanted. Be it ignorance, rudeness or callousness, it hurt all the same.

The coarse wool scratched, hurting her both outside and within. As she laced up her boots, she steeled herself for whatever challenges lay outside. She was unsure what status she had after the previous night, be it concubine or slave.

Stepping out of the tent, a bitter wind sweeping in from the bay immediately assaulted Affraic. She shivered, her exposed skin a blister of goose pimples. She wrapped her arms tightly around herself as she surveyed the bustling Norse encampment. Dark clouds loomed on the horizon, promising rain.

"This way," Einar's gruff voice cut through the din of the camp. He stood a few paces away, pointing towards the harbour where a group of women huddled around large swaths of sailcloth.

Affraic's brow furrowed as she followed his gaze. "What am I to do there?"

"You will work with the women repairing sails," Einar replied, his tone brooking no argument. "Everyone must contribute to the community, be they wife or thrall."

The words hung in the air between them. Einar stood staring at the ground. He knew Norse life was brutal and he could not afford to show weakness in front of this thrall especially since he liked her. Affraic's chest tightened as she searched Einar's stoic face for any hint of affection or reassurance. Finding none, she gathered her courage and asked the question that had been gnawing at her since she'd first arrived at the Norse camp and then ended up in his bed.

"And what am I to you, Einar?" Her voice was barely above a whisper. "Wife... or thrall?"

Einar's jaw clenched, his eyes hardening as he met her gaze. For a moment, Affraic thought she saw a flicker of something – regret? uncertainty? – pass across his face. But as quickly as it appeared, it vanished, replaced by his usual mask of indifference.

Without a word, Einar turned on his heels and strode away, leaving Affraic alone and shivering with her unanswered question and the biting wind that seemed to mock her predicament.

The sky had darkened to a bruised purple by the time Einar's hulking silhouette appeared on the horizon. Affraic's fingers, raw and bleeding, fumbled with the last stitches as she watched him approach. Her back ached from hours of hunching over the rough sailcloth, and her damp hair clung to her face, a constant reminder of the relentless drizzle that had plagued them all day.

"Time to go," Einar grunted, his eyes sweeping over her work with cold appraisal.

Affraic shook as she rose, her limbs stiff with cold. But she was determined to air the accumulation of the day's grievances. She thrust her hands towards Einar's face, displaying the cuts and bruises that marred her once smooth skin.

"Look what your 'important work' has done to me," she spat, her voice trembling with fury. "Is this how you treat a potential wife?"

Einar's laugh was sharp and sudden, cutting through the evening air like a blade. "Wife?" he said as he pulled his head back in fake surprise. "These sails will make us rich, woman. You should be honoured I've given you such a crucial task."

Affraic's eyes narrowed, her mind racing. "Crucial? This is thrall's work, and you know it."

"It's work that needs doing," Einar replied, turning away. "There are too few of us that we can pick and choose our jobs. Now come. It's time to eat."

As they walked back to the tent, Affraic seethed silently. *I am Affraic O'Braonáin*, she thought, *not some common thrall to be ordered about.* Her fingers, though aching, itched for something more substantial than a needle. Something that could prove her worth.

When they reached the tent, Einar began unbuckling his weapons, his mind already on the meal to come. Affraic's gaze fixed on the sword at his hip, an idea forming in her mind. Quick as a viper, she snatched the blade from its scabbard.

"Einar," she said, her voice steady despite the wild beating of her heart. "If you wish me for a wife, then give me a role worthy of my status. Make me a shield-maiden."

Einar's face darkened with rage. "Put that down, woman," he growled, advancing towards her. "Now."

But Affraic was beyond heeding his commands. She circled him, the sword held before her in trembling hands. "I can fight," she insisted. "I can be more than just a sail-mender. Let me prove myself to you."

For a moment, time seemed to stand still. Then Einar moved, faster than Affraic could have imagined. The sword was wrenched from her grasp, and she found herself pinned against his chest, his breath hot on her neck.

"You want to prove yourself?" he snarled. "Then you can spend the night with the other troublemakers."

Before Affraic could protest, Einar dragged her across the camp, tossing her unceremoniously into the thralls' pen. As the gate clanged shut behind her, Affraic realised that her gamble had failed spectacularly. But as she huddled in the damp straw, a small smile played at the corners of her mouth. That was the second time she had got an emotional reaction from Einar. She was learning how to get under his skin. Soon, he would be no longer able to resist her.

CHAPTER TWENTY-FOUR

A FRIENDLY SWORD IS NO SWORD AT ALL

T HE OARS DIPPED GENTLY into the water and the men pulled back, barely making a splash. The boat journey seemed to take an age, giving Finn plenty of time to contemplate the enormity of the task he had been given. Finn turned his attention towards the jetty to see if he could find his men. There were numerous bands of warriors disembarking from boats and gathering on the shore side. There were far more than a hundred men on the shore, making it impossible for him to pick out who he had been given to lead. A space on the mainland jetty became available, and the oarsmen guided the boat in. A rough hand reached down to Finn and hauled him onto the jetty.

"Ah, the orphan returns," Wart Face grinned at Finn as he let go his hand. "I was expecting a corpse, but you must've run like a rabbit with your toothpick as soon as your opponent unsheathed his sword."

Finn went bright red, for he did not know who he bore such insults in front of. For all he knew, he was standing in the middle of his men. He swallowed hard, for now was the time to assert himself.

"Let it be known you are talking to the leader of one of the king's finest bands of warriors. We are off to slay the Norse and send them back to the sea. If you apologise for your insult, I will let you attend our victory feast."

Wart Face howled with laughter so much it brought tears to his eyes.

"I don't know what is the funnier," he exclaimed as he took in gulps of air between gales of laughter, "the fact that the king would give you a position of responsibility or the look on the Norsemen's faces as you charge at them with your toothpick."

All the men on the jetty turned to look at what was the object of Wart Face's derision. The laughter proved infectious. Finn froze as everyone laughed. Aodh was helped up on to the jetty. Finn squeezed the grip on his sword so hard it left an impression on his palm. Wart Face stopped laughing and his face dropped.

"SWORD!"

His men turned on Finn and went for their weapons. Aodh's sword flew out of its scabbard and with one swish an arm was dismembered and flew in the air spraying blood in its wake before plopping into the lake. One of Wart Face's men howled in agony as he tried to stem the bleeding from the remaining stump of his arm. The men on the jetty turned pale and edged away from Aodh.

"No one insults an agent of King Malachy," Aodh hissed as he pointed the tip of his sword at Wart Face and his men, daring them to challenge him. "For if they do, they insult the king himself."

Wart Face signalled to his men to part.

"We will let you pass for we believe you rather than him," he said pointing at Finn. "But if we cross paths again, be careful for my men may seek vengeance."

Aodh gestured to Finn to move.

"You had better forget all thoughts of that for it was you at fault today. Note how quick I am with my sword for if we do meet again and I be not on the king's business, I may not be so merciful."

Aodh and Finn passed through the scowling faces and towards where the warbands were gathered by the shore.

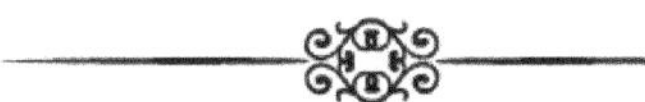

Finn and Aodh walked through the different warbands, Aodh with a determined stride, for he had to make up any shortfall in confidence the men may have in Finn, who walked in his shadow. The men stared at Aodh, shaded in silence for most were too young to recognise him, but most were afraid, for few dared to use violence not sponsored by the king in the shadow of his crannóg. Aodh raised his blooded sword and let the blood trickle down his arm.

"Who has been assigned to follow Finn O'Braonáin?"

The men in one group looked at each other until one man raised his hand.

"We have been told to follow you, Finn."

Aodh grimaced as he realised what he had done. He gestured for Finn to step forward.

"I am not Finn, but am also one of his followers. This is Finn."

Finn stepped forward and blushed.

The men turned to their group, and a cacophony of angry whispers erupted. The man turned to Aodh.

"We have no wish to die so the king can dispose of another of his useless bastard sons. Let us free you of his burden. We will happily help you drown him in the lake over the hill. We can do it so you are provided with a good story and we can all go back to our homes still alive."

Aodh glared at Finn and then shook his sword at the men.

"He is no bastard son, he has been appointed to his position on merit. The Norse camp will be empty for Malachy will drag all the warriors away and all you have to do is burn and loot the camp. This is the best opportunity you useless farmers will ever come across to be rich men. Now pick up your things for time is not for wasting."

The man looked at Aodh and then looked at Finn and his expression did not change.

"Are you going to do all his killing for him or is he actually going to show himself to be a leader?"

Aodh squared up to the man.

"He is happy to show his killing skills, starting with you if you wish?"

The man smirked and looked over Aodh's shoulder at Finn.

"Lead the way, please."

Aodh nodded and the men picked up their belongings and began to march south. Once all their heads were turned Aodh grabbed Finn's arm.

"You need to show yourself as a leader and quickly, or the men will kill you in your sleep so they can flee. There is only so much I can do or say until they cease to be afraid of me."

Finn gulped and nodded his head.

The column of one hundred men wandered south in a lackadaisical manner with Finn at their head and Aodh trying discreetly to give him advice on leadership. He also made Finn remember the men's names by heart and whatever other information he could glean from conversing with them without actually interrogating them. Wart Face had certainly unnerved Finn and Aodh's actions, while well intentioned, had only undermined him. Most of the men when seeking guidance about the route and what they may face ahead had consulted Aodh and glared disdainfully at Finn, only asking Finn for advice under pain of punishment by Aodh. Nevertheless, Aodh made sure to involve Finn at every juncture so he would get used to commanding men and gain their confidence, all in the hope his experience would rub off on him.

He was soon presented with an opportunity as one of their scouts ran back through the woods.

"Aodh, Aodh, there are plumes of smoke on the horizon to the south."

Aodh scowled and pointed to Finn. The messenger looked from Aodh to Finn, but Aodh's growl told him to address Finn.

"There are plumes of smoke coming from the south, Finn," the messenger said.

Finn turned pale, for immediately south of their position was his village.

"Let us march with all haste so we can stop the Norsemen in their tracks."

Aodh nodded and gave a brief smile. In the gravest of circumstances, Finn had given his first order.

CHAPTER TWENTY-FIVE
CHARRED DREAMS

FINN STUMBLED THROUGH THE charred remnants of his village, his eyes burning from the suffocating smoke that clung to everything like a burial shroud. The once vibrant community, filled with the laughter of children and the bustle of daily life, now lay below charred wood and ash.

As he neared the remnants of his family's home, a crushing weight settled in Finn's chest. The roof had caved in, leaving the walls as fragile spectres of what once was, barely standing amidst the devastation. He navigated the debris with a heavy heart, his boots grinding against shards of pottery and the blackened beams strewn across the ground, each fragment telling of the horror unleashed here.

Tears cascaded down Finn's cheeks as he took in the scene of utter ruin. Everywhere he turned, the scorched bodies of neighbours and friends lay frozen in their final, agonising moments, twisted grotesquely where they fell. The overpowering stench of burnt flesh and singed hair engulfed him, forcing him to choke back vomit.

But then, out of the corner of his eye, Finn caught a flicker of movement. He whipped around to see a group of children, their faces smeared with soot, their clothes mere rags, darting frantically between the ruins before vanishing into the shadowy woods beyond the village.

A fierce surge of hope ignited within Finn. Maybe, just maybe, some had survived the raiders' merciless attack. He wiped away his tears with a rough hand and charged after the children, his heart hammering violently in his chest.

As he ran, Aodh signalled for some of the men to follow him and others to circle around him in case they ran into a trap. Finn ran into the forest and soon came across a clearing where the villagers with whom he had spent his life lay huddled, crying and covered in soot.

Finn knelt on the damp forest floor and embraced the survivors from the village. He recognised their faces – gaunt, streaked with soot, eyes full of sorrow. They collapsed into his arms, clinging desperately.

"What happened? Where is my mother?" Finn demanded.

A woman sobbed, her voice breaking. "She went to the hillfort of King Tigernach. On a hunger strike, she said. To shame him for failing to protect us, now and all those years ago. And your sister—"

"What of her?"

"She is now a prisoner of the Norse."

Finn's hands balled into fists as white-hot fury coursed through his veins. The guilt for not being able to defend his family churned his stomach and he folded over to shield himself from the horrors of the village as if he could make it all go away. The Norse had first taken his father from him and now their curse hung over his mother and sister. The urge for vengeance consumed him. If he had not been able to protect his family then whose responsibility should it have been? There was only one answer.

He sprang to his feet. "Tigernach!" he snarled. "That craven wretch will pay for this. I'll tear his fortress down with my bare hands!"

Striding forward with deadly purpose, Finn suddenly felt a rough hand grab his shoulder. Aodh wrenched him around, fixing Finn with an iron glare.

"Have you lost your mind, boy? The Norse are the threat here, not Tigernach. They'll slaughter us all while you curse at Tigernach's walls." Aodh gestured at the huddled survivors. "Malachy has a plan. Let's stick to it. We're at his mercy, but it's our only hope. By all the gods Finn, think!"

Finn wrenched away, chest heaving, torn between his all-consuming rage and the cold reason in Aodh's words. He pictured his mother, frail and wasting away, and the fresh wave of anger nearly swept him away again.

But as he gazed at the terrified faces of the survivors, he knew Aodh was right. The Norse had to be dealt with first, or none of them would live to take another breath. Finn squeezed his eyes shut, forcing the fury down like bile. When he opened them again, they shone with grim determination.

"The Norsemen first," he growled through clenched teeth. "And then Tigernach will answer for his crimes. On that, I swear my life."

Aodh nodded, a flicker of relief in his weathered face. "Aye, that's the way of it. But first, you need to win back the confidence of the men. They'll follow strength, Finn. Show them the fire in your belly."

Finn took a deep breath, squaring his shoulders as he turned to face the ragged band of warriors. "Listen, men, and listen well!" he bellowed, his voice ringing through the trees. "The Norse think us broken, but they're wrong. We'll march on their camp and teach them the true meaning of Hibernian fury! We'll make them pay tenfold for every drop of blood they've spilt!"

A few scattered cheers rose from the men, but Finn could see the doubt lingering in their eyes. He had to do more. Striding forward, he clapped a hand on the shoulder of a burly young warrior. "Conall, your father was a mighty fighter. I see his courage in you. Will you stand with me?"

Conall hesitated, then nodded firmly. "Aye, Finn. I'll follow where you lead."

Emboldened, Finn moved among the men, calling each by name, invoking the memories of their fallen kin, stoking the embers of vengeance in their hearts. Slowly, the tide began to turn. Backs straightened, jaws set, and hands tightened around sword hilts.

As the men began to rally, Finn turned to Aodh, lowering his voice. "My mother... she can't be left alone. Tigernach's a snake, but even he wouldn't dare harm her openly. Not yet, anyway."

Aodh's face softened. "I'll send Babo to watch over her. He's quick and clever, and fiercely loyal to you. He'll keep her safe."

Finn clasped Aodh's arm, gratitude welling in his chest. "Thank you, old friend. I won't forget this."

With a final nod, Aodh slipped away to find Babo. Finn watched him go, then turned his gaze to the path ahead, his blood singing with the promise of battle. The Norse would learn the true strength of the Hibernians this day. Then, with his honour restored and his men behind him, he would march on Tigernach's hillfort and claim the justice his family so desperately deserved.

CHAPTER TWENTY-SIX

NO TIME TO PLAY THE HERO

THE ACRID STENCH OF fear and desperation suffocated the air as Babo trudged towards Tigernach's hillfort. Ominous, dark clouds churned violently above, poised to unleash their wrath with merciless intensity. Before him lay a chaotic sprawl of ramshackle shelters, a shanty town birthed from necessity and sheer terror, clawing desperately at the fort's entrance.

Babo's eyes searched the sea of unfamiliar faces, searching for any sign of Gormlaith. The woman he sought was as elusive as smoke, and he squinted in his search for her. Where could she be in this chaos?

As he pushed through the throng, a withered hand grasped at his cloak. "Please, lord," croaked an old woman, her eyes sunken with hunger. "Have you any food to spare?"

Babo shook his head, his voice gruff but not unkind. "Babo no food."

The old woman's grip tightened. "You look like a man of violence. Perhaps you'd consider vengeance instead? The Norse burned my village to the ground. I'd give you all I have left if you'd make them pay."

A chorus of agreement rose from the crowd gathering around him. Babo's hand instinctively went to the hilt of his sword, but he forced himself to remain calm. These people were desperate, and desperation could turn ugly in an instant.

"Babo no time for revenge," he growled, as he pulled his cloak out of the woman's grip. "Babo seek someone important."

A man with a scarred face blocked his path. "More important than justice? Then protecting the weak?"

Babo's patience wore thin.

"Babo no time," he warned, his voice low and dangerous. "Babo no hero. Here to protect Gormlaith."

The crowd's murmurs turned hostile, and Babo tensed, ready for a fight. But before things could escalate further, a peal of thunder split the air. The first fat drops of rain began to fall, and the people scattered, seeking shelter.

Babo breathed a sigh of relief, but the guilt gnawed at him. "Babo no hero. Babo here to protect Gormlaith," he kept repeating to himself.

He pressed on through the muddy paths between shelters with renewed determination. The rain intensified, soaking through his cloak and plastering his hair to his scalp. But Babo paid it no attention. His eyes remained sharp, searching for any sign of the proud, fierce woman he'd been sent to find.

As Babo rounded the corner of a dilapidated shelter, he spotted a huddled group of women near the gateway to the ring fort. His heart leapt as he recognised one figure among them, but he had to squint to make sure it was her such was the change in her appearance. Gormlaith sat swathed in rags and a tattered blanket, her eyes hollow with hunger but burning with determination.

"Babo question the gods," he muttered, his chest tightening. "Gormlaith look ill."

He approached cautiously, noting the hostility in the eyes of the women surrounding Gormlaith. They clung to her like limpets to a rock. Their gaunt faces trembled, but they dared not cry out. Babo reached out with his hand towards Gormlaith. It shook as it slowly made its way towards her.

"Babo look for Gormlaith. Why sit out here so?"

"It's that pig Tigernach's fault!" one crone spat as Babo drew near. "Sitting up there in his fort while we starve! Too afraid to come out and face us, that's what he is."

Gormlaith's eyes lit up at the sound of a familiar voice. She raised a trembling hand. "Peace, Aileen. Save yourself for when Ultán or his men pass by. Sit, Babo. Tell me, what brings you here?"

Before he could speak, a commotion at the gate drew their attention. Ultán strode through, flanked by armed men. His eyes glittered with malice as they fell upon Gormlaith.

"Well, well," he drawled, loud enough for all to hear. "You're still here? The dogs haven't eaten you yet?"

Ultán's men laughed. Babo's hand tightened on his sword hilt.

Ultán continued, addressing his men but projecting his voice. "Did you hear the news, men? We've struck a deal with the Norse. A prisoner exchange! And guess who we're getting?" He paused dramatically. "The lovely Affraic, daughter of this crone!"

Gormlaith's head snapped up, her eyes wide.

"Oh yes," Ultán gloated. "And once she's here, I'll make her my bride. Whether she likes it or not!"

Gormlaith sprang to her feet, her finger jabbing the air between Ultán and herself. "You miserable worm! May your seed shrivel in your sack! May rabid dogs feast on your manhood! Over your dead body or mine, you'll never marry my daughter."

Ultán's men drew their swords. "She's threatened the prince!" one shouted. "The Brehon's protection is no more!"

They advanced towards Gormlaith, threatening violence. Babo sprang into action. His sword sang as it met the air, connecting to flesh with a sickening crunch. An arm flew off and twitched midair as it refused to let go of its sword in its hand. The pommel of Babo's sword connected with the other guard's front teeth, who fell to the ground in an explosion of blood. Ultán stood back and put his arm out in front of his remaining men, for he could see the violence getting out of control.

"Babo protects Gormlaith," Babo growled, positioning himself between Gormlaith and the remaining soldiers. "Brehon protects Gormlaith. Sent by Malachy."

Ultán's eyes bulged, but he held up a hand to order his men to back off. "This isn't over," he hissed, before retreating into the fort.

Babo's heart raced as he watched them go. He lowered his sword when the fort gate began to shut. He exhaled deeply. A crowd had gathered and he searched the faces to find those of foes. But when he turned and saw the gratitude shining in Gormlaith's eyes, the tip of his sword hit the ground.

Gormlaith's shoulders sagged as the tension drained from her body. She looked up at Babo, her eyes a mix of gratitude and resignation. "It has been a long time, Babo," she said, her voice hoarse. "Thank you for your bravery, but you needn't have bothered. I've lost everything. My family, my home..." She trailed off, her gaze distant. "What's left to live for?"

Babo's heart clenched at her words. He bent down beside her, his voice low and urgent. "Babo sent by Finn. He lives."

Gormlaith eyes blazed with renewed fire. "Finn? My boy?" She whirled towards the fort's entrance, to where Ultán had disappeared. "You lying, scheming bastard!" she bellowed, her fist raised in defiance. "You'll not have my daughter, you hear me? I'll see you rot in the deepest pits of hell before I let that happen!"

Several of the refugees huddled nearby flinched at her outburst, but Gormlaith paid them no attention. She turned back to Babo, grabbing his arm with surprising strength. "Tell me everything," she demanded. "Where is he? Is he safe?"

Babo glanced at the darkening sky, feeling the first drops of rain on his face. "Babo feel rain. Gormlaith get shelter."

Gormlaith's laugh was sharp and mirthless. "Shelter? Here?" She gestured at the muddy, overcrowded shanty town. "You're welcome to sit beside me, brave warrior, but I hope you don't mind getting soaked to the bone." She settled back onto her threadbare blanket, patting the space next to her. "Now, tell me about my son."

Babo lowered himself to the ground and he sat beside Gormlaith. His face twitched as if he were trying to smile. But he could not manage it because of his head injury. But Gormlaith smiled back, for she understood. The rain began to fall in earnest, but neither of them noticed as Babo began to recount his tale.

CHAPTER TWENTY-SEVEN
BLOOD AND ANGER

AFFRAIC TREMBLED IN THE corner of the pen, seeking warmth without having to huddle with the monastery priests who were her fellow prisoners. The priests were by now hollow-eyed skeletons, nearly worked to death by the Norse. They spent most of the time huddled in the opposite corner making a constant racket hacking up phlegm created by their numerous ailments. They no longer had the energy to pray for themselves, never mind anyone else. Affraic could barely recognise the faces she once looked up to, for they were now such wretches you could only look down upon them.

Dawn broke, but the only difference it made was that shafts of light made their way through the wicker wall riding on the cold breeze. With the daylight came the crows for they could smell death. They hopped around on the wicker roof cawing as they impatiently waited for their next victim. Affraic thought they must prefer the executed more as there was less chance of eating themselves ill than by eating someone worked to death.

But Affraic's anger warmed her heart. It may have kept her awake all night but it was better than a tearful night in the cold. How could Einar have done this to her? Of course he could. She saw what he did to Étaín. Was she to end up like her? Was this the action of a stupid man who bowed down to his embarrassment and ego? From his strutting around the camp the days before, Affraic thought he cared nothing for what anyone thought, except for Thurgest, as he could have you killed far quicker than you could work out why he was having you killed. He should just take her and be glad there was someone willing to warm his bed that would not stab him in the throat if they could smuggle a knife under the covers. But she would make him pay for this night when he eventually returned. If there was something her mother taught her, it was how to make men squirm.

She could hear the sound of distant voices. Those who had recently been enslaved crowded towards the door for starvation had got the better of them. Those veterans of the pen crowded in the corners, for they would rather stay and die in the pen than be beaten to death hauling logs. Affraic made herself visible but not near the front for she did not want to appear desperate. It would give Einar the opportunity to see the error of his ways and to pretend to himself that he had 'rescued' her. She could sacrifice a small portion of her dignity so as not to have to sit in the cold all night because his ego was dented. She could wait and make him pay later.

The guards came to the door and one untied the rope. He began to heave it open until the edge of the door was swamped by the hands of those inside trying to push it open.

"Get your hands off the door or I'll cut them off," he said in a voice that betrayed he already had the ailments of Hibernia.

The hands were retracted and the door dragged open through the clumps of soggy earth.

"Get out. Those who don't work, don't eat."

Those who wished to eat piled out leaving only Affraic and the ill priests in the pen.

"Get out now before I set fire to the pen. Let's see if your God comes to save you then."

Affraic decided she had made her point and could make her dramatic exit. She stormed out looking angry. But all she was met with was the cold wind. She stopped and looked for her intended audience. She only saw the stony faces of the guards.

"Where's Einar?" she demanded.

"The leaders are busy, as you should be," the guard replied. "If the sails are not finished today, there will be beatings for you all and no food. Now move."

Affraic received the butt of an axe in her back to get her to move. She looked over her shoulder to see the guards kicking the sides of the pen until all the priests got up. No one was avoiding work today.

Einar stood legs astride on top of a small hill that overlooked the black pool, which the Norse had converted into their harbour. The priests were dragging logs towards the unfinished palisade, delivered by boats which had brought them from the forest beside the newly constructed bridge over the Liffey. Norse guards whipped and taunted them so much that it would not be long before they would be in their graves to meet their God, whom they loved so much. But before they went, they could do their enemies one last favour since they were so kind to send them to heaven. Einar smiled as the construction project he was overseeing was going well.

The thralls from Affraic's pen were herded past him.

"You hadn't the nerve to come and see me this morning?" Affraic snarled as she passed by.

The guard lifted the butt of his axe to smack her in the cheek for disrespecting his leader, but Einar signalled for him not to. He admired how her spirit still burned so brightly even after a night in the pen. He must not douse that flame, for she would more than likely die before becoming a broken thrall. The guard settled for pushing her onwards.

The thralls were now gathered around the sails that had been carried up from some of the ships below. Einar ignored Affraic and stood in front of the thralls. He raised his chin and puffed out his chest.

"Today, you face a choice. These sails need to be repaired by tomorrow because your new leader, Thurgest, needs to set sail. If you succeed, you will be allowed to warm yourselves before a fire and will be well fed. If you fail us, you will be punished. If you defy us, you will be tied to the dragon's head on Thurgest's ship and left there until you drown. Do not think your Norse overlords are all bad. If you serve us well in our time of need, you could be rewarded with the status of free people within this new Norse land. This is the new world, so get used to it. Now get on with your work, for if you demand my attention again, all you will see is my fist."

The thralls looked to the ground as the sewing equipment and materials for patchwork were distributed. Affraic sat on the ground on a cowhide to keep her from getting wet and began to sew a patch onto a sail. The waves crashed on the rocks below as she saw the Norse ships dominate the bay, coming to and fro unimpeded by any Hibernian vessel. She lost herself in her dreams that she was a Hibernian princess on the shore looking out on all the lands that were hers, commanding the sea and the lands equally by the force of the Norse navy. Einar was beneath her on the hill but at her command, obedient to the point of kissing her hand.

"Get back to work or Thurgest will skin you alive and use your skin to patch up his sails," came a shrill woman's voice from behind her.

Affraic cursed and jammed her bone needle through the edge of the sail, for it was the only spiteful thing she could do.

"OW!"

Anger had robbed her of attention. She looked down, and to her horror, the needle had gone through her finger. Blood haemorrhaged from her finger and dripped all over the sail. The Norse woman ran up behind her and hit her on the back of the head.

"Thurgest likes the blood of his enemies on his sail. Is this the gods revealing you are an enemy of Thurgest? If so, we'll tie you to the rocks on the cliffs below and let the sea take you."

The pain blazed in Affraic's brain, so she was unable to stop herself from lashing out.

"I am Einar's mistress. Are you too stupid to realise what he will do to you when he hears you treating me like this?"

"All I hear is a bed thrall giving me cheek. We all answer to Thurgest, even your bed master, and the gods have declared you Thurgest's enemy."

The woman towered over Affraic, baton in hand, about to deliver the decisive blow.

"Stop."

Einar had heard the commotion and grabbed the woman by the wrist.

"We need all the thralls we can lay our hands on, so you cannot kill them on a whim. Leave this one to me and I will take care of her."

The woman shook off his grip and smirked.

"I know you will, but is it not a bit early in the day for that sort of thing?"

"The only sort of thing we'll get up to is a visit to the healer," Einar snarled. "Now get these sails repaired. You have until sunset or you may find yourself as her replacement as a thrall."

The woman snarled and turned to face the thralls repairing the sail.

"WHAT ARE YOU LOT LOOKING AT? GET BACK TO WORK BE-
FORE I FLAY YOU ALIVE."

Einar grabbed Affraic by the wrist. She gave a contented smile
as he dragged her away, her blood dripping onto the grass as
they walked.

CHAPTER TWENTY-EIGHT

LET THE HEALING BEGIN

EINAR DRAGGED AFFRAIC BY the arm across the building site that was the camp of the Norsemen. Affraic stumbled along in the wake of Einar's brisk pace. She smiled to herself for Einar dared not look back at her even though she was merely a wounded thrall.

As they marched towards the healer the priests and other men captured by the Norsemen dragged logs from the boats. They were cut to the right size, and one end was sharpened and one end flattened so it could take the blows of hammers. They were then lifted into place with the sharpened end placed into the ground. They hammered the stake into the ground. Such was Thurgest's ambition that he drew out a plan for the size of his own town and would not compromise. This left gaping holes in the palisade which his men had to camp in at night to dissuade potential attackers.

Inside the patchwork palisade, the Norsemen had a town of tents and within those tents they had begun creating permanent structures. Some were laying out the foundations of Thurgest's long hall, from which he planned to rule over Hibernia. Some worked on the docks, on wooden quays to which they could tie their ships. Some worked on the network of wooden paths, from which they could bring their loot and thralls. Some worked in the storerooms, where they could accumulate food to get them through the winter or any sieges the natives may subject them to. Some worked on the thrall pens for the slave trade which was what they reckoned would make them rich. Some worked on permanent homes, so they could lay their roots firmly into the soil.

But if Affraic was upset by any of this, she did not show it. She only cared for what Einar thought, for from what she had seen of him, all of this could all be his. He only had to see off a few of the elder Norse, but if he was lucky, they would soon tire and leave the new town all to him. By that time, she would have made him hers and they could rule together. Much better than any life the oaf Ultán could offer her, or any of the village men come to that. She did not want to be a farmer's wife or be like her mother, the widow of a dead warrior who frightened off any man who came near her. No, the life of a Norse chieftain's wife was what she wanted and she would do all in her power to get it.

Einar came to the tent of the healer who had set up his stall outside. On top of the fire, a cauldron was suspended to which he added various powders which were vigorously stirred in. The healer picked up a yellow vial of liquid, held it to the sky and pondered its colour. When momentary contemplation did not yield a conclusion, he shrugged his shoulders and threw it in anyway. Einar strode up to the man and pointed back at Affraic.

"Can you heal this stupid girl?"

The healer did not look up.

"There is no cure for stupidity here. The fastest cure I can think of is to get her to charge towards the Hibernians with only a weapon. They will soon lop her head off and put it on a spike. They like that sort of thing. One head cured of stupidity and one happy Hibernian chieftain who can lie peacefully in his bed leaving the job of frightening off his enemies to the head of a stupid girl."

"Please," Einar said, well used to the caustic wit of the healer. "Lift your head up and look at her finger."

The healer snarled at his attention being diverted from making his potion.

"What makes this girl so special that I have to delay myself from brewing a potion for the Hibernian ailments that plague your men?"

The healer pointed to a row of men sitting on the other side of the fire. They waved the smoke out of their faces as they simultaneously did battle with sniffles, sneezes, and shivers. The healer raised his eyebrow, thinking he had made a very valid point. However, when he clapped eyes on Affraic, she blushed and looked to the ground.

"Oh," the healer said as he tried to extricate himself from the conversation he had started.

"It's her finger," Einar growled, trying to hide his embarrassment. "This thrall, to her detriment, has a better talent for making mischief than for repairing sails. Heal her finger so she can get back to work and I won't have to make an example of her to the other thralls."

The healer had to hide his face after Affraic blushed again when Einar said he would make an example of her.

"If you ask nicely, I'm sure the healer will give you a potion for later," Affraic said coyly as she batted her eyelids at Einar.

Einar went a peculiar colour red as anger and embarrassment merged on his cheeks.

"Just bandage her up so we can leave," Einar snarled through gritted teeth.

"Be patient and give the healer a chance," Affraic said. "It is not even dark and we have all night."

"By the gods, you have a wicked tongue," Einar snapped, "but I have no time to be whipped by it. Stay with the healer until he is done. My men will come and collect you when you are ready. I have far more important tasks to do than stand around and wait for you."

Einar stormed off and Affraic gave the biggest grin to his back. She had got under his skin.

"I hope you know what game you are playing," the healer said as he took her hand and examined the deep cut on her finger. "You are playing for your life."

"That is the only game a thrall can play and I mean to win," Affraic said as the smile evaporated to reveal a granite face of determination.

"Indeed I do," the healer said. "For I was once a thrall from Northumbria and I played your game, too."

Affraic gave a knowing nod.

"Then bandage me up well, for I have no wish to bleed on his bed furs. My best work is done in the night."

The healer examined the cut and sprinkled it with ground medicinal herbs. Affraic could not help but howl. Einar turned from his conversation down by the moored ships and looked in Affraic's direction. He dispatched his men to collect her, for he knew she was almost ready.

CHAPTER TWENTY-NINE
MAKING A CHOICE

IT HAD NOT BEEN long since Affraic's life had changed completely, maybe a few weeks at most. Her brother was missing, but considering what he had got himself into, more than likely dead. Her mother had lost her two children and she was more than likely dead too. Affraic knew that she would have been straight to Tigernach and Ultán to complain about how she had lost both her children and how the Norsemen were now camped by their door, yet they had done so little about it. Her mother did not lose an opportunity to curse at Tigernach and his useless son ever since her father had disappeared, yet failed to explain why she laid so much of the blame upon him. Affraic gagged at the thought that Ultán had proposed to marry her on several occasions. Yes, it would have lifted the status of the family quite considerably in the village. It may even have earned her brother the privilege of commanding some of Tigernach's men. But the thought of that ugly fool's hands all over her was too much to bear. All that she would have gained would have been lost in a nocturnal fit of rage for she would not have been able to resist the urge to stab him to get his grubby hands off her.

But now she had Einar, who was everything Ultán was not. He was handsome, with his piercing blue eyes and set jaw. His matted blond hair set him apart from most of the Hibernian men she had met. He was strong and a great warrior, or at least everyone said that, for she had never witnessed it herself. But from the way he wielded his sword when he practised in the morning, she knew he would take some beating. He was covered head to toe in tattoos, something she heard showed the status of a man in the Norse world, or at least that was what she wanted to believe. But it was Einar's status in the newly established Norse colony that attracted her the most.

Affraic noticed that Einar was a busy man. Her eye to spot something for her own advantage was certainly not wrong on this occasion. Einar seemed to be second only to Thurgest, with Torstein his main rival for his master's attentions. But with ships coming and going all the time, Einar seemed to be the only constant. He was hard-working, had the respect of the men and showed good building and carpentry skills. There was much to turn his hand to. The ships needed repairs, the sails required maintenance, and a palisade needed to be constructed. Thurgest wanted the great hall to be constructed straight after the wall was finished. It was a never-ending list of chores, but Einar applied himself to them with diligence and without complaint.

Affraic watched from the hill, incapacitated by her wound but resented by the women and thralls alike for it was one less pair of hands to help them with their work. But she treated their words like the biting wind from the bay that licked the hill. She wrapped herself in another blanket, covered her head and congratulated herself on such a shrewd choice of potential spouse.

She saw some boats arriving from up the river Liffey that looked crowded with people. On closer inspection, it looked as if warriors surrounded a clutch of people, more than likely locals who had been freshly enslaved. Affraic ran down the hill to see if any of the people who had been captured were from her village.

The bitter wind whipped off the sea, carrying with it the stench of fear and desperation. The docks were crowded with people all gathered around the gangplank of the lead boat that had come downriver. Some warriors from the boat marched down the plank to part the crowd so they could lead their new thralls straight to the pens to be allocated. Some would be put to work on the construction of the Norse town, some would be sent to till the soil, some would be servants, some would be bed thralls. The rest would be sold to the merchants and dispersed across the Norse world. Affraic knew what would happen to the people and positioned herself in the crowd so she would have a good view, but not be conspicuous.

The thralls came off the ship heads bowed, with some of the women wailing and pleading for leniency for their fate. The docks creaked and groaned beneath the weight of so many bodies, the weathered wood slick with sea spray and the blood of those who had resisted. They were chained together, and most were covered in mud. Their faces bore the blackened stain of smoke, and their cheeks were running with tears.

The first batches of people all wore faces of misery but none were known to Affraic. When the second batch came Affraic could have almost cried there and then. The Norsemen forced her former neighbours and friends off the boat at sword point, beating them if they tried to resist. Affraic had to hold herself back from reaching out and grabbing some of the children and trying to hide them in the crowd. But the throng that had gathered around the disembarking ship was only two or three people deep, maybe one hundred in all. Most of those were Norse warriors who snarled at or kicked and prodded at the new thralls for as soon as they had broken their spirit the sooner they could be set to work. There was nowhere for the thralls to run. As soon as they broke away they would be shot down with an arrow. It was a fatal choice. To live as a thrall and see if one day you could escape and be free, or to die in one last futile grasp at freedom.

Affraic swallowed hard. She wanted to be the wife of a Norse chieftain but did not want to see the dirty parts of where they got their power from. Especially if it was at the expense of people she knew and loved. But she had to make a choice. She swayed from side to side as the next batch of thralls came off the boat. She did not know any of them. She wiped the tears from the corners of her eyes, pretending it was the wind instead of seeing her loved ones enslaved. She swallowed hard. Her heart hardened. It was the same stiff resolve her father told her she had to have when they had to kill her favourite cow in the middle of winter so the family could eat. Her choice was to survive. Just like a lone wolf whose pack was killed and then she has to go off and join another. Unfortunately, this wolf also has to witness the new pack finishing off the old. She walked over to Einar who was inspecting the thralls as they came off the boat. She squeezed his hand to let him know she was there. He smiled briefly at her, then returned his attention to making sure the boat was unloaded without incident.

CHAPTER THIRTY

FOUR-LEAF CLOVER

S EVERAL DAYS PASSED, AND Einar began to seek out Affraic's attention, which she dangled seductively in front of him, being careful to only pay him attention as a reward for doing what she wanted. It was as if her attention was a dancing shadow on the woollen walls of the tent, elusive but all the more seductive for it. The air hung thick with the earthy scent of burning peat mingled with sweet notes of honey mead. Furs and woven rugs in intricate knotwork patterns carpeted the packed dirt floor. The air was heavy with the scents of wood smoke, mulled wine and fragrant oils – all carefully arranged by Affraic as if she were a she-wolf drawing a sheep into her trap. It was early days, but she thought he was falling for her without the need to resort to one of her mother's love potions, whose potency she used to brag about. If they were so potent, why did she have two unmarried children?

He could be sweet and affectionate when properly motivated, nothing a slap around the face could not fix should he prove resistant or claim to be tired, and all talk of returning her to repairing sails had now gone. She managed to convince him she was a really slow healer but her hand injury did not affect how she was in bed and he should take advantage while nobody was looking for her to get back to work. He took her words to heart and he made up in bed for all the times he spent at sea before he landed in Hibernia.

But Einar still had duties to perform for Thurgest, and this morning, he turned his back to Affraic as he got dressed, which aroused her suspicions. She crept over to his side of the bed.

"Where are you going this morning in such a rush that you have no time for your bed thrall? Would you not like to give me a proper good morning so you can then go out and take on the world? I can put you in chains if you wish to play the thrall?"

"Do not distract me with your trickery this good morning, woman," Einar scowled, hardening his voice in a vain attempt to intimidate her. "I have important business to do, one which requires all my wits and does not require me to have all my energy previously sapped by a woman."

Affraic swooned back on the bed.

"Oh, and which cruel master has you doing all of this? If you were your own man you could do as you please. You could have me first, then go out and command."

"That is not the way of the world," Einar snarled as he ripped away his shirt from underneath Affraic who was trying to hide it from him. "Be quiet and let me think. What I need to do is serious."

Einar pulled his shirt on, stood, and picked up his best wolfskin, throwing it over his shoulder.

"You had better be here when I get back," Einar snarled as his hand paused on the flap of the tent. "I want you to get up to no mischief today."

He closed the tent flap behind him, and Affraic stuck her tongue out at his departing back. But he did not know Affraic at all. She leapt out of bed as soon as the tent flap flopped to the ground.

Where is that pompous ass going at this time in the morning? It is something to do with Thurgest or else he would not be so nervous. He is the only one who inspires any fear. It has to be something important for him to bark at me first thing in the morning when I am offering myself to him. Then he tells me not to get up to any mischief. Could he have made it more obvious he is up to something?

Affraic quickly got dressed and threw a shawl over her head so no one would immediately recognise her but she would fit in with all the women. She ran out of the tent to follow Einar.

Affraic saw Einar at the bottom of the hill, by the gate below the village of tents of the lesser-status Norsemen. Even though there were numerous gaps in the ambitious palisade Thurgest had ordered built, they gathered around the temporary gate. That was to be replaced by a gloriously decorated portal, something that she had heard Einar already planning, but it seemed somewhat symbolic that they would gather there. Thurgest and Torstein were there alongside Einar, and the surrounding warriors were in full battle dress. But they were not preparing to leave the compound, which would be the first conclusion for them waiting at the gate.

"What are you doing here?" came a harsh voice from her right-hand side, but the corner of Affraic's hood obscured the man from sight. "Are you here to harm our leader?"

Affraic immediately bent down and picked a handful of four-leaf clovers and stood up again. The Norse guard was now snarling in her face. But Affraic thought the best way to deal with this was to fight fire with fire.

"And who are you to come and harass Thurgest's cook?" Affraic snarled back at him. "Our master has ordered me to make him a fabulous meal for his esteemed guests. What do you think he is going to say when he chews on a bland hunk of beef and I tell him that you prevented me from picking any herbs?"

The guard's eyes widened as he searched for a riposte.

"They're not herbs," he exclaimed as he pointed to the bunch of clover in Affraic's hand.

"Oh, you're a cook now, are you? Why don't you make his meal then?"

Affraic thrust out her hand and threw the clover in the man's face and stormed off. He stood there flabbergasted, not able to move. The sound of horns blared through the air. He ran after Affraic.

"Please, please woman, forgive me for my folly. Please, pick the herbs and I will make sure you get what you need."

Affraic halted and smiled to herself. But she turned around with the sternest of frowns.

"Now I will do it, but only for the master's sake for you have insulted me. I don't need your permission for anything nor do I want your help nor want you following me around."

The guard bowed in apology.

"You will have the freedom of the hill. If anyone interferes with you direct them to me."

He then paused when he got a full glimpse of Affraic's face. He squinted as he tried to remember where he had seen her before.

"You're Einar's woman, aren't you?"

Affraic's face hardened.

"That does not make me any less of a cook and gives you even less reason to interfere with me."

The guard bowed again.

"Please, if you tell Einar about me, tell him of my diligence, not of my insolence."

"If you see that I am not further interfered with, he will hear only praise."

The guard nervously surveyed the hill.

"Where is best for you to collect your herbs that have not been trampled to the ground?"

Affraic glanced down at the gate and estimated the best position for her to remain anonymous yet be within earshot.

"Down there," she pointed. "It may be trampled upon but I also need some roots."

The guard swung his arm in that direction.

"Take what you wish and I will see you are not interfered with."

Affraic gave a smug grin and walked in the direction the man's arm was pointing.

CHAPTER THIRTY-ONE

A GULP, BUT NOT SURPRISED

AFFRAIC CROUCHED DOWN BEHIND a tent, peering around it at opportune moments. She crept closer, her leather boots silent on the damp grass. She kept low to the ground, feeling the damp earth beneath her fingers and the rough canvas of the tent against her cheek. Listening to the men gathered around the gate was easy, for Thurgest had a booming voice and loved to brag. She had to come this far down in case anyone else had something interesting to say and not be drowned out by Thurgest. She heard Thurgest laugh.

"So who is it that wants to make a treaty with us?" Thurgest said to Einar, who obviously had made contact with these potential Hibernian traitors.

"It is the king," Einar said, bowing his head in deference and hoping this underhanded move would place him in higher esteem with the Norse leader.

"Is he?" and Thurgest paused momentarily to remember back to his previous raids in Hibernia. "What's his title, the High King of Hibernia?"

A bead of sweat rolled down Einar's face for he feared he may have been tricked.

"I know not his title, except the one he told me, that of king. Maybe of a place called Brega."

Thurgest squeezed his fist for he thought his time may be wasted.

"You can be king of a hill, a pig pen even, here on this island. There are so many of them, that you are nothing if you are not a king. If he does not prove useful cut his head off and hang it from the gate." Thurgest turned and put his face into Einar's. "Then you will be king of my pig pen until you learn not to be taken in so easily."

Einar went pale and nodded. He gulped, stared at the gate with a burning intensity, determined to milk the most of those who came through it.

The gate was opened and the dignitaries walked into the bounds of the camp. Affraic poked her head up above the tent but she could not see over the line of Norsemen. Thurgest's finest men happened to be the tallest too. The Hibernian guests were greeted warmly and presented with gifts by their Norse hosts. Affraic could not hear what was going on for part of the display of power Thurgest had arranged inconveniently involved the blaring of horns. The dignitaries were invited to the great hall situated down by the harbour, which conveniently contained the Norse fleet, the biggest symbol of their military might and the most appealing for any ambitious Hibernian king. The dignitaries found themselves amongst a throng of Norse guards so Affraic had to run among the tents to keep up so she could glimpse them.

But Thurgest had sent his men along the route to clear it of Hibernian thralls for he wished to hide his true intentions temporarily. Affraic covered her face and snuck around the tents and the half-finished buildings and waited for them in the throng of people especially invited to meet the Hibernian king. She took her hood down, and nobody said anything to her as they recognised her as Einar's woman. Thurgest and his guests rounded the bend in the hill and the tents and marched towards the great hall. The guards parted, and Affraic's face dropped. Tigernach and Ultán were there tucked in between Thurgest, Einar and their giant guards. Tigernach grimaced, face firmly forward as if he was here to complete one single task and forsake all else. Ultán walked as if he were a wooden puppet with his eyes fixed firmly to the ground as if he did not want to admire Thurgest's display of fully armed warriors about to be unleashed on Tigernach's lands.

Thurgest smirked as his guests squirmed. He was enjoying the moment but wanted to squeeze it for all he could get. He turned outside the half-finished great hall and directed his men and his guests to turn and face the gathered crowd.

"Look, men," Thurgest boomed across the square in front of the great hall. "We are here barely a hundred moons and look, the Hibernian kings come to pay homage to us. All your efforts will not be in vain. Stick with me, men, and you will soon carve out your farms full of thralls in this green and glorious land."

The men roared and shook their weapons above their heads. Tigernach and Ultán looked like they wished a hole would come and swallow them up, for they were already in hell. Thurgest took Tigernach by the arm and led him to the great hall. Affraic ran to see if she could get up beside the hall so that she could listen in. But there was no chance of that. Burly guards blocked her way, and they were not for fooling.

Curiosity definitely got the better of Affraic. She was forced back to the tents by Thurgest's guards with the other free women. Despite the display of the supplicant Hibernian king to his men he still wished to keep parts of the visit a secret. Affraic returned to the tent and sat in the cold wind that perpetually seemed to swirl around the hill. She had a view of the great hall and would be able to tell when Tigernach and Ultán left and when Einar would return. She mulled over in her head how much she would tell him she had done that day. But the whole camp had come down to watch the humiliation of Tigernach so she would not have to keep many secrets from him.

Day turned to night, and eventually an escort of fire torches went from the great hall to the gate. The gate shut behind them and Tigernach and Ultán were released into the dark. The Norsemen sang a quick war song as the final act of derision against their guests. They cheered, laughed and then the fire torches dispersed around the camp. The majority of the Norse came up the hill. Affraic strained her eyes to make out Einar in the blur of light against the dark. He strode through the light and to the front wearing rosy red cheeks and a large smile on his face.

"A lot of ale at this meeting of yours?" Affraic said, arms crossed, eyebrow raised.

"That is how men do business," Einar replied. "And how is my little flower today?" He angled his face to kiss her and closed his eyes. He was met with her raised hands.

"Not well enough to put up with the fumes of ale in the tent all night."

Einar smiled and bobbed his head playfully from side to side trying to get past her hands. She responded by gently slapping her hands on his face and dragging them down until his closed eyes and puckered lips were revealed. She rewarded his patience with a kiss.

"You would have been so proud of me tonight," Einar said, his rosy cheeks desperate to be lavished with praise.

"Why is that?" Affraic said, giving his outstretched cheek a peck.

"We had a Hibernian king visit us today. We ran rings around him. He was practically begging us to rid him of his master. The fool does not know what it is to make a bargain with Thurgest. It is almost as bad as making you his enemy."

Affraic wrapped her arm in the nook of his elbow and pulled.

"Why don't you come back to the tent and sit by the fire and I will fetch you some ale. Then you can tell me all about it. I may be of some use, you know."

She winked at him, and he smiled back.

"You are as cunning as a fox," he replied, "and as beautiful as the finest pelt."

He smiled and saluted her. She scrunched up her face.

"The fox can't have been that cunning to get skinned alive."

Einar frowned but Affraic smiled back at him to mellow his mood.

They got back to the camp and Affraic settled Einar by the fire and gave him an ale. She wrapped her arm under his and gave him a big smile.

"Now, tell me about your adventures today."

But instead of bragging came silence and a thought struck Einar. He raised himself from their entwined bodies and looked Affraic in the face.

"You are from around here so you may know of this local king."

"I told you, I may be of some use," Affraic said, smiling.

"We had as our guests King Tigernach and his son Ultán."

Affraic paused momentarily to stop herself from smiling. All the humiliation her family and especially her mother had suffered under Tigernach and Ultán would not go unanswered. Now was the perfect moment for revenge.

"I know both these men well and can provide you with much insight," Affraic said before pausing. "But since everyone else is making a bargain why shouldn't I?"

Einar's eyes burned.

"You are not a thrall. You have the privilege of being known as my woman and being free. What more could you want?"

Affraic took a sharp intake of breath. This was her opportunity. Her face hardened.

"If I provide you with enough information to rid yourself of Tigernach and take his lands, then you will make me your wife."

Einar laughed.

"Tigernach is a weak fool. We can burn his lands and hang him from a tree any time we wish. Why do I need anything from you?"

Affraic gnashed her teeth.

"Because I know things you don't. Tigernach is very unpopular and his people would easily side with you if you stopped enslaving them. I know what their weaknesses are."

Einar was tired and saw that this conversation was only going to end in an argument. But he did not want to go to bed with an angry woman. If he was to get any sleep that night, he had to broker a compromise.

"Since you hold such a lofty opinion of yourself and demand so much, we can only strike an expensive bargain for the both of us."

Affraic stiffened up and drew back. "What do you propose?"

"If we overthrow Tigernach with your help, and I am granted his lands, I will marry you in his hillfort and declare you my wife for all to see."

"And if you do not get his lands?"

"You will be my bed thrall for life and I will be free to marry whoever I wish."

Affraic scowled and brought her fists to her hips.

"You seem to do rather well out of this either way."

Einar tilted his head.

"I am the Norse lord and you are the conquered."

Affraic slapped him in the face, which made Einar laugh.

"You may be feisty, but you are still the conquered."

"I want more from this bargain," Affraic said, "and how do I know you will keep it?"

It was Einar's turn to be serious.

"I will have to do most of the hard work for this bargain and am in a far better bargaining position, as I'm sure you will agree. If you doubt that, you can reconsider your position in the thrall pens for as long as you wish to stay away from the bargaining table. Until Tigernach's lands are taken, you are a free woman. By that I mean forever. If we never take them, you will always remain a free woman. So it depends on whether you wish to marry me or not. So you now also have an incentive, as to whether you remain loyal to your Hibernian roots or if you wish to become Norse and marry me. So, what is your answer to this proposal?"

Affraic immediately stuck out her hand.

"Is this the way you Norse conclude a bargain?"

Einar beamed and took her hand.

"It is."

The hands shook, both smiled and Einar had a restless night of the more pleasant kind.

Affraic reached into the basket and took a piece of damp clothing with one hand. A rope stretched from the tent's mast to the mast of a nearby tent, linking all the Norse tents together. She fastened the wet, clean clothes to the line with a peg and let the wind from the bay dry them. Affraic had to remain vigilant of Einar, ensuring he did not notice how much she could actually use her injured hand, which might lead him to send her back to work. She had been staying with him for several days now, with the healer advising him that she needed to rest her hand and should not be working. Affraic attempted to earn his favour, hoping he would keep her as his war wife rather than sending her back to work. His responses encouraged her, but she would leave nothing to chance.

She was joined by some other women, all red-faced and wrapped in shawls. While it may have been strategically prudent to build the Norse base on a hill beside a natural harbour, with only a small proportion built, it left the inhabitants exposed to the elements. Some of the women had travelled from Norway. Not many, for those that came in the first wave were the warriors meant to carve out some land, and the women were to follow. Some had, but the ship space was mainly needed for new war-riors and supplies so they were only arriving in dribs and drabs. The rest of the women were like Affraic, trying to make the most of being captured and taking up with the enemy, for they had no friends.

But every head turned when the sound of drums came from the harbour. The men rushed out of their tents, picked up their weapons, and ran toward the sound. Thurgest stood by the ships on a hastily erected platform, arms folded, chin pointed towards the sky. The men ran down and surrounded him, lowering their weapons. Thurgest knitted his brow.

"Why would I call you here and want you to lower your weapons? Has all the rain made you soft?"

He surveyed the faces of the men, and few had the nerve to look back at him. There were some murmurings from the back of the crowd from those who had taken his words as an insult.

"But do not worry, I am here to save your standing with the gods. While you have grown fat and lazy and helped yourself to the local thralls, I have been out spotting more prey. For those who wish to bask in the glory of the gods, get on the ships. They are ready and waiting for you. Those who wish to be fat farmers and wait until you are ripe and then the Hibernians kill you, stay here."

Thurgest threw his arms open wide.

"Now, come and join me."

The men flooded forward and boarded the ships.

"Don't worry," Thurgest assured them. "You'll be back within a week and all the richer for it."

Einar looked back at Affraic, her long black hair flowing behind her in the wind. He took a couple of strides forward to walk into the blade and shaft of an axe.

"The motivational speech was for the men, not the masters," Thurgest said as he grinned behind his axe. "You are to serve by ensuring the palisade is completed by the time I get back. I can't have my base burned down while I am out raiding."

Einar nodded. His words grated on his dry throat for he had been taken by surprise. Thurgest looked to the hill and his grin got wider.

"You like the Irish thrall? We are here to take, so take. Do not be embarrassed for that will only show your enemies your weakness. If you show your weakness, you will both soon be dead. Now go back and join her. Watch me leave and then whip her priests to finish the walls and trap her inside."

Einar curled a smile at the side of his mouth.

"Now go and command," Thurgest said. "My father, Haakon, your grandfather, will be here soon, and then everything will change. You need to secure your position before that."

Einar saluted him and walked back to Affraic to watch the main body of Norsemen leave.

CHAPTER THIRTY-TWO

A CONFIDENCE TRICK

Finn and his one hundred reluctant men made their way south towards the Norsemen's camp. They kept to the less trodden paths and the denser woods, for they wished to avoid any Norse patrols. Aodh wanted them to move quickly for they had to exploit the small advantage they had as it would take the Norsemen some time to learn the terrain and the best roads to travel. But every time the sun moved in the sky the one hundred would become less.

Aodh had noticed the desertions, but as he looked at Finn's stiff determined face he knew it was a mask and beneath was a nervous frightened boy. It was just like when the king would send his boy out to battle for the first time and Aodh had to manage him. However, the king would arrange it so the boy would safely blood his sword without placing himself in excessive danger, for Aodh was there to take the brunt of the fighting. This boy would not be granted such favours. He would be fortunate if he led the charge to turn his head and still see his men behind him. He knew he had to buttress the boy's authority if he were to stand any chance of succeeding. So he came up with a plan. The hardest part would be convincing the boy.

Finn strode ahead of the men, not daring to look back for fear he would be met with disapproving faces. He was determined to attack as soon as he arrived, no matter Aodh's opinion. The more he delayed, the more men would desert and the greater the chance of failure. A hand gripped his forearm. He turned, furious his line of thought had been disturbed. They would pay for their insolence. He had to assert his authority.

"Finn," Aodh said firmly, as if trying to get the attention of an insolent boy. "Guile. This battle can only be won with guile. You smashing into the camp will only result in all your men being killed in the time it takes for the crows to take fright at the din of battle and fly away. Come, let us rest and let me give you some advice."

"Not in front of the men," Finn snarled and wrenched his arm back.

Aodh sighed.

"Not in front of the men."

He pointed to a clearing in the woods where the men could rest and he could slip away with Finn. Aodh paused and signalled for Finn to be quiet. The men stopped and Aodh listened to the rustling of the leaves. He dropped his hand.

"We are alone, at least for the time being. May the fairies and the wood gods make our steps silent so we may keep it that way. Let us rest, for we are near the Norsemen's camp."

Aodh signalled to the men to sit and rest. Amidst the towering oaks, their trunks gnarled with age and their leaves whispering in the breeze, the warriors found pockets of shelter. The dense canopy overhead filtered the sunlight, casting a dappled pattern on the forest floor. The air was filled with the sounds of clanking metal, rustling leaves, and low voices as the warriors went about their tasks. Moss-covered boulders and fallen logs became natural seats and tables, their surfaces worn smooth by countless years of exposure to the elements. They took out whatever little foodstuffs they carried with them and resentfully ate. Aodh had forbidden them from hunting in case they accidentally alert the Norsemen to their presence. Aodh surveyed the men and once he was assured most of them would stay put, for he knew any loftier aspiration was foolishness, signalled to Finn to follow him.

They crept slowly through the wood, watching the ground for precariously placed twigs that may snap underfoot and give away their position. Aodh pointed the way, far enough from the men to get some privacy, but near enough so the men would not sneak off and desert. They climbed over an ancient fallen oak, covered in a bouncy green moss, a haven for beetles and insects alike. Aodh stopped on the other side of the tree trunk and Finn shrugged his shoulders. Aodh pointed to a dry stone and Finn sat. Aodh sat opposite him and smiled. He tried to smile like a father who had not abandoned his children, but he had no experience of that. So he resorted to the reassurance of master and apprentice.

"To lead men into battle you have to have confidence. But ultimately, no matter what is in your heart, you must exude confidence."

Aodh leant in.

"I know the men are deserting and I know you feel pressure. But we should stop here, for I have something that I think will help you."

Finn gnashed his teeth for Aodh's words were a wicked poison being stirred into his already boiling pot of emotions.

"The best way to get the men behind me is to attack," and he dramatically stabbed his sword into the ground. "That way they do not have the chance to run away and we catch the Norsemen unawares."

"For good or for ill, fate has chosen me to be your master," Aodh said, his face cold and stern. "I am telling you to go to the seer who is just beyond the hills. He will tell your fortune and what fate the gods have decided. Once you know your fate, the men will follow you. They will not follow your words for now, but they will follow the words of the seer. What say you?"

Finn's grimace faltered as he contemplated his master's words. Aodh had protected and been honest with him up until now and it was not in his interest to change it on a whim.

"As long as the men do not desert in my absence, it seems like a good plan. Lead the way."

"I'm glad you think so," Aodh said sarcastically. "We can only pray the seer can teach you what I cannot."

Finn knitted his brow.

"Does that mean we are going to be there for a long time?"

"Not long enough," Aodh sighed, "not long enough."

They returned to the clearing in the woods, distressed that the men had not placed adequate sentries around their resting place to prevent them from sneaking back and easily penetrating it. However, they were pleased to find the same number of men there as when they had left. Aodh called the men together in the centre of the circle.

"Finn and I are going ahead to scout out the enemy and work out the best way to attack. We expect that King Malachy and his men will draw the main host of Norsemen north, which should enable us to destroy their camp while they are gone.

"Remember, King Malachy will reward those who successfully take part in the attack, especially those who present him with the heads of our enemies as evidence. Those who desert will be hunted down by his dogs as cowards. Do not disgrace yourselves to be cast out in shame by your families and villages. Be brave warriors and earn your rewards."

There was faint clapping and cheering by the men. Aodh studied the faces of those who stood before him, looking for those who sowed dissent and fear. Too many faces registered both and it was too much to take on now, especially when he was protecting the boy. He turned to leave and the men sauntered back to their previous spots to finish what they had been doing.

"Come Finn, before the dark sets in."

Aodh pointed in the direction of the Wicklow mountains. Finn hesitated, thinking this was the last time he would command men, for by the time he returned they all would be gone. Aodh went over and put his arm around his shoulders and led him in the direction of the mountains.

CHAPTER THIRTY-THREE

RIDDLES AND CIRCLES

AFTER WALKING FOR TWO days through woods and forest, they came to the foothills of the Wicklow mountains. Finn was nervous and tired, for he had been gone so long that he was sure all his men had deserted him. Aodh saw he was faltering and was quick to offer encouragement.

"'Tis not far to go until we are in the mountains. Then you can see all that you can be."

Finn scowled.

"You exhaust me and take me away from my men. Then you speak to me in riddles. If it were not for how highly my mother and father spoke of you, I would think you are trying to take me away from my enemies."

Aodh tried to reassure him with a smile.

"I do a far greater thing for you, that is to show you your destiny. It will give you the confidence to be a man and a leader. Now, double your pace and do not slack. You will both be enlightened and fighting fit by the time this adventure is over."

"I hope I live to see both," Finn replied, doubt growing in his mind.

They continued on for another half a day until Finn heard a stream amidst the rustling of the woods.

"May we stop?" Finn said, his voice faltering with tiredness. "I need to drink, bathe and consider if you are spinning me a yarn, and if I am caught up in your web, why would you trap me so?"

Aodh laughed.

"It is your mind that is trapped in cobwebs and none are attributable to me." Aodh pointed to where the trees rose to climb the mountain. "Look up there and tell me what you see."

Finn followed Aodh's finger but could see nothing but trees, ferns, grass and mud. The same sight he had been seeing for the last couple of days. He was at the edge of despair but vowed to himself that following the finger would be the last part of this journey. If he found nothing, he would stop at nothing to force their passage home. He walked until the path began to gain steepness as it climbed the next hill. He looked around and saw nothing worthy of his attention. But he had to humour Aodh if he was to persuade him to come back to the men with him.

"Am I looking at an old fallen tree?" he said, sarcasm getting the better of his tired mind. "Am I supposed to wallop the old hollow tree trunk and whatever way the beetles fall out of it is supposed to tell my destiny?"

Aodh lowered his head.

"If there is one thing I have taught you in our time together it is to observe. You cannot lower your attention on the battlefield no matter how tired you are, or else you are a dead man. Now, what else can you see?"

Finn sighed and threw his hands in the air.

"Is this some kind of trick? Why would you trick me so? Have you so little faith in me that you have to trick me into leaving the men?"

"This is no trick," Aodh said, his voice now buffeted by a guttural growl. "Tell me what you see. If you wish to decline, I can say your apprenticeship is over and I can return to my home in peace and you can do whatever you wish to do with yourself. But do not leave your poor mother with a corpse."

Finn gritted his teeth. His head hurt, his limbs ached and his belly rumbled. He had to find something of significance on that hill and fast, or else he would be abandoned as wolf food. He strained his eyes for he knew he had one guess.

"There are some old ruins up there. It looks like a wall. Is that a fat crow sitting on the edge of the wall? Is he guarding the way to the seer?"

Aodh gave a faint grin, a slight relief that all his efforts were not in vain.

"The crow has feasted on the eyes of many a naïve young man. They will be circling above the woods as we speak. Be smart and try not to be part of their next meal."

Finn snarled at him but did not put his protests into words. They walked up to the ruins and the crow cawed and took to the skies. It landed in a tree and was soon joined by several other crows who stared down at them.

"Ignore them," Aodh said as he brushed past Finn. "Follow me. The seer is this way."

They picked their way through the discarded rocks of the old church, the words of forgotten prayers carved by dead hands into them. The rocks had by now become consumed by moss and grass and shat on by the crows. Finn gulped and hoped he would not meet such an ignominious end.

"Come," Aodh said. "He is down by the river."

Finn could suddenly hear the gentle splash of water, and the soil beneath his feet seemed to grow softer. The crows cawed above his head as they appeared to be following him.

"Ignore them," Aodh said. "The seer uses his crows as his eyes in the forest. He saw you coming a long time ago. They are just making sure you are friendly and going in the right direction."

Finn looked over his shoulder to see the lead crow land on a branch and whack his beak off the branch as if to show how hard it was and that he could easily poke out Finn's eye. He gulped as he walked into a tree and banged his head.

"I hope that is not the first part of your prophecy," Aodh said in a light tone, but could not disguise his worry.

Finn rubbed his head and cursed.

"Be wary of what gods you call upon in these woods," Aodh said. "The spirits of the old ways roam amongst the trees and the shadows."

"The only spirit I wish to contact is that of my father, to inspire me to throw the Norsemen back into the seas."

Aodh ground his teeth, for this youth was grating on him. But he owed it to Finn's father to mould him into the best warrior he could with the clay given. He took a deep breath and regained his composure.

"Still, mind your tongue. You need to guard your feelings, for he can rip right through you."

Finn was intrigued by this revelation.

"You went to see him?"

"When I was a young man, about your age. He made me the man I am now. In repayment, I took to the hills to protect him. There are many a priest who would hire a warrior to come and kill him, thinking his death would be a blow for the old ways. All become feasts for the crows."

"If you had told me that I would have come all the sooner."

"If I knew you took far more after your father than your mother, I would have taken you all the sooner."

Aodh stopped and gulped for he had brought the young man to meet his destiny.

"We are here, prepare yourself."

It would be up to Finn now.

CHAPTER THIRTY-FOUR

WHATEVER YOU DO, DON'T BURN THE STEW

INN AND AODH CAME to a clearing in the woods beside a gushing stream, which wound itself past some large protruding boulders in its path. Moss and other aquatic plants had made their homes in the nooks and crannies of the rocks and in the still pools protected from the rushing water. The stream was encased on both sides by huge slabs of granite that, over hundreds of years, the stream had cut its way through. The stream brought life to the lush green woods, and a curtain of drizzle ensured the stream never ran out of water.

Finn felt for his water flask, for he was taught never to miss an opportunity to fill up at a clean stream, for you never know when the next one is. He bent over and was about to fill his flask.

"No, there is no time for that," Aodh said, a stern tone to his voice. "He is here."

The smell came first. Mould, maybe? Definitely sweat, like he had just fought a strenuous battle, but there was a pungent smell of the woods and outdoors as when men spent a long time out fighting, away from women who may want them to tame the smell. Almost a smell of neglect. Finn looked up to see a pair of dirty feet in front of him. The toenails were long and broken, blackened by both bruises and dirt. They gave way to mud-strewn legs with splotches of red rashes from both the cold and the nettles and brambles of the woods. Then came the brown tunic of a priest; the Lord himself only knew when the man last took it off. The beard and hair were wild and unkempt, a mass of grey that leapt out into the world, dirty and matted, evoking enough fear to drive any warrior away that did not come to specifically seek his attention. But the eyes. Those eyes that protruded from beneath all that hair. They burned as fiercely as any berserker Norse warrior he had ever seen. Finn shuddered at the sight of him, but Aodh stood behind him to prevent him from running.

"Who are these warriors that have come to smite me in my home?" the seer bellowed. He lifted his staff and Finn saw the knurled lump of unhewn oak at the end. If the seer could swing that with enough force and land it on his opponent's head, he could take out most warriors.

Aodh held out his hands to reassure the seer he had no weapons.

"It is me, Aodh. I seek your counsel. I am not here to cause harm."

The seer squinted hard. Finn thought he must be old to have so much grey hair and also to be taken by the blindness, not because of a battle wound or torture.

"I know you," the seer said pointing at Aodh, "but I don't know you." His finger settled on Finn. "Your future looks troubled. Much confuses you. But for now your source of confusion is me."

Finn opened his mouth to protest but Aodh silenced him with a glare before any words could come out.

"May we sit, for it is the boy's future I come here to ask you about?"

The seer scratched his beard.

"We may sit, but I need something to base my predictions upon if I am to be of any use to you. I am old and frail and the crows give me scraps to supplement what food I can find in the plants of the woods. But I like rabbit." His eyes grew large at the thought of rabbit stew. "But they are far too quick for me and to my detriment, I am yet to befriend a hawk. If you get me some rabbits, I can read their entrails and you can make me a stew."

Before Finn could protest, Aodh had slapped him on the arm and picked him up.

Finn soon found himself in the woods looking for sturdy sticks to sharpen.

"It would be so much easier if we had bows and arrows."

Aodh shook his head.

"It would be so much easier if the rabbits would run up to our feet and drop dead in front of us. But it's not going to happen. We must make do with what we've got. I can set a couple of snares and we can sit and wait until they get hungry. It may take a while, but it will be worth it."

Finn followed Aodh's instructions and with the sharpened sticks and some string, Aodh had set the traps. All they had to do was wait. Aodh found a sheltered, dry bank of grass and settled down to sleep.

The seer sat upon a rock and raised his face towards the morning sun. It shone brightly but gave away little heat. But most of the seer's face was covered in mud or hair which made it difficult for the sun's rays to penetrate all the way to his pale skin. This was his favourite time of the day when his crows had gone off to hunt for food and he could enjoy the other birdsong without the constant cawing in the background. He heard a twig snap behind him.

"I hope you do not come back empty-handed," the seer said. "I have made a bargain with you and one day you may realise a glimpse into the future is worth a lifetime of rabbits and I only ask you for one meal."

"I have your rabbits," Finn said, his voice betraying his tiredness but from his hand dangled his trophies. "I hope you can tell me how to become a great warrior in return."

The seer shook his head and smirked.

"I made you no such bargain. All I offer is a glimpse into your own soul. If you do not wish to take up my offer, then throw your rabbits onto the rocks so the crows can have them. If you are lucky, they will guide you out of the woods, and you can continue your quest to become the great warrior you so want to become. But if you do not want to heed my words, heed those of your master. For he knows as well as I do that great warriors do not exist. Sure, they may brag in the king's hall and get the honour of becoming his bodyguard or be the first in battle to meet the enemy's swords. But he will be haunted by the ghosts of those he has slain, destined to see in his dreams how his sword entered another man's belly or how he severed limbs, or gloriously put women and children to the sword, again and again and again."

Finn turned to Aodh and held up his rabbits. His face twisted and he shrugged his shoulders.

"They are not for the crows," Aodh said sternly. "You didn't know what was waiting for you when you came, did you? Going to a seer can be life changing but it can also rip out your soul. You are about to lead an attack on a Norse camp with a bunch of men who will run at the merest of excuses. I will do whatever I can to protect you, if not for your sake then for the sake of your father. Present the man with his prize, then sit and listen to what he has to say."

Finn held out the rabbits for the seer to inspect. The seer shook his head.

"They are no good to me like that. I need them gutted so I can read their entrails. I need a pot, water, fire and herbs. It is as if I only told you the good parts of your life, which for you would make a short story. You promised me a stew, not a handful of dead rabbits."

Finn sighed and put the rabbits down on a rock and went to fetch firewood. A crow flew down and began circling the potential meal.

"Is that your decision made, that the meal is for the crows?" the seer said pointing at the proximity of the crow to the rabbits. "I'm sure they will be grateful."

Finn turned and chased the crow away. The seer smirked and shook his head.

"Don't get on the wrong side of your guide home. He can eat the entrails of the rabbits when I have finished with them. The entrails will be fed to the crows after I have read your future, just as your body will be fed to the crows when you have met with said future."

Finn shuddered.

"Is that your prediction? That I will become crow food? I have gone to all this effort just for that?"

The seer turned to Aodh and shrugged.

"He is so jumpy, Aodh. His head so full of stories yet he knows nothing of the world. Why did you bring him here if he is going to jump under the first blade he meets? Is it because of the guilt you feel?"

Aodh gulped, for he knew the futility of hiding anything from the seer when he got his hooks into you. He needed to deflect the conversation back towards Finn.

"I have an obligation."

"Is that the name guilt goes under these days?" The seer raised an eyebrow and Aodh looked away. "I see you do not want to say. If the rabbits are just from the boy I will read his future but you may wish to tell the boy your secret sometime soon while you still have control."

A bead of sweat broke out on Aodh's forehead.

"Thank you for your kindness in giving me a free reading, but the rabbits are from the boy."

The seer gave Aodh a knowing grin which brought out the perspiration on the small of his back.

"I do not want to take up any more of your precious time than I have to," Aodh said giving a meek grin. "Shall we return to the boy?"

"Cut the rabbits open and display their entrails over there," the seer said, directing Finn towards a flat piece of rock. "I will examine the entrails while you will make my stew. But be careful, boy. I do not know how the entrails will possess me and I will be deeply unhappy if there is no stew after I examine your future." The seer turned to Aodh. "So, have your wits about you and be ready, Aodh, to save my stew."

Finn glared at Aodh, but nevertheless gutted the rabbits and threw the entrails on the rock. The seer stooped and immersed his hands in the entrails, seeking some kind of divine revelation. The crows quickly joined him and pecked at the edges of the entrails. Finn worried they may eat the important parts and spoil the revelations. But he concentrated on making the best stew he could for that was the only way he could think of to gain favour with the seer.

Suddenly, the seer jerked bolt upright and threw his hands to the sky. The crows fled and Finn almost spilt the stew. Aodh nudged him out of the way and took over stirring the stew. He pointed to where he thought Finn should stand, directly in front of the seer. Finn stared at the top of the seer's head as he shook and gyrated. He sprang up and Finn was face to face with him. The seer's eyes had glazed over and he shook as if he was possessed. His murder of crows flew down and perched on the edge of the rock, again forming a crude circle.

Finn felt his heart sink into his stomach as the words of the old seer echoed in his mind. With a rush of blood to his head he felt as if he was falling into a dream world, as if the stream, the rocks, the crows and the woods suddenly became unreal.

Finn found himself alone on an ash-covered plain. He baulked as he heard the crunches as he walked. He looked down to see that he could not avoid treading on ash and bones such was their proliferation. Smoke climbed from the smouldering remains of thousands of lives and curled around his legs like serpents slithering in unison, then winding around his body and up into his nostrils. Finn broke into a coughing fit. He coughed and coughed until he finally expelled the lingering smoke of death from his lungs. When he looked up it was as if the landscape was the corpse of a skinned and gutted rabbit with all life stripped away. In his despair Finn's voice wavered as he called out for his father, his words swallowed by the vast and mocking emptiness.

Then in the distance, he saw a lone figure, with their back turned, a tawny cloak whipping in the wind with his sword but a shadow. The figure seemed achingly familiar. It appeared as his father had once done in Finn's childhood memories before he disappeared into the landscape and went to war. Finn ran towards the figure, his heart a wild drum of hope and desperation. If he could reach him he could save him and then they could go to war together and save the land.

The landscape stretched impossibly, cruelly elongating the distance between them. With every step he ran it seemed as if a small strip of courage fell from his body, like a snake shedding its scales. With each falling scale, his pace slowed. He took his sword from his belt to show his father who he was in the hope he would turn and come to him, and that seemed to renew his courage and gave him the energy to run faster. But no matter how fast he ran, the figure remained maddeningly far, his form flickering like a mirage.

The ground suddenly shuddered beneath him, a deep, resonant tremor, stopping Finn in his tracks. His breath came in ragged gasps, his chest burning, as the earth beneath his feet cracked and split. A distant roar echoed, and Finn turned to see a massive, sinuous shape slithering towards him. It moved with terrifying speed, its scales glinting obsidian-black in the fiery light. Finn froze, his heart hammering in his chest. The serpent reared up, its eyes cold and knowing. He knew those eyes in a more human guise.

Aodh.

The name was a hiss through his mind, a whisper of betrayal. A great fissure opened close by, spewing molten fire and smoke into the sky. The serpent slithered after his father. Aodh the snake had no problem in catching him. He coiled around the leg of the silhouette of his father only to release him above the smouldering pit below. The figure disappeared in the chaos of the smoking fissure and Finn screamed, the sound lost in the roar of the land tearing itself apart.

A massive shadow crept forward from the horizon and darkened the sky. It was Thurgest the tormentor of Hibernia, but not as a man, rather as a demonic dragon beast, as if he had been spat out straight from hell. His wings unfurled and from the scales dropped ash which covered the earth. Angels flew down from the clouds but with a blast of dragon fire, fell from the sky, their wings burnt to cinders. The dragon descended, jaws agape, torrents of fire spewing forth to scorch what remained of the earth. The ground sizzled and spat around Finn as he stumbled, the flames a deadly crown surrounding him. He could feel the terrible heat searing his skin, his face, his very soul.

Then, there was Aodh again, serpentine and elusive, like a coiled snake, his scales glistening and eyes sharp with a knowing cruelty. Finn reached out, pleading, but Aodh slithered away, vanishing into the safety of the shadows. His mocking laughter mingled with the dragon's roar and the crackling of the burning earth.

"Liar," the whispers returned, a chorus of betrayal.

Finn fell to his knees, the ground beneath him blistering and alive with molten fury. He lay sprawled, the skies above a canvas of fire and smoke. Thurgest circled, his massive form casting a shadow over Finn and condemning him into a darkness more profound than night. The dragon's eyes glowed with a vengeful, ancient malice, and Finn felt the weight of the creature's hatred pressing down upon him like the whole of the heavens collapsing. Finn raised his father's sword to fight the beast but the sword became red hot and he was forced to drop it. The smell of burning flesh made him turn over his hand and burned onto his palm was the hammer of Odin. Finn screamed in pain.

The air was now overwhelmed with the smell of burning flesh. He could barely breathe, every ragged gasp filled with ash and despair. Thurgest swooped down, the monstrous heat of his breath singeing Finn's hair and skin. He could do nothing but lie there, helpless, as the dragon's ferocious maw loomed closer and closer.

His mother and Affraic appeared in the distance running from the dragon. There was only Finn between the beast and the remains of his family.

Finn rose to his feet to defend his family. The dragon swooped down again. With merciless precision it pressed its claws down on Finn's shoulder until he had bent the knee and his head bowed to mitigate the searing heat from the belly of the beast. A ring appeared on his finger and immediately turned red hot and burned itself onto his finger. His screams pierced the inferno, but there was no one left to hear them. Only the unrelenting void, the dragon's vengeful roar, and the white burst of light that swallowed him whole.

The seer collapsed to the ground and seemed to come out of his trance. He rolled around on the ground gasping for breath as his crows hopped around him seemingly trying to revive him. In the meantime, Finn had fallen on his behind and stared pale-faced at the fallen seer. His features were still as if he was in shock at what just happened. Aodh was in a similar state of paralysis until the stew began to bubble over and a drop of the boiling liquid landed on the hand that should have been stirring. Aodh's yelp of pain brought the other two back to life. The seer sat on the rock and shook his head to clear it. The smell of the stew wafted up his nostrils.

"I hope you haven't burned my stew. Revealing the folly of youth is a very hunger-inducing occupation."

"No, no, of course not," Aodh mumbled as he stirred the pot to move all those solid items that had stuck to the bottom.

"Good. We would not like you ruining your dinner to bring you another bout of bad luck, be it all created by your own hand."

Aodh grimaced.

"We all seek to be masters of our own destiny, but circumstances keep getting thrust upon us."

The seer frowned.

"I hope that explanation works on the boy, for only a good stew will work on me. Now get some bowls for it is time to eat."

Aodh got some bowls from the cave in the rocks nearby that served as the seer's home. He dished out the food and they all sat in silence and ate. The seer smiled, playing with his food as he sat and muttered to himself. Aodh wondered if this whole adventure had backfired and whether Finn had copped on to what the seer was talking about when he ridiculed him. Finn barely touched his food for he was trying to remember exactly what the soothsayer had said to him and what it meant.

A large crow landed on the rock and cawed loudly in the direction of Finn. The seer smiled.

"He says it is time to go. The storm is coming and your destiny awaits. You certainly will not meet it sitting here eating the rest of my stew."

Aodh hurriedly finished his bowl and took Finn's off him for he had not eaten much nor ceased to play with his food.

"We thank you for your guidance and your wisdom," Aodh said as he bowed his head in reverence.

"I hope you remain thankful. Bring better rabbits if you come back again. Ones with a bit more fat on them. Now go, before the crow gets bored waiting for you."

Aodh saluted him, hooked his arm around Finn's, and they left.

CHAPTER THIRTY-FIVE

STOUT HEART, WEAK STOMACH

THE SHANTY TOWN AROUND Tigernach's hillfort had by now grown quite large, for the news of Gormlaith's protest had spread far and wide. A great clamour came from the people moving north to get out of range of the Norse raids that destroyed their villages and looted their monasteries. Most were women and children as their menfolk were required to fight the Norse threat. Some of these women took up residence with Gormlaith and set up around her. Some of the men who were deemed not fit enough to serve their masters to throw the Norsemen into the sea also took up with Gormlaith. They stood with Babo at his position by the gate of the hillfort, allowing Gormlaith to distribute curses and abuse as she pleased.

Gormlaith enjoyed the protection of the Brehon and the law for as long as her hunger strike lasted. Her action meant for her and the world that her king and protector had neglected his duty to her and not provided adequate provisions and protection and it shamed him in the Hibernian world. For Gormlaith to forsake the hunger strike would be to accept the protection of the king and to abandon the quarrel she had with him. But she would never do that, such was her resolve at the start of the strike.

Some of the women who had sought refuge in her camp joined her in her hunger strike but some did not. But Gormlaith did not judge. She knew, from the first, that she was the focal point, that it was her that Ultán and Tigernach stared down their walls at, that it was her at whom they pointed their ire.

But everyone knew that it was Gormlaith holding the camp and the hunger strike together and she was becoming visibly frailer. Her curses no longer had the same bite or venom and she took more to sitting out in front of the gate these days rather than stand and shake her fists at the occupants. Ultán spotted an opportunity as he observed from the ramparts.

The morning was bright and the air crisp with a slight breeze that would first linger and then spread. Ultán stood on top of the earth walls and looked down on Gormlaith's tent. As surely as the sun rose over the horizon Gormlaith emerged from her tent, disappeared into the woods and then returned to take up her position sitting outside the gate. She appeared to have a stoop today and was slower and stiffer than most mornings Ultán had observed her. He gave a smug grin for the conditions were perfect for him to execute his plan.

Gormlaith sat in front of the other women and stared at the gate. She felt dizzy this morning, the hunger seemingly especially bad. Her bones creaked and she found it difficult to get comfortable. She thought of the stupidity of her children and how it was all their fault she found herself in this state. But it had all got out of hand. It was not now just her own foolish children but those of the mothers that sat behind her. She now bore their pain and that of all the dispossessed in the camp on her ever-weakening shoulders. It would be so much easier to walk away from all of this and find another king to live under, but then all of this death and suffering would have been for nothing.

The gate to the fort creaked open. Ultán came forth with a tray of fresh bread, followed by his men who also had trays of bread. They laid them down in front of the seated women and let the gentle breeze do its work.

The bread was warm, its crust a burnished gold, and Gormlaith felt the heat from it rise into her lungs as she inhaled the beautiful aroma. She sat squat-legged on the cold earth, her cloak wrapped tightly around her shoulders, the wind hissing its disapproval at this temptation. It had been weeks since she began the hunger strike. With each day that passed, the gnawing in her belly became another voice, another plea, another small betrayal of her own will. She could smell the bread, the yeasty sweetness, and her mind unspooled a hundred visions of tearing into it, the softness inside, the swell of it under her fingers.

But she was Gormlaith, she was a woman of her word, and she would starve this body before she broke her pledge. If she reached for it now, if she let her resolve crumble like the bread she so wanted, what would remain of her? She was not a woman to be bent or bought, not by the king or his son, not by hunger. She had sat through rainstorms, through the jeers of the men from above the fort walls, through the pitying eyes of women who shook their heads as they passed.

Her skin lay tight against her bones, and her vision danced with light as if the sun had fallen into the sky and shattered there. But with each pang, with each moment of weakness, she found herself growing stronger in other ways. The bread was a temptation, a reminder of what was soft inside her, what could be swayed by the simple needs of the flesh. She closed her fist. She would be hard like the whites of her knuckles. She would not let it win.

She closed her eyes, imagined it – the first bite – how it would fill her, how it would end this. Tears streamed down her face as if she was trying to wash the temptation from her eyes. She wondered if the king could feel her defiance from his high seat. She wondered if he laughed at her or feared her, if he thought her foolish or brave. And she wondered if she could have ever been so defiant, so fierce, so certain of herself without this hunger to drive her.

The bread sat there, its smell curling around her like a cruel embrace, the devil putting his hands on her shoulders, hands creeping down towards her breast. She opened her eyes, drew in the cold air, and let it fill her.

"You cannot tempt me, Ultán," Gormlaith said in a stern voice, her gaze firmly fixed on her tormentor. "I can feel how tempted these women feel, for I am one of them and I cannot lie and say that I do not wish I could cast my hand forward and devour all the bread in front of us. But I cannot, for my cause is righteous and although my body may weaken, my resolve and the support from my sisters grows every day. You must be desperate to do such a cowardly act and it will be seen as such, for I will spread it far and wide what you have done today. Now, be gone, you heinous wretch. Fetch your father and the rest of your loathsome family and abdicate for the people do not want you here."

Ultán snarled and kicked over the trays of bread and the loaves lay in the puddles until the dogs came and devoured them for they were hungry also. Gormlaith and her sisters remained seated outside the fort, consoled that they were not tempted to break their fast that day and resolving not to stop until King Malachy gave them a sufficient remedy.

CHAPTER THIRTY-SIX

A SHARP TONGUE

SEVERAL DAYS PASSED AND Ultán had to slip out of the fort un-detected by Gormlaith and her followers. He gulped as he and his men approached the gate on their return. The fort was positioned in such a way that there were only two entrances, and this was the main one, which faced south. Since Gormlaith had taken up residence, Ultán would often go around the fort and use the northern entrance as he had done days before. But today he could not. For today, he could not look weak and go around to avoid the howls of a mad woman. Today, he had to look strong, for he had a delegation from the Norse camp with him. He ordered his men to stand between the crowd and the Norsemen, hoping that the people in the camp would not notice who he was escorting into the fort. But hoping that no one would notice three burly wolf-skin clad tattooed warriors as they walked past them with a full escort was the dream of a fool.

Gormlaith leapt to her feet at the sight of Ultán and the Norse-men.

"What are you up to, you little shrew?" she hissed at Ultán as his men blocked her path to him. "You're too much of a coward to have captured these men yourself. Did you lay an ambush for the brave warrior that captured these men, then slit his throat and rob his glory? That would be just like you, you little turd."

A flush came over Ultán's face and he went for his sword. His men held him back.

"Remember the words of the Brehon, master. You cannot harm her, for she is under your father's protection."

Ultán threw his men off and put his sword back in its sheath.

"Damn her to hell, and you can take my father with her. Who would allow a prince to be insulted so at the gates of his own fort?"

Gormlaith saw her opportunity to drive the dagger in.

"Your cowardly father, that's who," Gormlaith said as she pressed her head between the two guards who held her back. "At least you can say one good thing about him, that you can frighten him into obeying the law and obeying the priest."

"No one tells my father what to do," Ultán said.

He gnashed his teeth and lashed out a fist in Gormlaith's direction. Luckily, one of his guards had the foresight to block him but the misfortune to receive the full force of a fist in the back. He collapsed like a heavy sack of cabbages.

Einar, who was one of the emissaries from the Norse camp, remembered what Affraic had told him as part of their bargain and began to laugh.

"Look," he whispered to one of his men. "He cannot even control his old woman."

Ultán's nostrils flared, and he cracked his knuckles to prepare himself for violence when he overheard this. He could not look weak in front of the Norse if he was to lead the negotiations with them. His men looked at him in wide-eyed panic. Ultán said a prayer to ask for forgiveness and lowered his head to charge at Gormlaith like a bull. His men jumped out of the way. Ultán charged, but he dared not look for, in his haste, he thought that if he was dragged up before the Brehon, he could plead he charged towards a general insult and not at Gormlaith per se, and it was all an accident that led to her death. But he found himself off his feet and airborne. He went head over heels and landed with an almighty thud on his back. He went red, for in his daze, he did not know whether he had slipped or been manhandled. He looked up and saw Babo towering over him.

"Malachy sent Babo to protect the woman. He who hurts her hurts Malachy, for she is in his protection. Do you want to hurt Malachy?"

Ultán shook his head and raised himself gingerly to his knees and took the extended hands of his men. He dusted himself down and stormed off towards the gate in silence.

"It seems like we should have negotiated with Malachy," Einar said to his men as he laughed and followed behind Ultán.

Gormlaith beamed from ear to ear and threw her arms around Babo.

"I like you. You can stay."

Babo smiled back.

CHAPTER THIRTY-SEVEN
SHE IS NOT MY MOTHER

THE NEXT DAY ULTÁN was still seething about his humiliation at the gate the day before. His Norse guests smirked every time they laid eyes on him, and it stole his opportunity to impress his father. Ultán had brought the Norsemen here to see if they could negotiate an alliance against his father's master, King Malachy. But Gormlaith had robbed him of his gravitas and his father had quickly noticed. His father took over the negotiations and reduced him to the role of assistant. Ultán had to sit in silence as his guests ate and made merry while making jokes at his expense. His father forbade him from carrying out any acts of retaliation against the Norse for fear that killing the Norse emissaries would be the death of them all. Now it was morning and his father's words rang in his ears. The only way to regain any credibility with the Norse was to escort them out of the fort again and past Gormlaith for anything else would signal to the Norse they were afraid of her and the Norse would see this as weakness. Weakness would mean certain death.

The fog swirled around the ramparts of the fort and the dew glistened on the grass. Ultán stood red-faced in the cold with a blanket slung across his shoulders. The animal pelts he would normally wear were left at home for he did not want to look like a Norseman should they be ambushed as he escorted them back to their camp. He sent his men to rouse the Norse as he waited outside with the armed escort. Ultán had become quite cold and damp by the time the three Norse stumbled out of their hut, still drunk by the looks of it. They saw Ultán waiting for them and they all smirked at him.

"Are you going to bring us to see your mother again before we go?" Einar said.

"She is not my mother," Ultán said through gritted teeth, his cheeks now turned crimson.

"You can tell her, her cooking last night was.... adequate. Your ale was like piss, but drinkable piss. As long as you drank enough of it you could wash down her food. We may take her as a thrall, but only if she learns to cook better."

"I'm glad you enjoyed my father's hospitality," Ultán snarled through gritted teeth. "I will give your compliments to the men who cooked it for you and say a prayer for the deer that gave their lives to entertain you."

"I did not know your pale Christ cared so much for deer," Einar replied as he placed his hand on Ultán's shoulder. "Pray that he cares as much for you."

"I did not know it was Norse tradition to threaten your hosts after you had received their hospitality?"

Einar laughed.

"Oh, these are just words that trip off the tongue when men have ale. Do you not like to have a joke when you have a drink, or do you hold your hands to pray every time you have a swig of your ale?"

"Have you got everything you need?" Ultán said for he tired of this conversation. "It is time for you to go."

Einar walked over with a big smirk on his face and put his arms over Ultán's shoulders.

"You should come back to our camp next time and we'll serve you some real food like we did before. And bring your mother. She was far better entertainment than anything your father pro-vided."

Ultán shook his arm off and stared at the north gate. If he went that way the Norse would know exactly why and he would never live it down. He had to face Gormlaith.

Ultán's men hauled open the gates and the fog-laden breeze directly from the sea wafted in. Ultán stood beside the Norse-men, his mouth a tangled grimace of humiliation and anger. The camp outside was still, for Ultán had chosen to leave early in the morning, hoping everyone in the camp would be asleep. He knew many of the women were on hunger strike to show that his father was incapable of protecting them and that Malachy, the king of Mide, should get rid of him. The hunger should make them weak and therefore more likely to sleep so he may get away without meeting Gormlaith. However, the Norse had other ideas. They ran ahead before Ultán or his men could stop them.

They ran towards the tents they had passed the day before and began lifting the flaps.

"Oh Ultán's mother," Einar cooed. "Where are you? We want to say goodbye and thank you for the food."

They moved from tent to tent searching. Ultán stood apoplectic but frozen to the spot, overcome with panic. He wanted to pick up his sword and smash it through Einar's skull but he could not. If he killed the Norse emissary it would be the highest of insults, the end of any prospect of an alliance and almost certain death or enslavement to his people. But he could not allow this to continue.

Babo emerged from his tent with his sword in his hand wondering what the commotion was. Einar placed his hand on his throwing axe tied to his belt.

"Peace, my friend," Einar said. "We come to say goodbye to your mistress. There will be no violence while we are here."

Babo lowered his sword and pointed to the tent beside him. Einar grinned and signalled for his men to join him. Ultán stepped forward but one of his men stuck his arm out. Ultán swallowed his words. He realised it might go better if Gormlaith did not know he was there.

"Oh Ultán's mother, we are here to say goodbye."

He opened the tent flap to see Gormlaith stirring in her sleep. She looked old and frail, her skin pale and her bones showing. Her blankets were torn and tattered and the tent smelt of illness.

"Your son should really let you stay in the huts in the fort," Einar said, grinning. "You would be far more comfortable there."

Gormlaith eyes sprung open to the horror of seeing a Norseman sticking his head into her tent. Her heart almost leapt out of her chest. She edged to the back of the tent hoping she may find a means of escape.

"You're not allowed to kill me," was all that came out of her dry lips.

Einar smiled and creased his brow.

"No, you have me all wrong. I came to say goodbye to Ultán's mother for showing us such entertainment yesterday." He shook his head apologetically. "I do not blame you for him being so dull."

All Gormlaith needed was the vaguest reference to Ultán for the furies to rise again.

"That waste of sperm is no son of mine," she spat.

Einar laughed and held out his hand.

"That's the spirit. My men and I would like to say goodbye to you outside. But before we go, I hear you are protected? By who?"

Gormlaith scowled.

"Those two useless oafs, the king and prince, are just puppets. They play at being hard men but he is just the local warlord. Malachy is the king of Mide and I have his protection. By the law I am allowed to forgo food to show the king is not looking after my welfare. He cannot interfere for if he does it would probably mean his kingdom. Malachy must have it in for him if he would give a lowly woman like me his protection."

Einar undid the string that held the bottom of the tent flaps together and he knelt and held Gormlaith's hand.

"I have a Hibernian woman with fire in her belly just like you."

Gormlaith tutted.

"She probably has fire because you made her one of your thralls."

"Don't get high and mighty with me. You may not call them thralls, but you have slaves all the same."

"If you set her free she would probably be a lot nicer to you."

Einar laughed.

"She broke any chains as we put her in them. She is like a wild and untameable horse. But yet alluring all the same."

Gormlaith took her hand back and crawled towards the door.

"Well, I'm sure you did not come to me to ask me for advice about what to do with your woman. Let me lay eyes on Ultán again and at least you can leave entertained."

Einar rose from the door of the tent to see Ultán sweating and swallowing hard.

"We need to leave," Ultán said firmly, "while it is still safe for both of us."

Einar gave a fake smile.

"We were just saying goodbye to your mother. Let us see you embrace her before we go. It would give such a wonderful impression to the lord of the Norse world in these parts, Thurgest, that you love your mother so."

Ultán stood transfixed for he knew not what to do.

"She is not my mother," he growled. "Now let us leave and do not test the patience of your hosts so."

Einar raised his chin and his eyebrow and strode over to Ultán.

"Now why would your father put you in charge of the party of Norsemen he is negotiating with so he can betray his king?"

Einar began to circle Ultán.

"But wait. He did not. As soon as we arrived he took over from you and cut you out of the picture. Does your father think you weak?"

Ultán's nostrils flared as his cheeks went red.

"It is not wise to insult your host when you are heavily outnumbered."

Einar advanced towards him but Ultán put his hand on his sword grip. Einar stopped and eyed up his host. He raised his hand in a peaceful gesture.

"I bring you peace, my friend. Maybe our Norse sense of humour does not translate too well when we cross the water. We don't mean to insult you. Let me say my goodbyes and I'll be on my way."

Einar walked up to Gormlaith but in such a way as to block Ultán's view. He took her face in both his hands.

"Goodbye, Ultán's mother. Next time we meet I will bring you his head."

He let go Gormlaith's face and was gone.

CHAPTER THIRTY-EIGHT

A SWORD, RATTLED

FINN AND AODH FOUGHT their way through the brambles of the woods back to the clearing where they had left their men. The ancient oak wood loomed around them, the dense canopy blotting out the sky and casting the forest floor in perpetual twilight. Gnarled roots twisted underfoot, ready to snag an unwary ankle. The air hung heavy with the musty smell of damp earth and rotting leaves. The crows quickly abandoned them. Aodh thought it was because they considered the pickings off the rabbits poor. They were wary of man or beast jumping from the shadows for these woods had become far more dangerous since the Norsemen came. Both wolves and bandits had been driven back into these woods by the rampaging invaders. But Finn was battling with something more pressing.

"I could not make out hide nor hair of what that seer was saying to me. Do you know what he meant?"

Aodh sighed, but did not turn around. He slashed at the protruding brambles with a little more aggression.

"I wasn't in your dream and the imagery was from your own head. The message contained was for you and you alone to work out. The messages were reflections of your life and where it is heading. You are supposed to think about it and work it out yourself."

Finn did not contradict him for Aodh the snake was one of the main messages he took from the dream. But considering he was his mentor and he still needed him, he decided on another approach.

"He seemed to have plenty to say about you," Finn said pointedly.

"Ignore that," Aodh growled. "He is upset that I went off on this quest with you when I am the guardian of his forest. He likes to create a bit of mischief."

Finn had not heard this before.

"Why were you made guardian of the forest?"

"You have too many questions, boy."

"And you have many interesting tales to tell. Why don't you tell me this one to pass the time?"

"There is no tale to tell," Aodh said, turning to Finn as he was by now rather agitated. "Your father, Babo and I were amongst a war party driving Norse raiders from the bay. There were many of them, but way more of us, since Malachy had unleashed his full wrath against the raiders, for they had desecrated so many churches. We pursued a rather cunning band of Norsemen into some woods beside the sea. We thought their ships were hidden near there, and being young and foolish, we wished to slaughter them before they could get away.

"However, they jumped out and ambushed us. Babo received a blow to the head with the butt of an axe and fell almost immediately. Your father was at the front of our group and was cut off. I was towards the rear and was driven back and forced to flee for the ambush was well planned and we lost most of our men in the first few moments. I ran to get help and met Tigernach and his warriors. By the time we got back to the woods the Norsemen were gone and they had taken their dead and wounded and left ours. Babo was found unconscious in a bush but there was no sign of your father or any of the men who had been with him. We assumed they had been taken to have their heads cut off to decorate the Norse ships so they could claim some kind of victory to their kin.

"Babo was brought back to your village and was nursed back to health by your mother. It was something for her to fixate upon while we looked for your father. But we never found him or his body."

"So he could still be alive?" Finn said, his eyes wide, begging for hope.

"I would not like to say what I think they did to him for at best, they tie enemy warriors to the bows of their boats and let the waves have them. Now, let me return to Babo because he was never the same after that. It was my duty to look after him because we were like blood brothers, bonded together as warriors. We retired to the woods and made our home in the caves. We soon befriended the seer and he helped to look after Babo and his health improved somewhat where he had a healthy body but the mind of a child. In return, I cleared the woods of bandits and of the worst of the beasts. But the Norse came and the bandits returned in greater numbers than ever. That is why he is bitter against me for now he only has the crows and trickery with which to defend himself."

"Yet, he still talks to me in riddles," Finn said, fixating on only the parts of the story that affected him.

Aodh shook his head at the lack of acknowledgement for any of his troubles.

"Shake your head of doubt, boy, for we have jumpy men who will pick up on any sign of weakness. We must lead the attack while Malachy still gives us some sort of advantage by drawing away the main force."

Finn nodded and was silent. Aodh returned to the front and took his frustration from the raising of buried memories out on the brambles. They did not get very far.

"Who goes there?" and several men jumped out in front and behind them.

"It is us, you fools," Aodh growled at the men they left behind. "You were wise to hide and ambush but we are no strangers."

"We cannot be too careful," one of the ambushers said. "Many of the men have deserted, and bandits pester those who remain."

"Lead us back to the camp," Aodh said, his voice laden with authority. "We must attack before our strength is sapped any further."

It was not far from the place of ambush to the remains of the camp. Nothing had prepared Aodh and Finn as to what a shambles it had become. At least half the men had fled. Those that remained cared little for how many fires they started or who knew they were there. Few bothered to perform sentry duty and talk was of why should they be foolish enough to stay when Malachy could not punish them all. Aodh was furious.

"Gather all the men into the clearing," he hollered. "I will remind you all of the wrath of Malachy and how I have managed to avoid it for so long and will not succumb to it now."

The men ambled off in various directions leaving Aodh to stew in his anger. Even Finn decided to leave him alone and also joined in finding the men to assemble them.

A short while later they all stood in front of Aodh. Finn sheepishly went and stood beside him but ensured he was not directly in his line of sight.

"Thirty-eight of you. That is all that is left. Thirty-eight."

Aodh turned and spat on the ground.

"Those who deserted will be hunted like dogs. Remember, Malachy sent us here to act as a distraction while he engaged the main army. We were supposed to free those we could from bondage and destroy the camp if we could. But what can we do with thirty-eight?"

Finn twitched as if something in the seer's nightmare had inspired him. He knew what to take from the seer's dream now. It was courage. His father's memory was wrapped up in his sword. This was it, this was the moment he had been waiting for. He reached down and grabbed the hilt of his father's sword. He stood in the centre of the circle of men and raised his sword to the sky.

"WE CAN ATTACK," Finn exclaimed, much to everyone's surprise. "Thirty-eight men can each carry a fire torch, thirty-eight men can set fire to half-built walls, thirty-eight men can set fire to a fleet. All we need is the element of surprise and we can cause chaos."

Finn paused for effect.

"For God, for king, for family, for revenge, for Hibernia. No matter what motivates you, we must rid the land of this Norse curse. Are you with me, men?"

Finn vigorously shook his sword in the air. Much to Aodh's surprise the men copied him and they raised their weapons and roared.

"Let us leave then, and wait hidden by the Norse camp for the moment to strike."

The men roared again. Finn pointed his sword in the direction of the camp and the men set off after him. Aodh was left standing, mouth agape at this turn of events.

CHAPTER THIRTY-NINE

THE SEEDS OF SUSPICION

EINAR WAS ENJOYING HIS new domestic arrangement. Affraic seemed to put in so much more effort once their bargain had been struck. But it was partly just a front. She spent her days when he was busy doing Thurgest's work, talking to the Hibernian women who had been made thralls trying to obtain information. Most of what she gathered she kept to herself, for she always deflected when Einar asked her questions. But his meals were most pleasant and she was very active in bed so he saw himself with little to complain about. Long may this arrangement last, but he was not naive and knew everything moved in cycles and there was always some sort of bad news around the corner when you had given your life to be a Norse raider.

The horns blared from the harbour just as he sat down and Affraic had handed him a bowl of rabbit stew. Einar's attention was immediately stolen as he cranked his neck towards the harbour.

"Do you have to go right now?" Affraic pleaded. "You don't know what an effort I had to put in to claim the prize rabbit from the hunters."

"My name carries much weight, be it in the claiming of prize rabbits or the summoning of horns," Einar said in dismissal of her claimed efforts. He lifted his spoon to his mouth and slurped. "However, I must give all credit to you for what you did with the rabbit once you obtained it. It is a delightful meal to return home to."

Affraic stood over him and frowned.

"Well, eat as much as you can before that horn blows again. One of the other men may take a fancy to me if I have to give all your food away and they find out how good it is."

Einar's eyes flashed with a tinge of jealousy.

"They can eat all the rabbit they like, but they will never lay a finger on you."

The horn blared again.

"I've had enough of your blathering. Now eat. You only have a short time."

Einar shovelled the food into his mouth and wiped it with his sleeve. He kissed Affraic on the cheek, giving her a full whiff of the rabbit on his beard. She squeezed his hand.

"Now come back quickly."

"I will come back as soon as I can," Einar said gruffly. "I am on Thurgest's time, not my own."

He let go of her hand and walked down the hill towards the harbour. As soon as she thought he would not look back at her, she grabbed her shawl and snuck down after him. She smirked to herself as she thought of her vengeance for his being so arrogant towards her. But it would start by finding out what he was up to.

Einar arrived at the bottom of the tower where the horn blower was stationed. The sea in front of them was still lit by the dying summer sun and the shadows of the clouds crept over it.

"What is so urgent that you have to disturb my dinner like that?"

"Look out on the horizon and see," the watchman called. "It is a large fleet summoned by Thurgest all the way from the homelands. I knew you would want to come and see."

Einar scowled.

"We never know who is on these ships, be they friend or foe until they disembark," Einar said. "Alert the men and have an armed guard ready to greet them as they come off the ships. I will go to the great hall to make preparations in case we have any distinguished guests. Make sure there is enough space on the docks for the ships to moor."

There was a flurry of activity on the docks as the Norse prepared for the arrival of the new fleet. Affraic found herself a comfortable spot on the hill from where she could observe the coming and goings without the danger of Einar accidentally passing her. It was best he did not know that she was up to mischief. She watched as the fleet drew nearer and nearer, about twenty ships in all. Were all of these ships slavers coming to take her former neighbours to faraway places to end their days toiling for their Norse masters? Should she do anything about it or was she just powerless doing her best not to end up a thrall herself? Some of the Norse free women sat down near her to watch the fleet pull into the harbour. She noted the apprehension on their faces, as if they could not confidently predict what was going to happen. She watched as Einar returned to the docks with armed guards alongside him. He was leaving nothing to chance.

Einar rubbed his chin as the ships came into harbour and threw out their ropes to the men onshore. Slavers, merchants and unknown warriors. What were their intentions?

"Einar," called a familiar voice from one of the lead boats. Einar squinted but could not locate the voice. That was until he looked at the face beneath the waving hand on the third ship. Torstein had returned.

The docks were soon full with warriors disembarking, merchants unloading their goods and slavers eager to return home readying their ships to receive their cargo. Einar sifted his way through the crowd to find Torstein who had disembarked and must be on the docks somewhere. He found him supervising the unloading of a large chest from his ship. He was too engrossed to notice Einar coming.

"Abandon your work momentarily and come and greet me," Einar said.

He opened out his arms and Torstein reluctantly embraced him.

"How are you?" Torstein said. "How are things in the colony?"

Einar let go of the embrace, smiled and put his hand on Torstein's shoulder.

"Good, good. Thurgest continues his raiding and has left me in charge in his absence. He should return soon, with ships filled with thralls and gold and jewels from the churches of the pale Christ."

"The richer we get, the better for the colony," Torstein said. "It was easy to get traders and other warriors to come. I had to hardly embellish my stories at all, and they were all champing at the bit."

Einar looked at the new warriors crowding the docks; their faces, tattoos and shields indicated they were not all from the homelands.

"Where did you get this lot from?" he demanded.

"They were all in our towns and villages, but they came from all over. Some are from the Orkneys, some are from Rus. We even have a band of Hibernian warriors who have come and joined us."

Einar scowled.

"We will have to keep our eyes on them to ensure they remain loyal. Or else their heads will soon be decorating the spikes on our gate."

Torstein laughed.

"At least with Thurgest you are never short of a head for your spikes."

"Did you bring anything else back with you from the homeland?" Einar said, changing the subject.

"We brought Thurgest's father back with us."

Einar's face dropped and then it occurred to him not to reveal his true feelings.

"Thurgest will be pleased."

"His brother, your father, was not. He called Thurgest every name under the sun after he found out we took his father without his specific permission."

"But what can he do about it now?"

"I would not underestimate Thurgest or any of his family or what they will do. All I hope for is Thurgest is happy and finds a good use for your grandfather."

"We will know fairly soon for he should be back from his raids any day now."

Torstein slapped Einar on the shoulder.

"Then we must clear the docks for his return. All thralls occupying pens must be sold quickly and the slavers dispatched so Thurgest can refill them. Let us have a market in the morning and by evening all ships should be gone."

Einar nodded in agreement and he started ordering his men to put their plan into action.

CHAPTER FORTY

LEARNING TO SPY

IT WAS ONLY HALF a day's march to the camp, thankfully free of Norse patrols. The forest provided them with natural cover for their movements. They soon found a grassy knoll for the men to hide behind while Finn and Aodh waited until dusk to scout out the camp.

Finn had young eyes that could pick out minute details in the distance, while that skill had long deserted Aodh's. He was left to rely on intuition, which, as luck would have it, was quite strong in him. They made their way across the flat lands south of the camp, which were once the homes of Hibernian farmers; those farms were now abandoned, and most were burnt out. The Norse did not occupy them, for they lacked the confidence and resources to defend them from the inevitable attacks from the locals wanting their land back. There were some woods and streams as they passed through the lands, which did provide some cover, but they soon became suspicious when they found no Norse to confront them. They went to the hill below the camp, for it had expansive views of the bay and was a prominent landmark to occupy if you wished to command the bay.

The hill was covered in woods, but Finn knew the area well, both from his own explorations and from when he was young, shadowing his father. But these woods also contained the Norse. They had to carefully make their way uphill whilst avoiding the enemy patrols. They eventually made it to the small plateau at the top of the hill, only to find a small Norse camp. On top of the hill was a large wooden beacon which several Norsemen guarded. Perched on this hill, they could see right over the bay to the north, on a clear day maybe as far as Wales in the east and as far as the Wicklow mountains to the south. They could see any enemy army coming at them several days in advance of their arriving at the Norse encampment.

"Clever," Aodh said to Finn as they hid in a dense bush to observe the Norse. "They are laying proper roots in the land. If we do not cut them out now while they are weak, we may never be rid of them."

Finn clenched his fist.

"But we are only forty if you include us. At least half the men would be needed to ensure the beacon is never lit while the rest take the camp."

"We can never do that. We do not have the men. Darkness is our friend. If we can cause enough chaos and hope there are some fighting men amongst the slaves they have taken, then I think we may take the camp."

"But they seem dug in all over the bay."

Aodh frowned at him.

"We have been given one task and not enough men to do even that. Pray to whatever god you wish that you get to make it back to Malachy's fort to complain to him how many men you have been given. Now, let us leave for we need to inspect the walls of the camp under the cover of darkness so we can find a weak point."

But before they could leave they found themselves disturbed.

"What are you doing here, hiding in the bushes?"

They turned their heads to see two large Norsemen standing behind them, axes in hand. Finn grabbed some dirt from the ground and flung it at their eyes. They both staggered back, groaning as they raised their hands to shield their eyes.

Aodh unsheathed his sword and struck the nearest Norseman on the side of his face with the pommel.

"Run."

They took to their heels and small branches pelted their faces and bodies as they bounded their way through the thick woods. The Norse behind them had recovered enough to sound their horns which meant they would now be getting hunted. Horns sounded around them both near and far. Finn paused to look around them to see if they were trapped. But Aodh waved them forward. The horns sounded again, this time as if a circle was closing in upon them. Aodh signalled to Finn to follow him and Finn obeyed even though he had the beating of Aodh in any kind of foot race. An arrow whizzed past Finn's head and thudded into a nearby tree. Finn could see no end to this forest for he was on the Wicklow side of the hill, the one less known to him, and this forest spread as far as the mountains themselves. But Aodh was sure-footed and looked like he knew where he was going. Fast-moving shadows now appeared left and right as the Norse called to each other that their prey was within sight.

Suddenly the woods ended and Finn and Aodh ran into the daylight. Before them lay a cliff and beyond that the glorious Killiney Bay. Finn came to a sudden stop and Aodh halted when he noticed.

"Trust me, Finn, and so exactly as I tell you."

Finn began to shake and immediately went for his sword for he thought they were going to make a last stand. An arrow whizzed past his ear and fell over the cliff. The Norse now halted at the ring of the woods and grinned at the thought their prey was trapped. Those not armed with an axe took out their daggers and they crept slowly towards Aodh and Finn.

Finn bent over and took out his sword.

"Put it back in its sheath," Aodh said as he took out his dagger.

"Why?"

"Just do it."

Finn obeyed and took out his dagger,

"Now, jump," and Aodh jumped off the side of the cliff.

Finn shook, but the Norse now all came for him. He ran after Aodh and threw himself after him.

CHAPTER FORTY-ONE

A LIGHT IN THE DARK?

FINN FOUND HIMSELF IN mid-air looking out at the beauty of Killiney Bay. If this were the last thing he ever saw while he was alive,e he thought himself lucky. But before his life could flash before him, he collided with a branch of a tree that broke his fall. He landed on his feet and his knees buckled and he fell to the ground. He could hear muffled shouting above and behind him. His body felt numb but he could move all his limbs. An arrow thudded in front of him. Suddenly everything became real again and the shouting and cursing were deafening and the arrows crept nearer.

"Come on, get out of the line of fire. You'll be safe in here."

It came from behind him. It sounded like Aodh's voice. Finn turned his head. Aodh was kneeling in the mouth of a cave, beckoning him to come and join him. Finn looked above his head. Two Norse archers were trying to negotiate the jagged rocks to aim at him. Both arrows hit the ground, narrowly missing him.

"COME ON," Aodh roared.

Finn picked himself up and ran into the cave. Aodh got up and ran ahead of him and waved him forward.

"Follow me. These caves lead to the beach. We can escape from there if there are no Norse ships around."

The darkness seemed to press in on them from all sides, a suffocating blackness that threatened to consume them whole. It felt as if some immense, ancient beast was swallowing them, the damp rock walls its gullet, the echoing drips of water its ravenous drool. Aodh's memory of the caves served as their only lifeline, a fragile thread preventing them from being forever lost in the belly of the beast.

Finn's heart raced as he clung to Aodh's hand, his palms slick with cold sweat. Each breath came in short, panicked gasps, the dank air thick and cloying in his lungs. The ground beneath their feet was treacherous, a twisted labyrinth of slick stone and murky pools that threatened to pull them under at any moment.

Aodh forged ahead, his steps sure even in the oppressive darkness. But Finn could feel the tension in his grip, the barely contained terror that mirrored his own. The weight of the mountain pressed down on them, tons of solid rock poised to crush them into oblivion.

Finn let out a cry of pain as his foot caught on a jagged rock, sending him tumbling to the ground. Aodh pulled him up, urging him on, but the fall had cost them precious time. The sound of their pursuers was closer now, the flickering light of their torches casting eerie shadows on the cave walls.

"Do not despair, Finn. I have climbed through these caves many times."

The air became stuffier and Finn felt the cave walls closing in on him. He wanted to cry out but his ego was still intact and he had no wish to look foolish in front of Aodh. If this was to be his tomb he would die like a warrior. He broke into a cold sweat and was on the verge of cursing God. Aodh looked back into the darkness and gripped Finn's hand tight.

"I can see it," Aodh cried, desperate joy filling his voice. "A chink of light, the merest chink of light."

"All I see is dark," Finn hissed as he slipped on some unseen slime on the uneven rocks.

Aodh yanked his arm up and tucked his forearm beneath the nook of his elbow.

"We are nearly there. Brace yourself for a little longer."

Faint shafts of light streamed down the walls of the cave lighting up Finn's heart and returning the spring to his step. Aodh dragged him along, his heart almost beating out of his chest. They reached the end of the cave and collapsed at the entrance. A shadow cast itself over Finn's face.

"What have we here then?"

Finn lifted his face from the cold rock only to see a Norse axe blade.

CHAPTER FORTY-TWO

BLINKING TO STOP THE TEARS

B OUND BY HAND AND chained by foot, Finn and Aodh were force-marched onto the Norse longship that was pulled up on the beach of the bay. They found themselves seated amongst a huddle of fellow prisoners, weeping women and children and humiliated men.

"Where are they taking us?" one woman said in Finn's ear as he was thrown down beside her.

"To their camp and then God knows where," Finn said, his words bitter but hushed. "Wherever it is, we are to be one of their thralls. Pray to God he sinks the ship before we reach the port for then we can at least die with our backs unbroken."

Finn received the back of a hand across his face.

"No talking," said the guard. "Only speak when spoken to."

Finn circled his jaw hoping the movement would relieve the pain. It only made it worse. It began to rain. The drops of water were soothing on his stinging face. He moved his jaw again. The pain was subsiding. The boat rocked in the waves and the already traumatised children threw up all over their mothers and the deck. Finn was reduced to sitting in a pool of vomit. He looked over to Aodh who just sat and stared at the deck, keeping his own counsel.

The ship came to a halt after what seemed like a couple of hours, but Finn could not see over the sides of the boat.

"Get up. Get up. Get up and meet your new masters," cried the guards.

They wrenched up those who would not stand voluntarily and forced them towards the gangplank. They gave Finn several punches in the stomach as they thought he might resist. Aodh took the wiser route to stand up himself and preserve his energy for whatever may come. Finn was forced down the plank bare- foot, for his shoes had been taken by his captors. He yelped as he caught a splinter in his foot. He limped along the plank until he reached the dock. He did not know it at the time, but as the latest batch of thralls was unloaded from the ship, they were divided into different groups. Finn was rejected by the slavers as being lame so he was allocated to stay on the colony. Aodh looked strong but troublesome so he was allocated to the building gangs in the colony, the thralls with the shortest lifespans. As they were staying, they were directed towards the thrall pens by the docks to await their first full day of servitude.

Affraic stood on the docks looking for people she knew that had been captured by the Norse. Einar and his promises of wealth and power had not fully conquered her heart but she could not turn her back completely on those she knew and loved. She believed it was only a matter of time before the Norse would deploy a large enough army to take over all of Hibernia, and she wanted to ensure she was aligned with the victors while she also wished to protect those she loved. Hence, she came to the docks to persuade her loved ones to come and join her so they could survive and prosper too.

The prisoners came down from the ship one by one. It took some effort for Affraic to make her heart cold but she managed to harden it for the crying women and children as they came off the boat. She knew none of these people so it was easy for her.

She found the wailing of the new thralls irritating and asked herself why she put herself through it. Surely her time would be better spent arranging Ultán's downfall and the rise of her future husband? Surely she should be busy making allies amongst the women of the Norse so she could see who she would have to elbow out of the way to become queen of this town. She turned to leave, but then heard a large yelp coming from the gangplank of the new ship of thralls. Such a cry pulled on the last of her heartstrings, and she turned to see what helpless soul was in so much pain.

My brother!

She did a double-take to make sure it was him. But as he hobbled along the gangplank, she had a clear view of his face. It was him. Her whole body tensed, and her howl of pain would have been louder than his had she not choked it down to the same place which held her feelings. But she could not stand idly by and let this happen. She had to free him. She lost control of herself and hurled herself forward in the crowd. It created a crush, for there was a ring of guards along the paths of the port, mainly to stop the thralls from escaping. But it worked as well the other way, and more men joined them to push back the crowd. Some in the crowd lashed out at Affraic, and one punch caught her full in the jaw. She fell like a sack of vegetables and the crowd began to trample on her, not always accidentally.

"Move out of the way," came a commanding voice and the crowd quickly parted.

Affraic woke up to see Einar kneeling above her.

"What happened?" Einar said in a kind tone.

Affraic reached her hand out and he helped her to her feet. She needed time to get her wits back before saying something she might regret. She looked into his eyes and then at the crowd of people around her. He could not be trusted, not in this context anyway,

"I felt faint and was caught in the crush of the crowd. I am sorry if I caused anyone to be hurt," she said, somewhat pathetically.

"It is you who have been the most hurt," Einar said. "Let me bring you back to the tent so you can rest."

Affraic took his hand and squeezed it.

"Take me back, but leave me to sleep for I know you have important business to do."

Einar nodded and led her by the hand back to their tent.

Einar brought Affraic to the tent despite her protests.

"I am not a child," she said, wriggling in his grip.

"Let me take care of you this once," Einar said tenderly, as he opened the tent flap. "If you are to be the wife of a jarl, you will have to look after me many times. In fact, I should train you how to use a dagger for that may come in useful to defend me from my enemies if I lie wounded in my bed."

Einar looked at Affraic's twisted smile and he quickly changed his mind. He invited her in and they both stood over the bed.

"We may leave those lessons until after we are married." Einar held Affraic in one arm and threw the blankets off with the other. "Get into bed now and rest. You have had a hard day."

Affraic lay down and squeezed one eye shut.

"If I promise to sleep will you leave me be?"

Einar could see where he was not wanted.

"I have much work to do this evening so I will leave you to sleep. If when I return you sleep soundly I will sleep in the great hall with the men."

"Don't you be catching any lice there or other ailments," Affraic said, scolding him with her finger. "I only combed the last of your lice out of your hair yesterday."

Einar pointed to his head.

"I will wear a firm hat to ward away the lice," he replied with a smile.

"Good, now leave so I can sleep."

He shut the tent flap behind him.

She lay in bed counting his imagined steps as he went down the hill. She leapt out of bed and cried out in pain at her aching bones and bruises that drained her of her energy. But this was no time to be ill. She would only have one chance to save her brother.

She searched the tent for some useful tools, in case she had to break him out of the thralls' pen. At last, a hidden dagger beneath the rim of the bed. Einar was serious about his fear of getting murdered in his bed. She gathered what clothes she could and stuffed them under the blanket, hoping they would fool Einar should he come back and check on her. She knelt, said a quick prayer for luck, and listened outside for silence. She would not get it that night for the Norse were celebrating something or other by the dock; she had yet to learn properly about their gods, the ways of the gods or their particular feast days. Beyond that, in the momentary gaps of the men making noise, was the hoot of owls and the howling of wolves. She would have to take her chances. She gently opened the tent flap. No one around. She stole out of her tent and into the darkness.

CHAPTER FORTY-THREE
SWEET SISTER

A FFRAIC'S HEART RACED AS she darted through the shadows, her breath coming in short, panicked gasps. The distant flickering torchlight cast dancing shadows across the hard-packed earth. She took a deep, shuddering breath, trying to calm her nerves. The crisp night air filled her lungs, carrying with it the scent of wood smoke and roasting meat.

High above, the star-strewn sky stretched out like an inky tapestry, the constellations glimmering like diamonds scattered across black velvet. The crescent moon hung low on the horizon, its pale light washing over the slumbering Norse encampment. Tendrils of silvery mist crept between the tents and across the open spaces.

Affraic crept along the edges of the camp, keeping to the shadows. Her eyes darted about, searching for any sign of movement. Raucous laughter and drunken singing drifted on the night breeze from the centre of the camp where the warriors were gathered around firepits, drinking and carousing late into the night.

As she drew nearer to the thrall pens on the outskirts, her stomach twisted into anxious knots. Armed guards stood at the entrance, their spears glinting in the moonlight, their faces hard and alert. Affraic's mouth went dry. She had no plan, no clever ruse to gain entry. Desperation clawed at her chest. Her thoughts were quickly interrupted.

"Who goes there?" called a voice in the dark. A large looming shadow came towards her until she saw the grizzled face of the guard. It was the same one she had encountered when she was pretending to be picking herbs. His head jerked back.

"Einar's woman."

She bent over and cupped her mouth.

"Yes, it is I. He has sent me here on a mission. One in which you can play an important part."

The guard's eyes widened and so did his smile.

"What can I do for Einar? If I do well, will you tell him? I hate being a guard at night. I can never get any sleep in the day, for I am eternally dragged into something else."

Affraic beckoned him to lower his head so she could whisper in his ear.

"We have a spy in our midst."

The guard jerked his head up and frantically looked around.

"Let us kill him and throw him in the river as a sacrifice to the gods. Then they will bless our town and it will flourish."

She called him down again.

"Shh, no, he is one of our spies. But he was captured and is now in the thrall pens. We need to release him but in such a way that it looks like he escaped. Anything less and we will ruin his story and the Hibernians will kill him."

The guard knitted his brow.

"Why did Einar send you to do this? Why did he not do it himself?"

"A Norse letting a Hibernian go into the night? A Hibernian letting a Hibernian go into the night? Which do you think looks better?"

The guard withdrew his scrunched-up face.

"I suppose. But how do we find him? We cannot open all the pens or they would all run out. Then we would be both dead and any spy would be meaningless to us."

Affraic turned her head and scowled. She had not thought of that.

"I will go from pen to pen and call his name and we will quickly find him."

The guard nodded and invited her forward.

She bent down beside the wall of intertwined twigs that made up the walls of the pen.

"Finn, Finn," she whispered. "It is me, Affraic. Come and speak to me through the wicker walls if you can hear me."

There were a few moments of silence.

"Finn, Finn, it is not a trick."

A pair of eyes appeared through the gaps in the wicker to check her out. Then came another, and then another.

"Finn?" Affraic's hands became clammy under the watch of so many eyes.

"I am Finn."

"No, I am Finn."

"None of you are," Affraic spat. "You do yourselves no good by lying. Tell me who the real Finn is."

"I am Finn."

"No, I am Finn."

"You can all rot in hell for all I care," and Affraic stormed off to the next pen only to be met once more by multiple sets of eyes and desperate voices claiming to be that of her brother. She sat between the pens and cried, mainly out of frustration and wishing she could fling open the pens and let everyone run and take their chances. But that would ruin whatever she had with Einar. There had to be another way.

She positioned herself between the pens and whistled half a refrain their mother used to sing to them when they were children. She looked around into the dark waiting for a response. There it came, broken and disjointed, but all the same the basic tune. She edged over to the correct pen and whistled the refrain once more. Some imitators took to the air but none could mimic Finn as he could never whistle anyway. She peered through the cracks in the wattle and saw a familiar pair of eyes, albeit not burning with the usual foolhardy energy and passion.

"Finn, it's me, your sister," she called as she clawed at the wattle, trying to stick her fingers through the gaps so she could touch her brother's hand. All she could manage was to stroke the tip of his finger with hers through a tiny gap.

"Sweet sister," Finn said rather meekly, "it may not look like it now, but I am here to rescue you."

Tears streamed down Affraic's face.

"I think it is me here to save you. I don't need saving."

"I'm in no position to argue," Finn said as he hung his head and his voice trailed downwards.

"I can let you out, but only you. If everyone is released they will hunt us all down and kill us."

"I have to bring Aodh with me," Finn said clawing at the wattle. "He is my friend. He served with our father. I got him into this mess."

Affraic's hands rolled into fists as she battled with her brother's request.

"You can have him, but only him."

Finn nodded but Affraic could only see vague movements in the gaps in the wattle. She signalled to the guard to open the gate to the pen. The guard shrugged his shoulders and shook his head. Affraic forcefully pointed to the gate. He crept over and fiddled with the knot, trying to keep one hand free so he could grab the axe stuffed beneath his belt if needs be. He failed to open the gate and Affraic glared at him. He used both his hands and undid the knot. He pulled the door open. Out rushed everyone from the pen and the guard was quickly overwhelmed and slain with his own axe. Some of the people ran to the other pens to free their loved ones and friends. Finn took Affraic by the hand.

"Come run with me and be free."

She looked around at all the prisoners running in various directions and heard the guards shouting from the palisade. She knew in the dark that she would be struck down before anyone would ask her if she was Einar's woman so she grabbed Finn's hand and ran. They ran as fast as their legs could carry them. The Norse appeared out of their tents or from their guard positions on the palisade and began to recapture the thralls or cut them down where they stood. Affraic squeezed Finn's hand and they both accelerated. Fire torches streaked through the night as the Norse ran up from the docks. They released the dogs on the escaping thralls. The sounds of snarling dogs, ripping flesh and screams filled the cold night air.

Affraic and Finn ran and ran. She felt the constant pounding in her knees every time her feet impacted the ground. Her heart beat so hard she thought it may burst out of her ribcage. She could hear the thumping of feet behind her and dared not look behind her.

"Over there."

Finn pointed to the right as there was a gap in the palisade and also no guards. Affraic veered right, her ankles straining as she changed direction. They ran full pelt towards the gap. A chasm of darkness lay behind the gap but they knew that was the forest within which they could lose any pursuers. The gaping chasm opened up before them. Then a figure leapt out from the dark, a long beard-scarred face and broken teeth. He screamed as the axe flew down towards Affraic. She flinched and raised her arms to defend herself. A fist flew through the air and landed on the Norseman's jaw sending him flying. Both Affraic and Finn came to a halt and turned to see Aodh standing over the Norse having separated him from his axe. Aodh grinned and threw Finn a sword.

"Are we escaping or what?"

CHAPTER FORTY-FOUR

RIVALRY REBORN

FINN AND AFFRAIC DARTED between the towering oaks, their hearts pounding in their chests as they fled deeper into the ancient forest. They appeared to have lost Aodh somewhere along the way. The woods seemed to come alive around them, the branches reaching out to shield them from their pursuers. Gnarled roots rose up from the earth, twisting and turning like serpents, threatening to trip them up at every step. But Finn and Affraic were nimble and quick, leaping over the obstacles with the grace of deer.

Behind them, the shouts of the Norse grew louder, their heavy footfalls echoing through the trees. Finn risked a glance over his shoulder and saw the glint of steel in the fire torchlight, the Norse warriors brandishing their swords and axes as they gave chase. Fear surged through Finn's veins, urging him to run faster, to push himself to the limit.

Affraic ran beside him, her black hair streaming behind her like a banner of defiance. She moved with the fluid grace of a huntress, her eyes scanning the forest ahead for any sign of danger. Together, they wove through the trees, ducking under low-hanging branches and vaulting over fallen logs.

Suddenly, Affraic's foot caught on an exposed root and she tumbled to the ground with a cry. Finn skidded to a halt and whirled around, his hand flying to the hilt of his sword. The Norse were gaining ground, their faces twisted with determination and bloodlust.

"Come on!" Finn hauled Affraic to her feet and they plunged onward, weaving between the massive trunks of oak trees that seemed to whisper and groan with ancient voices. The woods grew thicker with each step, the underbrush snagging at their clothes and hair as if trying to slow them down.

But the darkness closed in and the shouts and footsteps behind them became more distant until they eventually faded to nothing. They came across the trunk of a large fallen oak they could hide behind. Finn looked behind them from the cover of the oak and listened for any unnatural sounds from the forest. Once satisfied they were not being followed, they collapsed behind the oak tree.

Their chests heaved until they got their collective breath back. Finn was the first to recover, for he was most used to running for all the time he spent on the hurling pitch. He resumed lookout duty. There were no more distant screams from the Norse camp but only the howling of wolves and the hooting of owls from the forest. They could only assume they were the only ones to have made it this far. Finn was satisfied they were not followed nor had search parties taken to the woods. He returned to his sister.

"We should make our escape back to the men," Finn whispered. "I have seen enough of the camp to know its weaknesses."

A wave of panic and confusion came over Affraic.

"What? You are going to lead an attack on the Norse? Who put you in charge and when have you ever led men?"

Finn scowled.

"This is not the time nor the place to discuss these things. Just know that your brother has saved you and the camp will burn."

Affraic went red and grabbed Finn by the elbow and pulled him back.

"What kind of a fool are you?" she hissed through gritted teeth. "Your foolishness got all of those people killed just so you could escape. I had everything under control until you rushed the guard."

Finn stood tall, scowled and stuck his chest out.

"You were just a thrall until I freed you. How did you have everything under control?"

Affraic squared up to Finn for she knew who he really was and was not going to be talked down to by him.

"I am going to be married to one of the most prominent Norse in the camp, that's who I am."

Finn smirked.

"How much 'going to be married' are you? 'Going to be married' get in my bed or 'going to be married' have set a date?"

Affraic slapped him across the face.

"'Save you from getting murdered by the Norse', 'save you from a life of slavery' type going to be married. Now sit down and shut up for I have something serious to say."

Finn knew the look on Affraic's face meant that this was no time for backchat. Her finger protruded to tell him what to do.

"I am to be married to the most prominent Norse chieftain in the town and no matter what you say or what you do, they are here to stay and you just have to get used to it."

Finn scowled, but kept his mouth firmly shut as he knew his sister had not finished.

"Tigernach and Ultán have entered into an alliance with them."

She let the shock on Finn's face sink in.

"You always knew they were traitors out for themselves, so this can't come as much of a surprise."

Finn grimaced and then nodded in acceptance that he thought her words were true.

"My future husband has promised me that if they can take Tigernach's lands and they are given to him, and I help him in this endeavour, then he will marry me."

Finn leapt to his feet.

"This is what you plot and scheme? Are you Norse now as well as stupid? That will never work. He is stringing you along so you will willingly climb into his bed."

Finn staggered back from the wallop he received to the side of his face.

"Have you ever known your sister to fail? Have you ever known her to take an insult without reply?"

Finn held his cheek.

"There are only a privileged few in my life I would take such a blow from. But what you say is the folly of dreams. I was to return to the camp in front of a band of warriors and burn it to the ground. That my kin are getting embroiled in all their lies makes it all the more imperative that I do so. Now, you can remain hidden in the woods, or I can bring you to safety, whichever you choose. If you go back to the encampment, I cannot guarantee your survival, for you will have surrendered yourself to the fortunes of war. What is it to be?"

Affraic smiled.

"Look at us. Mother always said she had two headstrong children. Neither of us is going to back down. I will come with you and wait for your attack to fail. If I do that and you do fail, will you agree to help me in my plan?"

It was Finn's turn to grin.

"Since you let me go first and I will not fail, I agree."

Affraic threw her eyes to the heavens.

Suddenly, they heard a rustle in the bushes for their debating had distracted them. Finn went for his weapon as a figure appeared from the shadows.

"Have you finished arguing yet?" Aodh said with a cocky smile. "The Norse could hear you from miles away, so they didn't bother chasing."

Finn dropped his weapon and ran to embrace his mentor.

"We have a plan. One that can succeed."

"I'll be the judge of that," Aodh said with a raised eyebrow. "But you can tell me on the way to our camp and we shall see if we have enough men to carry out this plan of yours."

Finn smiled at Affraic and they set out after Aodh.

CHAPTER FORTY-FIVE

FLYING SPARKS

IT WAS NOT LONG before Finn and Affraic had made up and were joking and laughing with each other much to the consternation of Aodh.

"These woods are probably crawling with Norse by now, hunting down the thralls we freed. Be quiet or you will get us all killed."

Finn and Affraic looked at each other and hid their sniggers behind their hands.

Suddenly, a branch cracked in the distance. Aodh stopped and cocked his ears. He raised his hand for Finn and Affraic to be silent. He listened for a minute and then dropped his hand, satisfied the disturbance was nothing that should alarm them. They carried on walking.

"We should have been stopped by our men on patrol if they were paying attention," Aodh growled as they travelled further into the woods. "They will all want to be here, or Malachy will hang them along with the rest of those cowards who ran away."

They advanced a little further until Aodh started to recognise the trees. Aodh held his hand up again for silence. They crept through the bushes to where their men were camped. They observed the clearing at a distance to find it was more shambolic than ever. The tents were half collapsed, their hides sagging from the poles like the skin of a starving man. Bedrolls lay strewn about, stained with mud, mead, and worse. The fire pit was a mess of cold ash and blackened bones, the meagre flames sputtering and dying in the damp air.

The men themselves were a sorry sight. Their once-proud beards hung limp and matted, and their faces were gaunt and hollow-eyed. They huddled in small groups, wrapped in tattered cloaks, muttering to each other in low, desperate tones.

Aodh burst out of the bushes in such a fury he kicked the fire and burning logs, and sparks and embers showered those sitting on the other side.

"If I were a Norse warrior, you would all be dead now," he roared in the faces of the men in front of him.

Several of the men who got sprayed by flames and ash rose, cursed and grabbed their weapons.

"If you were not appointed by Malachy you would be dead now for doing that to us," said the bravest of them.

Aodh leapt over the flames and beckoned them forward to attack him.

"Any of you who wish to take up arms against me and survive the repercussions are welcome to take command of the attack on the camp. Do not forget, if you do not attack the Norse camp, you will soon find yourself trying to fend off demons in the pool of dead souls."

As the words penetrated the ears of the men the anger on their faces dissipated and their weapons slowly lowered.

"Good," Aodh said, his face still solidly stern. "We attack at nightfall. How many men are left?"

The brave man who spoke against Aodh rubbed his beard and looked to the ground.

"Thirty," he spat out, hoping the harshness of his reply would not bring further comment down upon him. He was wrong. Aodh whacked the tip of his sword into the ground with frustration.

"No matter," he growled. "Get your weapons, say your prayers and do whatever else that prepares you for battle."

The men grumbled but turned to collect their belongings.

Affraic smirked and playfully nudged Finn.

"My plan is much better than yours," she whispered in his ear.

She met his scowl with a large grin.

"The Norse camp will burn tonight," Finn growled. "You'd better find yourself another husband."

Affraic stuck her tongue out just like she did when they were children.

Aodh gave Finn a little slap on the back of his head, causing him to choke on his reply to his sister.

"Get your things," Aodh said. "If you are lucky enough to survive the night you'll have the rest of your life to argue with your sister."

Finn grunted but obeyed his mentor.

CHAPTER FORTY-SIX
DANCING FLAMES

The ancient oak wood loomed above and around them, its gnarled branches reaching out like skeletal ribs in the moonlight as if they walked in the belly of a beast. But they did not know whether they would emerge from its ass or its mouth. Finn and Aodh stepped cautiously into the shadowy depths, their hearts pounding in their chests. They had left the men behind them as they had gone to scout ahead. The forest floor was a carpet of fallen leaves, muffling their footsteps as they crept forward.

A cool breeze whispered through the trees, carrying with it the musty scent of decay and the faint whisper of something otherworldly. It was as if they were walking in the footsteps of their ancestors, those who had fallen in battles long forgotten. Finn shivered, pulling his cloak tighter around his shoulders. He could feel the weight of the forest pressing down on him, as if the very trees were watching their every move.

As they ventured deeper into the wood, the darkness seemed to close in around them. The moonlight struggled to penetrate the dense canopy overhead, casting eerie shadows that danced and swayed with every gust of wind. Finn's nerves were on edge, his hand never straying far from the hilt of his sword. The moon came back, almost by surprise as the woods began to thin again as if their final exit from the beast, be it from ass or mouth, was soon to be revealed.

Suddenly, Aodh held up a hand, signalling for Finn to stop. They crouched low, peering through the undergrowth. There, just ahead, was the Norse camp. They quickly found a large bush to hide behind which gave them an advantageous view of the camp.

The fires in the Norse camp burnt brightly, the shadows of the men inside betrayed by the dancing flames. All were easily observable through the gaps in the palisade. The flickering flames also betrayed Finn's nerves to Aodh at the edge of the forest.

"It is now or never," Aodh said solemnly. "Malachy will have engaged with Thurgest's raiders days ago and we must attack before the Norse come back with their tales between their legs."

Finn did not deviate from staring at the camp.

"That is if Malachy is successful."

Aodh gave Finn a harsh stare.

"If he is not successful, then all of Hibernia may fall. If we do not approach our mission with optimism then we have failed already and are needlessly throwing the lives of our men away."

"Men die for pointless reasons all the time. They are quickly forgotten, as are most men."

Aodh extended his arm and placed his hand upon Finn's shoulder.

"Listen, we must make a plan. You remember the layout of the camp as well as I do. Our only hope is to cause as much chaos as possible to cover our escape. We saw how freeing the slaves turned the camp into chaos. We use that chaos for our own means. One of us goes for the slave pens and the other for the harbour. We must set fire to their fleet but leave them with a means of escape. We do not have the men to fight a pitched battle and I am assuming we need some of the slaves to take up arms and join us. Which of these missions do you want?"

Finn had by now gone stiff with nerves, frozen in his stance under the cover of the tree. His brief stint as a thrall had frightened him to his very bones. If he were to go back into the camp and not escape, he was determined that he should die and die the death of a hero, for at least his name would be remembered, just like his father.

"I cannot make a choice, Aodh," he mumbled. "Give me the task I am capable of."

Aodh sighed.

"Think of the strength you gained from the visit to the seer. Think of how the vision of your father filled you with courage. Stride with confidence like you do on the hurling pitch. You free the slaves for you are far quicker than I to cover the ground from the palisade to the pens. Take the men to help you fight and free the rest and set them to run to freedom. You must engage the Norse or at least cause such a distraction as to draw them away from the harbour. For this task you take the bulk of the men."

Finn knitted his brow.

"What about you? You have a more important mission?"

"I need to be like the creeping fox with his eye on the hen house. You do not need a pack of foxes to steal the eggs if there is an adequate distraction."

"Then you choose your ten and I will make do with the rest."

Aodh took Finn by both shoulders and looked him square in the face.

"By whatever gods you follow, you can do this. You will do this. Find somewhere for Affraic to hide, preferably where she can come out and redirect any slaves that manage to win their freedom back to safety. Then I will meet you by the clearing where we camped, if it is still safe."

Finn gulped and purposely hardened his face so he did not appear afraid.

"This is normal," Aodh said. "Only fools are not afraid before they go into battle. Let us split the men and take up our positions."

Finn nodded and followed Aodh.

Aodh took the ten men he considered to be the most nimble but it was hard to differentiate between them since he knew them so little. The rest were given to Finn.

"You will go first and I will await your signal," Aodh said as he put his hand on Finn's shoulder. "I will circle around the left and enter through the gap in the palisade there. I will then make my way to the boats and set them on fire. If you have not run by the time you see the flames then drop everything and start running then."

Finn nodded.

"I will wait until it is darkest before beginning my attack. You will see a clear signal when I have released the pens."

Affraic had followed them as she wanted to see how foolhardy their plan was and give it one more go to persuade them to abandon it. She knitted her brow when she overheard them and could not help making her presence known.

"If you wait until the thralls are released you will surely bring the guards out upon yourselves. There will not be many thralls left after our breakout as many of them would have been killed attempting to escape. They have also had little time to restock."

Both Finn and Aodh flew around and drew their swords. Aodh cursed in frustration.

"What are you doing here?" he hissed.

"I have come to stop my brother from getting himself killed." Every word was spat as if it were a challenge.

Finn ground his teeth but realised Affraic was his problem to deal with.

"What else would you have me do?" Finn snapped but he soon changed his tune when he saw the response on his sister's face. "I have to do this. I have promised an important king."

Aodh saw it was time for him to go as Finn needed to sort this out himself.

"I shall wait for your signal," Aodh said. "My life and the lives of your men depend on it."

Aodh knew he had to have a final say for he knew how persuadable Affraic could be from his interactions with her mother.

"You know you can never defeat the Norse with only thirty men?" Affraic said. If *I told you so* was not emphasised enough in her voice, it was stamped on her face.

Finn walked away in an attempt to rid himself of her negativity. But it kept following him.

"I don't have to," he eventually replied. "All I have to do is give Malachy the chance to defeat Thurgest and my mission will be done."

"And you along with it," Affraic said. "You know my plan is so much better, yet you seem to think following the king's instructions no matter how much it endangers you is a wise course of action."

Finn shook his head and raised his hands.

"Stop with your objections, please. We already agreed this, remember? You need to wait here in safety. If I return and find I have been the victim of treachery, then we'll sit and talk and it will be the turn of your plan. For now, let me follow my path and know I have a supportive sister behind my back."

Affraic saw that he was trapped and not for persuading. She nodded and became solemn.

"May the road rise with you, brother, and I will pray that God has your back."

Finn smiled and embraced his sister.

"We will know by morning who has the better plan."

CHAPTER FORTY-SEVEN

A SIGNAL OF SORTS

F INN TOOK HIS PLACE behind a giant oak at the edge of the woods. He could see the silhouettes of two guards on the moonlit half-built palisade. He signalled to two of his most loyal men to sneak up on them on one side while he and another would approach them from the other side. Finn was moving around for the direct approach. He threw a stone to distract the guards and they were immediately attracted to the commotion. They began to search the nearby bushes. Finn leapt out from a bush behind them.

"Are you, by chance, looking for a missing thrall?"

The two guards whirled around to see where the voice was coming from. But before they could cry out and raise the alarm, their throats were slit and their lives gushed down their throats and chests. Finn put his fingers to his lips and signalled the men forward. They seeped through the gap in the palisade and hid among the shadows as Finn assessed what was in front of them. They had purposefully chosen the less populated section of the camp so they could penetrate inside with less risk of being molested for their troubles. Finn pointed towards the hill to where the thrall pens were. There were now a substantial number of guards allocated to watch over them. Finn signalled they needed to revert to plan two.

A group of men climbed the hill. Some walked in single file in the middle, and the rest herded them from the front, side and back. Finn was at the front struggling with what bound his wrists. Several of the guards stepped forward with their leader in the middle.

"Who goes there?" he called, his voice deep and harsh, as if it were the lash of a whip.

"More thralls for the pens," said one of the guards of the new batch. "They are to rest in the pens tonight and be allocated out tomorrow."

The Norse leader narrowed his eyes and put his hands on his hips.

"No one told me about a new batch of thralls coming in this evening and I have not seen any boats dock."

Finn saw the guards tense and hover their hands over their weapons. He threw off his loose ropes. He leapt upon the leader of the Norse before he had time to draw his weapon and plunged his dagger into the man's belly numerous times until the blood gushed. The rest of his men followed his example and set upon the Norse guards. But inexperience let Finn down for he had not made sure that all the guards were in easy reach to be killed. The ones on the periphery ran down the hill shouting at the top of their lungs.

"At least Aodh has a signal," Finn sighed. Finn looked around and assessed what he needed to do next. "Now, men, free the slaves and direct them towards the forest and take care of any Norse that come at us."

But the men proved ill-disciplined and were already freeing the thralls while some at the rear were already making their escape. Finn cursed but went to help clear the pens. Those that were in the pens were reluctant to leave at first for most had been recaptured and punished after the original escape. But when Finn announced who he was they quickly took to their heels and ran down the hill towards the gaps in the palisade. Norse charged up from their encampment and the docks. Finn sized up those who ran out of the pens and stopped the young men of fighting age.

"Here," he said as he handed them the weapons of the fallen Norse. "We need your help to free your people."

The young men reluctantly took the weapons, stared down at them and then at the huge Norse advancing up the hill towards them. They took off in the opposite direction, most discarding their weapons as they slowed them down. Finn cursed them but having so few men left he also took to his heels.

CHAPTER FORTY-EIGHT

A NIGHT OF FLAMES AND FANGS

ODH HEARD THE SCREAMS from the top of the hill. It was a signal, but not the one he wanted for he did not know who did the screaming, be it Norse, thrall or Finn and his men. He looked to the sky and saw the darkness was perfect. The other omens were mixed for the attack, but he knew he would not get a better chance. He reluctantly signalled his men forward.

They crept through the thickets on the perimeter of the woods watching the chaos unfold. Aodh smiled when he saw the Norse were being led away from the harbour, just as he wanted. They approached the gap in the palisade nearest the harbour and saw two guards still remained. Both were quickly felled by silent arrows. The way was open. They stole through the gap in the fence and stuck to the shadows beneath the completed palisade. Several of the tents along the way to the docks were still occupied and those unfortunates inside them were swiftly silenced. Aodh waved the men on.

Next came the prestigious half-completed buildings of the settlement, like Thurgest's home, Einar's future home and the barracks for Thurgest's bodyguard. All had been abandoned to pursue the escaping thralls. Aodh gritted his teeth as he passed these buildings by. These were the Norse laying their claws into the land and they would hang on for dear life to defend them. They must be burnt to the ground and then their foundations dug up and cast into the sea so the Norse curse would never return. But not now. He could burn them on his retreat when he had set fire to the ships. He could hear the screams of the dying coming from the hill and knew he had to hurry for the distraction would not last too much longer and the Norse would naturally return to the docks.

They were now on the edge of the path to the docks and Aodh signalled for his men to take cover on either side. Aodh paused to assess the situation. The docks were lit by fire torches all along the wooden pathways. At least one guard stood outside each of the ten ships moored to the dock. There were four guards at the entrance and several more guards sitting, weapons at the ready waiting to be ordered to assault the hill. Aodh's force were outnumbered by at least two to one and that was just from the guards he could see. Aodh always knew it was going to be difficult but there was much distance out in the open between each set of guards and he knew he would lose most of his men if not all. But he was old and was always prepared to die in combat situations. He was surprised he had survived this long so he thought he may be blessed. He certainly needed all the blessings he could muster now. He signalled to his two bowmen to get into position.

Aodh waved his hand and two of the guards at the entrance fell with arrows in their chests. The other two barely had a chance to raise their weapons before they were felled in a similar manner. Aodh gave the signal to charge. The men rose and rushed down the path in silence for they did not want to give away to the Norse that another attack was commencing. The guards from the docks rushed to meet them but they roared as loudly as they could for they knew they could win by sheer weight of numbers alone. The bowmen took out another two guards to even up the numbers before metal clashed with metal. Aodh's muscle memory was good for he blocked the blow from above with his sword and pressed into the belly of the man with his dagger to be rewarded by a cry and the gushing flow of blood. But he had no time to admire his work for another Norse was quickly upon him. The Norse wielded a heavy axe which he swung, relying on the weight to deliver the fatal blow. Aodh danced around the swinging blade but he knew he could not outlast the younger man who just lumbered from side to side. He heard a cry from his right as an axe blow to the shoulder blade almost sliced one of his men in two as his warm blood sprayed everyone around him.

"BOWMEN."

Aodh's cry was answered as the axeman opposite him collapsed with an arrow in the temple and the slayer received two in the chest. Aodh whirled his head around. His men were struggling but no more Norse had joined the fray. Aodh felt a blade whisper past his shoulder. He instinctively thrust his knife towards the breeze. It plunged into muscle and sinew until it met bone. He turned his head to see his blade embedded in the shoulder of a man who howled in agony. Aodh put him out of his misery. There were no more left to challenge him, so he plunged his sword into the back of a Norse, pinning down one of his men. The two remaining Norse fled.

Aodh's chest heaved with exhaustion. The bloodlust no longer pumped as it did in his youth for all his joints and muscles ached. He reached his sword over his head to silently signal their mission was not over and they had to set fire to the boats. But even that was a chore, such was the weight of his limbs in combination with that of the sword. He counted what men he had left. Six, including the two bowmen. How poor was the quality of the men he was given if even with the advantage of surprise and of two bowmen they lost nearly half their men. Aodh took a satchel off the back of one of his fallen men and distributed the fire torches and pointed to the nearest lit fire torch on the dock.

"We must hurry if we are to get out of here alive."

They went and lit their torches and the first couple of fire torches were lobbed onto the first boat. The raiders moved on but to Aodh's dismay the boat did not catch alight.

"Be careful men. We only have moments so look for something flammable so your comrades' lives will not be wasted."

The second ship quickly caught aflame as did the third and the fourth. There was suddenly a terrifying shriek and Aodh looked over his shoulder to see a group of warriors charging down the hill towards them.

"Do what damage you can," Aodh shouted. "We must leave for we have been rumbled."

The bowmen pulled back their strings and did as much as they could to reduce the number of warriors advancing towards them. Aodh greedily set one more ship on fire and lit a tar pot on the docks, spilling the liquid sludge as far as he could to do the most damage. But when he raised his head his men had fled and he was alone.

He could now make out the angry faces of his enemies as they set foot on the dock. He ran for if he stayed he would be cornered and quickly dead. The warriors were rapidly after him. He heard a hiss whizz past his ear. The nearest warrior fell in a heap. Another arrow and another warrior fell. At least the arrows were friendly. Aodh turned his head but slipped on a pool of blood on the pier. He fell in a heap on the ground. His dagger flew out of his hand. He rolled over onto his back and scrabbled for his dagger. A warrior loomed above him. He pinned down Aodh's arms and raised his axe above his head. He was grizzled, dirty with a long beard. Was this the last sight Aodh would ever see? He was hoping for Jesus. The man hesitated. Aodh squinted at him.

"Cathal?"

The man froze.

"Aodh?"

CHAPTER FORTY-NINE

A HERO RUNS DOWNHILL

FINN LOOKED AROUND TO see how many men had stuck with him. Five. He swallowed hard. How could five be enough of a distraction for Aodh? How could five destroy this entire camp? He realised he had wasted his time in the woods dreaming of being a hero without ever having to raise his blade in anger. The Norse were closing in on him. He would soon be outnumbered. Was this the dragon of the seer's prophecy coming for him? Was he to die on this hill? Not if he could help it.

"Run, men, run."

They ran as fast as they could down the hill. Finn looked over his shoulder to see some of the Norse change direction and come after him while others settled on easier targets. The gap in the palisade was ahead. Suddenly a band of Norse emerged from the shadows below with a blood-curdling roar. Finn raised his sword but did not drop his pace. It was just like running with a hurling stick with the sliotar at the end. He swung his sword in an arc with so much force that if it did not connect with something it would knock him off balance. It collided with a hip bone after slicing through a leather tunic, muscle and sinew. He keeled to the right as the juddering of the sword in flesh knocked him out of his stride. He heard a roar in his ear and continued his velocity right, narrowly avoiding a falling axe blade. He swung his sword in an arc and plunged it into the man's spine. The man howled as Finn withdrew his blade and warm blood spurted all over his face.

An arrow whizzed past his head and lodged in the back of one of his men. He looked around and found himself in the pit of hell. Norse ran marauding around the hill slaughtering all of those who could not defend themselves. The fire torches of the hunters looked like the trail of a demonic dragon swallowing the souls of all the hunted. Whereas before when they had their original breakout the Norse tried to recapture as many as they could, this time they showed no mercy and slaughtered all they came upon. It was as if they were attempting to cast a legend of blood upon the hill. One that would live on in the hearts of those they would enslave in the future. If they did not bow their heads and bend their backs, they too and their families would be victims of such slaughter.

Finn saw one of his men nearby being set upon by two Norse. He raised his sword and let out an anguished scream. He plunged his sword into the back of one which distracted the other enough for Finn's comrade to plunge his dagger into his belly.

"God bless you a thousand times," the man said, his face pale from exhaustion. "You did not have to come back and save me, but you did."

Finn brushed off such gratitude.

"We have not the time for this. We must save as many as we can and regroup in the woods. We can only survive if there are enough of us to defend ourselves."

They ran towards another of their number and freed him from his attackers before they could deliver the fatal blow. The Norse were small in number and relatively isolated but Finn could now see a mass of them charging down the hill. Finn raised his sword above his head, its weight juddered down his arm and into his shoulder.

"Retreat, men."

But it was pointless to anyone but him that he even said it. Everyone was already running towards the gaps in the palisade. The rain of arrows began to get heavier as the Norse gathered their strength and saved their energies by not chasing their foes. Finn took to his heels and ran as fast as he could towards the gap in the palisade.

Then, out from the shadows jumped a giant Norse, a troll of legend if ever there was one. He stood in the middle of the largest of the gaps and he scythed down anyone who came within his range. Finn put his head down whilst others slowed down to see if there was another means of escape. Finn spotted the two men he had just saved running down the hill to his left. He signalled to them to take the right side of the troll as they approached and he would take the left. The troll roared and swung his axe from side to side, daring them on. One of the men picked up a discarded spear and threw it at the troll. He easily batted it away and roared defiantly. However, Finn felt the slip of the wet grass underneath his feet. He remembered back to one of his favourite moves on the hurling pitch, one which the current rules did not outlaw, indeed he was often commended for it. He slid along the grass and at the last second before colliding with the troll's knee lifted his sword up and jammed it as hard as he could beneath the troll's kneecap. The troll howled in agony as the sword went through bone and sinew and the kneecap was sliced off. The three men jumped on the troll and stabbed him as many times as they could. They ran through the gap and into the forest followed by as many of the freed prisoners as had seen their feat.

CHAPTER FIFTY

TORN BETWEEN MERCY OR REVENGE

THERE WAS NO ESCAPE for Aodh. He lay beneath his former friend's blade not knowing whether he would plunge it through his chest or offer him a hand up. The world seemed to have stopped between them as both struggled with their memories of the past. Aodh decided since he had the sword pointing at his chest he should break the silence.

"Cathal. I thought you were dead."

Cathal sneered and spat blood from his mouth.

"Many times I thought I was dead and many more I wished it. But whatever gods float up there in the sky thought it best to keep me alive. It was a cruelty if you ask me. But no one asks me anything these days. They kept me like a dog on a chain until I knew nothing but to obey their commands. Now they set me like a wild dog upon the likes of you." Cathal gave an evil grin. "But I might like to kill you. You made me what stands above you today."

Aodh gave him a steely stare, one he was in no position to give, but he knew the old Cathal and wondered how much of him remained inside this beast.

"I did not abandon you. I searched long and hard for you but you were gone. I thought they may have strapped you to the front of one of their ships, but I doubt it, for you still stand before me."

Cathal's chin dropped.

"I often wished they had for it would have been over all the quicker. But any compassion and mercy were beaten out of me long ago. But what I do will be far more merciful than what they did for me. I will dash your brains out with one fell swoop and your soul will thank me for it as it sinks into the mud and down into hell."

Cathal raised the axe across his chest and over his opposite shoulder so he could get a good swing. He moved his left hip back so he could generate more power in his swing.

"It is time to pray if you believe in that sort of thing."

"Wait."

Aodh put up his hands to block the blow. Cathal narrowed his eyes.

"Why are you trying to plead for mercy? I am giving you a warrior's death. Far more than you deserve considering you abandoned me."

"Would you like to meet your son and daughter? I can bring you to them."

Cathal reeled back for he had long abandoned any hope of seeing them, having banished them from his mind when all alone in a thrall pen on top of a mountain in Norway with the snows coming. Even the memory of them flooded his heart with emotion, most of which he no longer had the fortitude to bear. His face clouded over with anger and he swung his axe. But he could not bring it down on Aodh's head for all he saw were the innocent faces of his children looking up at him, longing for his love and attention.

"What wicked trickery is this?" Cathal screamed, the saliva dripping from his mouth. "My children are dead. You are trying to fool me into escaping. You are not content with leaving me to the Norse, you have to stamp the remains of my heart into the ground."

"It is no trick," Aodh said, as he tried to keep his voice as steady and calm as he could. "I can bring you to them. It's not far, but we would have to come alone. You may say whatever you may wish to them and be free to return here. You and I will meet again on the battlefield, and we can sort out our remaining differences there."

"Are you going to finish him off?" came an Irish accent from behind Cathal. "We need to chase off the rest before the master returns."

Cathal gave Aodh a contemptuous look and pulled his shirt into shape. He stood away from Aodh.

"I am going on a scouting mission," Cathal announced. "The master will be very pleased with what I will bring back."

Cathal kicked Aodh and pointed to the gap in the palisade. Aodh had no choice but to obey.

CHAPTER FIFTY-ONE

THE LUCKY TELL TALES OF WOE

FINN RAN THROUGH THE dark forest, the twigs and small branches on the lower reaches of the tree trunks whipping him as he ran by. The little light the night sky above provided gave modest illumination for the ground below. The two men who helped him slay the troll ran along either side of him. They laughed at the joy of being still alive, free of the Norse camp and having the privilege of being whipped in the face with the twigs and feeling it when they had left most of their comrades lying dead behind them. Finn held up his hand and pointed to the right. They changed direction and followed him. They jumped over a moss-laden oak tree and hid behind it.

Finn returned the two men's smiles and peered over the top of the fallen trunk. He could not see much beyond the trunks of the nearest trees but could only hear screams in the distance. He ducked down behind the fallen oak and sighed loudly. It took him a few moments to get his breath back. His smile quickly faded.

"Did you see how many managed to escape?" he asked, moving his head from side to side to momentarily look both men in the eye.

"I saw many fall," one man said. "The Norse were quickly out of their tents and killed everyone they came across."

The other man nodded in agreement.

"We must go back to the meeting point and see who has survived this mission and then go back to Malachy to see if we aided his victory."

His two companions peeled themselves off the ground, their limbs limp and heavy, their eyes tearing up with the effort of having to run again. Finn gave them a warm smile of encouragement.

"We will have left mere foot soldiers and return heroes. For who else can give the king such a vivid description of the Norse camp?"

His companions gave him a weary smile but followed him all the same.

Finn set a brisk pace but did not break into a run for the forest was dark and dense and hid all sorts of hidden foes, be they animal or man. They also had to ensure they were not followed for the last thing they wanted for their comrades was to survive the ordeal of the camp only for the enemy to be led straight to them once they thought themselves safe. Finn circled around the meeting place twice until he was sure he was not followed.

They arrived at the camp and Affraic ran and embraced him as soon as she saw him.

"I was so worried I would not see you again," she whispered in his ear. She let go of her embrace and held him by the forearms so she could inspect him as he stood in front of her. She gave a faint nod of approval.

"Only scratches and you reek of smoke, but that only accentuates your usual odours. I think you'll live."

Finn scowled for he had no time for humour. He looked around the camp and saw ten exhausted men lying on the ground, at least half with visible wounds. He shook his head.

"Is this it?"

Affraic nodded with a downturned mouth.

"I went to the edge of the woods and could see the flames and hear the screams." She saw the disappointment linger on his face. "I will tell everyone you were a hero."

Finn turned away, for he did not want his face to give away his feelings anymore.

"I'm sure your Norse friends will be impressed," Finn said over his shoulder.

"I'm sure Tigernach and Ultán would be proud of your efforts," Affraic snapped in return.

Finn whirled around in a rage to strike down the offender since he had not lost the sensitivity of his battlefield wits. But he saw the shock on his sister's face upon him turning on her. His head bowed, his shoulders slumped and his hand went forth seeking reconciliation.

"I don't want your hand," Affraic said, her mouth down turned. "I want your promise. You said if your way failed you would try mine. Will you keep your word to me?"

Finn turned away and bit his lip. To keep such a promise would mean admitting the greatest failure. What would he tell Malachy about his raid if he entered into such a scheme with his sister? Surely Malachy would see through his lies. There had to be another way. Finn gulped for there was no greater discerner of his lies than his sister.

"If Aodh does not return then I owe him my revenge. Then, I cannot make such a promise to you."

Affraic cursed him, slammed her fists on her thighs and turned and ran. Finn smiled to himself. He could do without his sister baiting him now at the moment of his greatest failure. Surely if Aodh returned the mission would be a success?

Finn lay down on a blanket in the ferns and slept. It was as if the roots of the ferns had crawled onto his body, penetrated his skin and drained all of his energy from him. He had nothing left. He was as limp as a wet bow string.

CHAPTER FIFTY-TWO
IS THIS A TRICK?

AFFRAIC DECIDED TO PUT her anger with Finn to some good use. She let the survivors of the attack rest while she went out into the forest to see what stragglers she could find. She returned several hours later with six exhausted soldiers and ten escaped thralls. She led them into the camp, showed them where to sleep and asked those who had been there a while and had made rabbit stew to share their food.

"We cannot linger here long," she said to the weary faces. "Rest a while and then you must cross the river and head northwards."

"What about you?" asked one of the women. "Aren't you coming with us?"

"I have other things to attend to," and she set out to seek which bush Finn was asleep in.

A helpful soldier pointed her in the right direction. She rounded the tree behind which she believed Finn lay. She staggered back and drew her hand to her chest once she was on the other side. There sat Aodh, bloodied, bruised and covered in dirt. He glared at her.

"How long have you been here?" she said to cut through the atmosphere.

"Barely long enough to find a flat rock upon which to rest my backside. But I have little time for niceties as your Norse friends are waiting for you. Wake your brother and come quickly back to me for we have matters of great importance to discuss."

"Are these matters of victory or defeat?" she said with a cocked eyebrow.

"Enjoy that smug smile while you can for it will not return for many a moon. Get your brother, for I am serious about the matters we need to discuss."

Affraic gave Aodh a dirty look and momentarily dreamt of her Einar slowly strangling him for being insolent to her. She looked through the expansive bushes of ferns for her brother. She soon found the large indent in the foliage he had created for himself as he rolled around in his sleep to avoid the numerous damp patches on the ground. She looked at him sleeping and noted that even in that position he looked troubled. She kicked his outstretched foot.

"Get up, sleepyhead. You don't want to die in your bed."

Finn jolted upright and ripped his knife from his belt at the same time. Wide-eyed and dazed, he thrust the blade in any direction which he could locate a sound. Affraic jumped out of the way.

"It is me, your sister, you fool. Don't let me be the only person you have killed this day."

Finn shook his head and scowled.

"Don't even joke about that. I am no longer the boy you once knew. I am not even the man you knew yesterday."

Affraic sneered at such talk.

"I am not the girl you once knew nor should be spoken to harshly, for my husband-to-be will wreak any vengeance necessary for disrespecting me. Now get up, for Aodh wishes to speak to us urgently about some grave matter or other. I have had quite enough of stupid deaths this day and long to return home. Let him have his say and you can return with him to the mountains to play kings and quests or whatever it is you are doing."

"We do important work for the freedom of our people," Finn snarled.

"Pah! Our people. It's our people this, our people that until the farmer from the next valley stabs you in the back because he thinks you stole one of his sheep. The kings in our country are all out for themselves so why shouldn't I be out for myself?"

"Because it is at everyone else's expense, that's why not."

"Stop arguing and come and sit," Aodh shouted from the other side of the tree.

They both came around the tree, their faces contorted in anger, but they sat in front of Aodh and impatiently waited for him to speak.

"I have someone I wish you to meet."

Affraic slammed her fists into her sides and tilted her head.

"If it is not my husband-to-be, who can you possibly have that will not waste my time?"

Aodh signalled to someone to come out from behind the tree. Cathal shuffled into view, his head bowed, ashamed to look his children in the face for he had no idea what tales their mother had told about him but he assumed them to be bad. Affraic tutted and threw her hands up in disgust.

"Why are you introducing us to this dirty bandit? Do we have to hang him for some supposed crime? Just do it. Why waste our time with him when I need to get home and you need to escape?"

Cathal raised his head and looked straight at Affraic. He had not seen her since she was around five, he could not remember the exact date because of all the time he spent in a prison or a thrall pen. To him, she was beautiful, the same picture of her mother he had kept in his mind all those years. His last light of hope. She was just like her, headstrong, forthright and stubborn, but he loved her all the more for it. He wanted to reach out and take her hand but could not raise his own. He tried to tell her who he was, but his throat went dry like the deserts the Norse used to tell tales of. He reached down for his flask and glugged some of its contents. He hoped it would give him courage as well.

"Young woman," he croaked. "I am your father."

Affraic took one look at Cathal and then turned to Aodh and slapped him across the face.

"I don't know what your little trick was supposed to achieve but if it was to make me angry then you have succeeded. Have this man flogged for trying to deceive me or I will have my husband-to-be set his dogs on you as soon as I return to the camp. My father is dead. This is some trick to bring me to heel. Shame on you."

"But Affraic..." Aodh said, but it was to her back for she had already stormed off. "It is no trick."

Finn was more intrigued and eyed the man. He had little reason to doubt Aodh for he had been a faithful friend and saw no reason why he would try and pull off such a ruse. They had been beaten by the Norse, or else Aodh would have bragged about his success, but he wondered how he had run into such a man who would claim to be his father. He shook with nerves as he thought about all the stories his mother had told about his father, and his curiosity was piqued. But he could not take such a statement on trust.

"My father is dead," Finn said with a raised chin but hesitant voice. "That means if you are not an impostor, you are a ghost.

An impostor will meet my axe and a ghost the priest. Which is it to be?"

Cathal looked his son straight in the eye and held his gaze. Finn thought Cathal's eyes dead little dots in the upper echelons of his face, stars that had long since ceased to shine.

"My soul died many moons ago, far more than I can remember," Cathal said. His cheek twitched, but his face remained stony-cold. "Only my soul died. All I wanted was to see my children one last time before I died. The memory of your young, vibrant faces kept me alive for so long until I gradually forgot what you looked like. Hope was extinguished like a fire torch thrown into a pool of my own shit, spit, blood and vomit. Now here I am, and you don't even recognise me. I recognise you. You were much younger, and I tried so hard to forget what you looked like, never mind that you are alive. Now, I am a stranger to you."

Cathal lowered his head to hide his tears. Finn paused and looked long and hard at the man. He was thin but muscular. He looked as if he had suffered neglect for a long period of time and had the spirit beaten out of him. He looked more like a wild animal of the woods, a bandit long abandoned to the deepest depths many years ago. But when he spoke his words were captivating. His voice was a harsh rasp, but his words sounded true. They sounded like he spoke from the heart even though his was shrivelled like a prune. If this man was a liar, he was a very good one. But Finn was intrigued and had to get to the bottom of this mystery. He glanced once more at Cathal and turned back again to Aodh.

"You knew my father and he looked nothing like him," Finn said, pointing at Cathal. "What makes you believe that this is him?"

Aodh invited everyone to sit.

"I realise why you would be sceptical and it would not be a lie to say that earlier in the night this man held my life in his hands and could easily have killed me. But I would have gladly accepted death rather than bring the enemy into our camp to threaten the lives of you and your sister. But he knew so many things that any impostor, even though they may have spent a long time in a cell with your father, would not know. Hear his story, make up your own mind and then let us leave, for the Norse will soon come searching for us."

Cathal stood, not knowing whether to run or to stay, for at least if he was fighting there was a chance of death which he would welcome. This was far worse. This was resurrecting hope in a heart long devoid of light. If he were to gain hope only for it to be dashed once more, it just might be the last time.

Finn gestured for him to sit.

"I will fetch my sister and we will both sit and hear your tale. If I think you are a trickster at the end of it I will cut your head off for insulting the memory of my dead father. If I do not, then we shall see, for I have never seen a ghost before. Do we have a deal?"

Cathal nodded vigorously and found himself a rock to sit upon.

CHAPTER FIFTY-THREE

THE BOWED HEAD

FINN POINTED FIRMLY AT a rock so Affraic could be under no illusion this was an instruction to sit and listen. She snarled and lifted her skirt so she could sit comfortably. She turned her head to show her disdain for the man seated in front of her. Her brother may have ordered her about this time, but there was still room for defiance. She would bide her time for acceptance of her plan was more important than being seen to submit to her brother.

Cathal sighed. A tear came to his eye and his chin wobbled at the thought of having to rake through the embers of his life. But he looked at the eager face of one child and ignored the scowl on the face of the other. He knew it had to be done. He just did not know where to begin. He began to claw back through the remains of his memories.

"I remember back to when you were children, when we all lived in the village with your mother. I was always being called away on Tigernach's business, doing whatever his bidding was, no matter how foul the deed. That is where I met Aodh and Babo, and we were the finest warriors Tigernach had. Thurgest was a frequent visitor to these shores, and we spent most of the time marching up and down the coast trying to catch his men. I regret all of that, for it was time that I could have spent with you."

He looked at his children's faces but saw no emotional re-action, as if anyone could have been telling them that story. However, he had opened up his heart and this was the only chance he would get to reconcile with his children. He decided to carry on.

"However, one day Thurgest came back to our shores in strength. That raid was a brutal onslaught, with flames devouring villages, sacred monasteries desecrated, and women and chil-dren mercilessly dragged into the chains of slavery across the bay if not left for dead. Tigernach seethed with rage, and under

Malachy's relentless pressure, he rallied his warriors to hurl the Norse invaders back into the depths of the sea. I was sent out with our village warband to avenge the stolen cattle and women who had been taken as slaves. Aodh and Babo were at our head.

"We stumbled upon a Norse warband near our village, only to discover they had butchered some of our kin. Fuelled by wrath, we pursued them relentlessly. The Norse fled in disarray, but their numbers swelled as their warbands united. In our fury, we pressed on, becoming increasingly isolated from Tigernach's main forces who had joined the pursuit. However, the Norse lured us forward into their deadly trap near the coast. I was severed from the main body of men along with several of my comrades. Surrounded, and after a brief struggle, a sharp blow to my head sent me crashing to the ground. Aodh, leading the remains of our band of warriors, managed to escape, leaving chaos and blood in his wake.

"The Norsemen dragged me feet first to their ship, my senses jolted awake by the jagged rocks scraping my back, and a vivid trail of blood marked the path of my suffering. Intent on displaying my humiliation, they considered strapping me to the prow of their vessel, but Thurgest, ever vain about his vessel, balked at the idea of blood marring its sides. Instead, they picked another unfortunate soul, less visibly marred. According to Thurgest, Aegir, their god of the sea, would have been insulted if they had sacrificed someone who was already half dead and would have cursed their ship.

"I was clinging to life, and they crudely bandaged my wounds, dragging me back to their homeland like a trophy, a grim spectacle to be paraded, interrogated, and sacrificed to their insatiable gods. After enduring their brutal torments, I longed for the release of a sacrificial end, a wish for the gods' mercy through a swift demise.

"I spent the majority of the sea voyage drifting in and out of consciousness. Whenever I regained consciousness, my relentless vomiting would provoke their impatience, and they would mercilessly beat me back into darkness.

"Upon docking at their harbour, I was dragged alongside the other captives, paraded like trophies before the jeering Norse inhabitants. We were met with contempt, spat upon, and hurled into pens like cattle, left to ponder our grim fates. Fever ravaged my body, and I was abandoned to die in the squalor. As I lay sick, I knew the fever had robbed me of my chance at a quick sacrificial death.

"Yet, a shadow of mercy flickered in the form of a kindly old man whose face has now faded from memory. He administered strange herbs that pulled me back from the brink of death. Eventually, I somewhat recovered and was handed over to a remote village on the fringes of the Norse settlement, where I tended sheep for the villagers. Encircled by colossal mountains, sculpted by the hands of giants who gouged the rocks from the deep valleys to raise these towering peaks, I was trapped. On one side, snow-draped mountains loomed, while on the other, the sea opened into a fjord and from there into the vast, deep blue sea. My body, still ravaged by illness, lacked the strength to flee, even if escape was possible.

"The villagers gave me a meagre allowance of food for shepherding the sheep. It was a grim existence, but preferable to perishing in the icy clutches of the mountains.

"I think several years passed and times in the village grew hard and they had to raise money for food. They had to sell off all their thralls and since I was a former warrior, if I could fight they would get a better price for me. I agreed to willingly carry a sword again if only to repay their kindness and give them as much money as I could with my sale. We went down to the port and they promised me that they would find me a good master who would look after me the way they had.

"We arrived down in the marketplace, and as soon as I was displayed for sale, I attracted the attention of Thurgest. He was the most powerful man in the town, and once he had set his eyes on me, no one dared to bid against him. He got me for a cheap price, and all the villagers got were a few goats.

"Thurgest had me brought to his huge farm, where I was immediately set to work in his fields. I quickly noticed that most of his male thralls of fighting age were all from Hibernia. It soon transpired that he would pick the best of us to fight for him on his raids to Hibernia and those who failed to be selected would be killed in the cruellest way possible in front of the other thralls to encourage us to do our best to avoid such a fate. Those who did Thurgest's bidding were well fed and those who exposed traitors or those who tried to sabotage their master's efforts ate even better. Any camaraderie we once had was soon shattered. Many a time I found myself locked in a thrall pen for days on the side of a freezing cold mountain because one of my fellow Hibernians decided to tell tales so they could get a better meal. Thurgest also publicly beat anyone who showed any defiance or who did not immediately follow his instructions. We were all made to watch such daily spectacles and we were not allowed to bow our heads or to look away.

"The nadir of my existence was when he lured me into the suffocating isolation of his lair, and the torment would begin, relentless and brutal, until you shattered. He'd strap me down on his infernal table, sometimes on my back, other times on my front, dictated by his cruel whims. He declared himself the dragon, a predator soaring mercilessly above the valleys, while I was nothing more than a feeble rabbit, desperate and doomed. He would hold a flame in his extended hand and then nestle some liquid in his mouth and spit it out onto the flames. The burning liquid would then land on my body and burn a hole in my skin. Then he would wield custom-forged metal claws, instruments of pure agony. Donning thick blacksmith gloves, he'd plunge those claws into a roaring fire, just like a dragon's claws, heating them until they glowed a menacing red, before plunging them into my flesh. The searing metal ripped through my skin, a vicious blend of scorching heat and razor-sharp edges, forcing anguished howls from my throat as unbearable pain consumed me. Sometimes, blessed unconsciousness would take me; other times, I would remain trapped in the horror. When the stench of charred flesh became too overwhelming, his men would douse me with icy water, and depending on the season, cast me mercilessly into the biting snow only to take me back in before I started to freeze."

Cathal turned and lifted up his shirt to show them his back. Finn and Affraic winced at the deep gullies of red pain etched up and down his skin.

"I spent many years on Thurgest's farms tilling his land and tending his sheep, more years than I would care to remember. Then he called for fighting men to join him in his raids. I jumped at the chance for anything was better than toiling away on a freezing cold mountainside and then getting tortured at a whim. At the very least I would be allowed to die. But I was foolish for Thurgest had to torture every thrall who volunteered to ensure they were loyal only to him. So I crashed upon the shores of Hibernia, a beast in the service of Thurgest."

Cathal held up his hands, and looked to the skies as tears slid down his cheeks.

"So here your father stands, the husk of the man who left you that fateful morning. My soul has long since departed, leaving a mangled man, bastard halfling born of the dragon Thurgest."

He looked glazed eyed at his children to see what emotions it had stirred in their hearts. Finn looked teary eyed but Affraic's face hardened. Emotions swirled around her head, devils chasing angels. She so wanted to believe her father was alive, how he had endured and beaten Thurgest and was coming home to his family. But this man was nothing compared to the tales her mother told of her father being a heroic warrior abandoned by all his friends. He was nothing like her father, she remembered when she was a child. This man made a mockery of her image of her father the hero, of all the time she spent waiting for him, of all the hope placed upon her memory of him. This was such a mockery, it must be a trick. She squeezed her hand into a fist. She would do whatever was needed to survive the Norse but she would be strong, just like her father the warrior. And this was not him. It could not be him. She rose and towered over Aodh. She threw an accusatory finger at Cathal.

"I know why you believed this man when he held a sword to your throat but you should have disposed of him when he had outlived his usefulness. My father is dead, be it in body or in soul. What use is this tramp to us? Is he someone who was imprisoned with our father and wishes to tell his story to manipulate us into taking him in? Even if he is who he claims to be, his own story of all the torture he was at the wrong end of tells me he is loyal to only one person, that is Thurgest.

"What am I supposed to do with him when I return to the Norse camp? If I claim him as my father, if I were to bet, then my money would be on us both to die. If you bring him back to Tigernach you are most likely bringing a spy into the camp. At best, he will murder Tigernach and then murder you. No good will come from believing this man's story. The best thing for everyone is to slit this man's throat here and now, say a prayer for our departed father and revert to my plan."

Cathal stared at his daughter. A tear came to his eye and his chin began to wobble. She was hard-hearted, just like her mother. However, Finn shared his father's tears. Finn was more soft-hearted than his sister and had prayed for the day his father would come home. He was ready to believe, for even if this was not what he imagined had happened to his father, he could still save his soul. The image of his father from the seer's vision flashed into his mind. He could see a faint resemblance between the silhouette and the man who stood before him. Was the seer saying he would be reunited with his father? Was that what the vision was supposed to mean? He stood up and reached out for his sister's hand.

"I do not know if this man is who he says he is, but the only thing we do know for certain is that he saved Aodh's life. We need to repay this man in whatever way he wishes."

Affraic pulled her hand away. Finn felt the cold air between them. He turned to Cathal for he had to find out if what he said was true.

"It is hard for us to believe you are actually our father. You are nothing like we remember you."

Cathal's head dropped.

"However," Finn continued, "let us repay the kindness you showed to Aodh. Do you wish to be free? We can point you in the direction of whatever you remember from your previous life in Hibernia or wherever you wish to go."

Cathal sighed and his shoulders dropped.

"My dream has come true and I have set eyes on my children once again. It was foolish to expect any more. I have no place here anymore, I will return to the Norse. But hopefully we shall meet once more before I die and I can make up for all the time we lost out on."

Finn placed his hand on Cathal's shoulder. He unsheathed his sword from his scabbard. Cathal instinctively winced and cowered at the sight of the blade.

"Do not be afraid," Finn said as he held out the sword for Cathal to examine it. "I kept my father's sword and it gave me courage. I would charge at my mother when I was a child, claiming I was my father, the hero, come to slay the Norse. The sword took pride of place in the house all those years as we waited for our father's return. Do you recognise it?"

Cathal timidly leaned over and examined what he could see of the sword.

"It looks like a sword that I would have wielded. We were always poor so I could not afford the decorative sword of a champion, just the lowly one of a warrior defending his family."

"Pah," Affraic spat at her brother. "What do you expect him to say if you phrase it like that?"

Finn ignored her for he was basking in the awe of the thought that his father had returned.

"If you are my father, then you will rejoice when we get revenge on Tigernach and we may even kill Thurgest while we are at it. Escort my sister back to the camp but do not tell anyone who you think you are to her. If we find out you actually are our father, we will look after you."

Cathal's head dropped.

"I suppose that was the best I could have wished for. But make haste, for Thurgest will soon set his dogs on you. I have had their fangs on my legs many a time."

Affraic scowled for she was not happy with the arrangement her brother had made. She waved her fist at Cathal.

"If we are to go, let us go. If you are to slit my throat on the way, then let my ghost ever haunt the foolishness of my brother."

Finn went over and took her fist and unfolded her fingers until he could take her hand in his.

"I had my chance. Give our father this chance. Then we'll follow your plan."

Finn looked at her expecting her anger to dissipate, but got only scorn.

"It's about time. Oh, and I mean it," Affraic said as she jabbed her finger at her brother. "If he slits my throat, I'm coming back to haunt you."

She threw off Finn's hand and stormed off towards the Norse camp. Cathal gave a timid wave to his son in gratitude. He lowered his head and followed Affraic.

CHAPTER FIFTY-FOUR

FOR A DRINK OF WATER

ULTÁN STARED DOWN AT the shanty town camp that was ever expanding at the southern entrance of his father's hillfort. Even the constant rain had not put off the steady flow of women and children joining the camp. They even had a young Brehon camped with them, probably eager to make a name for himself ensuring the camp and its residents were protected under Brehon law. The camp was attracting a lot of attention especially from Malachy, the regional king. But Ultán had to stand and stare at the camp and listen to his father's ire.

"Why am I being subjected to this insult?" Tigernach spat. "The Norse have been raiding for years and no king has ever been able to drive them away for a sustained period of time, yet they camp outside my fort and they blame me?"

He threw his hands up in the air and turned and glared at his son looking for affirmation.

"They are just ignorant," Ultán mumbled, hoping that the conversation would end all the quicker if he just agreed with his father.

"But most of it is down to that damn woman," he said, pointing to the tent nearest the entrance to the gate of the fort. "What is her name, the wife of Cathal the mad-eyed or something like that?"

Ultán cringed for as soon as his father had named the perpetrator of all the unrest he knew the blame would soon settle on him. He had made too big a show of trying to woo her daughter Affraic and then humiliating her brother Finn when she spurned his advances.

"Gormlaith has indeed been troublesome," he replied in a monotone, trying to take the emotion out of the conversation, or at least to dampen it down. "But she has the protection of Malachy."

"Damn him. He is doing this on purpose to undermine me. How long will her hunger strike continue? Surely she should be dead by now? It is going on far too long."

Ultán's eyes sparkled for in his mind was the seed of a plan. It was not particularly subtle, for that was not in his nature. It was, however, brutish, which most definitely was. It just needed some refinement.

"Some say that she is a witch who is possessed by the devil. It is he who apparently gives her the strength to get up every day without food to curse you and spread falsehoods on your very doorstep, ungrateful for the protections you provide her from the pending Norse menace."

Tigernach gave his son a sly grin.

"They will be a menace no more if my plan comes together and we rid ourselves of Malachy." He put his hand on his son's shoulder. "Take care of the problem of Gormlaith for me and we shall see who our real allies are when Malachy comes to enforce the Brehon law."

Ultán gave a cruel smile as his father turned and walked back into the fort. He would take that as approval of his plan.

Babo awoke to groans coming from Gormlaith's tent beside him. He sat bolt upright, then collapsed down again with agonising pains in his stomach. He was no stranger to such pains for as a soldier out on campaign he would often get stomach cramps and see the white worm eggs in his shit as the illness worked its way through him. But he seldom had it in such a debilitating way as he did today. He could tell from the groans from the next tent that Gormlaith probably had the same illness as him but somehow it did not make sense. She was very ill while he seemed to be not too bad in comparison. It could not have been the food, as she was still on hunger strike and he was not. It must have been something else, and it was up to him to find out what it was.

He forced himself onto his knees and crawled out of the tent. He raised himself to his feet and looked around him. Everywhere were people crawling around on their hands and knees or rolling around on the ground holding their stomachs. Some were lying still on the ground, some red-faced and some pale. He looked to the gate of the ring fort and there stood Ultán grinning away to himself. Babo cursed and knelt to open the flap of Gormlaith's tent.

"Gormlaith, Babo come for you," he said only to be met by a series of ever louder groans. Gormlaith was doubled over and rolling around the tent.

"Come into the air, you feel better."

"I feel like I'm bloody dying," Gormlaith said, her red face scrunched up in agony. "We've been poisoned. He must've poisoned the well. He no longer leaves us food, and it is the only source of water outside the fort. That's the only explanation for it. I hear the moans from outside and it sounds like we all have the same thing."

"Everyone needs you," Babo said, extending his hand to help Gormlaith to her knees so she could exit the tent more easily. "They need you to tell them what to do."

Gormlaith took his hand and, with a considerable amount of struggle, managed to ease herself out of the confines of the tent. Babo helped her to her feet. She saw a worse apocalypse than Babo did, for women and children came crawling to her feet, begging her to help them. Everywhere she turned, people fell out of tents and crawled on the ground begging for help until they eventually collapsed from exhaustion. She looked up at the gate of the fort to see Ultán and his men gathered there.

Her hand began to shake as she reached out to take Babo's arm.

"We have to go. It is not safe here now."

Babo rested his arms on her shoulders and looked up to the gate. Ultán's men were lighting fire torches. Babo slung Gormlaith's arm over his shoulder and he stumbled towards the woods but via the shanty town of tents so Ultán would not see where they were going.

"Babo leave now. Babo leave now," he said to everyone he passed, but most could only grab at him as they collapsed to the ground holding their stomachs.

Ultán stood in front of his men at the gate.

"It is a terrible thing I ask you to do this day but it is necessary if we are to survive. The witch Gormlaith has brought plague down on her followers, probably in a desperate hope that it will spread into the fort and kill my father, me, and all of you. We must not let this happen. We must be ruthless and burn out this plague and kill all that could spread it before it kills us all. I do not want to do this any more than any of you but we have to if we are to survive."

Ultán raised his lit fire torch.

"ARE YOU WITH ME, MEN?"

The men roared back. They charged into the camp with a ferocious battle cry, their eyes blazing with a savage fury. They unleashed their wrath on everything in sight, torching every tent until the night was ablaze with flames that devoured all possessions. Anyone unfortunate enough to cross their path was cut down without mercy, leaving the ground stained with the evidence of their relentless onslaught. Ultán had cast his die and now waited for them to fall.

CHAPTER FIFTY-FIVE

THE DEVIL REARS HIS UGLY HEAD

THE LIGHT BROKE OVER the top of the hill when Affraic and Cathal approached the locked gate of the Norse camp. Affraic had deliberately walked ten paces in front of Cathal and proudly held her head high and refused to look back. He was no father of hers. He was not her equal. The sooner she could get Einar to dispose of this impostor the better for everyone.

Cathal sighed and walked dejectedly behind her. His head was down between his shoulders looking at the ground, daring not to look to see if she was looking back at him. She stopped when she reached the gate and allowed him to walk in front of her for he had a better chance of being recognised.

"I see the Hibernian dogs have returned," the guard scoffed from the watchtower. "And he has brought himself back a bone."

"I would be careful how you refer to me or else you will answer to Einar," Affraic shouted back up.

"Let's see what he says about his woman going feral, shall we?" the guard said with a smirk. "A lot has happened since you took to the woods."

Affraic sighed.

"Just open the gate. It is too cold to stand here and listen to your puerile jibes."

The guard laughed.

"You may find my company pleasant compared to what awaits you inside. But who am I to deny the request of a beautiful young woman?"

Affraic frowned, folded her arms and refused to acknowledge the guard in the tower above her head. She waited impatiently as the gates were slowly opened and marched straight through, ignoring those who had opened the gate for her. They laughed as she stormed past.

"Where are we going?" she called over her shoulder to Cathal, not slowing her brisk pace or looking back.

"Look at the harbour," Cathal said as fear shivered down through his voice.

Affraic looked to the harbour and she gulped. The harbour was now full of Norse ships with more sailing across the white seahorse waves of the bay to join their compatriots. Warriors marched up the hill, weary but jubilant. The two thrall breakouts her brother had been part of had only temporarily emptied out the pens for lines of new slaves were being marched up the hill to replace those who had been lost or killed.

"It must be Thurgest returning," Cathal said as he caught up with his daughter for what must have been the first time since they left Finn and Aodh. Affraic froze, for nothing was a greater threat to her plans than Thurgest's return.

"I must find Einar," she muttered.

"I would try the port," Cathal said, pointing towards it. His hand shook in the air. "If he is anywhere he is there, for Thurgest is the centre of power."

Affraic wondered if his hand always shook or if he knew something she did not. But they were here and nothing would be achieved until she found Einar. Everything would be all right when she found Einar. They proceeded down towards the port until they met some of the warriors who smirked and laughed at Cathal.

"Is the Hibernian dog returning to his master?" one of them said as he leaned in towards Cathal and smirked in his face.

"Is Thurgest there?" Cathal said, pointing to the harbour trying to ignore their jibes.

"Sniff him out, did you?"

"Is he there?" Cathal asked again, a little firmer.

"He is holding court, asking questions about what happened when he was gone. Doubtless he will ask what you were doing in the woods with Einar's woman," the Norse said as he smirked again.

"Thank you," Cathal said as he walked on.

Affraic tilted her head and pursed her lips as she also stared at Cathal and his strange reactions to the Norse. But Cathal also ignored her and quickened his pace as he walked towards the harbour ignoring everyone and everything around him. Affraic followed, but her steps became more cautious as her mistrust of

Cathal grew and grew. But she walked on for her best hope lay in Einar.

When Cathal reached the entrance to the harbour the Norse warriors were streaming down for an audience with the returned Thurgest. A crowd had gathered on the common ground in front of the great hall which was still under construction. Cathal weaved his way through the crowd completely forgetting that Affraic was ever behind him. He squeezed between the shoulders of two burly Norsemen until he was in the front row.

Affraic cursed Cathal as he took off towards the great hall. She slapped her hands on her thighs and stood with her hands on her sides. Then a shiver went down her spine. What if this had been a ruse all along and he was weaselling his way back through the crowd so he could tell tales to Thurgest? If that were the case, it would be up to Einar to use up some of his credit with his master to plead for a quick death for her, probably to be hanged on the docks. She instinctively stroked her neck to soothe such perceived pain. She set out after Cathal, calling his name, but it was his turn to ignore her. She, too, wriggled her way to the front. The eager-eyed Cathal was several people along from her.

Thurgest, grinning smugly, sat on a wooden throne especially made for him and brought out from the half-finished great hall. There was a fresh scar on his cheek and his hair was grey and matted. The crowds that surrounded him shared his jovial mood, sporting scars of battle and the weathered appearance of men having just gotten off a ship straight from battle. They were especially jovial because it was time to publicly distribute the spoils of war. Einar stood on the right-hand side and smiled when Thurgest looked his way. But Affraic saw his shifty glances from side to side when Thurgest was not looking. She estimated that Thurgest did not know what went on in his absence and Einar feared his reaction when he found out.

Thurgest raised his mug to be filled with ale and smiled at those around him. He looked tired and bleary-eyed from a night of hard sailing having just come off campaign. He looked out at the crowds of his warriors cheering him on and singled one out for special attention.

"Cathal, my dog. Your master has returned."

Cathal gave an almost embarrassed smile. Thurgest then signalled to the ships docked at the port and the prisoners were forced to the port side of the boats to see what would happen next.

"Cathal," Thurgest said, his voice now slightly stern. "Your master has returned. Don't make me wait."

The front row of men stood back to leave Cathal exposed. Cathal stood transfixed, staring at Thurgest yet unable to move. His body went rigid and a visible sweat broke out on his forehead. Affraic furrowed her brows and narrowed her eyes for she was perplexed as to what was going on. But she could not keep her eyes off it.

Thurgest waited patiently until his audience of prisoners had been properly lined up so they all could see. He then reached behind him and took a large collar with a heavy chain from one of his aides. He lifted up the chain so the collar dangled beneath it where everyone could see.

"Hibernian dog, your master is waiting for you."

Still, Cathal did not move. He squeezed his eyes shut only to open them and still see Thurgest holding up the dog collar. Something inside him kept him rooted to the spot as if it were the last piece of resistance left in his soul. Thurgest snarled and signalled to his aide who secretly passed him something. Cathal's eyes bulged as he strained to see what it was.

"Cathal, do we need to show everyone how I train my dogs?" Thurgest held up his claws and scraped the air with them. He did so with the cruellest of grins.

Cathal's hands shook, and soon fear infected his whole body. A wet patch appeared at his groin. He slowly walked forward as if he were under a magic spell, which compelled his feet to move forward in exaggerated steps one at a time. He found himself standing before Thurgest, who raised an eyebrow. Cathal fell to his knees and bowed his head. Thurgest placed the collar around his neck and tied it so it was firmly on, but did not quite choke Cathal. Thurgest tugged on the chain so he was cheek to cheek with Cathal. Cathal's heart almost jumped out of his chest.

"Tell me, what has been going on here when I was gone?" Thurgest said with a guttural growl. Cathal could not stop the words rushing out of his mouth.

"The... the Hibernians came and raided and freed the thralls. Einar's woman then fled into the woods to plot with her brother to overthrow the Hibernian king Tigernach. I led her back here... like a good dog."

Thurgest slapped him across the back of the head with the chain.

"You can be a good dog and sit quietly by my feet while I greet some of your compatriots. We shall deal with Einar and his woman later."

Einar cursed as Thurgest's men grabbed him and forced him to stay and watch. Affraic in turn cursed for it had not taken long for her to be proved right about her so-called father. She turned to escape into the crowd but she could feel hands crawl across her back and grab her elbows. She was firmly held in place by Thurgest's men. She too would be forced to watch and think about her own fate. Thurgest signalled to his men on the boat that he wished to see the prisoners he had taken in his last campaign.

A series of Hibernian lords and kings were paraded off the ships and forced to kneel in front of Thurgest. For those he wished to make allies of, he held out his ring for them to kiss. They all kissed the ring until one brave soul took it upon himself to spit on his hand. Thurgest sat back and smiled as an aide handed him a cloth to wipe himself clean. Then he gave a swift tug on Cathal's chain.

Cathal pounced on the kneeling man. He barely had a chance to lift his arms before Cathal swatted them aside, his teeth bared like a beast descending upon prey. Cathal sank his teeth into the man's head with savage force, tearing into the flesh and ripping off half an ear. Blood erupted in a crimson torrent, splattering across Cathal's face in a macabre mask. The man's scream pierced the air as he clutched at his mutilated ear, but Cathal was relentless. Fists rained down in an unstoppable storm, brutal and unyielding, until the man collapsed under the barrage. Cathal showed no mercy, delivering a flurry of vicious kicks, his foot an unceasing hammer against the man's skull. Each strike reverberated with sickening finality until the man lay motionless. Standing over the lifeless body, Cathal panted heavily, his body trembling, eyes wild and blazing with an unquenchable frenzy, drenched in the blood of his conquest.

"Good dog," said Thurgest, and yanked on the chain so that Cathal once more sat at his feet still trying to get his breath back.

"Next prisoner, please," and Thurgest signalled to his men.

There was no more resistance after that.

The Hibernian lords and kings were all held in one section of the meeting area surrounded by armed guards. Thurgest's scribes waited patiently for the meeting to be over for their job was to note and sort the pledges Thurgest had acquired into men, land and ships. The Norse warriors were by now ecstatic as one by one their leaders went forward and bragged about their exploits in battle and how many Hibernian warriors and priests had been killed. It looked and sounded as if they had won a resounding victory.

But Thurgest was not paying attention for he was deep in thought. His dog had proved faithful but provided him with some potentially alarming information about what had happened when he had left his nephew in charge. If this had been anyone else, he would have been thrown straight out into the square and after apologising in front of everyone and begging for his life he would have been left to the mercy of Thurgest's dog. But this was Einar, his brother's son. Not only did he trust him as he had always been honest and faithful, to kill him in such a humiliating way would be the final insult to his brother, especially after he had taken their father. No, he would have to deal with this in private and if there were any serious repercussions because of it, then they would have to be made public. He raised his hand into the air.

"Please, stop with your tales and save them for the feast. Slaughter the cows and prepare the fires. The celebrations will start straight away. We will have one day of celebrations."

There was a groan from some of the men for the length of the celebrations did not match the tales of glory.

"Do not complain, men. We are but one fort in a sea of enemies. What if we celebrated for three days and the raiders who took our thralls returned and burned the fort to the ground with us all in it? No, we must be secure in this fort and on this land before we can let our guard down in such a manner. The victory we won was great, but it was not decisive. Our enemy still left the field in reasonable order. They will be looking for vengeance, but the least we have is a day. Enjoy yourselves, men, and I will join you soon for unfortunately I have other business to attend to."

The men cheered. Thurgest leaned over to his aide.

"Bring me Einar and his woman to the great hall to meet me."

With that, Thurgest got up and left.

CHAPTER FIFTY-SIX

A BARGAIN WITH THE DEVIL

EINAR AND AFFRAIC STOOD in the half-built great hall with their heads bowed. Rain dripped from the rafters as the roof and some of the building had been damaged in the recent raid and Einar had not had the time to repair it yet. It was as if Thurgest had forced Einar to stand in his own failure and explain himself.

Thurgest sat on his throne, which his guards had carried in from the meeting circle. He stared at the ground, fatigue having set in from several weeks campaigning, and braced himself for any potentially difficult decisions he may have to make. Cathal sat at his feet with the collar around his neck and the chain tied to a round ring, which was specially added to the throne. His eyes were wild and distant, his skinny frame taut and upright as if his chain could be tugged at any moment. Thurgest was surrounded by his bodyguards in case Einar tried to kill him so that he could free himself. Thurgest finally raised his head.

"So, it takes a dog to tell me what my own nephew has been up to?"

Einar grimaced. His mouth went dry but the last thing he needed was not to be able to defend himself. He swallowed hard and summoned up what courage he could.

"It was not like that. You had just returned and got off the ship. You and your men were ecstatic. It was not the time to mention what petty raids I had to swat away. We are still here and we are strong. You won a great victory, which was not mine to spoil by reporting the exploits of a few rebels. It was no time to engage in recriminations based on the evidence of a dog."

Thurgest gave him a cruel grin.

"Oh, whether it is the right time or not is the sole preserve of Thurgest. I don't like things being done behind my back and having to rely on a spy to tell me. Do I, dog?" and Thurgest yanked on Cathal's chain.

"No, you do not, master. But you still want to know everything the dog sees, good, bad or indifferent."

Cathal stared up at Thurgest with a look of abject terror, waiting for confirmation that his answer was the correct one to give.

"Good Dog," Thurgest said before setting his stare onto Einar again. "If we have to hear any more evidence from Dog, there may be hell to pay. And we wouldn't like that, would we, Dog?"

"No, master," and Cathal turned around and stared at Einar.

Affraic stared at Cathal and swallowed hard in an attempt to hide the utter contempt she held him in. How could this shadow of a man, who was more like a frightened beast, have ever been her father, let alone still lay claim to that title? How could she have let Finn persuade her to trust this man who had led her straight into the arms of the enemy? She had been vindicated but she most certainly wished she had not been.

Thurgest arched an eyebrow.

"You hold a special kernel of contempt in your eye for my dog, young woman. Why is that so?"

Affraic gritted her teeth but she knew she had to give some sort of answer.

"I am wondering how this contemptible beast was ever a man."

Thurgest paused. He yanked on Cathal's chain to get him to rise. Cathal stood and broke into a sweat. Thurgest signalled to him to drop his trousers. Cathal's jaw dropped. Thurgest gave an almighty tug that almost decapitated Cathal. He dropped his pants and exposed himself to Affraic who reeled back and shielded her eyes.

"Yes, definitely a man," Thurgest said as he gave a cruel grin.

Cathal pulled up his pants and trousers and hung his head in shame. Thurgest examined Affraic's facial expressions and then held his finger in the air.

"No, that is not the truth. Now, tell me the truth before I have to ask the dog for I have a feeling the dog knows what it is. And he knows what will happen if he does not tell the truth."

Affraic clenched her mouth firmly shut as the guards who held her squeezed her arms to encourage her to talk. She glared at Cathal. *If ever you were my father, do not reveal this secret, be it true or not.* Thurgest grinned at Affraic's defiant face. He pulled on Cathal's chain.

"What's the secret, dog?"

But Cathal turned his head and looked the other way.

"So you still have some spirit left to defy me." He pulled so hard on the chain that they ended up cheek to jowl. "What is the secret, dog?"

"I cannot say. Please do not make me."

"CLAWS."

The aide immediately placed the claws in front of Cathal's face.

"What is the secret, dog? Or if you will not tell, face my wrath."

Cathal shook his head and started blubbering. Thurgest threw him to the ground and began to beat him with the claws and drag them down his back, which was soon a mess of blood and fragments of shirt. Cathal howled in pain but would not talk.

"Stop, stop," exclaimed Affraic extending her hand towards Cathal. "He claims to be my father."

"Claims?" Thurgest said raising an eyebrow. He yanked hard on Cathal's chain until he was beneath his knees. "Are you or are you not this woman's father?"

Cathal gave the faintest of nods. Thurgest laughed.

"That's more like it, Dog. See how much easier it is when you tell the truth? Now, if you tell me what you were up to with your daughter, then I'll send you to the healer. If not, I will roll you in salt and leave you outside until you beg me to bring you back in. And you had better beg quickly for only the gods know what will happen to you if I am forced to get a new dog."

Cathal bawled as the memories of the pain and abuse he suffered beneath those talons flooded into his mind and blinded him heart and soul. All he could think about was making the pain stop.

"I found her plotting in the woods with her brother," he said. He gulped to get some lubrication down his dry throat. "He had just assaulted the camp and freed all the thralls. I followed them there for I had captured an old friend of mine and he told me of them and as he bargained for his life he said he would take me to meet them."

Thurgest sat back and kicked Cathal away.

"I don't know how to take this, dog. Have my claws failed me so that you would put your own interests before mine? Or is it that the dog still has a bit of cunning left in him and all of this was a big ruse to expose this plot against me?"

Cathal threw himself at Thurgest's feet.

"It was all a ruse, master. It was all a ruse. Look before you. I have betrayed my own daughter and she stands here before you at your mercy. Your dog is faithful, your dog is faithful."

Thurgest carefully undid the chain from the steel ring and held up the end as he decided what to do with Cathal. He held the chain out and passed it to his aide.

"I am feeling a tad generous today for I cannot be cruel all of the time. Take him to the healer and let his daughter know her dog of a father has taken all the kindness and generosity on offer today."

The aide nodded and yanked hard on the chain, dragging Cathal across the room to the door.

Thurgest now set his eyes on Einar. Einar glared back at him in defiance and struggled with the guards holding him.

"I played no part in whatever plot you are thinking happened, Thurgest," Einar said firmly, knowing that Thurgest reacted best to a show of strength. "Whatever plot Affraic had with her brother, I had no part in it. All I did was faithfully defend the camp twice from assault, beating them off twice and making an example of all those thralls who chose to run."

It was Affraic's turn to struggle at what she saw was a betrayal.

"He claims to be part of no plot? Pah!" and Affraic spat towards him. "He was happy to plot with me to overthrow Tigernach as long as he could take his lands. I was in the woods seeking my brother's help to overthrow Tigernach. That coward promised he would marry me if I helped him take the lands."

Thurgest sat back and raised an eyebrow.

It was Einar's turn to break into a sweat.

"I only entered into this plot on your behalf, Thurgest. The lands would be taken in your name."

"And why would I want to plot to take something I could just steal or destroy?" Thurgest said, raising his hands and shrugging his shoulders.

Affraic realised she may be on to something and there could be a way out. It may also be a trap, but then again, she was dead anyway.

"The people hate Tigernach much more than they hate you. If you freed them from him then they may come willingly, which makes it much easier for you to establish a colony that will survive. Once you are settled, there are so many rival kings that at least one of them will ally with you, and then you are established in Hibernian politics, and the island could be yours if things go your way."

Thurgest stroked his chin.

"I can see why you fell for her, Einar. She is devious as well as beautiful."

Thurgest stood up and raised his chin.

"Young woman, I grant you your wish in advance. You shall marry Einar tomorrow. If you fail to bring me Tigernach's lands you both shall die for betraying me. Be thankful, Einar, that your woman's cunning has saved you."

Thurgest turned to his aides.

"Lay out a feast and invite the colony. Tomorrow we have a wedding and I will introduce the colony to my father."

CHAPTER FIFTY-SEVEN

SHADOWS AND PAIN

THE ANCIENT OAK WOODLANDS loomed above them, the gnarled branches reaching out like twisted fingers, grasping at the fading light. The canopy of leaves, once a vibrant green, now cast an eerie shadow over the forest floor, as if the trees themselves were conspiring to keep the outside world at bay. Babo gently lowered Gormlaith to the ground. Her breathing was shallow and laboured. He brushed a stray lock of hair from her face, his calloused hands trembling with a mixture of exhaustion and fear.

The forest seemed to pulse with a life of its own, a hidden energy that thrummed just beneath the surface. The air hung heavy with the scent of damp earth and decaying leaves, a pungent reminder of the cycle of life and death that governed these woods. The silence was deafening, broken only by the occasional rustling of unseen creatures scurrying through the undergrowth. Babo scanned the surroundings, his eyes straining to penetrate the gathering darkness. The trees seemed to close in around them, their trunks twisting and turning in a dizzying dance, as if they were alive and aware of the intruders in their midst.

Gormlaith stirred, her eyelids fluttering open. "Babo," she whispered, her voice barely audible above the sound of her own ragged breathing. "Where are we?"

Babo leant over her and took her hand in his.

"You no die on Babo," he said, tears welling up in his eyes.

"You need to take me to a healer," Gormlaith croaked, holding her stomach as it twitched in pain. "That little rat poisoned us and pretended it was plague as an excuse to kill us. I need to live to get revenge for all those he killed. Get me to a healer, then you need to get Finn."

"Healer in the mountains. You still be alive in the mountains?"

Gormlaith lay on her back and racked her brains. *What will keep me alive until I get to the Wicklow mountains? The gods provide for everything, especially in their sacred woods.*

"Leave me here and fetch me some dandelion leaves and some feverfew from the woods. Boil them in some water and give them to me. That should keep me going until we get to the mountains."

Babo nodded, took off his cloak and gently placed it over Gormlaith.

"Stop fussing and go. I'll be dead before you tuck me in properly."

Babo nodded and ran off into the woods.

Gormlaith lay on the ground almost perfectly still for her stomach was still gripped by pain. She could still hear the screams and shouts from the camp for they could not have travelled much of a distance given how much discomfort she was in. She lay on the ground and stared at the tree branches that lined the way to the sky and prayed to whatever gods she could think of to come and appear before her, bless her and grant her salvation.

She woke to the sound of more screaming, and this time it sounded much nearer to her. As the paralysis crept up her body, Gormlaith's fear intensified. Her heart raced in her chest, pounding against her ribs like a caged bird desperate to escape. She tried to take deep breaths to calm herself, but even her lungs seemed to be succumbing to the poison's grip. Each breath became shallower and more laboured, as if an invisible hand was squeezing the air from her body.

The darkness pressed in around her, suffocating and oppressive. The towering trees loomed over her, their gnarled branches reaching out like skeletal fingers ready to pluck her soul from her helpless body. The rustling of leaves and the creaking of wood filled her ears, mingling with the distant howls and shrieks of unseen creatures lurking in the shadows.

She dared not cry out even if she could. She felt her legs grow numb and heavy, as if possessed by a dark demon who sat on top of her waiting to make a sacrifice of her to his master. The demon spread up her body like a malignant mist slowly subsuming her body. She moved her limbs with much sweat and struggle but to her consternation, also noise.

She heard a crack of a twig in the distant wood. She froze, daring not to move as she felt so vulnerable and did not want to give away her position. Tears welled up in her eyes and rolled down her nose. The sensation tickled her face and she wished to scratch to relieve the itch. But she could barely lift her hand above her head. She lost control of her arm and it fell to the ground with a thud. At that moment all went silent around her. Then came again the rustling in the bushes as if it were a wolf working up the courage to search for the scent its nose deemed easy prey. Gormlaith became sleepy and even keeping her eyes open became a struggle. She began to recite her prayers once more as the darkness began to close in. She could still see the sky. Little droplets of rain fell through the spindly branches. They splashed on her cheeks and she could feel the cold when the raindrop exploded and dripped down the side of her face. She wished to scratch but could only cry because she still had feelings and she was still alive.

She heard a loud yelp from somewhere beneath her feet. She could hear a scuffle of some description and the thud of a heavy body off a tree trunk. There was silence. Then the mad scramble of feet that came nearer and nearer. Fingers forced themselves into her mouth followed by the slime of leaves and wet dirt. A hand was placed firmly beneath her chin. She could not swallow. She could not swallow. Her throat felt numb. Her mouth was yanked open. Her mouth was flooded with water. She shot up spluttering and coughing. The hand gripped her jaw again and she swallowed. She vomited and amongst the white foam was forest dirt. She immediately began to feel better. She lifted her head.

"Babo thought you were dead."

"Gormlaith thought I was dead too," she replied in a husky, worn voice. "Not as dead as the wolf you just killed over there." She pointed to the twitching body of a large adult wolf in a bush not ten strides away from her feet.

"Must go now before Ultán comes."

"Wait a minute," Gormlaith said before circling her palms in the dirt around her and then lifting it to her face and swallowing all she had gathered. She threw up all over her legs which had not yet quite shaken off the poison. She wiped her face and grinned.

"Now I'm ready."

CHAPTER FIFTY-EIGHT
NOT THE TIME FOR ROMANCE

EINAR AWOKE A BAG of shivers, aches and pains. It was far from the first time he had awoken a prisoner, nor even the first time he had slept in a thrall pen. But it was the first time he had done so with Affraic. She awoke shortly after him and wore a grin completely out of place for the predicament they were in. She rose from her heap in the corner, came up behind Einar and threaded her arm beneath the crook of his elbow.

"What are you so happy about today?" snarled Einar, shaking her arm off.

Affraic stuck her chin out and gave him a cute smile.

"Can I not be happy on our wedding day?"

Einar stood back and shook his head.

"You clearly don't know what this means. He means to wed us together so our destinies are intertwined."

"What's wrong with that?" Affraic said, her smile not diminishing.

"That means that if we fail, I die. As soon as I die, you die, for you are coming to Valhalla or wherever with me."

Affraic shrugged her shoulders.

"That is the same situation I was in when I was a thrall. The only difference is that we will be man and wife. It sounds like you are afraid, for you have become no better than a thrall."

Einar shook his head.

"But when you were a thrall, if I died, because you are beautiful another would have taken you and you would have lived. It would be luck if you had a second kind master but you have your charms and I'm sure you would have quickly had him wrapped around your finger."

Affraic snarled and slapped him in the face.

"Stop feeling sorry for yourself. You are still alive and you still have a chance with Thurgest. Don't fail. You have your fate in your own hands which you should be grateful for. Don't fail."

Einar rubbed his cheek.

"You know what they will do to you before they throw you on my funeral pyre?"

Affraic's chin stiffened and she slammed her hands on her hips.

"No, I do not. Nor will I ever, for you are not going to fail. Now put on a happy face for your wedding and pretend that Thurgest has given you a massive opportunity. For he has." Affraic's mood suddenly shifted from hailstones to sunshine. "For count yourself lucky. He has allowed you to marry me."

Einar tutted and looked to the heavens. Luckily for him the guard opened the gate before Affraic could slap him again.

"Come on, lover boy," the guard said as he beckoned him out. "Thurgest is waiting for you."

CHAPTER FIFTY-NINE

A DOG, A WEDDING AND A FUNERAL

EINAR AND AFFRAIC WERE paraded from the thrall pens all the way past the docks and up to the entrance of the great hall. Einar made sure he wore a smile and waved to everyone. He could see the faces change with confusion. Was this an actual wedding presided over by Thurgest or the prelude to one of his numerous sadistic tortures? Einar was not going to give them the pleasure of knowing.

They stopped in front of the great hall. Thurgest sat there as he did the day before on his throne. Today he looked rested and wore a huge grin. He signalled to his men. Einar and Affraic were stripped naked and then dressed in white robes and a crown of flowers was placed on Affraic's head.

"There, that is a much better way to dress for your wedding day. But today we have a special guest of honour." Thurgest held up the empty ring attached to his chair.

The warriors behind Thurgest parted and Cathal was led out with a collar and chain around his neck. He had been dressed in a red tunic and trousers, the brightest they could find so no one could miss who he was.

"And here we have the father of the bride," and Thurgest stood up and threw out his hands so the attention of the crowd turned to Cathal. The crowd turned to laughing and jeering and Cathal's face turned as red as his tunic.

"I will have a post with a ring on it erected outside your marital home so your father-in-law can come and visit." Thurgest laughed at his own joke and the crowd swiftly joined in the laughter.

Einar and Affraic's eyes remained firmly on the ground. Affraic slipped her hand into Einar's for she now knew what he meant. Now, they only had each other and it would be a battle just to survive.

"Normally, we would have a feast for the wedding of at least three days, but we all know the union before us is an insult to the gods, for it is not for love or lands that Einar here before us gets married today, but as a test of loyalty. He has taken it upon himself to conspire with the Hibernians while I was out fighting the same Hibernians for all of our glory and enrichment."

A ripple of boos went around the crowd.

"But now, he has seen the error of his ways and agreed to this marriage so he can conclude the same agreement he had with the Hibernians, but this time for the benefit of all of us."

The crowd cheered and jeered in equal measure.

"I will not insult the gods by involving them in this marriage," Thurgest continued, "but dog here will witness the consummation of the marriage and confirm it to us all before the lovers are cast out into the wilderness. If they do not return within a week with some good news or we hear a whiff of treachery, dog and his pack will be sent out only to return when they have chopped off their heads."

The crowd roared their approval.

"So, I declare thee wed and I hope you see the error of your ways and live a long, happy life. Now leave us, Einar, and stand and wait and think of a way you fulfil your plans and earn the forgiveness of Thurgest."

The crowd roared and Einar and Affraic were dragged away. Thurgest raised his hand in the air.

"And now, for the main ceremony. The consecration of my father."

The crowds parted, revealing six Norse carrying a large, highly decorated box, suspended between two long wooden poles. The procession wound its way through the harbour, the rhythmic thud of boots on the hard-packed earth echoing off the wooden buildings. The box, adorned with intricate carvings of battle scenes and mythical beasts, swayed gently with each step. Atop the casket lay the fallen warrior's sword, its hilt gleaming with precious stones and its blade polished to a mirror sheen. The crowds reeled back in shock, for it was well known that Thurgest's father had been a great warrior, greater even than Thurgest, but you would not say it to his face. But his father had long been dead, and his actual funeral was cast into legend for its extravagance. Yet, here he was, to be buried again in some colony in a far-off land, clinging on to its existence. No one knew what the gods would think of this reburial, never mind his family, and many feared this funeral would only bring curses down upon them.

Thurgest sat and looked at the faces of the warriors of his colony and noted those whose expression said they doubted him the most. He waved his hand and his aides and the warriors gathered the wood that was stored near the great hall and began to build a pyre in the middle of the meeting circle. By the time the procession had made it to the meeting circle the pyre was complete. Thurgest rose to his feet.

"We Norse say if you die on the land and you are buried there then it is your own land. However, I have no intention of dying myself."

A ripple of laughter broke the mood of shock in the crowd.

"But I have the next best thing. In the box you see before your very eyes are the bones of my father. Do not think for one moment that I disturb him in Valhalla for he loved war, loved conquest, and the shores of Hibernia were among his favourite upon which to blood his sword."

The surrounding warriors cheered, especially the older ones who remembered his father well.

"I sent my loyal man Torstein back home to fetch my father, who had some more conquering to do, albeit from the grave. My father will for the second time face the funeral pyre. The gods will welcome him in once more to Valhalla but this time with even more glory than before. Because when he is once more reduced to ashes he will be buried in Hibernian soil. His ashes will claim this soil for his people. For his ashes declare that this land is now ours for he is buried in it."

The men roared their approval once they realised Thurgest's plan. The casket was now placed upon the flames, and the men gathered and threw their mead and other flammable materials to help it burn. Einar looked at Affraic, both of them bound at the hand, and gulped. For he knew some of the consequences of Thurgest's actions. His brothers would come and with armed men, for they would be insulted at the desecration of their father's grave to serve Thurgest's naked political ambitions. But he also noticed how it reinvigorated the men. Einar could only hope he survived the night to see what being cast into the wilderness would bring.

CHAPTER SIXTY

A WATCHFUL EYE

AFFRAIC AND EINAR WERE escorted by Thurgest's men through the revellers with Cathal following behind. Drunken Norse shouted, cursed, raised their tankards and slammed them together as they celebrated Affraic and Einar's marriage and the burial of Thurgest's father. They paid little attention as the newlyweds passed by in front of them for they were more interested in the revelry than the bride and groom themselves. Affraic held her head high while Einar's fake smile was waning. The guards smirked as they poked him in the back.

"I hope you are going to be quick about this. We need to get back to the celebrations."

Einar had kept his emotions in check all evening but this goading from these low-ranking Norse proved to be the breaking point.

"Do you know who I am?" Einar growled back at them.

They just laughed for it was not often they got to ridicule nobility and get away with it.

"The husband-to-be and Thurgest's plaything," the leader of the guards said. "Whoever you think you are is far across the oceans. The best you can do now is do what he wants and then get out of Thurgest's attention while remaining alive. Take that from a friend. I have served with your father and know him well."

Einar glared at him but kept his thoughts to himself out of respect for the man's friendship with his father. If any of them could be made into an ally it was him.

They arrived at one of the recently completed timber huts.

"Here's where you'll do the deed," the leader said. "There's a bed in the back room and the men will arrange some chairs so we can be witnesses for Thurgest will want details. Now get in there and do what you have to do to prepare yourselves for tonight you have an audience, willing or unwilling."

Affraic held her head aloft and marched straight in. Einar held back, red-faced, and his head hung low. Thurgest had meant to humiliate him and he no longer had the strength to resist. Cathal followed behind, grim-faced, looking at the ground. The guard leader placed his hand on his chest and stopped him in his tracks.

"Not you. The master has something special prepared for you."

Affraic and Einar were forced to undress in the main room. They stood naked before the guards who smirked and sneered.

"You'd be lucky to get a willing woman with a body as good as mine," Affraic said as she glared at the guards with contempt.

"We'll be the judge of that. We'll see what you can do with what you've got soon enough," one of the guards sneered.

The leader opened the door of the bedroom.

"You can come in now. We have it prepared for you."

Affraic and Einar were shoved into the room, Einar pushing back as he took offence at the amount of force used. The room was small, dimly lit with a bed at the far end and two posts in the centre that supported the roof. Between the posts at the end of the bed sat an almost tearful Cathal, about to endure his greatest humiliation. He had his collar around his neck and two chains going from either side of the collar to a metal ring on each post.

"Thurgest said he had to watch," the leader said matter-of-fact-ly, "and if you do not, I am to poke your eyes out."

He then turned to Affraic and Einar.

"Well then, get on with it. The rest of us have a feast to get to."

Einar's cheeks flushed and he began to sweat. Affraic took his hand.

"Pretend they are not there," she whispered. "It'll be over with all the quicker. Don't show your anger for that is what they want."

Affraic climbed on top of the bad and lay down. She held her hand out.

"Come, Einar. It is only you and me."

The guards all laughed and Cathal looked to the floor. The glint of the candlelight on the blade of the leader's dagger fixed his gaze once more on his naked daughter. He was positioned so he could look right up the bed so he could see the very deed being done. But Einar became more and more angry as his manhood failed him.

"Come on, my love," Affraic whispered sweetly in his ear. "It is only you and me in our tent. All the noises and distractions are outside."

Still Einar struggled. He tried to inspire himself with his hand to no avail. He punched the bed in frustration.

"If you are not man enough then get off her and leave her to me," one of the guards said.

The rest of the guards all laughed.

Affraic rose and pushed Einar aside. She stood on top of the bed revealing her full nudity to all. The guards smirked but their heckles quietened. Cathal looked away to the side. Affraic walked down the bed and stood in front of Cathal, her private parts above his head.

"Look, you cowardly worm, who has the nerve to call yourself my father. Look into my womb."

Cathal looked up and balked at the sight.

"You may cower but it will be nothing to how you will cower in the future. A king will come from there and you all will bow to him. And he will despise you, man who calls himself my father. For I will tell him how low you have stooped. And he shall see how I have lived."

Affraic turned to all the Norse guards.

"Now, scum. Laugh all you want while you have the chance. Watch how kings are made."

She turned and slapped Einar on the arse and lay down on the bed.

"Come to me, kingmaker," Affraic cried.

Einar lay on top of her but still his manhood failed. She shoved him upwards with one hand and gave him an almighty slap across the cheek. The fire was in his eyes. Now he was in the mood to make kings.

CHAPTER SIXTY-ONE
INTO THE WILDERNESS

THE NEXT MORNING THE sunlight peered over the gate of the Norse enclosure that marked the doorway between the benefit of being protected by Thurgest and the dangers of the Hibernian wilderness. Einar and Affraic stood with their hands bound, but they had been given sufficient clothing both to survive the elements and to pass off as locals so they would not attract too much attention as they passed through the land. Einar recoiled from the hangover of a very poor night's sleep, as did Affraic, while those who surrounded them were hungover from the alcohol of Thurgest's feast.

Thurgest stood before him, picking at some annoyance in his ear, surrounded by his bodyguards. Torstein stood beside him and smiled smugly at Einar. He had taken over Einar's job of creating a town and was fortunate that his predecessor had laid some solid foundations. Cathal and the guards from the wedding night also stood beside Thurgest waiting to make their report.

"Was the wedding consummated last night?" Thurgest said with a smirk, looking directly at Cathal.

Cathal gave an embarrassed nod and the leader of the guards nodded in support.

"Good. Open the gate," Thurgest ordered as he rubbed his neck. "I wish to get back to my warm bed as soon as possible and not be standing out in this freezing mist."

The gates creaked open and the dark woods beyond unfolded before Einar. A mist crept along the land that would put shivers up the spine of the least believers in ghosts and spirits. But Einar tried to mute his reaction and show no fear for his best hope still lay in getting back into Thurgest's favour and he had not given up hope of doing so. Thurgest sighed, determined to keep any speeches short as he was serious about getting back to his bed.

"There lies the wilderness and any hope you have of redemption," he said, scratching away at his nose as it had become blocked in the cold of the morning. "You have a week before I set the dogs, or should I say your father-in-law, upon you. If you try to betray me, you, your wife and all her family and friends will be killed on sight by my men. You will be given safe passage for a week and then you become an outlaw. You are being given a fair chance despite your conniving. Believe it or not, I wish you every success, for your success is the success of the colony. Now go."

The guards cut the rope around Einar and Affraic's wrists and shoved them forward. Einar rubbed his wrists and looked Thurgest straight in the eye.

"I will not fail you."

He grabbed Affraic's hand and ran into the woods.

They ran and ran and ran until they were exhausted. Einar doubled over, panting heavily with his hands on his knees.

"Why did you run so far?" Affraic said between exaggerated gasps.

"Because," Einar said, now standing up, "you can never trust Thurgest, no matter what he says. I thought he might release his hounds. He always wants to keep you guessing what he is going to do, always to keep you frightened. But we must go far away from his camp, and you must lead. I only know the rivers as that is how Thurgest travels, so we must avoid them."

Affraic threw her hands up in the air and slapped her thighs for she was most tired, confused and frustrated.

"But you said that you wanted to get back in with him, and to do so, you need to be back at the camp within a week. How do you mean to achieve that if your plan is just to run away as far as possible?"

Einar advanced and took Affraic by the elbows.

"We must go and find your brother and whomever he was plotting against Tigernach with. We must take over their plans and use them for our own ends. But we must bring them along with us. Only by returning in a week to Thurgest with the support of the local Hibernians will we succeed in impressing him."

Affraic threw off Einar's grip.

"You mean betray my own brother? That would make me no better than my father."

"No," Einar pleaded. "Your brother seeks revenge and we can give it to him. Only we gain alongside him at the same time. I mean to create a situation where everybody wins, except the enemy we have in common. What's wrong with that?"

Affraic turned away to get a bit of respite to contemplate his plan. It did not sound like her brother would be a victim in all of this and they did have the same enemy.

"Come on then, and follow me," Affraic said. "I'm sure I can find him and convince him to help us."

It was her turn to take Einar by the hand and lead him forward.

They travelled for a day and a night and met some of the stragglers on the road fleeing south. That struck Affraic as being unusual, as to the south was the border between major kings, where bands of stragglers were treated with suspicion and prone to being set upon by the king's men or by bandits on the border. The normal safer route was to head north. They stopped to question some of the women and children as they fled past them.

"What are you running from?" Affraic asked. "Why do you not run north to come under the protection of Malachy?"

Affraic recoiled at the look of horror on the woman's face.

"Ultán, son of Tigernach, is possessed by some sort of madness. He declared the camp outside his father's fort where the women protested against him to be taken by plague and ordered his men to kill everyone. South seems so much safer."

"He would kill his own mother?" Einar interjected.

"Kill his mother?" repeated the woman. "I don't know about that, but I would not put it past him."

Affraic took hold of the woman's arm so she could not flee.

"Where are the menfolk? Surely there was someone there to protect you?"

"Most left with Malachy to fight the Norse, but rumour has it they were defeated. But some now occupy the woods near the fort. They are led by a boy from a nearby village and a band of men, whom he brags he freed from the Norse camp. He did not have the sense to flee so blinded was he by his mother's death."

"Who was his mother? What was her name?" Affraic grabbed both her arms and shook her hard.

The woman threw her off.

"It was Gormlaith if you must know. If you grab me like that again, you'll force me to take my dagger out from under my dress."

Affraic reeled back and put her hand to her face to try and stop the tears. Einar's head darted between the two women as he tried to decide who to deal with first. He held his hands out and pressed them downwards to encourage calm in the woman.

"We mean you no harm. We thank you for your information and wish you well on your way."

The woman scrunched up her face at Affraic's reaction but turned and ran after her companions who had stopped to wait for her. Einar then took hold of Affraic who collapsed into his arms and cried on his shoulder.

"I have had enough of horror and death without getting my revenge. Damn Ultán and his father to hell. Let us pick up our blades and send them there ourselves."

Einar released Affraic from his grip and looked into her tear-strewn eyes as he held her at arm's length.

"Do you know where we'll find your brother?"

"I have a fair idea, but if I'm wrong it won't take me too long to find him."

They set out in the opposite direction from the fugitives.

CHAPTER SIXTY-TWO

A CHOICE BETWEEN TWO DEVILS

FINN SLASHED AT THE bushes surrounding the clearing where they had taken refuge as he had to take out his fury on something.

"Aodh," he spat. "This is the final insult. He has insulted me all his life, lording it over me, stealing from my village, and he got away with it all because his father's men protected him. But no more, I say, no more. Revenge for my mother's death will be mine, and I will take his life with this very sword, or I will die trying."

Finn raised his blade to his face and examined the etches as if he were a man possessed. Aodh was unimpressed.

"You could have saved us the rest of your speech and just said you would die trying. We do not have the men to assault a hillfort and Tigernacht's bowmen will shoot us down before we even cross the empty space between the woods and his walls. Now sit, and let us use our brains instead of our brawn and think up a plan."

Aodh pointed to a spot on the fallen oak tree beside him and Finn threw himself down upon it like a petulant teenager. Aodh looked around the trees because he heard the cawing of the crows which had proliferated since they had settled in this one area and now seemed to circle them. Aodh pointed to a murder of crows that had occupied the branches above their heads.

"Look, death stalks us. They must have had a mighty feast today and in seeing us reckon they are in for a second helping."

Finn leapt from his seat.

"Shoo, shoo," he cried as he waved his sword around to frighten off the crows. He turned to Aodh once the crows had gone. "We must frighten off any bad omens that would discourage the men from fighting."

"Their hearts are already down," Aodh said. "After convincing them to attack the Norse camp I think there'll be no convincing them to assault Tigernach's hillfort. For one thing, you don't know how Malachy will react. In normal times, you would expect him to be happy at any misfortune that may strike at Tigernach, but these are not normal times. Malachy needs all the support he can get to hold off the Norse."

"Then what shall we do?" Finn howled as he threw his hands in the air. "If needs be I'll set off to kill Ultán myself."

At that moment there was a rustling in the bushes and all leapt to their feet and took up their weapons. Affraic and Einar stumbled forth. Finn immediately rushed forward and raised his blade towards Einar's throat. Einar dodged him and threw him aside.

"Stop. Stop," Affraic cried as she stood between them. "He is a friend." She paused momentarily. "No, he is my husband."

Finn froze with his sword raised above his head about to slam it down towards his brother-in-law. Einar looked at the blade pointed in his direction and stepped towards Affraic as she was his best hope of protection since he was unarmed. He raised his hands.

"I come in peace. I mean you no harm. In fact, I wish to become a good ally."

Finn gradually lowered his sword and looked to Aodh and Affraic for direction. Aodh broke the silence.

"Sit, Affraic and husband, and tell us of your circumstances. If you are hungry we have a little bread to share; otherwise, we can go foraging in the woods."

Affraic went and sat where Finn had sat a few moments earlier and invited Einar to sit beside her. Finn signalled to his men to lower their weapons but to post guards around the clearing in case it was a trick. Aodh offered his bread and mead bottle to their guests who eagerly took him up on the offer.

"What has brought you here?" Finn asked his sister once they had stopped eating.

Affraic wiped her mouth and passed the mead bottle to Einar so she could free herself of distraction to speak.

"I have come here seeking you and the promise you made to me the last time we met."

"And what was that?" Finn looked at her sceptically.

"That it was now time for my plan."

"And what plan would that be? There are two of you." He looked at his sister scornfully.

Affraic knitted her eyebrows.

"Do not doubt me, brother. You are sitting in a wood with a ragtag bunch of men with no one else to follow, and your adventures so far have purely been an exploration of failure."

Finn laughed.

"But you, with your high and mighty words, are sitting in the same woods with me. The only difference is that you need this 'rag-tag bunch of men' to execute your schemes. Have you perhaps come to explore failure with us?"

"Do not mock, brother, for we are in the same predicament and you need me more than I need you. For I bring you something far more valuable than you think. I bring you an army."

Finn laughed even louder.

"I know he is your husband but he is only one man. There is no need to try and fool us into thinking he is some kind of god."

There was a titter of laughter from the guards around them. Affraic's cheeks reddened and she leapt out of her seat. She pointed the finger of accusation at her brother.

"You have to decide what you want and what you'll sacrifice to achieve it. Tell me, what is it and what will you give up to do it?"

Her brother began to bluster but she was not going to stand for it.

"Come on, tell me. What do you want and what are you prepared to give up to get it? Tell me. You are the leader of men. Tell them."

Finn cut her off before she could embarrass him any more.

"I want to avenge the death of my mother and I will do anything to achieve that aim."

"Good. Now swear allegiance to Thurgest and you will have the Norse army behind you."

Finn stepped back and once it had sunk in what his sister had said stared at her as if a second head had sprouted from her shoulder.

"What did you say? Is this his influence? Did he make you say this?" Finn pointed the tip of his sword at Einar who did not flinch.

"Who do you hate more?" Affraic said. "Tigernach or Thurgest? Who is it that killed our mother?"

Finn started to pace up and down.

"Has it really come to this? A choice between two devils?"

"You have to think," Einar said, "who is the greater devil? Is it the man who killed your mother, who has humiliated you all your life, or the man who will help you kill him and make you a prince?"

"Who asked you?" Finn said turning round in a fury and pointing the tip of his sword once more in Einar's face. "You are just his agent and are a beast as bad as him."

"Sit and think, Finn, for this is a monumental choice," Aodh said. "Einar is right. If we wait in these woods until Ultán finds us then we are dead men. The best we can hope for is to become outlaws. Malachy will stab you in the back as soon as he is finished with you, but will not topple Tigernach for you. Einar may have brought you the best offer of a bad lot. You must decide what to do."

Finn collapsed to the ground, stuck his head in his hands and howled.

CHAPTER SIXTY-THREE

THE SEVENTH DAY

THE SUN FINALLY ROSE on the seventh day since Einar and Affraic had been banished. Torstein, Einar's replacement as master of the camp, had been busy and had filled in all the gaps in the walls of the palisade. They were now secure and anyone wishing to attack them would have to make a serious effort to overcome the defences to get inside. Torstein stood proudly on the gate tower and admired his work. He turned to the woods opposite the gate of which they now had a commanding view. He saw activity in the woods as if a large body of men were approaching them. It was unclear whether they were friend or foe. Torstein took the horn from his belt and sounded the alarm.

By the time Einar, Affraic, Finn and Aodh emerged from the woods in front of the gate of the camp the walls were bristling with well-armed Norsemen. But the four had an army of three hundred men behind them, gathered from those who had survived Finn's raid, those he freed from the camp and those he found in the woods, be they bandits or fugitives from Tigernach. The army was several times smaller than the men at Thurgest's disposal, but was impressive, nonetheless. Einar stood forward to speak, determined to make the seventh day his.

"Torstein. Tell Thurgest I have returned with a Hibernian army within the time he allowed me. I now come back to claim my rightful place at his side."

Torstein studied the men lined up outside the camp.

"These men come in peace and are prepared to fight for Thurgest?"

"Yes and yes."

Torstein snarled, for he had not wished success upon his rival and it looked as if he had achieved it.

"Only you and the leader of the Hibernians can come in. The rest can wait in the woods."

Finn raised an eyebrow at Einar who leaned over to him.
"They need you. I need you."
Finn nodded and went through the gate with Einar and Affraic.

Finn looked around at the difference several weeks had made to the Norse encampment. The docks were full of ships loading and unloading, and there was now a thriving market down at the harbour, trading in a wide range of goods other than slaves. There seemed to be an abundance of Norse warriors in the encampment as if new men were arriving every day. Soon, the camp would be bursting at the seams, and they would have to expand their walls. Was toppling Tigernach really worth encouraging the growth of all this? He could feel a pain in his chest as if it were guilt for sacrificing the rest of the Hibernians to satisfy his own rage.

As they walked, Torstein bragged about all he had achieved during the short stint of Einar's exile. Torstein made sure he had Einar's attention for each brag and emphasised how much praise Thurgest had heaped upon him. But Finn paid no attention for he was in a world of his own, wrestling with his conscience. He could be a hero for all time, his name a legend, living longer in the memory than any of the petty kings of Hibernia if he had the courage to leap on Thurgest and send him to hell. But then he would surely be horribly murdered afterwards for who would take his side and help him escape in the ensuing chaos? Would that be sufficient revenge for his mother's death, with the actual perpetrator still walking the earth and her only son mutilated in his grave?

"And here we have the great hall," Torstein said with a rather large grin on his face. He stopped everyone in the party so they could admire his work. "I even managed to complete the roof, so it is now watertight, something my predecessor conspicuously failed to do."

"Enough of your bragging and omitting I created a solid foundation for you to build upon," Einar said, most unamused. "Bring us to Thurgest for our axes thirst for the blood of his enemies."

Torstein gave a smug smile.

"As you wish. I hope he is glad to see you."

They were led into the great hall and made to wait as Thurgest was not ready for them. So long did they wait that Torstein was able to give Einar a lengthy lecture about how he fixed every rafter in the roof and what shoddy workmanship he had to overcome to do it. Einar had to stand and listen to it for he was only hours away from being declared an outlaw if Thurgest deemed bringing Finn and his men here as being insufficient atonement.

Thurgest eventually entered the room surrounded by his guards. Finn's hopes dropped for there was little chance of heroics today. He would barely be able to draw a blade before being killed, never mind being able to stab Thurgest. But they all had been disarmed before they entered the hall and only Thurgest and his men had weapons. The dreams of being a hero would have to wait.

Thurgest sat in silence and looked at his guests, staring them hard in the face. Einar knew this was a test and he held Thurgest's gaze when it came upon him. He was rewarded with a grin. Finn, however, did not fare so well as he quickly wilted and bowed his head as was the custom to do to a Hibernian king. His reward was for Thurgest to signal to his aide who exited the hall where Thurgest had entered. The aide quickly returned with Cathal and led him by a chain attached to the collar around Cathal's neck. The aide ceremoniously handed the end of the chain to Thurgest who pointed to his feet. Cathal sat silently on the floor. Cathal looked up at the guests then kept his eyes firmly on the floor.

Finn's eyes bulged at the sight of his father being humiliated so and his muscles tensed. He so much wanted to leap across and plunge a dagger into Thurgest's neck. He saw the cruel grin blossom on Thurgest's face. He must not show emotion. He must not show that Thurgest had got under his skin. This was his one chance to impress Thurgest and he had to take it.

"I see you have returned, Einar," Thurgest said in a low, measured tone. "It is the seventh day. The day you either return to the family or become an outlaw. Which is it to be?"

"I have returned to the family," Einar said as he bowed. "And I bring you a new ally. An ally that will open up Hibernia for you."

Einar looked over to Finn.

"Are you Einar's wife's brother?" Thurgest said, making no effort to hide his grin.

"I am," Finn said firmly.

"See," Thurgest said, pointing to Cathal sitting at his feet. "This is my Hibernian dog. Will you be like your father and lie at my feet?" Thurgest gave Cathal a kick in the side, but Cathal just took it and did not make a sound. "He's such a faithful dog, a ferocious fighter, but he knows his place."

Finn gulped and steadied himself. He raised his eyes so he could not see his father.

"I am here to be your ally, to be your equal."

Thurgest threw his head back laughing.

"I am Thurgest. No one is the equal of me. You may not wear the collar and chain, but you will still be my dog."

"Then I will offer my services to Malachy," Finn said, and he turned to leave. He may not get out of the hall alive, but at least he would die free.

Thurgest stood up.

"Do not turn your back on Thurgest in his own hall until he tells you to go," his voice boomed and bounced off the rafters.

Finn gulped again, put on a brave face and turned around again.

"Are you ready to negotiate as allies?"

Thurgest sat and smiled.

"I like an ally with a backbone, even if he doesn't know his place. Let's set aside your insolence for now for we shall come to that on another day. Now, what do you bring to the table that is worth me bargaining for, and what are your terms?"

Finn raised his chin high as this was his moment.

"I want to kill Tigernach and Ultán and be made king in their place," he said in a clear and commanding voice.

Einar glared at him for he had not shown these aspirations before. Thurgest looked unimpressed.

"I can kill them easily myself. As for you, I can set aside a field for you and declare you king of it if you so wish, and you can run around and be my dog inside it. As far as I can see, you would be as legitimate as any other king on this ridiculous island. So, why do I need you to do what I can do myself and give nothing away?"

Finn paused for he only had time for the most convincing argument. He tried to remember back to all the conversations he'd had with Aodh in the woods as he tried to teach him about the larger picture of war. Now, he had to put them together and come up with a persuasive speech.

"If you take to the field to destroy Tigernach you give up your advantages of mobility and speed that you have with raiding down rivers with your fleet. You have a sizeable army but as soon as you take to the land you will unite the Hibernians against you. Once you do that, you will soon be heavily outnumbered and you'll have to take the chance that you will not be so heavily defeated as to wipe out your colony."

Finn paused to size up Thurgest's reaction to his speech. He saw a giveaway twitch on the right-hand side of Thurgest's mouth on an otherwise stony face. He knew he was on the right track.

"But you can divide your enemies by allowing them to join you and therefore splitting them up. The difficult part is to persuade the first one to join you and then to treat them well as an example for others who may wish to join you. That is how I am valuable to you. I am the first and allow others to follow. That is, if you are victorious over Tigernach."

Thurgest pondered Finn's words momentarily, then lifted his hand.

"Whoever taught you, taught you well. These are wise words indeed from someone so young. I assume you can fight like your father?"

Finn glanced over at Cathal who looked away.

"His blood flows through my veins and I wield his sword."

"Good. However, for us to be proper allies you must swear an oath to me."

Finn narrowed his eyes. His cheek twitched as the seer's vision of the dragon forcing him to kneel before him flashed across his mind. He dismissed it as foolishness.

"We are allies. Why would I swear an oath to you?"

Thurgest leaned forward.

"You are nobody to me. You walk in with your sweet talk and offer me an army just like a drunken buck at a feast. But I am no naive wench to be wooed. If you wake up with a sore head and regrets in the morning, it will not be so easy to leave. Give me your oath that you will be a faithful ally or I will set my dog on you and find some other ambitious young Hibernian to whisper sweet nothings in my ear. It would greatly amuse me to see if my dog would kill his own son for me."

Finn gulped once more and looked across to Einar who gave him a firm nod.

"I swear on my life that I will be a faithful ally and not betray you."

Thurgest gave a smirk.

"Your sweet words come too easily from your lips." Thurgest signalled to his aide. "Bring me the oath ring."

"What is the oath ring?" Finn said.

"It is a tradition of my people that you will wear my ring to show you have taken an oath to me. If you remove this ring without our agreement you make yourself an outlaw and fair game for any Norse to kill and claim a reward from me. It is a heavy burden to wear my ring, only for the bravest of men."

Finn hesitated as the seer's vision came back to him of a ring burning itself onto his finger. But saw his sister out of the corner of his eye gesturing him forward.

"I will wear your ring," Finn said, "but I expect it to be replaced by a crown."

"Oh, I will give you a Hibernian crown. I will also give you a collar so you can run around your field. Now put on the ring."

Thurgest's aide walked over to Finn and handed him the ring. Finn took it and held his left hand out in front of him.

"I place your ring on my finger as a pledge of loyalty until our bargain is concluded."

Finn slowly slid the ring down his ring finger. Thurgest grinned.

"Still the elusive words of a young buck who thinks he can evade the way of kings. If you break your oath it will be your own father who will hunt you down. Consider us allies, but consider yourself also the vanguard of my army for trust has to be earned before we are proper allies. Go to your men and I will send word to you when we leave. But be ready for it will be soon."

Finn bowed and tried to hide his smile. The first part of his plan, to leave the Norse camp alive, had been a success. The ring to him was but an empty promise. The strength of the new alliance had yet to be tested on both sides.

CHAPTER SIXTY-FOUR

A RESTLESS SOUL

GORMLAITH LAY ON A bed made of straw covered in sheets in the back of a cave in the Wicklow mountains. She was pale, but still breathing. Babo sat by her side and held her hand having carried her in his arms most of the way up the mountains. His back still held the strain of all the effort.

"Give medicine and make her well," he demanded, his face contorting in wrinkles and red rage. Anger was the most dangerous emotion he could feel since he was permanently injured in battle years ago. It caused pain to sear in his head and him to lash out against whoever was the cause of the anger, or, if he was blinded by it and lost control, anyone who was in his vicinity.

Moira ignored the anger in his voice.

"You cannot hurry the medicines for they need time to mix and produce their magic," she said in a soothing tone. "You saved her by carrying her all the way here. She will be very grateful to you when she recovers."

"No want gratitude, want Gormlaith," Babo spat as he squeezed her hand. He mopped her brow with the cloth Moira had given him, being careful to capture every bead of sweat as he looked at her lovingly. Moira was curious as to why Babo had fallen so quickly for this woman, as she knew him from the caves of Wicklow, and Aodh and he had protected her from bandits many times, hence why she was repaying the kindness. Babo could read such questions in her facial expressions.

"Gormlaith made Babo well when had head problem," Babo said as he turned to Moira and spun his finger around beside his temple. "No Gormlaith, Babo dead."

"There'll be no one dying here today," Moira said as she ladled her potion into a bowl. She handed it carefully to Babo. "Now make her sip this when it cools a little and she has to drink all of it."

"Gormlaith drink all of it," Babo repeated in his own words.

He used his finger to test the temperature of the contents of the bowl and raised it to Gormlaith's lips. She sipped slowly and Babo waited by her side until she had successfully drunk all the medicine.

"There," Moira said. "All it requires is a little patience. Once she has taken all her medicine it is only a matter of time before she recovers. Are you going to return to your village or wait here with her?"

"Told to wait with her. Village," and Babo made the image of a village on fire by rippling his fingers upwards.

"'Tis the same all over. All those Norsemen have brought is destruction and there is plenty more of that to come. At least you know that you'll be safe up here in these mountains."

"You not know Gormlaith. Fly out from this bed will she at the first time of being awake."

"Then it is your task to make sure she gets her bed rest and does not leave until she is better."

"Harder to keep her in bed than to carry her uphill."

"Well, no better man than yourself to stop her from doing it."

Babo shook his head and went back to holding Gormlaith's hand.

Gormlaith slept for two days and then finally stirred. Babo awoke with a jolt for he had fallen asleep in the chair beside her, only leaving her beside to pee and to stretch his legs. Moira had not noticed Gormlaith stir and she burst back into the cave having been visiting one of the local villages in the foothills.

"Finn has joined the Norse and marches towards Tigernach's hillfort," she exclaimed, for she could not wait to tell Babo her important news.

"Finn has joined the Norse, you said," Gormlaith stated as she stirred in her bed and then tried to prop herself up on her elbows.

Babo turned and gave Moira a ferocious look before calming himself and turning his attention back to Gormlaith.

"Gormlaith rest now. Babo sort any Norse."

"Gormlaith will not rest now. There are things to be done." Her voice became fuller as her energy returned.

She groaned as she attempted to throw her legs off the bed but the tightly wrapped blankets proved too much for her. Babo placed his hands upon her and gently eased her down.

"Blankets beat Gormlaith, Norse beat Gormlaith."

"Nothing beats Gormlaith." But her eyelids began to feel heavy and she soon fell back asleep.

Moira crept up to the bed not wanting to make the same mistake twice.

"You won't keep her down for long. We need to give her as much medicine as we can give her before she forces you down that hill again."

Babo nodded and put his hands out for another bowl of medicine. He would keep her here for as long as possible but knew as soon as she could walk she would leave to find Finn. His task was to make her as well as possible beforehand. He squeezed her hand and returned to his prayers.

CHAPTER SIXTY-FIVE

NERVES TWITCH

AODH SAT WITH THE men in the woods outside the Norse camp. The men were on edge as the Norse had not reduced the number of guards they posted on the walls. They stopped opening the gate during the negotiations and did not communicate with the Hibernians outside. It was a siege in all but name. Some of the men had long known Aodh and sat with him beside a fire in the woods. They did not restrain themselves long from expressing their unhappiness.

"Your boy is taking a long time in there," said Dubán with a downward-turned face that barely ever broke into a smile. "He's probably dead now."

"Shut up, Dubán," Aodh said. "If he is dead then we're all dead soon. You have to have faith in the boy. He has a lot to negotiate with."

"Yeah," Bláán said raising a smile. "He's got him to negotiate with." He pointed at Dubán and everyone laughed.

"So why do we trust this boy?" Dubán continued, his anger stoked at being ridiculed. "What is he to you? Why do you protect him so?"

Aodh bit his lip for he did not want to spend his time waiting to see if he would live or die defending Finn.

"I owe it to his father and he will be a fine warrior one day. Now stop bothering me. If you have itchy feet make yourself useful and go and hunt some rabbits rather than sit there and annoy me."

Dubán rose to his feet and stomped around, restless. His eyes settled on the Norse wall. He searched for once evident weaknesses but they all seemed to have been fixed. He locked eyes with a Norse guard on the wall. Their eyes may have locked only momentarily, but the Norse broke into a smug grin which only inflamed the irritation Dubán already felt. His heart sank as his confidence deserted him. He turned back to Aodh.

"Why are we trying to fight on the side of the Norse?" Dubán said, spitting with fury. "No matter what Tigernach has done the Norse have done far worse, and if we give them a toehold they'll unleash chaos on our lands."

Aodh rose to his feet determined to put down this dissent before it spread.

"Sit down before I have you executed for treachery," he said as he extended his arm and pointed his finger firmly down.

But Dubán was having none of it.

"We all served Malachy for many years. He may have been a demanding master, but if you did as he said he treated you reasonably well."

"Hardly the most ringing of endorsements," Aodh said as his jaw stiffened and his muscles tensed.

"It is better than putting ourselves at the mercy of that monster Thurgest. It is said that God has cursed him, his colony and all his men to hell for all the priests they have killed and all the monasteries they have burned. And your response is to send a boy to do a deal with the devil?"

Aodh circled around the fire until he was nose to nose with Dubán.

"Ultán and Tigernach carried out the worst massacre in living history, slaughtering women and children who were exercising their rights under the law to protest outside his fort. If Malachy was such a good protector he should have avenged the people and killed them both for their actions. Yet he chose to sit on his hands. Is this the man you wish to fight for?"

"Better him than the monster Thurgest." Fear pulled a cloak over Dubán's eyes, and he drew his sword and lashed out like an animal. He brought his sword down in an arc thrust towards Aodh's head.

"Die, traitor," Dubán cried putting all his force into delivering this death blow.

But Aodh was quick despite his age. He kicked out and folded over Dubán's knee. Dubán cried out in pain as he crumpled over and he dropped his sword. Aodh saw a flash of panic in one of the other men's eyes as he realised it was now or never. Aodh swiftly went for his dagger. The man threw himself at Aodh, his weapon flailing. Aodh spun and plunged his dagger into the man's stomach. There was a cry of pain and Aodh felt the warm gush of blood before he plunged the dagger another three times to ensure the man would threaten him no more. The man fell to the ground with a thud and did not move. Aodh quickly circled around, swinging his dagger threateningly in case anyone else wished to attack him. But all the men backed off with their mouths agape. He searched for the perpetrator of this violence and all he saw was mud skid patches in the grass.

"Where is Dubán? Where is he?"

But the men said nothing and began to slink away.

"Stop him or he will alert the enemy," Aodh cried sternly trying to reassert his authority.

But none of the men moved.

"Let him leave if he wants to," one man said. "Better he run now than in battle."

"It is where he runs to that I am worried about," Aodh said as he signalled to the men to sit so he could restore peace and a sense of calm.

"This had better work, Finn," he muttered to himself as he stared into the fire. It would not be long until another rose to challenge him.

CHAPTER SIXTY-SIX
A CHANCE AT REVENGE

FINN'S HEART RACED AS he stepped out from beneath the gnarled branches of the ancient oaks, their leaves whispering ominously in the chilly breeze. The trees seemed reluctant to release him, as if they knew one of their wood dwellers was about to find themselves in peril right in front of their protective wall of trees. The open field stretched before him, a sea of swaying grass dotted with wildflowers. He was now exposed to what the world could throw at him – wind, ridicule, the edge of an enemy's blade. He gulped and a bead of sweat rolled down his forehead. His stomach felt queasy and his legs notably heavier, as if he was wading through mud. He looked behind him to see the reassuring smile of Aodh. He had been through all the routines Aodh had taught him on the march here so he could remember them in the heat of combat. But as Finn contemplated each momentous step he forgot everything except the overwhelming feeling of fear.

His men stood behind him as a show of strength dotted amongst the trees in the periphery of the woods so they were visible to the men on the defences of the fort. Three hundred men standing tall and strong. Three hundred men, cowering into themselves. Three hundred men having a fit of nerves, hoping their champion would have his challenge accepted so they would only have to stand and watch. They watched as Finn paused and they waited for his call.

Finn could feel the pressure of responsibility crushing down on his chest. He knew with every step he was placing himself in greater and greater danger. His body was stiff with nerves but he forced one foot in front of the other. His memories of his father no longer worked as inspiration for he had seen what his father had become. He dismissed the vision of the seer from his mind as all it represented was his doom. He thought of Aodh and tried to recall all that he had taught him. But he could dream no more as he was now in arrow range of the walls.

He looked at the walls of the fort trying to pick out Ultán, but no matter how much he squinted he could not make out any faces on the walls. He felt the wind on his face and feared it would blow away his courage, as fragile as it was. He had to do it now, but his throat felt dry. He coughed, regained his voice and threw his life into the hands of fate.

"Ultán, son of Tigernach, it is I, Finn," he shouted at the walls. "You have insulted me for too long for it to go unchallenged. I hold you responsible for the death of my mother, even though the deed may not have been done directly by your hand. Come down here and face me. Just you and me. Let us sort out our differences and save the blood of our men. What say you?"

There was stirring on the walls of the fort and sighs of relief from the men standing behind Finn. They all looked to the walls to see what would be Ultán's reply.

Gormlaith gripped the rough bark of the tree, her fingernails digging into the crevices as she steadied herself. Her breath came in ragged gasps, each one sending a sharp pain through her chest. She closed her eyes for a moment, gathering her strength. The surrounding forest was a blur of green and brown, the trees towering above her like silent sentinels. The air was thick with the scent of damp earth and rotting leaves, and the only sound was the distant chirping of birds. A warm hand rested on her shoulder.

"Babo say you should have stayed with healer."

Gormlaith raised her red-infused face.

"Gormlaith does not care what Babo says," she said with a wicked grin. "Gormlaith does not want Finn to throw his life away because he thinks his mother is dead."

Babo shook his head and held his hand out to help Gormlaith.

"Boy throw his life away for much lesser reasons than mother."

It was Gormlaith's turn to shake her head as she straightened her clothes.

"You don't have to tell me what a fool he can be. I should know, I brought him up."

Gormlaith pushed herself away from the tree, and her legs trembled beneath her. She had to keep moving, had to find her son before it was too late. She stumbled forward, her vision swimming as she tried to navigate the uneven terrain. Roots and vines clawed at her feet, threatening to trip her with every step. But she would not stop now. Not when her son's life hung in the balance. A hand was once more extended.

"Let Babo help?"

"Babo can help later. I'm sure there'll be plenty of heads for Babo to bash," she said, brushing his helping hand away.

Babo stopped suddenly and cupped his ear.

"Must be near fort. Can hear voices."

Gormlaith caught up with him and held her ear to the wind.

"I hear the voice of my son. What's he doing, shouting into the wind?"

Babo was about a foot taller than Gormlaith and towered over her skinny frame.

"He challenges Ultán to a duel because of mother's death."

"We were both right when we called him a fool," Gormlaith spat. "We need to stop this before he gets himself killed."

"Babo run and stop it."

"No," Gormlaith said firmly. "This is a mother's job since the mother is supposed to be dead. Only by showing him I am not dead can we hope to stop this."

"Too sick. Never get there in time."

"I might if you carry me."

Babo did not need a second invitation. He picked her up and ran towards the distant sound of Finn's voice.

It was not long before something stirred on the walls of the hillfort. Ultán poked his head above the palisade and gave a smile, as if he had been waiting all his life for this day to come. His head disappeared only for the gate to be slowly opened minutes later. There stood Ultán with sword, shield and breastplate, eager to take up Finn's challenge. He marched out of the fort with his men behind him. He walked slowly towards Finn without ever taking his eyes off him. His men lined up behind him in battle order. They were more numerous and better armed than Finn's men lined up at the edge of the wood. Ultán had more men on the palisade with bows at the ready waiting for his command. It all seemed too easy.

Ultán stood directly in front of Finn. He wore a huge grin and stared at him disdainfully.

"I have waited long for this day. I have often thought of challenging you myself but thought you too much of a coward to take me up on it. I also didn't think your sister would look too kindly on my proposals if I killed her brother. Hence, why I had to settle for challenging you in hurling."

Such insults steadied Finn's nerves and hardened his resolve.

"Well, I must be the better man if I am standing in front of the gates of your father's fort and making the challenge."

"No, it merely makes you a fool. So what are the terms for what happens after you die?"

Finn ignored the goading.

"It is just you and me, no one else has to die this day."

Ultán examined the faces of the men standing behind Finn and knitted his brow.

"But some of those men standing behind you are my father's men. Why would I take them back if they were foolish enough to follow you? Surely they realise it is a betrayal which my father will not let stand?"

"It is because of your father's actions or inactions that we stand here today," Finn said, swallowing hard for he was trying not to get emotional. "It is because of his neglect of my mother and his own people and the massacre you perpetrated upon them when your father owed them a duty to protect them."

Ultán laughed.

"They were all traitors against the good people of Hibernia, never mind my father or the Kingdom of Mide. They obstructed the actions of the king when trying to resolve the issue of the Norse with their protests outside the hillfort. Then they brought their plague and pestilence upon the land. All led by your mother, may the devil burn her soul for eternity in the fires of hell."

Finn gnashed his teeth for he could hold himself back no more. He swung his blade in an arc to crush Ultán's head but his blow was easily parried away.

"Finished making terms?" Ultán sneered as he took up a defensive posture, inviting Finn to attack him. "Where's that lovely sister of yours? Once I kill you, I'll throw your body into the woods to be devoured by wolves. Then I will take your sister to be my bride whether she likes it or not. Better than being destitute since her whole family will be dead."

Finn's face contorted with rage. He charged forward, swinging his sword in front of him, determined to blow Ultán out of the way, be it by skill or sheer force of anger. Ultán stepped to the side and hit Finn on the temple with the pommel of his sword. Finn crumpled to the ground. Ultán prowled around him like a wolf playing with its prey before it went in for the final kill.

"Get up," Ultán snarled. "Show me you're a man. Defend yourself. Defend your family's honour. Don't die like a dog. Get up."

But Finn's head spun and Ultán's voice was a tormenting echo. He staggered on his hands and knees trying to get up but always falling when applying pressure to his arms. Ultán kicked him in the ribs and he fell over in a heap. Ultán turned to Finn's men and raised his sword and shield in victory.

"Is this your champion? Is this all you have?"

As Ultán turned his back on him Finn managed to get some control over his spinning head and prop himself up on his sword and get himself standing again. He swayed from side to side as he regained his balance.

"It's a foolish mistake to turn your back on your rival," Finn growled as he spat blood from his mouth and positioned himself for his next attack.

"It was more foolish of you to get up for all it has done is set you up for more pain and humiliation. If it takes two blows to kill you, then so be it."

Ultán turned and dramatically arched his sword, forcing Finn to raise his shield to parry. Ultán was determined to milk the opportunity to publicly fight a weaker opponent for every piece of drama he could. This would be his redemption for all his foolish youthful mistakes in the past and for seemingly forever walking in his father's shadow. Finn skipped around him, avoiding his blows. He was attempting to wear his opponent out by coaxing him into expending his energy by always tempting him into the knockout blow. Ultán had the bulk to overpower Finn, but Finn had the manoeuvrability to avoid him. But he could not dance for long, especially as his head spun so.

"You make a fool of yourself in front of your men with your dancing feet. Do you think the Norse dance in their shield wall, or our warriors when they make the final assault of the battle?"

"Take every battle as it comes," Finn said between breaths. "You may have got me once but I still dance before you. Your men are probably wondering why you did not kill me when you had the chance."

"Now, so am I."

Ultán thrust another blow towards Finn's face and brought it forcefully down when parried. It only led to a clash of shields rather than Finn falling off balance. The shouting and jeering of both sides got louder and louder as they edged forward to limit the amount of space Finn had to dance in.

But Finn was tiring. He had taken a few blows but not given many back. As his lessons from Aodh taught him, he had to come out of the defensive at some stage and try and win. He mustered the last of his energy. He rained a shower of blows upon Ultán's head, forcing him to raise his shield and defend himself. But with each blow Finn could feel the energy being sapped from his arms. His sword felt heavier with each blow and each strike held less force. Ultán staggered back but yielded ground rather than the advantage. Finn heard a voice cutting through the cold air.

"Finn, don't despair. Your mother is still alive."

It sounded like the voice of his mother but he put it out of his head for he did not want the dead to distract him in what could be his last attack. He walloped his sword again and again on top of Ultán's shield. Ultán's rear knee buckled behind him. Finn slammed his sword down on Ultán's shield as he held it above his head.

"Go on, my son. Split the bastard open. He was always shit at hurling anyway."

Finn turned around as Ultán fell before him. He saw a vision of his mother bathed in the light coming from over the top of the trees in the woods. She was like a heavenly vision, an angel come down to earth as if she was beckoning him to join her in heaven. Finn felt a sharp pain in his knee as Ultán connected to it with his foot. He crumpled to the ground before Ultán. Ultán rose to his feet beaming as his nemesis lay before him almost helpless. Ultán raised his sword for the death blow.

"Babo, save him," Gormlaith cried, any resemblance of her being a spectre vanishing away in her panic.

Babo ran and shoulder-charged into Ultán's men but could not get past them. Ultán was distracted by the commotion and looked over his shoulder at Babo as he struggled with Ultán's men. It was all Finn needed. He saw Ultán's exposed belly beneath his breastplate above his head and reached for his dagger. He plunged it into Ultán's exposed midriff repeatedly, ignoring the gushing of blood down his arm and Ultán's cries of pain. Ultán buckled over in a pool of blood. Ultán's men stopped and watched their master keel over. Babo ran through the hole in their shields to Finn.

"Take hand, Finn."

The field descended into chaos as Tigernach's men charged to attack those led by Finn in revenge for the killing of Ultán. Babo hauled Finn up.

"Get up, must go."

"I must stay and fight," Finn said, still dazed as he watched Ultán writhing on the ground until he went still.

"Gormlaith got off deathbed to save you," Babo said as he scowled at Finn.

Finn looked down to the still twitching body of Ultán, his face and torso now covered in blood.

"Boy never been in proper battle before. People get dead be it by accident or on purpose. Boy must go now."

But the time for conversation was over as their foes had gathered around them. Babo broke off and had already disposed of one of them and was in the process of driving the rest off and creating a little space on the battlefield. Finn bloodied his sword and lowered his aching arms since his opportunities for rest would be few and far between. He looked around and saw his men were getting slaughtered. Tigernach had smelt blood and had charged out of his fort to rout his enemies. Finn raised his sword in the air.

"RETREAT, RETREAT!"

CHAPTER SIXTY-SEVEN

LESSONS IN LIFE AND DEATH

FINN STUMBLED THROUGH THE forest, over branches and rocks, for he did not have time to look where he was running, such was the general panic. Twigs scratched his face, and rocks, roots, and debris battered his feet as he ran. Arrows whizzed by over his shoulders and shuddered as they thudded into the tree trunks as he ran past. He glanced over to his right-hand side, his view partially obscured by the blurring of trees as he ran. Babo kept pace, struggling with Gormlaith, who would rather die than be on his shoulder when they jumped a tree trunk again. But Babo ignored her and gripped her waist ever tighter.

The Hibernians, or those Hibernians who had stayed loyal to Tigernach, swarmed behind them as Ultán's men had been joined by Tigernach's men. They ran like hunting dogs after a rabbit. Once they had got the scent nothing was going to distract them from achieving the kill. They screamed and shouted abuse and threats at their intended victims, not offering them an olive branch or a rope to climb down but merely the tip of a sword or a spear or a rope to swing off.

Most of Finn's men were by now dead or had fled. They had either been left in the field where Ultán lay or caught and killed as they fled in the forest.

"KEEP GOING, MEN," Finn shouted over his shoulder to no one in particular. "THE RIVER IS NEAR."

On the mention of the river everything seemed to go faster. The river meant some sort of salvation for there the men could abandon their weapons and hope to swim across to the other side unmolested and escape to the mountains. More men fell to Tigernach's pursuing forces who seemed to be funnelling them in a particular direction. Finn then heard a crash to his right. He looked across and could not see Babo and Gormlaith anymore.

"MOTHER!"

Finn ran across as fast as his worn-out feet would allow but the urgency surging through his veins blocked out any pain. He jerked his head from side to side but could not see them anywhere. As he stood looking he became a target for the darts and arrows which fell around him but much to his gratitude lodged in the trunks of the surrounding trees. He heard a yelp nearby. His senses tingled and he bit his lip. He threw himself forward. He found a shallow indent in the ground where his mother lay holding her arms up to protect herself. He felt a shoulder thud into him just under his armpit and he went flying. He rolled over and sprang to his feet as if he was on the hurling pitch losing the game and had little time to roll around and feel sorry for himself. He saw Babo struggling to fight off three men with his sword. They baited him like hunting dogs jerking forward to put him off balance but not giving enough for him to latch on to. Finn heard a roar to his right and on instinct jabbed his sword in that direction at waist height. It met some resistance but mostly slid in softly and Finn felt the now familiar gush of warm blood on his cold hand.

"You have no time to stand around thinking about it, Finn," Gormlaith roared. "Help Babo."

Finn ran forward and thrust his sword towards the nearest foe. The man turned and parried Finn's blow. However, he left himself exposed to Babo who gashed the man's back with the tip of his sword. The man screamed until Finn plunged his sword through his chest. The other man turned to face Finn but Babo put his sword through the man's head, spraying blood everywhere. The man fell with anguished cries into a heap. The third man lost his nerve and fled. Babo and Finn looked at each other and then at the oncoming charge of the rest of Tigernach's men.

"Don't just stand there," Gormlaith cried. "Pick me up and run."

Perspiration poured from Finn's forehead. The back of his soaking shirt flapped in the wind as he ran as fast as he could. He could see clear daylight beyond the trees ahead. A little further and he would be in sight of the river. Babo was still to his right, still running hard despite his panting. Tigernach's men were still gaining on them and the number of Finn's men running through the woods was dwindling rapidly. But one last burst and freedom would be in sight.

CHAPTER SIXTY-EIGHT

SHIELD WALL

THEY BROKE THROUGH THE bushes that lined the edge of the forest and into a burst of sunlight. But it was no time to be complacent. Finn looked over his shoulder and Tigernacht's men were still pursuing them. Finn faced forward towards the river. But his jubilant smile was cut short. A Norse shield wall was straight in front of him. Finn signalled to Babo to go around the wall. The first Norse missile hit the ground several yards in front of him.

"IT IS I, FINN," he shouted, draining his lungs of vital energy.

Another missile landed on the ground nearby.

"FINN. IT IS I, FINN."

Finn saw Einar peering over the shield wall. He waved his sword to instruct the men to stop firing. Finn ran around the shield wall and collapsed on the ground heaving air into his lungs. Every part of his body ached. He was covered in mud and sweat but worst of all, other people's blood. His heart pounded so hard in his chest he pressed it down with his hand so it would not collapse from all the overwork. He lay on the ground oblivious to the shouts of those around him.

"Finn."

He heard a voice calling but it was distant as if it was in a cave.

"Finn."

He raised his head and looked over to his right. There lay his mother, flicking bits of mud at him to get his attention. She looked pale, but quite lively for a woman of a certain age having been slung over the shoulder of a giant who had to run as fast as he could for several miles while being pelted with arrows and missiles. But all he could think of was how glad he was that she was alive when all the while he thought she was dead. As if from nowhere, a large sod of turf landed on his chest.

"Finn, your men need you."

He looked to see who the perpetrator was and saw his mother pointing up. He took the hint and lifted himself up, all the while every muscle and joint in his body ached. He stood up shaky at first but then found his balance. He looked around and saw only a handful of his men behind the Norse shield wall. Where were they all? He had started the day with three hundred men. Where was Aodh? He had not seen him in what seemed like hours. Were they all dead? Had they all run away? A panic overtook him and he stood rooted to the ground, his eyes bulging from his face when he contemplated what death and destruction he had brought, and it was not over yet.

There came a shrill blare of horns from the direction of the river. More Norse ships had arrived bringing reinforcements. They now swarmed like flies on the river, dropping off warriors then returning to their camp to fetch more. It was as if Thurgest had sent out a call in the limited time he had to other Norse settlements around the Hibernian sea and rounded up every Norse warband available for the battle.

Thurgest disembarked from the lead ship surrounded by his giant bodyguards with his Hibernian dogs running before him. Behind him disembarked the captured Hibernian nobility from his previous raids. Unsure of their loyalty, today Thurgest wanted to put on a display to all who witnessed it that it was futile to resist him so they should join him, the future High King of Hibernia. Thurgest's entourage paid little attention to Finn's stragglers sitting a distance behind the shield wall so Finn thought it safe to follow at a distance to see what would unfold. Finn positioned himself on some high ground to get a good view of the battlefield.

Finn's men were still running out from the forest when Tigernach's men spilt out across the clearing to the river like a tidal wave. Finn could see Tigernach's men hesitate a little but the momentum was too great for them and the charge continued. Thurgest raised his sword in the air.

"MEN, IT IS I, THURGEST, YOUR LEADER AND SCOURGE OF HIBERNIA. I ORDER THIS SHIELD WALL TO BRACE."

The Norse roared, raised their shields and the Hibernians charged straight into them. There was a cacophony of clashing steel and wood and the anguished cries of men filled the air. Tigernach's men forced them back several yards with the impact. Finn's stomach churned. Where were the rest of his men? Were they squeezed or trampled underfoot between Norse shield and

Hibernian spear? He had to rally the rest of his men so he could claim some of the spoils of victory if the gods of war should smile on his side today. He went and grabbed the nearest of his men who had lain down near him.

"Get up, get up. It is time to fight," Finn said as he forced his hands under the man's armpits and lifted him to his feet. The man shook him off and scowled at him.

"I have run like the fastest rabbit and brought Tigernach to Thurgest. What else will you have me do?"

"Fight," Finn shouted in his face. "Fight or you will end the day a thrall, I guarantee it."

The man went for the scruff of Finn's torn shirt but Finn knocked his hands away.

"Have you tricked me into coming here?" the man said.

"Don't be so foolish," Finn replied. "You know how wars go. You fight for your master and if you win you stick your hand out to get rewarded. Your day is not done. Stand behind me and let us gather the men. We can still win the day if both sides exhaust each other."

The man reluctantly stood behind Finn and he gathered up what men he could see until they numbered around fifty. As the men organised themselves again a figure pushed his way to the front and stood before Finn in a bloody and tattered shirt.

"Aodh, where have you been?" and Finn ran and embraced him.

"Running with the wind behind my back," Aodh replied. "But I regret not running past this place and back to the mountains for I fear something was agreed behind my back and I was not told about it." Aodh lowered his chin but caught Finn's embarrassment with a steady stare. Finn stared at the ground without the nerve to face his mentor.

"I had to prove my worth to Thurgest, so I agreed to his plan."

"And it is the perfect plan for Thurgest. He can have one foe kill another, and then finish the hurt victor."

Finn threw his hands in the air.

"What was I to do? I was lucky to leave the great hall alive."

Aodh slapped him on the shoulder.

"Do not concern yourself. Thurgest has run rings around all the kings of Hibernia he has encountered. Yet you live to tell the tale. You have a slim advantage for a narrow point in time. Sit on the sidelines and watch with your small band of men. When you see who is winning the battle, slam into the rear of whoever is losing and claim some of the spoils. Thurgest may have crippled you today but do not let him rob you of victory."

"But what about doing what is right?"

Aodh shook his head.

"Now is not the time for that. Now is the time for survival."

Finn shook his head but began to study the ebbs and flows of the battle.

The Norse shield wall was still standing, and Tigernach could only use missiles to break the deadlock, so the battle made little progress. Finn looked around to see how he could gain the advantage, but quickly noticed a steady stream of Norsemen were coming from the river boats, but few reinforced the shield wall. What was Thurgest up to?

CHAPTER SIXTY-NINE

ONE MORE PUSH

THURGEST ARRIVED AT THE rear of the shield wall surrounded by his bodyguards.

"HOLD THE LINE," he roared. "THURGEST IS HERE. AND WHEN THURGEST IS HERE THE GODS THROW THUNDERBOLTS AND OUR ENEMIES DIE. DO NOT APPEAR COWARDLY IN FRONT OF THE GODS FOR VALLHALLA HAS OPENED ITS DOORS THIS DAY TO WELCOME YOU IN."

The men cheered and tightened up the gaps and pushed forward against the Hibernians.

Einar, who had been entrusted to lead the shield wall, took Thurgest's arrival as a good sign. He did not regard being given command of the shield wall in the present circumstances as being an honour or a sign that Thurgest trusted him again. Rather, he viewed it as being placed in the heat of the battle where, as a Norseman and not an expendable ally, he was most likely to see the most action. His fate was in the lap of the gods. If he were killed, then good riddance, see you in Valhalla and no need for his family to get suspicious. If he survived, then he was blessed by the gods and should be allowed back into Thurgest's favour as had happened to others in the past.

He had to survive also for Affraic's sake, for no matter how he died they would give him a Norse funeral suitable for the son of a jarl, but they would treat Affraic like a thrall and send her from this earth with him. He shuddered when he thought of what they would do to her, as he had seen it done in his youth several times. He joined in with Thurgest's roar.

"PUSH, MEN, PUSH."

Einar pushed his shield forward with all his might. The weight the lines of Hibernians brought upon the shield wall was becoming unbearable. It would soon break. The grass beneath the men was being churned into mud. There was a yelp nearby as one of the men in the front rank of the wall slipped and was trampled to death by the Hibernians. The wall sealed up behind him as the Norse had to swallow their grief to preserve their own lives.

"HOLD, MEN, HOLD," Einar shouted. "Thurgest will come to our aid. We just need to hold them a little longer."

The Hibernians smelt blood and the front ranks of their line jabbed and slashed their swords over the top of the Norse shields hoping to injure and create a hole in the wall. The second ranks lowered their spears and jabbed along the ground, hoping to cripple and force the wall to collapse. Men started to fall from the wall and holes began to appear. Einar cranked his neck behind him while raising his shield to protect his head.

"We need more men, we need more men."

He saw Thurgest behind him count out a specific number of men and send them to join the wall.

"WE NEED MORE. WE NEED MORE."

But Thurgest ignored him.

"PUSH, MEN, PUSH."

More and more Hibernians were joining their lines and they began to slowly but steadily push the Norse back. Einar felt the battle was slowly ebbing away from him. The Hibernians changed their tactics. They would give a massive heave and push into the Norse ranks and then suddenly withdraw. The Norse were so invested in holding them off that the sudden withdrawal of pressure caused them to fall and the Hibernians made short work of those who lay on the ground.

"WE NEED MORE MEN," Einar once more shouted to the rear but once again, only those who fell were replaced.

The Hibernians switched tactics again, determined to push the Norse back into the river. There they would drown and a simple defeat could be turned into a decisive one once the victors destroyed the Norse fleet. But still Thurgest only replaced those who had fallen.

Einar pushed on his shield which grew heavier with each passing moment, not just with the fatigue of his whole arm and shoulder, but parts of arrows and broken spears were now lodged in it which both increased the weight and made it more difficult to manoeuvre. He tried to dig his feet into the ground but could gain no purchase in the ever-increasing mud. He looked behind him. The river was getting closer and closer.

Finn watched anxiously as the battle unfolded. Aodh observed him flinch every time the battle lines ebbed and flowed.

"It is not yet time," Aodh said firmly to calm Finn down. "Look over at Thurgest. Look at how calmly he is taking all of this. This is so unlike how the chroniclers have portrayed Thurgest in battle. Normally he charges ahead leading from the front, his axe swinging above his head. But not this time. This time he is calm, steady and patient. Watch for when he charges into battle for he is the master at spotting the decisive moment."

"Will I ever have the same insight and vision as you?" Finn howled in anguish. "I still feel like a boy but have been burdened with the responsibility to lead men."

"If you survive this, you'll have greater insight than most. Now watch the battle and tell me when you want to move."

They stood and watched for a few more minutes until the shield wall broke in the centre. The Hibernians charged through.

"Now?" Finn said, his forehead covered in perspiration as he prepared to throw the dice for his life and the lives of his men.

Aodh threw his arm across him.

"Thurgest has not yet made his move."

They waited a moment more.

"Look," Aodh said as he pointed to Thurgest, his bodyguards and his Hibernian dogs. "They pass around their potion that makes them wild before they fight. They say their war god Tyr himself mixes the potion and gives it to Thurgest. They will make their move soon. Be prepared."

Thurgest raised his axe in the air and his bodyguards sounded their horns. Thurgest, his bodyguards and his Hibernian dogs charged straight into the point of the Hibernian attack.

"Give the order," Aodh said as he raised his hand and pointed in the direction of the battle.

Finn knitted his brow.

"For which side?"

There was a mighty roar both beside them and from the other side of the battle. The Norse had used the woods as cover and wheeled around to the sides of the Hibernians and now abandoned their hiding places and charged at the Hibernian rear.

"Attack Tigernach in the flank," shouted Aodh.

Finn raised his sword in the air.

"WITH ME, MEN. INTO THE FLANK OF TIGERNACH."

The men roared and charged in behind Finn.

Finn seemed to find a temporary new lease of life. His limbs did not ache as much and his sword seemed lighter to wield. His feet pounded as his strides ate up the yards. The Hibernians did not turn to meet them as the right flank of the shield wall had maintained its formation and they were fully engaged fighting that. Finn gave out a blood-curdling roar and slashed his sword down the side of the nearest Hibernian he ran into. The man cried out in anguish and was then trampled to death as the shield wall broke ranks and charged into the faltering Hibernian line. The line broke and Finn and his men were left to hack men down as they fled. The Hibernian army collapsed and it became a slaughter.

Finn slashed and hacked his way through the Hibernian ranks, his sword a blur of steel and blood. He ducked under a wild axe swing and drove his blade into the exposed neck of his attacker, feeling the warm spray of crimson across his face as he wrenched the weapon free. All around him, the battlefield was a chaos of screams and clashing metal as the Hibernians were crushed between the Norse shield wall and Finn's savage assault on their flank.

A giant Hibernian warrior with a braided red beard charged at Finn, swinging a massive sword. Finn sidestepped nimbly and slashed his sword across the back of the man's thighs, severing the hamstrings. The Hibernian collapsed with an agonised roar and Finn finished him with a thrust to the heart.

Two more Hibernians came at Finn from either side, their spears levelled at his chest. He parried one thrust and twisted away from the other, then retaliated with a flurry of cuts that sent both men reeling back, their faces and chests streaked with blood. Finn pressed his advantage, beating their spears aside and carving great holes in their tunics until they both lay dead at his feet.

Gasping for breath, Finn paused and looked around, searching for his next foe. The ground was littered with Hibernian corpses, the churned earth soaked with so much blood it seemed more red than brown. All around, Finn's men were wreaking havoc, their weapons rising and falling in a relentless rhythm of death.

There were groups of Hibernians still in some distinguishable battle formations that were attempting to escape the field. The Norse harassed them but did not make an overwhelming effort to stop them from fleeing, as many of them had had enough, having been in the shield wall for hours. Aodh slapped Finn on the shoulder.

"I recognise that group over there. They are Tigernach's men, his personal bodyguards. If he has survived, he will be with them."

"Then I shall have my revenge," Finn said as he returned the slap on the shoulder. "With me, men. Tigernach tries to crawl from the battlefield like the coward he is. But we'll not let him slink away and not pay for his crimes. Remember the innocents his son slaughtered outside their hillfort? Whoever brings me his head gets the pick of the spoils."

The men roared and charged in behind Finn.

Thurgest swung his axe and decapitated another wounded Hibernian kneeling before him begging for his life. He looked around the battlefield and saw the retreating group around Tigernach. He took his horn and blew hard on it. Cathal and his Hibernian dogs came running. Cathal was head to toe covered in blood splatter with a rather large amount of blood running down from his mouth as if he had taken a bite out of one of his opponents and ended up with a chunk of flesh. Thurgest beamed back at him.

"My dogs fight so well I may one day set them free."

Cathal's lips trembled as if he did not know what to do without Thurgest.

"I promised you revenge against those who gave you to me and I will fulfil my promise this day. Beyond in that group is Tigernach who abandoned you that fateful day we met. I will leave him to you and your dogs and send none of my own men to spoil your revenge. But I do it on one condition."

Cathal bowed his head.

"What is that, master?"

"You must kill all you see."

"Why do you doubt us, master?"

"Why do you question my instruction? Do you want your revenge and to show Tigernach how you suffered?"

"More than anything."

"Then do as I say."

Cathal pounded his fist on the remains of his heart.

"Everyone shall die."

Thurgest took his hip flask and offered it to Cathal.

"Here, have some more of Tyr's juice. It will inspire you on your way."

Cathal glugged from the flask and handed it back to Thurgest. He howled to the gods and lifted his sword to the sky. His men ran after him towards Tigernach.

CHAPTER SEVENTY

A FORCED CHOICE

THE HARSH CLANG OF steel against steel rang out, nearly drowning the anguished cries of the fallen. Arrows whistled through the air, finding their marks with sickening thuds. The field was a scene of pure hell, the ground churned to mud by the trampling of countless boots and hooves, and slick with the blood of the slain.

Finn gritted his teeth, his eyes fixed straight ahead as he led his men through the heart of the carnage. Bodies lay strewn across the ground, their limbs twisted at unnatural angles, their eyes staring sightlessly up at the leaden sky. Some still moved feebly, their hands scrabbling weakly at the earth as they tried in vain to drag themselves to safety. Others lay still and silent, their life's blood seeping into the soil beneath them. But there was no time for pity, no room for hesitation. Every warrior knew the risks when they took up arms. This was the way of battle, the grim reality of war.

The stench of death hung heavy in the air, mingling with the acrid smoke from burning wagons and the coppery tang of spilt blood. Finn's lungs burned with each ragged breath, but he pushed onward, his sword gripped tight in his fist. All around him, his men fought with fierce determination, their faces streaked with sweat, blood, and grime. They had a mission to fulfil, and they would see it through to the end, no matter the cost.

Tigernach's men hastily formed a protective square around their leader, desperation etched on their faces as Tigernach bellowed at his retreating warriors to halt and fight. Yet, panic gripped their hearts, and some abandoned hope and surged past the square, fear driving their every step. Their sole focus was on escaping the impending doom, on fleeing the trap before the Norse sealed their fate. The path to the forest remained open, a glimmer of hope, and Tigernach's men pushed towards it with every ounce of strength they could muster. But despite their earlier exhaustion, Finn's men relentlessly pursued, their speed a menacing shadow that threatened to engulf Tigernach's struggling formation.

Finn reached the outer rim of the square and slashed down at the man on the corner. The man parried him away but the retreating square sealed up behind him as it advanced towards the forest. The man advanced towards Finn with grim determination for he had no time to make it back to the square to avail himself of its protection. He was bigger and stronger than Finn and had a larger shield and was determined to make the most of his short-term advantage. He slashed down at Finn narrowly missing his shoulder. But Finn was more manoeuvrable than the man and wheeled around and smacked him in the side of the head with the boss of his shield. The man staggered back and Finn thrust his sword into his stomach. He twisted it and then withdrew it and the man fell to the ground. The exhilaration of a clean kill surged through Finn's veins, lighting a fire beneath his confidence. Finn looked up and saw his men had brought Tigernach's square to a halt and were assaulting it from three sides. Tigernach stood in the middle waving his sword around and barking orders. Finn charged towards the square. He let out a blood-curdling scream and threw himself against the shields of Tigernach's guards, breaking their formation. His men swarmed through the gap. It now became bitter hand-to-hand combat as Tigernach's guards were picked off one by one.

A spear was jabbed towards Finn's face. He ducked, grabbed the shaft of the spear and pulled as hard as he could. The man juddered forward, off balance. Finn slashed down along the shaft. The spear fell along with three of the man's fingers. The man howled out in pain. Finn drew his sword over his left shoulder and slashed downwards and with one final yelp the man was silent. The next bodyguard came at Finn. He slashed downwards and nicked Finn's arm. Finn winced in pain and threw off his shield for his arm could no longer bear the weight.

"I need some assistance, men," he cried, not as a coward, but as a man who wished to survive to achieve his vengeance and not to fall to some unknown sword. He squared up to the bodyguard only for the bodyguard to fall forward and vomit blood all over him as the tip of a sword emerged from his stomach. The man collapsed and behind him was the blood-drenched face of his father.

Cathal's eyes bulged and gleamed with the shine of the blood-lust and the effects of Tyr's juice. He pulled his sword out of the bodyguard's back and fixed Finn in a cold stare.

"Leave here now, boy. Thurgest has commanded me to kill everyone here, but I will give my own flesh and blood one chance to leave before I am once more possessed by the Norse demons that control my life. Let us part now and you remember me as you did when you were a boy and not as I am now. Flee north to the Ú Neill, get as far away from Thurgest as possible, for no bigger demon resides in hell than stalks this earth."

Finn lowered his sword and held out his hand to his father, forgetting he was in the middle of a raging battle.

"Come with me, Father. You can escape in the thick of the battle. You can come back with me and live with your wife and your daughter. Live your life in peace and forget anything Thurgest ever subjected you to."

Cathal hung his head.

"It is far too late for me. My soul has been roasted on the fires of hell and barely resembles even embers. Leave now before it is too late for you too."

Finn grabbed Cathal's hand and felt his father's warmth. He saw something melt in his father's eye. Cathal jolted forward as he was shoulder-charged in the back. He flew face-first into the mud and scrambled to recover his sword. Aodh stood there in the glow of self-righteousness.

"Your father is beyond redemption, Finn. It is I he really wants. He only toys with your emotions, for what he felt for you when you were a boy is merely a faint memory in his heart. Go and fight and leave this to me."

Aodh shoved Finn away and Finn backed into another one of Tigernach's guards who immediately turned around and took him on. Cathal sprang to his feet, his eyes ablaze.

"You did this to me," he screamed as he launched a blow down towards Aodh's head. Aodh dodged the blow and swung a punch at Cathal's nose. Blood flew across the sky as Cathal fell to the ground. Finn launched a barrage of blows against the latest bodyguard who was too exhausted to fight off such a sustained assault. His sword hand became too weak to fend off the death blow and Finn plunged his sword through the man's chest. The man fell before him and Finn now found himself in the middle of the square. Standing in front of him was Tigernach, whose jaw dropped when he realised who it was. He held his sword up as if to make one last stand. Finn felt the hatred surge through him. He raised his sword. This sword would swing and take Tigernach's head clean off.

"You poisoned my mother and dozens of innocent people, all for protesting because you would not protect them."

Tigernach looked around him but none of his bodyguards were free to come to his aid. Then a glint of metal under the sunlight caught his eye.

"I see you wear Thurgest's ring," he said.

"What of it? It is only to get my vengeance upon you."

"That makes you no better than me or your father. Look around and see what is happening." Tigernach held up his hands to pacify Finn. "Look around. I'll not swing my sword. Look around and then we can talk."

Finn did not move his sword arm from above his head but paused momentarily to take in the raging fight around him.

"I see you are soon to be overwhelmed and are about to die," Finn said in a callous tone. "But I wish to take the pleasure of killing you myself."

"That is how it seems at first sight. But Thurgest's men are killing indiscriminately. They care not if you wear Thurgest's ring. They were more than likely told to kill you. On this occasion, where both our lives are at stake, we have a common enemy. Only together do we have an equal number of men to those of Thurgest so you will have to decide quickly. You can kill me and die or join with me and live. What is it to be? Quick now."

Finn lowered his sword to witness his father thrash his sword down towards Aodh who buckled under his father's strength.

"You did this to me," Cathal screamed at the bent-kneed Aodh, his face as red and angry as the pits of hell. One of Cathal's dogs ran past Aodh and slipped a dagger into his side, leaving blood streaming down Aodh's leg. Aodh winced as he felt the sharp pangs of pain from the wound. His energy seemed to leak out of the side of his body. But he could not give up on Cathal for that was the only way he could see to save them all.

"Thurgest did this to you. Remember that. I went to look for you but you had already gone. It could have just as easily been me and I wish it was for you had a young family and I did not."

"But it wasn't you, was it? You ran away."

Cathal hit him with a blow to the side of the head and Aodh buckled and fell to the ground. Cathal raised his sword and it descended without hesitation, chopping Aodh's head cleanly off his shoulders.

"NO!" Finn screamed and everything became a blur. Cathal's blood was up as Tyr's juice did its damnedest and he slashed away at everything that came between Tigernach and him.

"MEN, WE HAVE BEEN BETRAYED," Finn screamed. "PROTECT TIGERNACH AND WE'LL GET OUT OF HERE WITH OUR LIVES."

Finn's men and Tigernach's stopped fighting each other and formed a rough line to block the attacks of Cathal and his dogs. Cathal slashed away at the wall with the fury of an angry wolf but he could not get past the defensive line. Tigernach and Finn ran for the safety of the forest together.

Finn and Tigernach ran through the forest surrounded by what was left of both sets of men. Finn could barely lift his legs to put one foot in front of the other but knew that Cathal would not give up and return to his master until he had both their heads. Tigernach raised an exhausted finger and pointed to the clear sky at the end of the forest.

"We'll be safe in the hillfort. We can then send word to Malachy and he'll send help."

Finn nodded for he was too tired and his soul was in need of some hope after the battle and witnessing the death of his mentor. They began to run into groups of Tigernach's men who were by now walking for they felt safety in numbers. They reached the edge of the forest. Tigernach stared at the fort and his face fell.

"NO!"

Finn stopped and once he did so he collapsed to the ground so bereft of energy was he.

"What's wrong?" Finn said between breaths.

"I never locked the gate and all my banners have been torn down. They must have sneaked around us in the middle of the battle and taken the fort."

"So Thurgest made fools of us both. He used me to draw you out and you obliged him by rushing out to crush me."

Tigernach rolled his fist into a ball.

"I have other forts. This is not such a loss. All I have to do is to how Malachy what a good servant I have been to him and he will send his army to get my revenge."

Finn rolled into a seated position and smirked.

"He already gave you some of his army and they are now nearly all dead. Why would he give you the rest of it to meet such a fate? Then he would fall to Thurgest too."

Tigernach turned around to face Finn. He now looked like a frail old man, drained of both energy and hope.

"Well, I'll only die sitting outside my old fort waiting for the past to come save me. My only hope lies with Malachy. Come with me for you are seeking revenge too."

Finn got to his feet and looked north to Malachy's fort.

"No, my destiny lies on another path. I will go back to Thurgest and claim my part of the spoils for all the blood my men gave cannot be for nothing."

"Are you sure, Finn? Surely the Norse saw you flee from the battle with me?"

Finn gave a battle weary smile.

"I will tell Thurgest his dogs attacked me and I had to protect my men for there was no convincing them in the heat of battle we were on their side. I then pretended to be on your side but then turned upon you when the opportunity arose, but you escaped. Such things happen in the caldron of battle, especially when it is hard to distinguish between the sides."

Tigernach shook his head.

"That's a hell of a gamble. You're a braver man than I to do it. Why take the risk?"

Finn looked to the skies.

"I have just seen, my mother come back from the dead. To me, that is a miracle and this day I can only thank God for such small mercies. If she is alive it must be for a reason, and I must ensure she fulfils it. But I can only assume she is a prisoner of the Norse as they hold the battlefield. I must make sure she is safe and protect her."

Tigernach stuck out his hand and Finn shook it. He was too exhausted to wallow in the past and too traumatised by the death of Aodh to do any more killing.

"Thank you for today, you saved my life," Tigernach said sincerely. "But I will give you fair warning. The next time we meet we may not be on the same side. But if we are, I owe you."

Finn nodded.

"Our lives are in the hands of God. We shall see what he has in store for us next time."

CHAPTER SEVENTY-ONE

TO THE VICTOR, THE SPOILS

F INN STOOD IN THE ceremonial circle that was once the pride of Tigernach's lands but was now firmly in the hands of Thurgest. The stars sparkled in the sky, and the pale moon provided the backdrop for the Norse celebrations. Thurgest had won a decisive victory and had shattered the army of Tigernach as well as giving a punishing defeat to Malachy's main army. All of this for around one hundred and fifty Norse dead. The fort was a prize bargain even if obtained at twice the cost in lives. The Norse had erected huge fires and slaughtered the best of Tigernach's cattle, such was the grandeur of the feast. The Norse had cleared out all those who had stayed in the fort. All the Hibernian prisoners who had been taken in the battle and all those Hibernians who had fought on the Norse side were made to stand and wait for Thurgest to arrive and inform them of his judgment.

The Norse had helped themselves to Tigernach's supply of mead straight after the battle and they stood drunk, still covered in Hibernian blood and taunting their prisoners. Finn bit his lip and ignored them. He had by default filled the vacuum to lead those who had collaborated with Thurgest and those who now found themselves in his dominion. All the Hibernians stood behind Finn for they only trusted him to deal with Thurgest for he had managed to strike a bargain with him before. Finn was not so sure, but he could not show it. He no longer had the steady counsel of Aodh at his side for his father had taken that away from him. He knew he could easily die that day but by now he knew that was the price you had to be prepared to pay every time you faced Thurgest.

The horns blared and the Norse cheered. The man who had brought them successful raid after successful raid, victory after victory, had arrived. The Norse had raided Tigernach's house and had brought his ceremonial chair to the circle. Thurgest strode in front of his bodyguards, lifted the bottom of his shirt and sat on the chair. The Norse all cheered and the Hibernians all remained quiet.

Thurgest tilted his head to the side, gave a sarcastic grin and threw his hands in the air.

"I have the throne. Does that make me a king?"

The Norse howled with laugher and threw their mead at the Hibernians standing in the middle of them. Finn was especially pelted but he did not react when the mugs struck him. He just stood there stinking of mud, sweat, blood, grass and now mead. He twisted Thurgest's oath ring around his finger. Would it bring him the curses of hell or the luck of the gods?

Thurgest stood up and raised his mug to the heavens.

"We won a great victory today. All glory and honour goes to our warriors who now find themselves this day in Valhalla."

"VALHALLA," came the salute and all those that could raised their mugs to the sky.

"May we join them soon at the table with the gods, but not just yet. For there is plenty more to steal in this green and pleasant land."

More mugs and mead were thrown upon the standing Hibernians and the mead splashed Finn's face as the mugs hit his chest.

"Enough," Thurgest cried. "We must be good hosts to our Hibernian guests. But let us first show them what it is to serve Thurgest."

Thurgest snapped his fingers and Cathal and his dogs emerged from behind the throne. They were all still fully armed and covered in mud and blood just as they had been in the heat of the battle. Thurgest ordered them to stand in a line in front of their fellow Hibernians. Finn saw no emotion never mind compassion or mercy in their eyes. They were all cold-blooded killers and could be set upon them at any time. He knew they had been set up to intimidate him into agreeing with whatever terms Thurgest offered. But was this how Thurgest was going to conduct himself? If it was, he would prefer to die sooner rather than later with his dignity intact.

"Now," Thurgest continued, "it is time to see how all conducted themselves in battle and what they deserve from the spoils." He turned to his aide and whispered some instructions in his ear. The aide disappeared behind Thurgest.

"Firstly, bring me Einar and his Hibernian woman and let us see how they served in the heat of battle."

Einar came out of the crowd holding Affraic's hand, who walked behind him. He was no longer under armed escort, which certainly gave him hope of a reprieve. Einar bowed deeply before Thurgest, and Affraic followed suit.

"Well?" Thurgest asked.

"The line held with the minimum of men until the end," Einar said with confidence holding aloft his words. "Just like you planned."

"I remember the line broke in the middle and I had to come and support you."

Einar bowed his head again for it was not wise to contradict Thurgest, especially in public.

"That is true but it breaking only supported your ingenious plan. The line breaking only sucked more Hibernians in. It made it much more difficult for the main body of the army to escape before you sprang your trap."

"That is true," Thurgest replied with a smug grin and a nod. "You may have been responsible for most of the Norse deaths in the battle but you did play your role well and to my specifications. I seem to recall we struck some kind of bargain before the battle. What was it again before I ask my scribe to read it back to me?"

Einar gulped for he knew now was his chance.

"You promised me this hillfort if I helped you take it."

Thurgest raised an eyebrow. He glanced at his scribe who gave a hurried nod. Thurgest scowled for he considered it a hastily made promise.

"What did your woman do for me?"

Affraic moved forward and bowed her head but Einar spoke.

"She facilitated the alliance with the Hibernians and tended the wounded and dying on the boats both during and after the battle. Therefore, she served you to the best of her abilities."

Thurgest sat back in his chair.

"If she believed in the gods it sounds like she would make a good Norse woman."

"I am grateful for the strength of her belief in our cause."

Thurgest smirked again, determined not to give away the spoils of battle too easily.

"Torstein actually took the fort. Why should I not give it to him?"

Torstein, who was standing beside Thurgest gave a greedy grin.

"He could not have done it without my men holding the shield wall," Einar growled. "The bedrock of the victory was that the shield wall held. Therefore, I delivered on our part of the bargain so you should uphold yours."

"Do not forget your place, boy. It is the gods that provide and Thurgest is their hammer to their thunder. However, I need your family and their resources to support me." Thurgest stood up. "Therefore, the fort is yours. You may call yourself king if you wish for all the Hibernians seem to require to pronounce themselves kings is a pigsty. Now you have yours. I will leave the throne. You may populate your lands with Hibernians if you wish but they will make way if the influx of Norse farmers comes from the homelands. Congratulations."

The men who survived the shield wall cheered the loudest while Torstein spat and scowled. Thurgest's actions filled Finn's heart with hope as he watched Thurgest's other commanders get rewarded for their part in the battle. But now it was his turn.

Finn was called and he walked up calmly and stood in front of Thurgest. He did not bow his head or offer any form of reverence, for he wanted to be seen as an ally and not subservient, irrespective of whether he wore the oath ring. It did not help that he was covered in mead. Thurgest curled his lip and fixed his stare on this defiant-looking youth.

"So what did you do for me in the battle?" Thurgest said with a sneer.

"Gave the lives of most of my men to lure the enemy into a trap that neither they nor I knew about. I then took part in sealing the ambush. For these actions, I ask for my just reward."

"You ask and you do not bow?"

"I am your ally and not your servant."

Thurgest removed his gaze for he was distracted by Cathal twitching below him.

"Have you something to say, dog?"

Cathal turned around, his face a tormented grimace of fury. He could barely get his words out.

"He killed my men. He saved Tigernach."

Thurgest curled his lip into the cruellest of grins.

"Are you telling me, dog, your son is a traitor to our cause?"

Cathal nodded vigorously for he could not put his betrayal into words. Finn threw an accusatory finger at his father.

"I was about to kill Tigernach and bring you his head when this animal came and killed my men. He also killed my friend and mentor. I could not fight both. Why was he set upon me?"

Thurgest sat back and smiled while his men jeered.

"Because all Hibernians look the same," came a shout from the crowd.

"Silence," Thurgest said. "Let my dog tell why he bared his fangs."

Cathal could barely lift his head to face the cold stare of his master.

"Well, dog?"

Cathal bowed his head for he could not betray his master. He fell into a swirling nightmare of images of his children and his wife and of Thurgest tearing down his back with his claws. Just the mere thought of it brought back the smell of his own burning flesh into his nostrils. He began to blubber and cry. Thurgest threw his hands in the air.

"I cannot even rely on my dog to tell me what happened. Have him flogged for insolence." Thurgest turned once more to Finn. "Since we cannot verify your accusations we'll just put it down to the fog of battle. Therefore, for performing your part of our plan, what do you ask Thurgest for?"

"I only ask for what we agreed. I consider I paid a high price in blood for it."

"We won a great victory but not much land to dole out to all my captains and all of those who performed bravely in battle. There-fore, most will have to be paid with a promise. But a promise from Thurgest is one that will be kept. You can have the forest beside the hillfort. Your people would inhabit it anyway as bandits but you can control them for me. There will be more battles and more lands to distribute, so stay loyal and you will get more to add to it."

Finn stepped forward.

"I will accept your offer on one condition."

Thurgest stood up and scowled.

"No one dictates terms to Thurgest."

"That I can offer all the Hibernians here a place to live on my lands no matter what side they fought on."

Thurgest sat down and laughed.

"Take them. It means more farmland for my men so all the better for me."

Finn bowed.

"Thank you, Thurgest. I am grateful."

"Good. Now get out of here before I change my mind."

Finn bowed again, grateful to be still alive. But Thurgest smirked and raised his finger.

"But before you leave, I wish to witness the game you call hurling. Your father has told me a lot about it and says you are good at it. I think my men will like it since it is like training for battle. We shall meet out in the fields surrounding the fort tomorrow morning. You had better pick your best men for I shall pick mine."

"As you so wish."

Finn bowed once more and departed, a chill creeping down his spine. Doubt gnawed at him. What devious plan was this? He could not bring himself to trust Thurgest. Was this the path that would lead to his downfall? Yet, trapped in a fort brimming with Norse warriors, what choice did he have? He needed to play the game and emerge victorious, for losing would surely mean death. Frustration and anger welled up within him as he faced the daunting task of assembling a team from mostly injured men, strangers to each other and the game, yet somehow they had to conquer the Norse. He went to search for his mother to ensure that at least she would be safe.

CHAPTER SEVENTY-TWO
I TOLD YOU SO

S EVERAL HOURS SLIPPED BY as Thurgest meticulously completed the solemn duty of honouring his valiant men who had fought bravely in the battle, bestowing upon them gifts that reflected their courage and loyalty. One thing he was known for was commending the men who had served him well and it was a reputation he was determined to keep.

Meanwhile, Finn manipulated his time with calculated precision, and engaged in fervent conversations with as many Hibernians as he could find. He generously extended offers of sanctuary on his lands, meticulously assessing potential allies who might be persuaded to join his hurling team for the coming day. He was careful with how he phrased his offer, for he knew there was a strong possibility he was condemning them to death. But who knew if they would survive the next couple of days anyway? The Norse always went on the rampage after their victories.

On his journey through the fort and its surrounding areas he came across his sister Affraic and her husband Einar. They both looked exhausted but elated that Thurgest had kept his promise to give them the hillfort. That did not make Affraic any humbler with her brother. She ran to him. She embraced him and then held him out in front of her.

"You look like you barely have a scratch. Did you do any fighting at all?"

Finn shook his head.

"This is no time for jesting, sister."

But she ignored him and circled her arms around her to show Finn all the lands they could see.

"See? I was right. Now we're a king and a queen when once we were the son and daughter of a disgraced warrior."

"And we defended our father relentlessly to our mother, neighbours, Ultán and Tigernach, and anyone else who spoke badly about him, but little did we know of his true disgrace. I watched our father behead my friend and mentor Aodh today," Finn said as his words drifted off and his head dropped.

Affraic grabbed his head and nestled it in her bosom.

"You must leave now, for I am convinced Thurgest wishes to kill you."

"Being a king under Thurgest only puts a target on your back," Einar added.

Finn pushed his sister away.

"I am the last leader our people here have. Aodh taught me to be a man of honour and I will respect his memory. I wear the oath ring for Thurgest, which I mean to remove at the first safe opportunity, but I also owe a duty to my people. I will show Thurgest that we are honourable and strong by beating him in hurling tomorrow. Then I will leave and establish my kingdom."

Affraic tilted her head.

"You really want to be dead, don't you?"

"I told you, do not jest, sister. How about you and your predicament? When is Thurgest going to turn on you? You had to come and get me to help you survive the last time."

Affraic just smiled.

"I have Einar, and Einar has his father who is more powerful than Thurgest and will soon come to our lands. He will depose Thurgest and establish a mighty Norse kingdom. We shall establish ourselves in this hillfort and wait for my father-in-law to come."

It was Finn's turn to embrace Affraic.

"Now you have become the dreamer. May the blessings of the gods be upon you, be it whoever you believe in now, if you actually believe in anyone but yourself."

Affraic laughed.

"If you are foolish enough to proceed with this hurling match tomorrow I will do my best to help you, but I cannot guarantee anything."

"Thank you, sister, and I hope that we meet again."

"So do I."

Affraic smiled at him and Finn turned to Einar. Finn shook his hand and with that, was gone.

CHAPTER SEVENTY-THREE

A BITTER REUNION

FINN EVENTUALLY STUMBLED UPON his mother, who was being tended to by Babo. She sat on the ground, her complexion ghostly pale, her frame fragile and frail, a haunting shadow of the vibrant spirit he had once known.

"Mother, are you well? Did you hide during the battle?"

Gormlaith gave a faint growl.

"You were lucky I arrived when I did, for you were about to get yourself killed. If it wasn't for Babo we'd be at your funeral now." She paused a second. "What's that on your finger?"

Finn was about to respond when he felt a presence. A shiver went down his back. He drew his hand up his thigh in case he had to reach for a weapon. He turned and looked over his shoulder. Cathal stood transfixed, staring at Gormlaith. His face was pale, his eyes bulged, his jaw locked, his mouth devoid of words.

"What are you looking at?" Gormlaith demanded from what she saw as a dark stranger.

But Cathal could only stare. Babo became twitchy and as a precaution his hand slipped up towards his belt. Finn felt compelled to break the tension, if only to be rid of the man who murdered his mentor.

"Mother, believe me when I tell you. This is my father, and your husband."

Finn lowered his head, ashamed to admit the truth.

"Cathal?" Gormlaith said, her face a sea of confusion. "Is it really you?"

But the memory of Aodh's death plagued Finn's mind. His father would receive no solace while Finn could speak freely.

"Before you get reacquainted, Mother, you should know his deeds. He is a willing slave for Thurgest and does his worst murders for him. He is a man devoid of morals, devoid of a soul. He is the man who murdered Aodh in front of my eyes."

Babo immediately went for his dagger. Finn threw himself in front of Cathal, for he knew if they killed him here it would be certain death for all of them. Gormlaith's cheeks went a peculiar shade of red.

"GET OUT OF HERE, YOU HIDEOUS GHOUL," Gormlaith screamed at Cathal. "If I ever see your face again, I'll let Babo cut it off and throw it in the fire."

Cathal jumped back and cowered down for even the invitation to fight could not overcome the shock of meeting these ghosts of the past. He ran off into the night.

"Gormlaith leave before monsters come back," Babo said as he looked around for any of Cathal's compatriots hiding in the dark. Gormlaith patted him on the arm.

"Let me say goodbye to my son first."

Babo stepped away and Finn bent down and kissed his mother.

"Look at the state of you," Finn said. "Come with me and let me protect you. It's dangerous out there. Way more dangerous now that your husband has returned."

Gormlaith took him gently by the hand and looked into his eyes. His mask of bravery quickly melted and it looked as if he was going to cry.

"I'm not the person I used to be before the Norse first arrived," Gormlaith said. "I'm old and frail and the attempted poisoning has taken it out of me. I have been condemned as a witch and it has stuck, so a witch I shall become. Babo has agreed to come with me to the Wicklow mountains and there we shall end our days."

"But how will you live? Come and live with me and I'll protect you."

Gormlaith gave him a knowing nod.

"Before the sun has set seven times you'll be a bandit in the woods. That is, if you survive the next sun."

Finn smirked.

"Is that your first prediction as a witch?"

"Give or take a few sun settings. You'll see I'm right. But I'll get better with practice."

Finn kissed his mother on the cheek.

"If you are going to leave, I would leave now. Everyone is distracted and no one will notice you."

"What'll you do, Finn?"

Finn's face hardened.

"I've got this hurling match to play and if I survive that, I'll go see what lands I've been given."

Gormlaith signalled to Babo and he helped her to her feet. She leant over and embraced Finn.

"Good luck, my son. But be warned. The match is probably a trap. I'll muster up what gods I can to protect you. But if you survive that and don't fancy being a king, there'll always be a place for you in my cave."

"Thanks, I may need it."

With that, Babo picked up Gormlaith and they set off for the woods.

CHAPTER SEVENTY-FOUR
THE WAY OF KINGS

As DAWN BROKE, THE sun slowly emerged from its shrouded place behind a cluster of thick clouds, its light piercing through and casting a brilliant glow over the landscape. The stubborn clouds, put to gradual retreat, began to lose their hold, dissolving one by one until they were mere wisps in the sky. The world below, touched by the sun's gentle and warming beams, sparkled with life as dew glittered on every surface. All seemed good in the world as the sun brought a new day. That is, until its creatures awoke with spite in their hearts and revenge on their minds.

Finn awoke, a jumble of nerves after a restless night. His mother had gone, Affraic was with her new husband, he now saw his father in a completely different light, and his mentor was slain. He felt strangely alone that morning. He thought of his mentor Aodh and the seer's vision. He saw that parts of the seer's vision had come true but that the vision was not destiny. The vision was merely a path he could go down when fates collided. Fates had been thrown around like thunderbolts by the gods but this was a new world that day. One, for the time being, dominated by the whims of Thurgest. Finn reached over and put on his oath ring. How long more would this define him in the eyes of men and be a burden upon him? But he had one more duty, one more hurdle to overcome before he could be free of Thurgest. That is, if he survived the day.

Several hours later, Finn strode onto the hurling pitch, his heart pounding like a war drum, with the twenty players he had managed to gather from the remaining Hibernians who had not yet fled. The Norse, a sea of wild and unruly warriors, encircled the pitch like a tempestuous ocean, and their roars and cheers thundered through the air, fuelled by the copious amounts of mead they had consumed, even though the day was not yet half over. Their voices were a cacophony, a fierce collision of chaos and revelry.

Thurgest exuded authority and menace as he sat on Tigernach's old throne, while Torstein and Einar flanked him on either side. They stood as pillars of intimidation, taking the place of Ultán, their eyes sharp and focused like predatory hawks, locked intently on the players below as if assessing their every move.

Finn was accustomed to unfriendly crowds, but this one seemed intent on tearing him apart. The jeers were deafening, and ale tankards flew dangerously close as he stepped onto the pitch with his team. Finn noticed at the corner of his eye that Affraic had come to watch but she looked stone-faced amongst a crowd of jeering Norsemen. Finn struggled to keep his composure and steady his team's nerves as they moved to the centre, to await their opponents.

The other team emerged from behind Thurgest. Cathal ran out in front, his face a picture of determination and concentration. Most of the other players were his Hibernian dogs, all familiar with the game and the last of the players to emerge were some rather hefty Norsemen who Finn thought were too heavy and unmanoeuvrable for the game. They passed a mug of Tyr's juice from man to man preparing for the game as if it were a battle.

Finn saw his men were losing their nerve. It was like they were a sacrifice for the entertainment of Thurgest, hemmed in as they were by his men surrounding the pitch. The Norse on Cathal's team grinned. They were going to enjoy this. Finn walked as steadily as he could to the centre of the pitch to start the game. Cathal walked over and stood in front of him and wore the same stoic expression he had just before battle. He leaned over to Finn's ear.

"There will be no mercy shown to those who disown and dishonour their fathers."

Finn pushed him away.

"You know nothing of honour and are, to me, a beast of the woods rather than my father. When I plunge my sword through your heart, I will be showing you a mercy."

Cathal's expression did not change.

"Shall we throw the sliotar in the air and see what fate has in store for us?"

"Do as you please. I am ready for you anytime."

All eyes followed the sliotar as it soared in the air. The hurling sticks followed and clashed as Finn and Cathal fought for control of the ball. An elbow swiftly followed the stick and Finn shrank to the ground from being winded. Cathal and the sliotar charged down towards Finn's goal leaving everyone who tried to stop him trailing in his wake. As Finn got up he saw Thurgest grin and clap on the sidelines.

"I LOVE THIS GAME," Thurgest roared.

The game restarted and Finn wrestled for control of the sliotar with his father once more. He shouldered his father out of the way and bounced the sliotar at the end of his stick. This time he was mobbed by the dogs and relieved of it. Finn lay on the ground holding his ribs. He was suddenly covered by a shadow.

"This is from Thurgest," and one of the bulky Norse punched him in the face.

Finn's head spun. He saw the clouds passing overhead and the patches of blue between them. His mouth stung. His head ached. His heart sank into his stomach. He heard the roar of the crowd faintly in the distance. He lifted his head and saw the bodies of several of his men lying on the ground. Some moved and some lay perfectly still. He saw his father and his dogs jump up and down in celebration as they scored again. Finn realised this was all a trap by Thurgest. He had to decide. Should he get up and fight or lie still on the ground and hope to survive the day by them thinking him dead? This thought soon dissipated as he saw one of the dogs stab one of his men as he lay on the ground. They meant to kill them all and it looked like there was no escape.

Finn picked himself off the ground once more. He knew they would want his head for a spike to put on the gate of the fort, a lesson for all those who passed through it. He looked over to the crowd, and Affraic still stood there. She looked tearful and seemed to give a signal just before she walked away. Finn scowled. What did her hand gesture mean? Was that goodbye? Why would she walk away when he needed her most?

He saw the sliotar flying in the air coming towards him as if it were a cursed comet from hell. He saw Cathal and his dogs turn and run towards him. Their eyes lit up with the frenzy of Tyr's juice. They grinned and slobbered as if they were real dogs about to pounce on a hunted fox. Finn gulped for he knew there was no point in running as he could never get away. He saw the dogs pull out their concealed daggers and plunge them into the stomachs of any of Finn's remaining men as they made their way towards him. The crowd roared for blood. Thurgest leapt off his seat.

"FINISH THE TRAITOR, DOGS. FINISH THE TRAITOR."

Finn closed his eyes and prayed to whatever gods he could think of. His heart throbbed in his chest. He heard the sound of the wind above his head and opened his eyes. A volley of arrows appeared from the sky and landed between him and the dogs.

"RUN, FINN, RUN."

It was a familiar voice. Was it in his head? Was this what happened just before you died?

"RUN, FINN, RUN."

He turned towards the voice and a gap appeared in the crowd in front of him as some of the Norse spectators were felled in a hail of arrows. Chaos ensued as no one could see where the enemy had come from. The Norse scrambled to get their weapons and to regroup. Finn looked into the woods and from behind a tree his mother appeared.

"RUN, FINN, RUN."

She waved him forward and Hibernian bowmen appeared from behind the trees to provide him with the cover of arrows. Finn turned and ran for his life as arrows whizzed over his head. His feet slipped as they connected to the mud yet he still ran as fast as his legs would carry him. He reached the edge of the woods to see his father murder the remaining men from Finn's team and the Norse charging from the other side of the pitch. He tore the oath ring from his finger and threw it in the mud.

"Come on, Finn. Your dawdling will get us all killed," Gormlaith said as she waved him forward.

Finn took one last look and ran into the woods.

Thurgest charged across the pitch but halted at the edge of the woods for the Hibernian bowmen were covering Finn's retreat. Cathal caught up with Thurgest and stood, impatiently waiting for orders. Thurgest saw the glint of the edge of Finn's oath ring as it lay in the mud. He bent down, picked it up and cleaned it on his trousers. He signalled to Cathal to hold out his hand. He placed the ring on Cathal's finger.

"I make you a free man for your service to me," Thurgest said.

Tears welled up in Cathal's eyes as all that he had been through to become a free man flashed through his mind. He blinked to rid himself of the tears for to show emotion to Thurgest was to reveal a weakness.

"However, you will wear your son's oath ring. You have until the year's end to bring his hand to me with my ring placed upon it again. If you do not, you will become the lowest dog again, never to rise. Do you understand?"

"I do. It is my son's hand for my life," Cathal said as he sniffed.

"Then go and fulfil your mission," and Thurgest extended his arm to invite Cathal to pursue his son through the woods.

Cathal howled like a dog and signalled to his men. They ran into the woods determined to hunt Finn down.

About Author

If you enjoyed this book, please join my mailing list for release updates and offers.

https://landing.mailerlite.com/webforms/landing/i1l1n2

C R Dempsey is the author of Viking Dawn and also the 'Exiles' series, set in Elizabethan Ireland. He has plans for many more, and he needs to find the time to write them. History has always fascinated him, and historical fiction was an obvious outlet for his accumulated knowledge. C R spends lots of time working on his books, mainly in the twilight hours of the morning. C R wishes he spent more time writing and less time jumping down the rabbit hole of excessive research.

C R Dempsey lives in London with his wife and cat. He was born in Dublin but has lived most of his adult life in London.

C R can be found at:

https://www.crdempseybooks.com/,

https://www.facebook.com/crdempsey,

https://www.instagram.com/crdempsey/,

HISTORICAL NOTE

In the year 841, after years of raiding the Irish coastline the Vikings created a longphort or base off the river Liffey beside an inlet known as the black pool. It was the perfect sheltered harbour and defendable site to use to continue their raids along the coasts and rivers of Ireland to raid monasteries and to take slaves who they would sell to slavers from across the Viking world.In doing so, they also founded the city of Dublin.

This story is about the main Viking responsible for that,Thurgest and his exploits in Ireland. The only people who write about Thurgest are Irish monks who thought he was the devil incarnate. They knew so little about him they did not even know his real name. Turgesius is his most common name used, but it sounded too Latin to me, so I settled on Thurgest as it sounded the most Norse. Few facts remain about him except for his death and his extensive raids. Therefore, most of what I have written about him is fictional.

As for those who opposed him, Tigernach was the King of Brega, but little is actually known about him so again, he is mainly a fictional character. Malachy is a real king whose real name was *Máel Sechnaill mac Máele Ruanaid.* Malachy is the English translation of his name and I used that as I thought it to be a bit more reader friendly. The other characters are fictional.

I refer to Ireland as Hibernia and the Irish as Hibernians as the concept of Ireland did not exist at the time. Ireland was broken up into a myriad of small kingdoms all in a near state of constant war with each other. It did not take long for the various Irish kings to view the Vikings as potential allies against their traditional enemies rather than foreigners to be driven out.

I refer to the Vikings as the Norse as the original meaning of Viking was to go a viking, i.e. to go raiding. I use Viking in the book title as it is the more common term but Norse in the body of the book as Ithink it is more accurate.

Dublin was originally established for and thrived upon the business of slavery. I have not shied away from this subject nor the brutality of life around this period. The Hibernians also took and used slaves as slavery was a fact of life around this time.

The concept of going on hunger strike to show your king did not offer you adequate protection was real and intrigued me so much it was one of the initial pillars of the story.

Thank you for reading this far. I had a great time doing all the research for this book and I hope you enjoy it too.

C R Dempsey

August 2025

ALSO BY

If you enjoyed this book please would you leave a review on the retailer where you bought it.

To read more books in the *Exiles* series click on the QR codes below to be brought to your favourite online ebook store.

Bad Blood

★★★★ *"A new piece of Irish historical fiction that pulls you in through its protagonist, and is full of plenty of action," - Reedsy Discovery*

★★★★ *"To say this book is rich with action, adventure, and deep meaty history is putting it mildly," – The Historical Fiction Company*

★ ★ ★ ★ ★ *"a tale that is filled with twists, including stabbings-in-the-back, and one that puts readers on the edge of their seats," – The Book Commentary*